DESIRED

THEA DEVINE

DESIRED

BRAVA

KENSINGTON PUBLISHING CORP.
http://www.kensingtonbooks.com

BRAVA BOOKS are published by

Kensington Publishing Corp.
850 Third Avenue
New York, NY 10022

All Kensington titles, imprints and distributed lines are available at special quantity discounts for bulk purchases for sales promotion, premiums, fund-raising, educational or institutional use.

Special book excerpts or customized printings can also be created to fit specific needs. For details, write or phone the office of the Kensington Special Sales Manager: Kensington Publishing Corp., 850 Third Avenue, New York, NY, 10022. Attn. Special Sales Department. Phone: 1-800-221-2647.

Brava and the B logo Reg. U.S. Pat. & TM Off.

ISBN 0-7582-0322-5

First Zebra Paperback Printing: June 1994
First Kensington Trade Paperback Printing: December 2002
10 9 8 7 6 5 4 3 2 1

Printed in the United States of America

To Sylvester McGee with all my love

Prologue

Orinda Plantation, Bayou LaTouque,
St. Foy Parish, Louisiana Spring 1854

She came riding out of the swirling morning mist through the curtain of hanging moss that obscured the shoreline where Bayou LaTouque met the parched sweeping lawns of Orinda.

Her appearance was so unexpected that it instantly took on the quality of a dream.

He had no idea who she was. She was like no one he had ever seen before, and she was exactly like the woman he had always wanted.

She was beautiful, her body melting into the stride of the horse as he bounded up onto the small pier, her hand guiding gently, her legs beneath her long gauzy drenched skirt gripping his flanks tightly, her golden hair streaming out behind her.

She was the creature of a man's imagination, her terrain the torment of his heart and soul.

She did not exist.

He moved slowly among the thick trunks of moss-laden trees between them, and he watched her every movement with reverent fascination.

The instant her mount stepped onto the soft yellowed sod of the lawn, she slipped off of his back and stood looking at the crumbling facade of Orinda.

She was so lovely, her profile so pure, her skin positively translucent in the pink-gray morning light, and the expression on her face was so perfect: the ineffable sadness of one watching a beloved slowly die.

And that was as it should be: it was his dream, and the woman in it should feel all the violent sorrow that he had felt on returning to Orinda twenty years after he had turned his back on it. It was right that this was the place to which she wanted to come.

She began the slow climb up the graded hill that led to the cracked and peeling columns that fronted the verandah and circled the house like so many guardians of the past.

Orinda was not the grand towering home of an impoverished but refined social climber who had married well and subsequently increased his wife's fortune.

No, Orinda was scaled for comfort and daily living, the first place he had thought of when he had considered coming home.

So when the woman of his dreams mounted the verandah and pulled forward a caned rocker and sat down and just stared at the morning light as it rose fitfully above the bayou, he felt it was just and equally fitting that this was how she had chosen to spend her morning.

He followed her silently, expertly, creeping closer and closer to where she sat so very still, her hands clenched in her lap, her body forcibly at rest, her face serene, but her eyes blazingly alive and as blue as the sun-rising color of the sky.

He heard the whickering of the horse, and the skittery chittering of birds, and he inhaled the perfume of the moss-choked earth and the woman-scent of her luring him into her mystery.

In his dream, he needed only to walk forward, stretch out his hand, and she would come to him wordlessly, willingly, and he would gather her into his arms in all her beauty and volatility and he would possess her forever.

But he did not move lest he disturb the ambient quality of the moment.

She sat still for so long, the saturated material of her dress molding her tensed body like a statue, her expression immobile, implacable, except for the living blue of her eyes.

The heat rose with the sun, shimmering, immutable, and he watched her, surrounded solely by the matte silence and the raw buzz and drone of insects and nature.

He did not know how much time had gone by: he was curious about the raw tension in her, about why she did not move or explore the grounds—most likely because she had been here before, perhaps many times, perhaps every day.

He had only been back a little over a week himself, and he had gone nowhere except to town for supplies and gossip, secure in the fact that no one would remember Flint Rutledge, the pariah.

But they were still talking about Clay Rutledge, the murderer.

His father had been dead and buried six months past and his brother Clay was running through the money like it flowed from some headwater up the bayou, undiluted, undiminished, a constant and changeless flow, and the details were still the food of gossip.

Only now, his father's death at the hands of his brother over the slave Meline had taken on an insidious twist after a hundred sanctimonious retellings: any man would have succumbed to that kind of provocation. And any honorable son would have defended Meline.

And so Clay had killed his father, and Southern manhood had been avenged.

Flint was so tempted to leave Orinda and never look back, just as he had done twenty years before.

He couldn't decide, and on this sweet spring morning when his dreams were haunted with the possibilities of other fulfillments, he could have been seduced into anything.

But when his mind cleared of the clutter of the past and his ruminations about the realities of the present, he saw that only one thing was clear: his imagination had been playing him false.

The woman was gone, and it had to be the sudden brisk breeze that accounted for the fact that the rocking chair was still in motion.

Someone was watching her.

She sat achingly still and keyed up with excitement, knowing it was Clay, certain he would show himself at any moment.

It was their usual rendezvous at the usual time, confirmed in secret and delivered in private lest her father find out; she had timed her arrival and she was awash in that bone-melting moment of anticipation, always broken by the whiskey-deep tone of his voice breathing her name into the crackling silence.

She was tense with longing to see him: her body flexed against the revealing drape of her wet dress.

Clay . . . they had known each other forever, drawn together secretly, dangerously in rebellion and in opposition to their families' shared history.

But the past, the infractions, the newest scandal, his reputation had never mattered. Nothing mattered but that he wanted her and she could command him, and she had what every simpering flower-faced belle in three counties would have given her life to have: Clay Rutledge at her beck and call.

Her agitation grew. Someone was hovering in the shadows and she was suddenly not so sure it was Clay. It wasn't like him to draw out things this way. He had no patience for that; he wanted everything instantly, at the moment. He had no time to waste.

Neither did she.

She sat very still, her hands clenched tightly in the valley of her lap, the wet of the fabric chilling her skin and her heart.

Surely it was Clay . . .

She sensed the merest breath of a movement and a dissonance in the air and she felt a growing certainty that Clay would not come.

But she had no tolerance for his nonsense today; things were getting too far out of hand at Montelette and it was time to take action.

And she had meant for Clay to devise the obvious solution.

But this was just like Clay: he could sense trouble like a dog on a hunt and he could slip out of a trap or a delicately woven spider's web with the ease of the wafting morning breeze.

So he was avoiding her until she cooled down and thought better of approaching him with any kind of unpleasantness.

He was so sharp. He could read the lines of tension at a hundred paces. And he was so spoiled, he wanted everything his own way.

Well, it was time Clay Rutledge grew up, she thought grimly. It was time to pay him back in his own coin.

And she was as good at tracking a wily fox as anyone.

She slipped out of the rocking chair and crept stealthily around the corner of the verandah, and into the house.

Someone was living in the house.

In the parlor, spread out in front of the fireplace, there was a bedroll with a saddle at the pillow. On the hearth, there was a coffeepot, a tin frying pan, a mug, a plate, and some utensils.

And there was a change of clothing folded neatly on the muslin covered sofa.

She couldn't tell if it were Clay; anyone could be living at Orinda: nothing was locked in or boarded up.

But Orinda belonged to them: and in its musty halls and bedrooms, Clay had taken her on a voyage of discovery which was meant to culminate soon—*today* she had thought, and she felt a kind of rage that she could not force him to do anything she wanted and maybe, just maybe, she was not enough for him.

Not enough? She, Dayne Templeton, not enough for him?

She kicked the bedroll in a fury of frustration.

Not enough? He would prefer one of those fan-flapping hothouse flowers who never spoke a single word they ever meant?

Something fell to the floor in a tangle of blankets, and she knelt down to pick it up. . . . a rifle . . .

A rifle?

What would Clay be doing with a rifle? she wondered, hefting it onto her shoulder.

Not enough? She knew exactly what she would be doing with a rifle if she ever got hold of him.

More than enough. She checked the ammunition. Loaded. Nicely loaded and balanced and perfect to go hunting a rampaging bull whose game was to lure other women to Orinda and make love to them there.

She edged over to the window and pulled aside the curtain.

She could see nothing toward the front of the house except the stretch of desiccated lawn that slanted down to the bayou.

But he was out there. She was sure of it.

And she knew how to stalk wild prey. You had to be smarter and faster—and shoot first and ask questions later.

The perfect way to deal with Clay.

* * *

There were trees close to the house and she was so slender, she could just slip behind one thick trunk after another and make her way softly, silently, covertly, around the grounds of Orinda after her secret quarry.

Damn Clay, damn him—

She skirted the edge of what had been the orchard, listening, listening.

The heat rose in shimmering waves with not a breath of air to leaven the enveloping thickness of it.

Already her dress was clammy and dried in tight patches against her skin, and the rifle felt like it weighed a hundred pounds and she was certain that lifting it against the hazy thickness of the air would almost be too much for her to handle.

But she was going to handle Clay Rutledge and his illicit activities; she would blast his perfidious soul to hell and then *one* of her problems would be solved.

The silence was unnerving. Everything sunk into hiding as the smoldering sun rose high above the bayou.

And she should have been back at Montelette long before this . . . she moved again, lightly, confidently, to the far side of the house, which faced away from the water and toward the barn . . . and there he was, his bared back to her, his head submerged in a barrel of water.

Perfect. She could whack him on his bottom—just as a warning.

Clay? But Clay was not that tall, that muscular. . . .

She bit her lip as he lifted his head and the long, lean, sundappled line of his back to the sky and shook off the water like a contented cat.

And then he turned, almost as if he could see her hiding behind his back.

She flattened herself against the tree trunk, her heart pounding.

Dear Lord—not Clay . . .

Who . . . ?

She couldn't stay still for a moment. For all she knew, he might be three feet away from her, reaching out to grab her . . .

She edged her body impatiently around the opposite side of the tree—

Safe...

But she wasn't safe at all: he had stripped off his remaining clothes and he was vigorously washing his body...

Dear heaven—his body—

He was so long and lean and hairy and brown...nothing like Clay—Clay who bathed in private in his room and who would never, even in their rough and tumble play, remove one faultlessly pressed item of clothing...

So much hair—all over his chest and arms and legs and down and around the firm curved line of his buttocks...

And how fascinating—how different...his arms, so long with large capable hands moving with brisk efficient strokes all up and down his body—

Let him turn...

Her legs felt like rubber, her hands were so shaky she almost dropped the rifle.

Let him turn—

This—this she needed to know. This was a man's promise and a woman's fear. This was the thing that Clay refused to reveal to her. This, Clay said, was preserved for his wife, and reserved for a wanton, and he never was ready to declare her one or the other.

And she needed to understand what was so sacred and so profane all at the same time.

Let him turn...

She caught her breath as he slowly moved his body sideward so that she could see the tactile contour of his hip where it joined his muscular thigh, and he began mercilessly scrubbing the long flat line of his hairy chest, down and down toward his stomach, and still further down...

She bit her lip, her mouth dry, parched with the need to know the one last mystery of his body, the one last mystery about herself.

Let him turn...

He insinuated his freshly moistened washing cloth between his legs, tenderly bathing the most inviolable part of him, and she felt a violent little dart of pleasure attack her vitals.

And then he turned and she thought her heart would just stop beating.

He was just out and out beautiful, his body so perfectly formed and triangulated, tapering from his broad shoulders to his narrow hips, with the line of his wiry hair caressing every inch, all the way down to the wedge between his legs where the essence of him nestled . . . *the hard part.*

How it lay, neat and quiescent as if it slumbered—with no hint of how or why it could be roused to a towering firmness by a man's mere thoughts—or his actions.

She knew all about that part—the hard thrusting part, when a man's emotions raced out of control because of the unobtainable temptation of *her.*

Eve, Clay had called her, *the destructor, the temptress,* pushing him beyond all manners, morals and restraint.

How did it happen that the merest kiss or touch could reduce her to jelly and magnify him to stone?

And how was it that the merest glimpse of a strange man's naked body evoked such a response in her that she was already comparing him to Clay?

It was insanity. He was an interloper, illegally camped at Orinda and she should be shooting off the most tender part of him instead of making calf eyes at it and imagining . . . things—

She took a deep breath and girded herself. Surely she would be doing Clay a favor by confronting the intruder—

Or myself?

She clamped down on that unruly thought, mindful that her gaze had not moved an inch from the naked fascination of his male root.

Or did she want to see it move?

Did she want to *make* it move because there was nothing between her and it and all the forbidden knowledge she could grasp in her hands?

Or did she just want to scare him to death because he was at his most vulnerable now?

Damn, damn, damn . . .

Did he know she was there?

He was scooping buckets full of water and pouring them all over himself, and the rivulets streamed down his body into every concave muscle, down every indented line, through the thick wiry hair, down and down and into and onto the deep dark mystery of him, caressing him in all the places where she imagined following with her fingers, her hands, her lips, her tongue—

No!

Damn it, damn it, damn it—she was committed heart and soul to Clay Rutledge whether or not he was ready.

But he would be . . . soon, he would be . . .

"Who's there?"

His voice boomed out at her, startling her; she grabbed the rifle reflexively and lifted it to her shoulder.

"Damn it, who's there?"

His voice was like a god's—deep, commanding, as hard and inflexible as mahogany.

But how did he know? *How did he know?*

She could just see that he had wrapped a towel around his hips and his clothes were slung over one arm, and she didn't dare try to see more.

She had seen enough . . .

She didn't dare move and she didn't know if he were walking toward her or making his way to the house . . . She could tell nothing by the sounds—but he was barefoot; there would be no noise whatsoever; he could just sneak up on her . . .

"Who the hell are you?"

She reeled backward at the sound of his voice so close to her, ten feet away on the opposite side of her protective tree.

And his darkling black eyes didn't miss the rifle, either.

She steadied it against her shoulder, feeling the power of it playing oddly with her momentary feeling of helplessness.

"I'm the one with the gun," she said softly. "And who the hell are you?"

He smiled then, a lazy little smile that curved up the edges of his firm lips but did not find its way to his opaque eyes.

"I'm either your most ravishing fantasy or your worst nightmare."

She hated the smug nasty look in his eyes. Her hands trembled slightly as she forced herself to look him over, forced herself to shrug off her reaction to his obvious attributes.

"Oh—I don't think I would lose any sleep over you," she said insolently.

And there it was, he thought: a man nursed a dream of Eden and he wound up with a viper in his garden. How perfect.

"I think I'll torment your dreams, especially if you kill me." *Or I'll die of snakebite instead . . .*

She felt that wobbly disconnection of her knees. Damn him, he was too riveting with that knowledgeable voice and those eyes—and the rest of him . . .

She gritted her teeth. "Who are you?"

The heat rose between them for the space of a heartbeat.

"I'm the man you want to sleep with, sugar. And maybe that's all you need to know."

She made a strangled sound in her throat. "I wouldn't be too sure of that, stranger. *I'm* the one who's got the gun."

His obsidian eyes made inroads all over her body, touching her in places she would not have believed possible.

"I beg to differ with you, sugar . . ."

Dear Heaven—her eyes strayed, just for the zillionth of a second to his towel-wrapped hips—and he was there, all there, and it would take just the bold jut of the rifle barrel against the towel to reveal to her all his secrets.

". . . so easy to pull the trigger . . ." he murmured, following her avid gaze, waiting, just waiting for the right moment to reach for the rifle and—

Blam!

The shot cut a six-inch-long furrow into the ground beside him.

"As you say, so easy to pull the trigger," she said complacently as she racked up the next round. "Now—we can talk—or it can talk . . ."

He smiled again, and leaned against the tree, unmindful of the rough bark scraping the skin of his arm.

"I know all about how nicely *it* can talk, sugar. I'd much rather have that between us than a round of buckshot."

"Well, your buckshot can get me in a lot more trouble than mine, stranger, and let me warn you, no one looks twice at murder when property's involved."

"Is that so, sugar? You own all this land and house?"

"Do you?"

"I'm just passing through, sugar; the place is abandoned and no one will mind."

"I mind. The owner will mind."

"Let him come get me then, sugar. Or maybe I'll come get you." He made a move—and she fired again—*blam!*—inches from his feet at the root of the tree.

"Likely you killed the tree," he said blandly.

"Likely I'll fell a different tree if you don't start answering my questions," she said grimly, waving the rifle at him.

He caught her then, as if he'd been waiting for her to make that one little mistake, that one little hesitation, that one little movement that would cost her the precious second she would need to regain her balance and control.

He grabbed the rifle barrel, twisted it upward, and jerked it and her against his hard, wet body just as she pulled the trigger once again.

Blam! into the air, and then she was in his arms and gazing up at the burning coal-black of his eyes, her body strained against the iron-hard poker that would stoke her heat.

"Sleepy, sugar?" he murmured, and then his mouth took hers without preliminaries or apologies or lies.

And she fell into its swooning hot wetness as if she had been waiting for this kiss all of her life.

She felt her grip loosen on the rifle and then the bunching of the muscles in his arm as he tossed it over her shoulder.

She felt the bone-melting possession of a man's determination, and the thrusting demand of his body, which was separated from hers by a yard's width of material.

She felt the shafting coiling heat of a grown man's desire, held in check only by his mere will.

And above all, she felt a shimmering radiant fear that it would be too easy to succumb to this lush torpid world of the senses. She was halfway there on her curiosity alone, and it took all the strength she could muster to keep from reaching down and actually *feeling* that massive naked push against the thin material of her dress.

Clay had never aroused her like this . . .

The moment the thought skittered through her dazzled mind, she wrenched away from him violently.

"Sugar kisses . . ." he murmured, drawing her toward him again. "Hot . . . sweet . . . sticky—"

"Oh God," she groaned. She couldn't, she just couldn't let him seduce her with such sweet talk.

Clay . . . Clay . . . Clay . . . she chanted his name like a litany, pulling away and pulling away from him—and he let her go.

He let her go just when he could have overpowered her and made her bend to his will; and as she faced him, panting, across a space of a foot, with no protection now except his will, she understood for the first time the honor of a man.

"Sleep tight, sugar," he murmured, divining her every thought. "Pleasant dreams."

She whirled away from him and she ran. She ran from his eyes and from his all-encompassing mouth; she ran from his hard steely body and his equally steely determination.

And she ran, most of all, from herself.

Chapter 1

Montelette Plantation

Dayne Templeton stood leaning against one of the thick ornamental columns that dominated the verandah of Montelette Plantation, her arms crossed over her midriff as if she were protecting herself.

Protecting myself from what? A scurrilous stranger? A spoiled rakehell who was playing games with me? Or just Nyreen—who is more dangerous than the two put together?

She could hardly bear thinking about the afternoon, and it seemed that the only way to keep the two humiliations at arm's length was to pretend to be everything she was not.

So she was dressed properly now in a cool muslin dress, which had four deep flounces at the hem, correctly supported by those insufferable steel hoops, and her arms were covered by two decorous coy lace undersleeves peeking out from beneath two funnel shaped sleeves.

All prim and prime, she thought mordantly, tarted up to look like a proper young lady from her hem to her hair, when in truth there was nothing proper about her at all.

She was ready for warfare, she thought, even though she must play by the enemies' rules.

Enemies who now even included Clay . . .

"Oh, look at you, Miss Priss—standing there as if butter wouldn't melt on your biscuits and all rigged out to look demure and innocent. Why if your daddy ever heard about the trick you pulled yesterday at the Purdys' barbecue, I swear, he would marry you off to the first itinerant salesman who wandered onto Monte-lette."

"Well then, you must be sure to tell him, Nyreen. You can't wait to get rid of me anyway, can you?"

Nyreen chose to ignore her. "I just don't understand your thinking, Dayne—riding that old horse right up to the Purdys' reception like a cowboy and then jumping off so everyone could see your drawers *and* that you weren't wearing a hoop or *anything.* . . . If your mother were alive . . ."

"But she isn't," Dayne interrupted briskly, "and you have no right to scold me about anything. Besides, you were just jealous of all those handsome men sitting at my feet and falling all over themselves to hear about the Boy and his chances at the next Go-Down Race Day. It just proves that men really do like ladies with spirit."

But what she meant was, Clay liked ladies with spirit and he had told her so often enough.

"They don't marry ladies with spirit," Nyreen retorted, "or didn't your mama teach you that?"

"Did yours?" Dayne shot back without missing a beat and was gratified to see Nyreen's lips tighten.

"I know better than to chase those River County bayou babies who aren't seasoned enough to know which end is the rudder that steers the boat. I prefer an older man with experience any-way."

"Yes," Dayne said drily, "it is quite obvious that you do."

Nyreen did not rise to the bait. "And you—salivating all over Clay Rutledge. Your daddy would just about die—"

"My daddy is blind these days to anything but the business at hand," Dayne said acidly. "And anyway, that stupid feud is meaningless after all these years."

But she knew that wasn't true and that she was playing with fire by *publicly* encouraging the recklessly profligate and devastatingly handsome Clay who was still just on the edge of being socially acceptable after the *incident* that resulted in his father's death.

How hard had it been to watch him flirting and talking with other women at the barbecue when her lips were still warm with the heat of his kisses.

But he couldn't appear to favor her, not in front of all her father's friends and their neighbors who were still slightly wary of him and the circumstances of his father's death. He had been on his best behavior just because of that, and he had flirted so outrageously just to bring the ladies around to his side.

"Ladies love a scoundrel," he had said, his lips brushing hers as he bid her farewell, "but I love only you."

She gloried in the knowledge that he wanted her; and when the time was right, he had said, they would tell everyone and they would get engaged and not even her father or that ridiculous old feud could stop them. She had nursed that promise like a tender seed while she met him in secret.

"Oh? *I* wouldn't call it *meaningless*," Nyreen said consideringly. "You are such a child, Dayne. I sometimes wonder how we can be of an age."

"We obviously aren't," Dayne returned silkily, "and it's perfectly plain that you are so much more experienced because of the company you keep."

She heard the satisfying intake of Nyreen's breath as she digested the implication of that statement.

"Well," Nyreen said, "we shall see if there are repercussions when your father returns from town."

"I suppose we will," Dayne said, shrugging. "You will race to be first with the news of my intractable behavior and so—"

"You are impossible."

"*You* are not my mother."

"You need one!"

"I won't tell you what you need," Dayne said grimly.

"You're fooling no one."

"Neither are you."

"I won't listen to this."

"Fine then—go *away.*"

She heard Nyreen inhale deeply three times as she struggled to control her temper.

"Perhaps it might be better if *you* go away," she said maliciously, and Dayne felt a hot wash of foreboding.

She could do it—she could do it. She could convince my father—and then . . . and then . . .

Her father, whom she could have sworn was no fool—even her father had been taken in by the fawning fantasy of a sweet young thing distressed by the realities of life.

Nyreen was kin, he would say, but she wasn't blood kin, and neither Dayne nor she ever forgot it. Nyreen was only the daughter of her father's brother's second wife, and the couple had sent Nyreen to live at Montelette while the two went westward to build their dreams.

And Nyreen was now maliciously destroying *hers*.

Nothing had been the same since Nyreen had settled in at Montelette. And her parents had not come, nor had they sent word in four long years.

Dayne had been stuck up in the sickroom with her deathly ill mother while Nyreen—who was supposed to have helped her in exchange for staying with them—Nyreen had made herself indispensable to her father instead—and in ways Dayne did not care to think about.

She felt closed out and abandoned.

She remembered exactly the day it had happened, the day her father had absolved Nyreen of all responsibility of helping in the sickroom.

"My dear Dayne," her father had said in that sickening this-is-the-best-for-everyone tone of voice, "we all know you are so much more attuned to the demands of care giving. Look at how many hours you've spent in the stables with a sick horse, or one about to foal. You have so much more patience and strength. It makes sense, Dayne, really it does . . ."

It had made no sense to her that he had allowed himself the pleasure of Nyreen's company while Dayne presided over the sickroom, held her mother's boneless hand and assured her that everything was as it should be when she really felt that everything was falling to pieces.

The hard truth was that her father was attracted to Nyreen's youth and the exotic carnal aura that surrounded her. Nyreen was encouraging him and teasing him and pushing *her* slowly and inexorably out of her father's life in the process.

. . . better if you go away . . . you go away . . .

The words resonated between them: Nyreen was so sure of her power.

Dayne felt the shift in Nyreen's emotion as her fury died down and she insinuated herself into the righteous guise of mentor and advisor.

"My dear cousin, enough of this nonsense. I just want you to understand you can't keep your follies secret much longer. You underestimate the gentleman's code: Mr. Purdy—or someone who was at the barbecue—will surely tell your father what happened. Men will talk: they gossip worse than women when they get together for meetings and such. And they will say one thing to your face and another behind your back, and where will that leave you?"

"Why exactly where you want me, *dear* cousin—in disgrace and with my father loathing the very sight of me."

"I give up."

"You should never have tried."

Nyreen shot her a look of pure hatred. "And neither should you," she spat and she stalked away.

Two weeks after he arrived in St. Foy, Flint Rutledge returned to Bonneterre.

It was exactly the way he remembered it, as if time had stood still, and Bonneterre had waited for him.

What he didn't expect was the pull of the land, the fierce possessive sense of kinship with the ground he walked on; he had never thought he felt it. He had thought that he had run from it.

"You're late," his mother said and she was the only thing about Bonneterre that bore the stamp of the passing years.

His sudden appearance did not faze her. She had long ago come to terms with the destructiveness of the one son and the blind disrespect of the other.

She had no warm words of welcome for him after twenty years: she had never been warm and cossetting; she had always been removed and censuring.

And she had always loved Clay the best.

"Let me look at you," she commanded when he said nothing in response to her words.

"Have you not been?" he asked softly, and she felt in an instant the same old resistant streak in him that was never amenable to taking orders—especially from her.

Just like Verne. And not like Verne at all—a throwback, rather, to her own tall and lean father with the same family features: the hard high cheekbones, the world-weary lines etched around his eyes and sensual mouth, the glittery jet black gaze that missed nothing and skewered everything, the well-defined brows that were the one indicator of his emotions.

And his stance—his father come to life again. And the hands, the hair, so thick and laced now with strands of gray.

"Where have you been, boy?" she said, ignoring his awareness that she had been feasting on his very appearance. "Not that it matters. It's too late; there's nothing you can do, nothing. I don't need anyone's help. *Anyone's,*" she added fiercely. "Sit down. Tull—bring a chair for Mr. Rutledge."

"Yes'm," Tull said obediently, and brought forward a large, stiff chair.

He sat.

She stared at him. "You didn't have to go."

"I couldn't have stayed."

"It killed me."

"I was old enough. Verne wanted me out of the way, and he was right. You couldn't stop him and neither could I. The easiest thing was for me to leave."

Her face crumpled for a moment and then she visibly pulled herself together with the hard won stoicism she had cultivated all these years. Olivia did her crying in private.

"The cycle never changes," she said cryptically. "Your father is dead, Clay is a wastrel, and you squandered twenty years that you could have given to Bonneterre. I wish my letter had not found you. I wish you had never come back."

He stood up. "I can just as easily go, Mother. There is obviously nothing here—" but he wasn't at all sure that was true now.

However, her barbs and pointed disapproval could not blackmail him after all this time. He was immune to her, and he wondered why, in his youth, her least little rebuke had had the power to diminish him.

"Don't go!" The words spilled from her lips almost unconsciously and she looked stricken, as if she wanted to call them back.

"Don't go," she said again as if in that split second she had measured the worth of them and decided there was some reason to detain him.

"As you wish," he said coolly.

"I want to know—" she said and stopped again. She could never ask for anything, not even the most basic information; nor could she seem even remotely overjoyed that her oldest son had returned to her.

"We have to talk," she said finally. "We have to talk—you could stay a day—or two . . . a week perhaps?"

The hospitable mother, whom no guest on a day's outing could ever refuse. The sensibility remained the same: the guest must be entertained. Conversation would flow, and food and wine. Verne was gone and Clay might not be able to fill his shoes, but the appearance of bounty and hospitality had to be preserved.

He felt just a tingling stirring of pity, an emotion his mother would have quashed in a moment. She had grown so old and she was still the indomitable mother of his memory.

He could not say no.

From her third floor window that overlooked the rear gardens of Montelette, Nyreen watched in satisfaction as Dayne made her way to the stables. Dayne did this every morning, and Nyreen liked the fact that she could count on this routine.

There was something very nice about people being exactly where they were supposed to be at any given time.

And she loved the fact that she did not have to be anywhere.

Such a luxurious life, something she could never have conceived of barely a year ago.

Sometimes the gentility of life here grated on her nerves; and sometimes her tormenting and teasing of Harry provided all the excitement she could ever want.

All she had to do was figure out a way to get that hot-headed snit of a daughter out of the way before Harry found his conscience.

She had to mercilessly bind Harry to her so that if he ever had to make a decision, there would be no doubt whom he would choose.

Things were becoming explosive between them. The air was ripe with the burgeoning heat of their passion and Harry's resentment of Dayne's presence, which allowed them no privacy whatsoever.

And now Dayne had played right into her hands with her silly party tricks at the Purdys'.

The timing was right: it was merely a matter of helping Harry along.

She had ever been a risk taker. It was time to finally reap her reward.

Her father had returned too late from town and so Dayne did not know until morning what he had heard or even whether he had heard of her antics at the Purdys'.

And there was nothing from Clay—not a word, not an apology—and that immediately set her nerves on edge.

"Miz Dayne? G'd mawning, Miz Dayne."

She sat alone as usual at one end of the table, after her sojourn to the stables, as Zenona solicitously served her eggs, grits, fruit, and biscuits.

"Mistuh Harry wish to see you, Miz Dayne, right aftuh you takes yo' breakfus'."

"Thank you, Zenona," Dayne said briskly. *So—he had heard, or Nyreen had rushed to tell him the minute he came in the door.*

How late must she have awaited him? And what did he suppose they did after Nyreen had told tales on her?

She *hated* her, just *despised* her.

She ate slowly, simmering with rage against Clay and Nyreen both.

Clay was too confident of her, she thought angrily. Maybe he had shown up yesterday after all and the arrogant stranger had killed him.

Oh my yes, she did like that scene because it pushed the other more guilt-inducing pictures out of her mind: herself in the arms of the stranger, willingly accepting his kisses.

She hadn't thought about it all night in her fury over Nyreen. And now she had to deal with her father before she could even confront Clay and his perfidy.

Well, her father would be in his office now even though he had no pressing business. Everything ran with effortless efficiency in the hands of his overseer, Bastien who was quick with punishment and a hard driver of men; if someone sloughed off, Bastien was the one to attend to it, not Harry Templeton.

Her father had no need of an office. She suspected sometimes that he merely used it as an escape when the household got to be too much for him.

And if he were hiding there this morning, she couldn't quite fathom why he particularly wanted to see her.

Unless he wanted to chastise her away from Nyreen's prying eyes.

Which would be the first time he had taken her feelings into consideration for a long time.

The office was situated in a separate building, away from the house and beyond where prying eyes could see. And yet it was re-assuringly in plain sight and her mother's sickroom windows overlooked it, and every morning her mother would watch for him as if just seeing him made her feel that everything was just as it had always been.

But nothing would ever be the same again, and she could not resign herself to it.

She stepped up onto the verandah that mirrored the one on the main house.

The door was locked.

The door was never locked, especially if he were expecting her.

And there was no need anyway: she had the key.

She slipped her hand into her pocket and then something compelled her to stop.

A feeling of dread washed over her and eddied away, leaving her face burning, her resolution shaken.

She pushed away the forbidden thought that rushed immediately into her mind: *what if someone else is there?* Taking a deep breath, she removed the key and inserted it into the lock.

The door swung open, silently, smoothly, and framed the picture of her worst nightmares: her father and Nyreen, together, Nyreen naked and straddling his legs and offering herself, her breasts, her mouth, her body, her dark unholy mystery to the man who would greedily accept and worship the hot mystical sex of her.

Chapter 2

"Bonneterre is deeply in debt," Olivia said, her voice showing no vestige of emotion. "We live on credit from season to season, hoping the last will bail us out of the succeeding one. There is little liquid money, and what there is, Clay is slowly throwing away with his everlasting debts of honor. This year or next, Harry Templeton will finally have his way: I will accept his offer to buy Bonneterre if no other way out presents itself."

But of course it would: she was laying the groundwork for that. She only wanted her unflinching oldest son to have some idea of the hole into which his leaving and Verne's death had cast them.

She wanted to stack the deck as much as possible because, in her heart of hearts, she wanted him to stay.

But she would never ask.

"I see," he said, his expression as impassive as hers. He was truly his mother's son; only he knew she could get to him, and he saw the frustration bloom for an unguarded moment in her eyes.

And then she went on: "Clay is in New Orleans even now, redeeming the deed to Orinda, which he used as collateral in his last round of play."

Ah, that got to him—she saw it in his bottomless jetty eyes—the thunderstorm of anger finally that meant he had some feeling for his patrimony.

"I just hope he does not squander it on yet another game," she continued slyly, "but that is of no concern to you, is it, Flint my boy?"

"Not in the least," he said politely. "Is there anything else, Mother?"

"Let us pray that Orinda is the least of all he could lose to his gaming," she said coolly. "Or perhaps it might settle the question more easily than my signing over Bonneterre to Harry Templeton. Perhaps I should not be fighting so hard to hold on, now that it is evident that Clay does not care and you are perfectly prepared to turn your back on us again."

"Perhaps," he said noncommittally.

She felt a volcanic frustration with him and his obtuse desire to commit to nothing. He had been in the house barely two days, had walked around it like some stranger seeing it for the first time, and she could not tell from one moment to the next what he was thinking.

He was so different and everything else was so much the same. *What was he seeing?*

What was he *feeling?*

"*Flint,*" she said, and her voice neither commanded nor begged, but still there was that pleading underlying her absolute refusal to say anything more than his name.

The word said it all: she had named him well, and the name had gone from honoring her father and her family to representing the indelible impression of what he was.

He was her son; she felt it, she wanted it, she denied it all at once. He had never been lovable, and he still wasn't. But he was strong, and she needed that essence of him at this moment.

She didn't even want explanations. She wanted only his unflinching strength to lean against and depend upon.

And it was the one thing she could not ask.

She sniffed. She wondered what he was thinking.

No, she didn't care. It was like the winding up of the family circle: he stood linked with no one within and she no longer had to worry and wonder about the possibilities his twenty year absence had created.

Now she knew: she must go on as before. His presence made no difference; and in the end, the result would be the same as if he had never come back.

* * *

It was the final straw, and once Dayne had slammed the door and Nyreen had contrived to close out the vision of her horrified face and bring him back on his sojourn to ecstasy, and once he had attained that long awaited lust-driven culmination, Harry Templeton knew exactly what he had to do.

He had put it off too long; his friends had warned him—and he had finally had enough of Dayne's pathetic attempts to claim his attention. She was a grown woman, for God's sake—and he should have married her off years ago. Would have . . . but of course—her mother . . . Dayne had been particularly useful for taking care of that, especially after Nyreen had come to them.

He couldn't fault Dayne's devotion; it was her childishness, her snooping, and poking her nose where it didn't belong that infuriated him.

And her stubborn dislike of Nyreen.

He felt a glimmer of excitement at the thought of Dayne leaving Montelette. No longer would he have to worry about anyone overhearing them, or walking in on them.

He would be alone with Nyreen forever.

He looked up as she slipped into the office and locked the door behind her.

"The brat is gone," Nyreen whispered.

"We'll get rid of her."

Nyreen eased herself onto his lap and nuzzled his neck. "I had a wonderful idea."

He tried to kiss her. "Tell me."

She evaded his mouth. "It's the perfect solution, Harry. It will get you everything you ever wanted."

"I can't wait to hear it," Harry murmured, distracted by Nyreen's tempting curves and her eager mouth.

"Clay Rutledge."

He felt as if she had dashed cold water in his face.

"Are you crazy?"

Nyreen stood up and moved away from him. *"Think* about it for a moment, Harry. He's close, he's the heir apparent; you've been after Bonneterre for years—as you've taken great pains to tell me. She likes him—oh yes, don't look shocked. I *know.*"

She saw him wrestle with it, resisting it, hating it. And then slowly, slowly he comprehended how perfect the idea was. He could see it, the big picture: Dayne gone, Clay worthless, Olivia frantic, and Bonneterre needing some astute management—for a percentage of the profits—and he would have everything he ever wanted, just as she said.

She smiled maliciously and began walking toward him seductively and unbuttoning her dress as she came closer and closer. "But listen Harry—this is the best part—" And then she knew she didn't even have to say it. Harry understood the whole in that instant and he loved it and he would do it—because it would just kill Olivia Rutledge.

Dayne's mind was clear and she was as calm as the bayou water as she walked to the stable, saddled up the Boy, mounted him, and guided him slowly out to the long pasture and the road to Bonneterre.

She was not going to stay at Montelette a moment longer, and Clay must make good on his promise to marry her *now*.

Besides, she thought hardheadedly, he had nothing to lose. Montelette was the paying proposition, not Bonneterre; but over and above that, it would make her father furious—so furious she didn't know what he might do.

It didn't matter; he did not matter. Every ounce of love she had for him had gushed right out of her heart the moment she opened his office door that morning. She had nothing left—nothing.

She felt so cool and calm. It made perfect sense. Clay wanted her; she wanted him; and her father wanted Nyreen. The solution was simply at hand. Clay could not refuse her.

She rode through the sun-dappled fields and up and around the rise that led downward to the cane fields, which stretched for hundreds of acres in two directions.

Montelette's harvest, its riches, its lifeblood.

She felt a momentary sharp terror at the thought of leaving it.

But she wouldn't be leaving: she would be with Clay, just down the road, just as she had always dreamed, and just as they had planned.

* * *

Olivia was waiting when Clay returned from town. "We have a guest."

"Why, that's fine, Mama," he said carelessly, tossing his hat to Tull and stamping into the parlor. "I remember how Daddy loved to entertain."

"Daddy loved to show off," Olivia said tartly. "I didn't *love* to do anything—not that it's any of your business. I hope that Dupin has returned the deed to you?"

"Now Mama—"

"Of course you will give it to me now for safekeeping."

"Well, no—I can't rightly do that, Mama. I left it with my banker in New Orleans."

"Did you now? How fortuitous. With M. Bertrand? Yes, I thought so. He did your father many signal favors over the years; of course he would cosset you and assume things would go on the same way forever. Which harvest have we put into his pocket this time? No comment?" she taunted as Clay turned on his heel and stamped to the window. "I didn't think you would tell me."

Clay wheeled around to face her then. "Orinda is safe, Mama—that's all you care about anyway."

Olivia drew herself up. "What if we could reckon on a more productive harvest at Bonneterre? What if there's a chance we could reduce the debts and elevate our reputation in St. Foy?"

"We've been over that, Mama. It can't be done."

"That's very interesting, Clay, because I have been talking to someone who says it can be done—someone who *wants* to do it."

"Nonsense," Clay said sharply. "There's no one around for two hundred miles who has the time and energy to devote to overseeing another crop."

"Oh—but my guest—"

"Who *is* this fool?" Clay snorted derisively, just about at the end of his patience with his mother's cat-and-mouse game.

"Me," a burnished voice said behind him, and he whirled to confront the vision of his darkest dreams: his god-incarnate older brother, who had absconded, decamped, and deserted them, and who now stood there like some biblical patriarch just waiting to claim his birthright and mow down the mere mortals who stood in his way.

"Either he goes or I go."

Clay made the ultimatum confidently, knowing full well Olivia could not bear to lose him, counting on the fact that she adored him and had always had nothing but derogatory words for the beloved older son who had walked out of their lives without looking back.

Flint's defection had almost broken her spirit: she had been counting on him to temper Verne's hotheaded ways. She had known from the beginning that Clay was just like his father and she would get no help there.

But Clay had also known that he had that same seductive, reckless magnetism and that she was not immune to it. He had gotten by on it for so many years, and he cared nothing about Bonneterre except insofar as it provided him with enough to get along.

And now, in her last years, the old witch was going to put her heritage before her heart and turn the thing over to that changeling brother of his?

Never! He would leave first. He would convert Orinda into cash and show the old crone who had the power all along.

He even knew she could read it in his face, and his insolent derision of her stupidity.

She wouldn't want him to sell Orinda. He saw all the possibilities warring in her expression, and he was certain she would make the right choice now.

She looked so old suddenly, so defeated: he wished Lydia were here to see him triumphing over his mother's better instincts. She would have loved seeing Olivia backed into a corner, and bowed by the decision she must make.

Olivia knew that Clay would not back down. He had made his choice, too. So it was only a matter of her telling that usurper that he was not welcome here, and that he, Clay, would be managing Bonneterre just as he had always done.

"Well," Olivia said briskly, the word coming out like an exhalation of great tension. "Well—" She could hardly bear to go on. Clay was going to pull the very life from her and not give a damn that he was doing it.

Careless, reckless Clay, always depending on the things that he knew were unchanging. Never thinking of consequences or ramifications. Always seeing her as the bottomless bulwark of the family fortune that would float his ship time and again because she would be dead—and he would be dead—by the time there was nothing left.

He never did understand, she thought remorselessly, feeling the creak and crack of her age and the unforgiving motion of letting him go.

"Well," she said again, knowing very well the threat that would follow, "your heart and soul have always been in New Orleans, Clay. I expect you'll like living there full time."

"I expect I will," he said coolly, meeting her hard flat eyes. "I expect I will, once I position myself properly. You understand what I mean, Mama."

"Indeed I do," she said, and she found that it didn't hurt a tenth as much as she had thought it would. "But of course I was weak-minded enough to make the deed over to you. So it is no surprise you will do with it as you please."

"Mama—" he caught himself. He wouldn't beg, he wouldn't . . . but in a flashing instant he saw everything he was relinquishing by taking this hardheaded stand: the power—the unlimited mind-boggling power he had over lives he could do with as he wished. There would be none of that in New Orleans unless he were willing to pay for it.

But why not? he thought, lifting his chin. The bastard changeling would pull money from this place, get it on its feet and then . . . and then—accidents could happen. And meantime, he could sell off Orinda for his immediate needs, and maybe the thing would come right anyway.

And if it didn't—*if*—there was always that mewling Dayne Templeton: there was money there, lots of it, and he would be perfectly willing to marry her to get it— providing Harry made up the right marriage settlement.

And if he wouldn't, well . . . time to work out those consequences later; surely Dayne would not expect her father to live forever . . .

So it would all work out in the end: his mother could have the family traitor. In truth, he was probably good for just one thing: getting Bonneterre back on its feet and productive again.

And when the money was flowing and Olivia was missing him desperately, he would waltz back into their lives again, his pockets stuffed with gold from the real work of the gaming tables.

He had only to have some patience, then Bonneterre and its riches would be his once more. Everything else could wait.

"I will pack and be out of here as soon as possible," he said stiffly.

"I didn't expect anything else," Olivia said.

He started from the room and turned back. "This is so stupid, Mama—to let him back here and hand him over the plantation and you don't even know what he can do . . ."

"I know what you *can't* do," Olivia said. "He couldn't do much worse. And you could have done a lot better."

"Lydia will have a tantrum."

"I'd be pleased if you would invite her to stay with you in New Orleans then."

"Mama—"

"No more threats, Clay. I'll deal with Lydia when she returns from St. Francisville. Have the goodness to let me know your direction when you are settled. Otherwise, I have nothing more to say."

"Nor have I, Mama," he said resentfully as he mounted the steps. "Remember—it was *your* choice, not mine."

"Oh no," Olivia murmured, watching him until he disappeared. "Oh no, it was your choice, my boy, and you made it a long, long time ago . . ."

She had never been this close to Bonneterre; they had always met in the fields of Montelette or down at Orinda where no one ever came, but never had she come within shouting distance of the white columns of Bonneterre.

She felt her knees turn to water as the long tree-shaded drive came into view, and she reined in the Boy.

The prospect was daunting; she had not thought for one moment about how she was going to get to see Clay, but if she had to, she would just walk up to that forbidding ten foot double door and summon a servant.

She was crazy to have come. What if Olivia Rutledge happened out onto the verandah and saw her? What if her father had someone following her? What if Clay weren't even there?

She debated her course calmly and coolly as the Boy stomped and danced impatiently, waiting for her to make a decision.

She couldn't go to the house—at least not at first. There was something about the notion of facing Olivia Rutledge that was positively unnerving.

She bit her lip. She didn't know why she was so intimidated: Bonneterre was no different than her own house with its encircling two-story verandah and the secretive rooms deep within its shadow. And the man who had lived there, her father's worst enemy, he was dead, so what could Olivia Rutledge do to her if she found her on the property?

She could run her off, Dayne supposed, but that would be an amusing sight: Olivia with a broom, whacking at the Boy and screeching at *her*. No, Olivia would never lower herself to do it.

She'd probably invite me in for tea. Appearances must always be preserved.

She had learned that lesson at her mother's knee, and it was probably why she could not lower herself to have a screaming tantrum about her father and Nyreen.

And she certainly ought not be at Bonneterre in pursuit of Clay before he was ready to declare himself.

But she couldn't think about that now that she was here. She had come this far—she could not leave without seeing him.

She just couldn't get up the gumption to go up to the house. If he were home, he probably wouldn't be there anyway. Clay's second home was the stables, and it would be a lot easier to ask someone there to summon him to meet her.

And if that didn't work, she would resort to more desperate measures, like banging down the front door.

She eased the Boy back down the drive and looked for a break toward the fields behind the garconniere that flanked the house.

It was easy enough to trail behind the houses and past the overseer's cabin, and the dairy house, skirt the edge of the fields and the vegetable gardens to the carriage house and stables which were on the far side of the property.

She did not go unnoticed and here and there in the hum of activity, one and another of the servants and workers stared up after her, likely debating whether or not to tell the overseer that there was a stranger prowling Bonneterre.

But someone would find out soon enough, she thought, as she ducked into the stable and called out Clay's name.

Immediately, the largest black man she had ever seen in her life appeared and she jumped in fright.

"What you want, Miss?"

His voice was so deep, it seemed like it rumbled up from someplace near his toes.

"I'm looking for Mister Clay," she said boldly.

"Yas'm. He be loadin' up in de cah'rage house."

Loading up? . . . loading up?

She whirled away from him and raced out of the stables, pausing only to drape the Boy's reins over a post, before she charged into the wide open doors of the carriage house.

"Clay! Clay!"

There were kerosene lamps burning to augment the natural light, and he pulled up sharply at the sound of her voice, the trunk he was hoisting in one hand falling into the arms of the house servant assisting him.

"Jesus . . ." he muttered, swinging down from the carriage that was ominously loaded with boxes and suitcases. She didn't hear him, however, and she saw nothing, only him, as she flew into his arms.

"What the hell are you doing here? Are you crazy?"

"Clay . . ." she murmured, winding her arms around him; he felt so solid, so safe, so sure.

"Dayne . . ." As tactfully as he could, he set her away from him, and as he caught the sheen of tears in her eyes, he lifted her chin so he could clearly see her face.

"Something's wrong. You never would have come here if something weren't wrong. Dayne . . . your father?"

Did his tone sound too hopeful? But still, if something had

happened to Harry—it would be a way out that could salvage his pride.

"Oh yes," she sniffed, "my father, my stupid, unthinking, uncaring, randy father—" She couldn't hold back the tears that spilled from her eyes. ". . . and that . . . that . . . Nyreen—they . . . they—" She took a deep breath as she sensed his impatience with her. "I walked in on them. They were together—alone . . . rutting animals—And my mother not dead a year. . . . He's going to marry her, Clay, I just know it, and I cannot stay another minute on Montelette with her. I *can't.*"

Shit. He felt the word forming, and he clamped down on his temper and his instant feeling that everything was falling apart before he could even make one rational plan.

"This makes no sense, Dayne. Your father—and *Nyreen?*" He was appalled at the thought of it—Nyreen was so young. And so luscious. And so available . . . All alone with Harry on Montelette . . .

And then he felt a stab of envy that Harry was going to win once again and leave him, Clay, with nothing.

Dayne heard the tone of his voice very clearly—the rational tone, the one that accused her of making up stories. She should have known that feminine wiles never worked with him. And that she was the last person he expected to resort to them.

Her tears dried up and her determination rose with a steely intensity.

"They were together—in his office. I *saw* them. I won't ever be able to look at her without seeing them together—like *that.*"

She didn't have to say more: the picture was too clear—Harry and that tempting hot-eyed nymph—a picture that could arouse him even in the starkness of her words.

Damn it, damn it, damn it . . .

He didn't want to say it—but he didn't like being backed into a corner—especially by *her.* His plans didn't include *her*—not yet, maybe not ever.

So he said it, because he wanted her to define the solution. "What do you want me to do, Dayne?"

She did not disappoint him. She was so beautiful, with her

glittery blue eyes that were assessing him a little too acutely for comfort. And that beautifully shaped mouth.

He watched her perfect lips form the words that no lady would ever say out loud to a man: "I want you to marry me."

He knew he heard them; and he knew, gentleman that he was supposed to be, he ought to have offered the moment he heard her tale of woe.

But still—that pulsating beat of a minute, two, three passed and he said nothing, and Dayne thought she would die.

Except that it was so like Clay, she should have expected it.

"I'm going to New Orleans," he said finally because he had to say something. "Listen to me, Dayne, I've got to leave Bonneterre. It's a matter of honor . . ."

"It always is," she said bitterly.

"I would have you in a minute," he protested, warming to his story, "but something happened that neither of us could have foreseen—my brother came home and my mother made a choice, and now I have no other option but to leave. You have to understand, Dayne. She's handing the whole thing over to him, over my head and behind my back, and I can't—I won't—let that bastard take my inheritance right from under my feet. I need time. You have to give me time. That's why I have to leave—"

"No, you don't," Dayne said tartly, meaningfully.

"I have to leave," Clay repeated, "but I'll—I'll send for you the minute I get settled, Dayne. I swear. Nothing will change between us. We'll live in New Orleans, and we'll live like kings. Everything will be just the way we planned it, Dayne, I promise."

She drew herself up. This would be the hardest thing she had ever had to do. But the bastard deserved it. He was running out on her and Bonneterre and it was time for her to do some plain speaking.

"I need it to be that way now, Clay. I have to go back to that house—and I have to live with the knowledge of what I saw and what my father is really thinking. It could take you months to make your way in New Orleans. I can't wait that long."

"Not even for me?" he asked, thinking to cajole her—just a little, so that he wouldn't precipitately lose one of the options he was counting on.

"Especially not for you," she said pointedly, wheeling away from him so he could not witness the humiliation that would only give him more power over her.

Oh, she was finished with him; he was as meaningless to her as snow.

"Dayne—wait! What are you going to do?"

"Find someone to marry me," she said tightly from the carriage house doorway, her words as decisive and piercing as arrows. "And soon."

God, he hated them all: his stupid mother, his bastard brother, and that insipid Dayne who couldn't even wait one month for his plans to come to fruition.

One stinking month—he knew a half dozen women who would have waited a year, let alone a month—that stupid little fool . . . after all his patience courting her! He had played her masterfully, reeling her in and casting her away. . . . He'd been so good at it, and now all his work would be for nothing.

He finished tying the last of his trunks onto the carriage and dismissed his servant.

Moments now before he left Bonneterre and he was seething with rage at Dayne for throwing this new complication into his plans.

If only she had kept quiet and kept her peace—for a month—for one damn month. Harry would not have done a thing about Nyreen in a month. Between them, they could have figured out something, in a month. He would have come down to Orinda on weekends, and they could have planned something. . . .

Damn, but she had caught him by surprise—a man couldn't be expected to say yes to a proposal when everything was dumped on his head all at once.

Hell—Montelette would solve all his problems, and Dayne Templeton was like biscuit dough in his hands—he should have just said yes . . .

He *would* say yes—

"Mistuh Clay . . ."

His head jerked up as he heard the sibilant sound of his name.

"Mistuh Clay . . ."

"Who is that?" he demanded sharply.

"Me, Mistuh Clay," the voice whispered seductively, "li'l ole me . . ."

"Meline . . . ?"

"Cain't fool Mistah Clay none, can I?" she murmured seductively as she sauntered out from one of the carriage stalls.

"You shouldn't be here."

Meline patted her tummy. "I be needin' to talk to you, Mistuh Clay."

"We've already talked about that," Clay said pointedly.

"Ain't nuthin' you can do, I know dat. But dey's somethin' else, Mistuh Clay, and maybe you be wantin' to listen befo' you go runnin' off and leavin' m . . . yo' rightful place."

He felt like shaking her. The last thing he needed on his way out the door was a scheming uppity house servant who was no better than she should be. His father was dead because of her and his mother already suspicioned the worst possible explanation, the truth of which he would never admit.

Everywhere, eyes watched him. Even now—

"You got to stay, Mistuh Clay—me an' the chile—we got a secret; we got powuh—"

"Voodoo mumbo jumbo," Clay snapped, grabbing his coat. "What the hell are you talking about?"

She felt flayed by the anger and rejection in his tone. She reared back, and her eyes narrowed. It was always like that between them—master and slave, except when he wanted something. And now he didn't want anything because *he* had taken everything he possibly could.

But she always had hope. Her mama had taught her to have hope, and to find a way to get some power.

Well, she had the power, and now she wanted the man, so she tempered her anger into something more conciliating.

"You come see Meline, Mistuh Clay, jus' like you used to, and you make it up nice wif me, and den maybe I tell you—"

He was losing patience. He could not be caught with her and she could have nothing to offer him *now*. Nevertheless, he knew that his rebuff would not deter her. That wasn't the way it

worked with Meline. He had to be nicer, to preserve her pride—
and their secret.

"Tell me *what?*" he said finally, swallowing his fury.

"I got a secret, Mistuh Clay, and I been savin' it fo' de time
someone be needin' it."

"We both know your secret, Meline—"

"No, no, no, Mistuh Clay, dat ain't what I'm talkin' 'bout,"
she said coquettishly. "You come see Meline and maybe I tell you.
Dis a secret fo' a man; a woman cain't do nuthin' wif it—'spe-
cially *me*. But a smart man . . . a man who know to keep a
promise . . ."

"I kept my promises," Clay said softly.

"As much as you can," Meline contradicted him. "But dis
way, you be keepin' all yo' promises, Mistuh Clay. You be findin'
de way, and all you got to do is come find Meline when you is settled in yo' fancy N'Awlins place. You find Meline and we sweet
talk, Mistuh Clay, 'bout promises and powuh and what my
mama done tole me."

His eyes kindled suddenly. "The jewels . . ."

"Now Mistuh Clay, how it gonna be if I tell you everything
right now? You be doin' what you gotta do, and den you come
find Meline when you is ready."

He reached out for her the moment she disappeared into the
shadows.

The jewels . . . oh God, he hadn't thought about that old story
for years . . . *the jewels* . . .

God, what a thought—

But how could it be so? Meline's mother had died and they
had burned—Olivia had said so . . .

And he was a fool to even remotely believe a desperate, lying
house slave, even if she were carrying his baby . . .

Or was he desperate enough to believe *anything?*

Stupid woman . . . !

"George! George!" he shouted, swinging into the carriage as
his driver came running. "Damn it, man—where have you been?
It's time—let's get the hell out of here!"

*   *   *

Know thine enemy . . .

Deep in the shadows of the carriage house loft, Flint Rutledge crouched as silent as a Sioux, his glittering eyes following the movement of the carriage as it lurched out into daylight.

A man could trust nothing, he thought dourly, not his family, not his dreams, not even his instincts.

He couldn't even trust himself.

He didn't move until the grating sound of the carriage wheels receded in the distance, and even then he shifted his body cautiously, deliberately, levering himself slowly off the edge of the loft and dropping softly and silently onto the carriage house floor.

From the open double doors, he could see the long vista of the winding drive and the towering trees sheltering it on either side.

In his mind's eye, he could see the whole map of Bonneterre, every dependency, every field, every track and bush, the big house with its thick columns and shaded verandah, and his intuition responded, overriding every other emotion:

Mine . . .

He crushed the thick envelope he held in his hand.

How quickly he had come to that.

Mine . . .

He had spent twenty years to find that he wanted only what had been his to begin with.

Mine . . .

All of it—Bonneterre, the woman, the banishment of Clay— everything he wanted, he held in the palm of his hand.

Slowly he smoothed out the thick, wrinkled envelope, which Tull had handed him just before he had followed Clay out to the carriage house.

Mine . . .

It was addressed to Olivia in an unfamiliar hand.

But when he turned it over, he found Harry Templeton's name engraved on the flap.

Mine . . .

Mercilessly, he tore open the envelope and scanned the contents.

My dear Olivia,

I take the liberty of writing to ask if I might call on you tomorrow evening to discuss a matter of some benefit to us both.

Mine . . .
Everything—and he wasn't nearly as gullible as Olivia.
He had made his choice, the die was cast.
He crumpled up the letter and headed back to the house.

Chapter 3

Montelette Plantation

"How dare you, how goddamn *dare* you push your nose into places it doesn't belong? What the hell is wrong with you?"

She looked up at her father mutinously. *But someone wanted me to see, dear Father; someone arranged it so very nicely . . .*

"When I think—" her father went on furiously when she didn't respond, "the very last thing I promised your mother, the very last thing she asked of me was to see you suitably wed—"

Dayne reacted instantly. *"Never!* I will *never* marry!"

"Had your mother lived—"

"—that she-cat would never have come one foot near your office or your bed," Dayne hissed. "Or does a man's code of honor nowadays include seducing house guests as well as house servants?"

"You mistake the matter entirely . . ."

"I mistake nothing. You want to get rid of me so you can devote all your time to seducing *her.* Don't deny it, Father; don't add lies on top of lies."

His face set; she read her fate in his expression. He did not even have to say the words.

"I want you married off, my girl, and soon—and that is the end of it. I will make the arrangements."

"Send me away instead—like you did Peter."

"Ah, Peter. Yes . . . Peter will be home in a short time, and I guarantee you, my girl, he would be perfectly willing to accept my wishes in a matter like this."

Peter is a milksop, she thought rebelliously. "He wouldn't be willing to see you sell me to the highest bidder. And that is just what it will be—you'll send out invitations and someone will come along and bid."

"You will silence that flashy mouth, Dayne, and you will leave everything to me—which an obedient daughter would be happy to do."

"Fine," she snapped, refusing to bow down to him, hating—just hating—the power he had over her. "Fine."

It was just like a man: things don't go his way and immediately he begins issuing threats. But what could be worse than Clay refusing her and her father already arranging a union with some godforsaken planter's son?

"Why don't you just hold an auction, Father?" she added nastily. "Why don't you just set up a platform right on the front lawn of Montelette and come one come all to bid on your daughter. Dress me in rags and invite everyone to come up and examine the merchandise: 'She's strong, gentlemen, and she's young. Look at the musculature, the teeth, the fine head of hair, the wide hips—she's a breeder, gentlemen, and can't you just imagine—'"

Whap! He slapped her. Hard. Stinging. Her gush of words stopped just for an instant as she touched her cheek in shock.

And then she bit back her tears and smiled. "How different is it, Father? Am I not little more than a slave with whom you can do whatever you like?"

Curiously, he felt no regret: she had deserved it with her deliberately goading words. She deserved everything that would come to her now, he thought vindictively. She had no right to interfere with his life, and he had every right to mandate hers.

What she didn't understand was that she was not supposed to know it. He hated her for knowing it and pinpointing with her snide know-it-all tone exactly how it was going to be.

And he wouldn't back down either, or cover it with pretty words or a soothing sensibility.

"That's exactly how it is going to be, Dayne, and the sooner you come to grips with that, the better off you will be."

"Fine. I'll tell you what, Father. It makes no difference to me. I'll marry the first man who walks in that door."

He looked at her in disbelief. But of course she had made that snide offer without knowing that even as she spoke a stranger had been shown into the room and stood looking at her with a mixture of awe and amusement.

"A tempting offer, sugar," his voice drawled behind her, "but I wouldn't have you on a bet."

Dayne froze. *Dear Heaven—he was real . . .*

"I don't blame you," Harry said cordially, not in the least discomposed by the intrusion because he did not put it past Dayne to have arranged it. "Definitely a wise choice in spite of my daughter's rash statement. But perhaps you don't know exactly what you're turning down."

"Believe me, I know."

Dayne felt her face suffuse with color. *The jackass . . .*

Harry applauded. "Nicely done, Dayne. Very nicely done. Your timing is perfect; you merely neglected to give him his lines to read. Where did you find him?"

He walked forward to grasp the stranger's hand. "You changed your mind just in time. A wise choice—a very wise choice. You were supposed to say 'I accept.'"

"No, I believe that was your play," the stranger said pleasantly. "But of course the actor you cast in the role of savior couldn't bring himself to say the lines, either, and so I am here in his stead."

Harry snatched his hand away. "Who the hell are you?"

"Why, I'm your nearest and most devoted neighbor," he said. "Did I not introduce myself? Flint Rutledge, late of Rockridge, Montana, and now the new overseer at Bonneterre Plantation."

Dayne closed her eyes in futility. His brother—Clay's long-gone, ever-feared brother. The one who had just walked in and taken everything away from Clay. And her.

His worst nightmare—and now hers.

She turned slowly, gathering her composure around her like a woolen shawl, curiously unmoved by her father's obvious shock.

Dear Heaven, he was everything she remembered and more. His clothes only enhanced the line of his body and everything she knew lay underneath.

She lifted her head and met his glinting jetty eyes. She was not going to let him discompose her—even if his heated gaze settled on her trembling lips like a kiss.

She wasn't going to remember that kiss, either.

"Well Father, now I can feel secure: Mr. Rutledge will not up the ante. I'm ever grateful."

She smiled at him, her most beguiling smile, while she simmered with a fine rage that the knowing light in those deep dark eyes didn't flicker and they didn't move one inch from her face.

"Oh, I think not," he said lazily. "I believe it is your father who wishes to play hazard, not me."

She whirled on him. "Father?"

Her father sent her a stolid mind-your-own business look. "Where is Olivia?"

"I come in her stead, of course, since any business relevant to Bonneterre now devolves on me. You did want to discuss business?" he asked mockingly.

"It's none of *your* business what I wished to discuss with Olivia," Harry said sharply, covering up his dismay with pure bluster. "And I *will* speak with Olivia, and not *you*, and so I bid you good evening, Mr. Rutledge. I think you can find your own way out."

Harry stamped out of the room, never minding that he was leaving Dayne with that Rutledge monster: it would serve her right, he thought vengefully, if the vagabond of Bonneterre cut her down to size. It might make her more biddable, humble even, to know not every man succumbed to her charms. Hell, the son of a bitch might have some use after all.

Dayne felt trapped, like a butterfly pinned to a display. How could she make a graceful exit after her father's exhibition? Flint obviously was enjoying her discomfort enormously.

She hated him. She should have shot him in his damned poker . . . part. And lived with the consequences.

He was just staring at her with that amused fascination almost as if he had never seen her before.

But of course, she looked so different today—she looked like her father's daughter, the one he wanted to hand off to the first available male—which, thank the Lord, would *not* be the arrogant Mr. Flint Rutledge.

She stiffened her shoulders. *Mr. Rutledge had declined, thank you—as if Bonneterre were some great treasure that he would choose to bestow on some simpering mealymouthed belle sometime in the future . . .*

Lord, she hated him!

"It's so tempting to be rude, Mr. Rutledge, but I was raised to have manners. I believe *your* business is concluded."

"But the business between us . . . ?" he murmured, positively intrigued by her lady-of-the-manor aspect.

She bit back a sharp retort. It was time to put Mr. Flint *I-wouldn't-have-her-on-a-bet* Rutledge in his place.

"Business between *us,* Mr. Rutledge? Surely you must be mistaken. We have no business. I've never met you before this night. And I hope never to meet you again."

And she turned on her heel and floated out of the room just the way her mother had taught her back in the days when she had been willing to listen, her hips swaying gently, her back ramrod straight, her chin held high.

She would show him, she would. She could play the haughty sugar-coated Southern lady better than anyone.

Stupid men—that was all they ever wanted anyway: a stupid woman they could put on some pedestal, where they could admire her while they rooted after more willing prey.

But she was the daughter of Montelette. And he was no one—and she would show him just who was going to reject whom when push came to shove.

She simmered about it for days while her father put out the subtle call for eligible suitors and spent the steamy mornings in Nyreen's arms.

Well—she didn't know—but she was almost sure. There was a throbbing silence in the house, a pulsating and drenching silence that almost suffocated her as she went about her daily routine with the Boy.

And even the Boy felt the unease in the air, in her.

It was as if time stopped and she was waiting, waiting and she did not know for what.

How delicately her father was handling it. If she hadn't known, she never would have guessed that he had a list as long as her arm of planter's sons who would fulfill his requirements for her husband.

. . . a tempting offer . . . I wouldn't have you on a bet.

His words replayed and replayed in her mind, and his kiss lingered on her lips like a bruise. How could the one have nothing to do with the other, unless it was the true nature of men to be so devious?

He was devious; and so was her father. And Nyreen—with her mysterious smile and hot, knowing eyes that said, as surely as if she had spoken, that Harry was going to take care of things and Dayne would be out of their lives forever—*soon*.

She hated them all: her father was going to throw her away for the worthless Nyreen. And Clay's obnoxious brother had summarily rejected her before anyone had even asked him if he would have her . . . !

She wanted to make him pay for that. She wanted him groveling at her feet. She wanted to have the same hot, sensual power over him that Nyreen had over her father.

And when he capitulated, she wanted to throw him away. . . . *I wouldn't have you, Flint Rutledge, if they paid me.* . . .

It was such a lovely daydream. She ruminated on it in the following days as she exercised the Boy and as she languidly followed one track and another through the working fields of her childhood.

She knew every acre of ground, every fragile row of cane, which miraculously grew from seed cane every year or from the leavings of the previous year's crop. They had plowed and furrowed in February and now the workers were cultivating the growth, digging drainage ditches or gearing up for the harvest. Those who weren't in the field were gathering the wood that fueled the sugar house, or building the barrels and hogsheads in which the sugar and molasses were shipped.

The fields of Montelette were a beehive of activity, where everyone had his job and knew his place.

Only she was the outcast of them all.

So I have something in common with Clay's brother after all, she thought dourly.

. . . And sugar kisses that melted on the tongue like candy—sweet and sensuous and gone in a moment . . .

Dear Lord, she wanted to make him sorry—

She veered across a short track that linked two fields and nudged the Boy up the ridge that overlooked the whole of Montelette and some of the parched acreage of Bonneterre.

Clay's heritage until two days ago.

How did a man just walk back into his family's life after disappearing for twenty years? How could Olivia let him?

But the answer lay before her in the scorched and unproductive fields of Bonneterre: Clay had done nothing, had left everything to a succession of overseers who hadn't given a damn about Bonneterre or its legacy.

Clay had gone to New Orleans and even if his brother hadn't returned, he still would have been there now. Even if he had agreed to marry her, she was sure he would have left her soon enough for the seduction of the city.

That was the way it was with Clay and, in her heart of hearts, she knew it. But at least she would have had Bonneterre, and she would have—she could have—run it.

Yes, she would have taken things in hand and she would have made it work, and she would have had Clay and Bonneterre, too, instead of this insidious and gnawing desire to lash out and get revenge.

Bonneterre was dying—which was just what Harry had always wanted. And so, he would marry her off and then pursue Bonneterre, oblivious to the return of Flint Rutledge and so certain that one outcast older son could not make a difference within this growing season.

He would have offered Olivia the earth and she would have accepted—beaten down finally by the inability of either of her sons to do *anything* right, and then Harry and Nyreen would have lorded it over the whole of St. Foy for the rest of their lives.

The only thing Dayne didn't understand was why Flint Rutledge had turned up at Montelette that night.

Business, he had said.

What business?

And between Harry and *Olivia?*

Harry had been planning to offer for Bonneterre *now?* But of course he had not known about the return of Flint Rutledge.

And he still had to deal with *her*—so what could he possibly have wanted to speak to Olivia about?

They hadn't spoken in twenty-five years and suddenly he wanted to discuss business?

What kind of business?

The dynastic kind, a canny little voice in her mind whispered insinuatingly. *The kind where he gets you off his hands and insures Bonneterre will become his all in the same process . . .*

NO!

She couldn't think it—she refused to link it—her father offering her to Clay in order to get Bonneterre—using *her* as a pawn to further his own plans, fostered by his nasty lust for Nyreen . . .

It was too awful—and how would he know anyway?

But of course he knew—Nyreen would have told him just as she told him everything else.

Dayne had never had any secrets from the moment Nyreen had come to Montelette.

She felt sick.

She felt like the top of her head was going to blow off from the sheer pressure of the elegant truth of her deductions.

Would Clay have accepted . . . ?

No . . . no—he would have reveled in the fact that Harry was, for one moment, in his power.

And he wouldn't have gone away, either . . .

If Clay had known that Montelette was in the offing, she would be planning her wedding today . . .

And she would have been ecstatic about it because she would never have known anything about her father's machinations behind the scenes . . .

She almost had to admire Harry's plot: what better scheme than to foist her off on the spendthrift son of the man he most hated and reap his final reward by taking over the plantation he would have given his fortune to own.

By the simple expediency of pairing his scapegrace daughter with Verne Rutledge's rakehell son, he would have accomplished both of his purposes.

It really was masterful.

And it was the only answer to why Flint Rutledge had shown up at Montelette four days ago: Harry had sent for Olivia in order to sell her to Clay.

And she would have played straight into her father's schemes: if Clay had agreed to marry her, Harry would not have had to offer anything at all.

She would have done the whole thing for him.

So Harry must have panicked at the appearance of a stranger, even if he did turn out to be a Rutledge. He could not have prepared for that.

She felt a moment of vengeful pleasure at the thought of Harry's carefully laid plans turned topsy turvy by the defection of Clay and the arrival of Flint Rutledge.

It was perfect, just perfect. He looked like a *purposeful* Rutledge—someone who would not be susceptible to Harry's manipulations.

Not that she cared . . . he wouldn't have her anyway—*on a bet.*

And all she wanted was the sweet release of chewing him up and throwing him away.

Why not . . . ?

She thought the words as she simultaneously caught a glimpse of a rider coming through the desiccated backfield track of Bonneterre.

She couldn't see who it was, but it had to be him. Who else would be taking the futile trip through the backfields?

She nudged the Boy to a less conspicuous place—under a tree and behind a small copse of bushes.

Why not? What did she have to lose? She had gambled everything and she had not come up a winner.

The deck was stacked: men had everything their own way. She couldn't stop Clay from leaving, and she hadn't been able to deter her father. Could she make just one man bend to her will? One man—the man who had rejected her out of hand—could

she entice him to the point of wanting her so she could have
the pleasure of slapping him down and casting him
aside . . . ?

Did she really want to play such a dangerous game with Flint
Rutledge . . . ?

But how dangerous could it be, when Harry was getting set to
sell her to the first interested party? Her prospective husband
would not even be buying her—he would be buying Montelette
and all its riches, everything Harry had to offer that would not go
to Peter, or that bitch Nyreen . . .

There would be papers and promises: any husband-to-be
worth his salt would insist on it. And she would have no choice in
the matter and no recourse whatsoever.

. . . sugar kisses . . .

And honeyed words—a woman got stuck any which way.

She watched thoughtfully as the rider swept slowly and thoroughly through the backfields of Bonneterre and then disappeared from sight.

He rode the desiccated fields of Bonneterre and he hid his
anger under a mask of impassivity. Nothing ever changed.
Nothing. And all the rattlings and rumblings in Charleston and
Washington wouldn't make a damned bit of difference when the
cutting season came and the field hands at Bonneterre refused to
work.

For three days he had crisscrossed the acres of fields, half in
plantings now and the other half gone to seed and fallow. And
the gardens were a mass of weeds. Olivia had let it happen, and
he didn't know just what he was going to do about it all.

Except that Olivia was counting on him doing something.

He felt no sense of his father's hand as he roamed the backfields of Bonneterre. And certainly no sense of Clay's.

He felt as if it had belonged to him from the beginning of time
and that the land had been waiting, dormant, for his return.

And that there was something in him laying dormant, waiting
for the first moment he stepped foot back onto Bonneterre.

It was his, had always been, and always would be.

The rest would follow—in a year or two or three . . .

It didn't even shock him that he was thinking in terms of permanence. And in spite of the fact he hated the system. He had always hated the system.

But now it was his, and he would deal with it and make it work.

And nothing could stop him—not even the crassness of Harry Templeton and his vicious plan to buy Bonneterre using the enticement of his money and his daughter's body as collateral.

Harry had meant to bargain for Clay, using Olivia as the broker and offering the riches of Montelette as persuasion—and Clay would have leapt at it in an instant. Harry's overseer would have absolved him of all responsibility for Bonneterre and Clay would have been able to draw on all the ready money Harry would have provided in his daughter's dowry.

A nice tidy package for Clay—too bad his scapegrace big brother had gone and spoiled it all.

Now Harry's daughter paced the futile boundaries between their plantations seeking what? Vengeance for his callousness?

She hadn't escaped his acute eye, which was so used to scanning for the enemy on the plains: she was unmistakable that first afternoon even though she quickly ducked behind some trees and bushes.

And she was there again the second day, and then the third.

Plotting what? Armed with what? He wouldn't put anything past her in her fury. And he would sooner trust a rattlesnake than a woman in a rage.

The fourth day he climbed up the rise and hoisted himself high up onto a thick tree branch to wait for her.

It was an interesting perspective. A man got a totally different view of things when he was ten feet above the ground.

He could see for miles around and down to the bayou. He could see the fertile fields of Montelette and the movement of the field workers as they cut their way through the stands of cane with hoes and rakes and wagons. He could see the slant of Montelette's roof and the verdant green lawns beyond.

But when he turned in the opposite direction, he saw profligate waste, a squandering of the wealth of Bonneterre, and the end of the season before it had even begun.

Clay's legacy and Clay's future because Harry Templeton would have taken it over and made it his own.

But not now . . . not now—

He wondered if Harry knew that Clay had absconded when faced with the challenge of the older brother he hated.

And then he saw her coming, and it was the same as it had been the first time he saw her.

She came riding so slowly up the hill out of a haze of sunlight and into the shadow of the trees that dotted the rise that her appearance instantly took on the quality of a dream.

She was dressed as before, in a loose-fitting lightweight dress which allowed her to straddle her mount, and her golden hair was bound up this time and pinned on top of her head in deference to the shimmering afternoon heat.

She slid from her horse and tied him to the tree and then she leaned against the trunk and just stared at the same vista that had occupied him moments before.

She could not be hiding a thing under that dress except dreams and determination.

Nor could she disguise the anger in her that radiated out of the tense line of her body, or the ineffable bitterness in her eyes.

She was in a fury once again, and containing it by dint of pure self-control as she gazed out over the bustling fields of Montelette.

Had she wanted Clay? The thought hit him like a thunderbolt. *She's beautiful; she isn't crazy . . .*

But that was the woman of *his* fantasy. He had no idea what she was like, except she had a wasp's tongue and she could pinpoint a target at a hundred feet.

And Harry was ready to sell her off to anyone who could shoot faster than she.

Or maybe it was just a ploy to flush out Clay—

He can't have her . . .

It was almost as if she heard the thought: she whirled abruptly toward the prospect of Bonneterre and whispered fiercely, "Damn you, Clay. Damn you to hell for your lies and your treachery—"

Her shoulders heaved. "Dear Lord, show me what to do—show me a way . . ."

His timing was perfect—he slid slowly off of the tree branch and swung himself gently against the perfect posture of her rigid body and toppled her down to the ground.

She was soft, so soft. He felt as if he had melted into her, as if the hard part of him had found a soft and giving home in her.

His dream . . . his reality—

He felt the earth move as he looked into her blazing eyes and read the animosity there.

But it didn't matter: he wanted those lips and the soft honeyed taste of her tongue.

He dipped his head—he savored—

Mine. He felt it as elementally as he felt his yearning for the soft mother earth of Bonneterre.

No one else—no one . . .

She writhed frantically against his weight and his strength and his seductive possession of her mouth.

Sugar kisses. . . . How could she forget?

He covered her, he enveloped her with his intensity to possess; it was all there, pure, male, latent, waiting to be unleashed—

He felt it in himself, he felt the faint tremors of emotion in her: she was not invulnerable. Her strength lay in the fact that she would die before she would admit it.

Such strength . . . her body heaving, her mouth defiant, curious, testing—her hands pushing and pulling against him as if she had the power to move him.

She had no power against the buttery movement of his mouth against hers. Her body shifted and sought to melt against the soft and the hard—his pliant lips and the compressed thrust of his body against the sinuous undulation of hers.

Just like before—God, she was not immune to the rich commanding pressure of his mouth, not at all, *at all.*

Or could anyone have taken her, just anyone, and she would have surrendered simply out of the rebellion in her heart?

Oh—but not him . . . *not him—*

"You bastard—what the hell do you think you're doing?" she hissed, wrenching herself violently away.

"I'm kissing you," he murmured, his voice laced with reason

as he cupped her face between his large hands. "There are no boundaries here, sugar, no plot of land that belongs to Templeton or Rutledge. Nothing to possess at all—except me and you."

"*Never!*" She slapped at his hands, pushed at his unyielding chest. "*Never!* Get your hands off of me, Mr. *Flint* Rutledge."

She was so angry that she had loved his kisses.

He was amused by that contradiction in her and he obligingly shifted his body, levering his weight onto his hands, one of which caught the sleeve of her dress.

Instantly, she rolled away from him to the horrifying sound of her flimsy dress tearing from her shoulder to her hem, leaving her vulnerable, exposed.

She wore hardly anything underneath: a chemise which had torn at the shoulder and now flapped over to mold the shape of her heaving breasts, a petticoat under which he could see the lace trim of her drawers, her black lisle stockings and her feet encased in soft kid slippers which tied around her ankles.

His eyes kindled as he swept his heated gaze over her.

I want her.

His desire was so keen he almost thought he'd said the words out loud.

Or maybe he hadn't had to. Maybe she was really so experienced with men, he had no need to say or do anything at all.

And she saw it; she saw everything in the explosive silence between them.

He watched her change before his very eyes like a chameleon—a frightened doe one moment, a sleek and pouncing lioness the next, assessing her prey.

If she had had a rifle in her hands, he would have been a dead man.

And that look—that glittering, almost feral appraisal— woman to man, yes. Dangerous, that look. Venal. She thought she was going to chew him up and spit him out.

She thought she understood the nature of men when all she knew was how to plot and plan to get her own way.

But what she didn't know was, it was going to be the other way around. He was going to devour her, and he was going to make her love every minute of it.

Chapter 4

She knew the exact moment she realized her power. It was like a revelation from the heavens, a lightning bolt of perception that illuminated an endless kaleidoscope of possibilities.

Later, when she was alone, it was a moment she savored and examined and enjoyed from every possible angle.

It gave her a sense of being in control. It freed her from the passivity of having to accept her father's dictums with no recourse whatsoever.

It gave her back a sense of her own femininity and made her feel less like a commodity to be bargained away to the highest bidder.

That would come, of course, as day followed night; Harry was determined, but no more so than Nyreen, and Dayne had no expectation that her father would bend to Nyreen's wishes in the matter.

But until then—oh, until then . . .

It was a most delicious thought—Flint Rutledge wanted her—no, not her exactly. He wanted her flesh, her body, her kisses. His desire was oh-so obvious in the way he looked at her . . .

Clay had never looked at her like that . . .

Nor had any man.

It was potent, heady; it conjured up dreams. It drenched her imagination with forbidden images of him as she had seen him, naked and so primitively, forcefully *male;* it evoked all the wanton things she could envision doing with him—only him.

And then—and then—

When he was totally beguiled by her, utterly under her spell, she would slap him down as fully and forcefully as he had done her . . .

She would crush him under the heel of her boot and leave him begging for mercy.

Yes—that was sweet, rich—and raw . . . the jagged edge of pain seeping beneath the honey.

She would make sure of it. Nothing would be out of bounds for someone who was to be sold as a slave to whomever had the money to buy her.

Nothing.

She looked at herself in the mirror and saw herself as *he* must have seen her, all tousled and bared to his gaze, her lips pouty from the force of his kisses.

This then was what a man wanted—not intelligence, not a partner, not a helpmate. A man wanted a warm body and lush lips and a woman's willingness to surrender.

And that was the only hard part. But she could play with that too because it was the only way to hurt her father.

But it was more than that: it was the only way to find out and understand what drove him into the arms of Nyreen. And it was the only way to satisfy her own curiosity as to what might have been between her and that dog Clay before he had so precipitously run away.

In all, she thought, it would be a most enlightening investment—and the only price was her purity.

She wondered if her father was going to guarantee her virginity.

"Shhhh—she's in the next room."

"Oh Harry, I can't stand this, I can't. Everywhere I go in this house, I feel like she is waiting to intercept me. And everytime we want to be alone, I'm scared witless she will knock on the door and interrupt us. There's nowhere we can go for privacy— *nowhere.*"

"God, I know, I know. Nyreen . . . I need you . . ."

"I can't. Not here. How can I? Do you know . . . do you have any idea how much I want you—right now? Think of it, Harry—

if she weren't here, in the house, I would strip off my clothes right now and I would give you everything you want—right here, right now . . ."

He groaned and reached for her. She slapped his hand away—

"If she weren't here, Harry, we could make love anywhere in the house, anytime you felt like it. I could just . . . walk into a room, any room, and you could say—'Take off your clothes.' " Oh yes, yes, she could see him salivating already, her words arousing him unbearably, perfectly. She knew just how to play him. It was so easy, and Dayne was so stupid.

She licked her lips, running her tongue erotically over the shape of them. "I just love that idea, Harry. I could sit on your lap—right there, right in this big old pristine parlor of yours—I could be naked this minute . . . if she weren't in the house. And you could be feeling my body, Harry, all willing and waiting for you."

Abruptly she turned away from his outstretched hands.

"But of course, that's only my dream. Did you know I think about us together, alone and naked, in this house with no one to disturb us? And I imagine all the delicious things that we could do, if only we had some privacy?"

Harry swallowed and pulled her back to him and pushed her onto his lap where she could feel his ferocious need for her.

"What would you do, Nyreen?"

She pressed her body against his and nipped his ear. "I would never get dressed, Harry. I would be the slave of your desire. It's all I've ever wanted since I came here. Think of it, Harry . . ." She squirmed against him, feeling his protuberant sex expanding beneath her bottom. "Oh God, I can hardly stand it . . ."

He nuzzled her neck. "I'm doing everything I can. That scoundrel Clay is in New Orleans and that damned Flint Rutledge is back on Bonneterre and there's no hope there. I wouldn't even approach Olivia again."

She stiffened and shook off his hands and his mouth. "But it was such a perfect solution."

"Well, the bastard is up and gone and that's the end of it, Nyreen. Next time, I'll prepare more thoroughly, I promise you."

"Oh God, it would have solved everything. And now it's going to take so much longer . . ." She began stroking her breasts. "Just think if she weren't here . . ."

"Let's pretend she's not . . ."

"Harry—it's impossible—" She cupped her breasts and marveled at her protruding nipples outlined against the thin material knowing Harry's mouth was wet with wanting them.

"We'll go upstairs . . ."

"And how much time do you suppose *that* will give us?" she asked cuttingly.

"Enough time to do exactly what we want," Harry muttered, dipping his head to get at the hard peaks of her nipples.

She pulled herself back before his tongue could touch them. "We could have so much more time—"

"We will, I promise you. I'm working on it now." He reached for her breasts again. "Let me, just let me—I'll have everything in place sooner than you think."

"Promise me?" she whispered poutily.

"I want what you promised me," Harry growled. "I want it *now.*"

He didn't notice her knowing little smile as he pulled her from the room.

But even then, he couldn't wait. He thrust her into the closet beneath the stairs, ripped off her clothes, and took his fill of her ready and willing body.

She smiled contentedly in the shrouding darkness as she wrapped herself around him and bent him to her will.

The rise was neutral ground between Montelette and Bonneterre, just as he had said. She could legitimately ride there in exercise of the Boy, and it made perfect sense that she would stop there to rest because of the profusion of shade trees.

And if she happened to look down toward Bonneterre—well, she was merely scanning the horizon of a view she had seen hundreds of times before.

Except this time, he was part of the view and an aspect that could not be ignored.

It was a game. As Harry got closer and closer to refining his list of candidates to marry into the family, she became bolder and bolder.

Nyreen's barbed comments and pointed looks spurred her on. She endured Nyreen's lectures on the proper behavior of a lady and did as she pleased.

And every day, she stayed away from the constricting atmosphere of Montelette for longer periods of time, which only made Nyreen more vicious in her criticism.

"Who, I ask you, will want her when word gets around about her loose behavior?" she demanded of Harry. "She spends hours away from the house—she'd never be at home if there happened to be a caller—"

"I see—I'm to spend my time *waiting,* just in case someone *happens* to call—which is to say, if father *happens* to arrange it," Dayne interposed rudely.

"Exactly right, young lady," Harry said forcefully.

"She's never home," Nyreen went on, "and she's had nothing to do with overseeing the servants for weeks and weeks and they've gotten slack and lazy and they won't listen to me . . ."

"They'll have to, once I'm gone," Dayne said nastily.

Nyreen ignored her. "She's doing everything possible to ruin her chance with anyone who might be favorably disposed toward her, and I'm getting sick of her flaunting my rules and doing whatever she pleases. It isn't acceptable Harry, not in your house or for a suitor. So what are you going to do about it?"

"I'm going to marry her off as soon as damned possible," Harry said succinctly. "You hear, young lady? I'm going to find some poor fool who'll put up with this nonsense, and then I'm going to have daughters who will appreciate what they've got—"

Nyreen froze, and then she looked up and saw Dayne's speculative blue gaze resting on her.

She shook herself. "Indeed they will, Harry, I promise you that."

"Well fine," Dayne said, *"I'm* not going to sit around waiting for that to happen, Father dear. I beg you'll excuse me. If the white knight who wishes to rescue me walks through that door, I promise you, I will fall into his arms. But until then, my time is my own, and since Nyreen is to all intents and purposes now the mistress of Montelette, it seems only fair that she should do the work. Don't you think, Father?"

"What—?" He had been so utterly absorbed in the thought of Nyreen bearing his children that he had blanked out all of Dayne's diatribe, and now he scrambled to put together the sense of her words.

"You will help Nyreen with the servants, young lady, until I say so. And you will—"

"But I won't," Dayne contradicted. "I wonder whether you have some distant relative whom I can visit for the next twenty-five years, Father. Preferably someone who lives in—oh— England or France? Canada perhaps?"

Harry reined in his temper. He had the candidates finally and it was only a matter of time. He needed to rope them in slowly and inexorably, exposing them first to Nyreen's exotic charm and then to the breathtaking beauty of Dayne, and he had to hope she would keep her mouth shut and they would keep their eyes on the money he would offer in the settlement of the dowry.

Simple really. Probably she could have been the worst shrew and still he could have married her off if the money were enough.

She was just plain too much. She hadn't given him time to make a come-back. She was out the door already, above Nyreen's protestations and for the moment, beyond his reach.

Dayne wondered how stupid she was to give Nyreen all the time and space she needed to cement her hold over her father.

But no, that had been a lost cause from the moment Nyreen walked into the house and twitched her hips in the direction of her sex-starved father.

She could not have prevented that any more than she could have prevented her mother's death.

So it was only a matter of time now; she had seen the look in Harry's eyes. The Dayne Dragoons would be marching any day now to assault the hallowed doors of Montelette and take her away from the scene of her sins.

Fanciful . . . a column of knights, marching in precision, intent on storming the castle—

One knight—astride his mount, galloping purposefully across the backfields of Bonneterre, viable and visible from the rise above.

"He's there, Boy," she whispered into the stallion's ear, and she felt a sudden frisson of excitement.

She didn't know what she was doing; the sense of power had dissipated days ago. Now she understood she was tempted to tumble headlong into pure trouble.

And maybe she wanted to. Maybe she was waiting for just the right moment, just the right event.

Maybe it was him and that awful rebuff. Or just possibly she had been courting trouble ever since she had gotten involved with Clay.

But why think of that? Clay was gone and his brother was here, and she was as likely to fall into the one's arms as the other.

Hadn't she welcomed their kisses?

Wouldn't she love more?

Would she?

Wasn't that why she was there every day watching and waiting?

But no—he had disappeared, there one moment and gone the next, almost as if he were goading her to follow him.

He wouldn't . . .

She remembered his eyes, his jetty unfathomable eyes glittering with some indescribable emotion as he looked at her.

Wouldn't she?

She licked her lips and tasted—sugar . . .

She couldn't . . .

She tasted salt.

She wanted to—and she didn't know how the daughter of Montelette could urge the Boy down that slope and on the path to her downfall.

All the families up and down Bayou LaTouque and the surrounding Parishes knew each other. Harry Templeton was certain there wasn't a candidate for Dayne's hand whom she did not know of, at least by reputation, and he had to plot and plan very carefully just who he would invite to the house and who, ultimately, would be Dayne's suitor.

The money was the key, but there was plenty of that. Time was his only enemy; his desire for Nyreen raged out of control. The more she let him take, the more he wanted, and she cleverly fed his need by describing in graphic detail everything they would do once Dayne was out of the house.

If he could have gotten away with murdering Dayne in order to have Nyreen, he thought he could have done it.

Every moment of his day, his thoughts were crowded with fantasies of Nyreen, playing upon the lascivious scenes she created as she firmly denied him and aroused him all in the same breath.

He did not know how he could stand another day and another without sinking himself into the sinuously sinful body of Nyreen.

He knew he was being manipulated, but he didn't care. He wanted her musky, dusky sex and he would do anything to insure their privacy so he could take her every prurient and exotic way she had described.

She was the essence of woman, open and giving one moment, pouting and withdrawing the next, leaving him with images of how things could have been—if only . . .

He wanted to create the perfect realm for her, one in which he was master and she was both his queen—and his willing subject—

"Harry darling . . ." Her voice, low and seductive.

He looked up. She stood by the doorway to his office and as she met his lust-darkened gaze, she shut the door behind her and began walking toward him in that slow deliberately enticing walk of hers.

Simultaneously, she began unbuttoning her bodice until it fell away from her bosom and exposed her naked breasts beneath.

He caught his breath; his manhood jolted to protuberant life. The contrast between her ladylike dress and her naked breasts with their tautly pointed nipples aroused him to an almost animalistic need.

Cunningly, she let him gaze his fill, reading in his eyes the quotient of his control. He hardly had any; obviously, all her lust-filled fantasies were working on him just as she had intended, and she could read him as clearly as a book.

She sashayed around behind the desk, behind him, and bent over his shoulder.

"I hope you're working on something very profitable, Harry," she whispered huskily, making sure that one stone hard nipple point settled neatly into his ear.

He swallowed as he felt the taut peak, and the soft flesh behind it, press into him.

"Right here," he whispered. "Right now." He turned his head to take the invading nipple into his mouth, but she had moved to lean over his other shoulder.

"Tell me who—tell me how . . ." she breathed, brushing his neck with her taut-tipped breasts.

"Let me touch—"

"Harry, darling . . ." she murmured scoldingly, moving away from him again, "this is a prime example of how things are as opposed to how they could be. Here I am, just yearning to spend a long afternoon sitting naked in your lap—and I have to worry about who might knock on your office door. I ask you, is that fair to me? Is it? We can't even plan ten minutes together during the day . . ."

"Surely ten *minutes* is possible . . ." Harry growled, reaching up to grab one of her breasts with no ceremony whatsoever. "Tell me ten minutes is possible, Nyreen. Tell me I can have ten minutes. You know what I can do in ten minutes."

She bent over him and let him have the feel of one naked breast. "Oh, no one knows better than I, Harry darling; but you know how one thing leads to another and—"

But his voice was already thick with desire. "I don't care, Nyreen. I don't care. Let me—let me . . ."

"Promise me . . ." she whispered, jamming the other breast against his neck.

"Anything you want," he rasped, his fingers kneading the keen point of her nipple. "Anything. Anything. Tomorrow—I'll have someone come tomorrow and we'll see what . . . we'll see what happens . . ."

"Tomorrow, Harry?" Oh, she was in clear control—a moan here, a groan there, the scalpel question that demanded his promise . . .

"Yes," he groaned, and she gave him his reward, sliding around his shoulder so that he could take her straining nipple into his mouth.

It was hot, so very hot, hot inside Montelette and out, and Dayne had to escape it, the flooding fever of Nyreen's resentment, and the torrid heat of her own imagination.

The waiting was the hardest. Sometime soon her father would begin parading her before the most willing aspirants for her hand.

Miss Dayne Templeton, gentlemen—sound of breath, body, and breeding; a man doesn't need a woman with a mind—

They would probably look at her teeth, too, just as if they were buying some damned brood mare—

Damn it! They *were* buying a brood mare, she thought angrily, and the only thing they cared about was getting sons and founding a dynasty. And once they had done that, they could and would take their own pleasure whenever and wherever they wanted and they would leave her immured on the plantation and expect that she would take care of things.

After all, that was what she was born and raised to do, wasn't it?

She felt a seething, all-enveloping rage as she contemplated the end result of her father's driving lust for Nyreen.

And in the end, he would have what he wanted, too: she would be gone, Nyreen would be his, and it would be as if no one else existed. And if Peter dared come home and interfere, her father would just flush him out of his life, too, with no qualms and damn the consequences.

Oh, to be a siren who could arouse such possessiveness. . . . How did Nyreen do it?

What was it about her that sapped her father's willpower and made him a slave to his lust for her?

But Dayne did know. She had caught a glimpse of it in a man's dark eyes. She had felt the potency of it for one coiling moment—an eternity of knowledge and power all for the surrender of her virtue.

And what was that worth to the potential husband who would only use her and abuse her?

They did treasure modesty and chastity, these purebred planters' sons . . .

Yet they could be manipulated by some carnal sorceress just like her father had been . . .

Just like *his* father had been—

So the only thing she could conclude was that it was infinitely more interesting to use a man's bloodlust against him than to be his subservient wife.

So therefore—why shouldn't she?

Why couldn't she?

Hadn't she been on the very precipice of . . . ?

And wasn't she aching with curiosity about . . . ?

Wouldn't she just love to use some man's desire for her against him—

Someone like that obnoxious Flint Rutledge?

Oh, but she wouldn't think about that—she wouldn't. It was too easy to consider falling into the spirit of it.

Too easy . . .

And it was too hot—

So very very hot . . .

She rode down to the cool lapping shore of Orinda, the only place where no one would think to look for her.

It felt like she had been away from it for years; it had been merely two weeks—maybe—but so much had happened.

Too much.

And too soon she would be forced to leave.

As the Boy stood in the water, she slid off his back, deliberately wetting the hem of her dress and her bare feet.

Here, on Orinda, she did not need corsets and hoops to define her femininity. Here she could be free of all constraint and manners. Here she dared to dress to serve her needs, naked beneath her dress and clothed to the world.

She could walk through the lank grass and feel the sun-dried prickle of it under her feet. She could rock on the rotting verandah and curse the feckless Clay.

And she could sit in the shade of a moss-draped tree and weave her erotic dreams.

It was enough, enough to think about them. Enough to imagine the possibilities. Enough to have seen the mysteries of a naked man and to have tasted his kisses.

Enough . . .

"Sweet sugar in the tall grass . . ." a voice murmured behind her.

She stiffened.

Or had she hoped . . . ?

She didn't turn; let him have the view of the proud set of her shoulders. It was all he deserved.

"Heaven help me," she said caustically, "a snake in the grass and right here at Orinda."

"Your bite is more lethal than mine, sugar," he murmured as he dropped down beside her.

"I'd love to take a bite out of you," she hissed.

His eyes glinted with amusement. "You're pure poison, sugar; I wouldn't get within ten feet of that viperous tongue."

Oh God—she felt the power, right then, right there. He was doing absolutely nothing and she felt the pure unreasoning flex of her femininity jolting up against his mocking words.

He wanted her. He just wasn't going to let her get the upper hand.

And she wanted it so badly.

"Even Adam was tempted by the snake," she murmured, making a show of smoothing out the thin gauze of her skirt against one of her tucked legs.

She even liked how the material molded itself to the shape of her thigh, so thin and fragile that he could make it melt away with just a touch.

Just like that. Just.

"I just like to think old Adam was fascinated by all that convoluted movement—" his voice lowered, "all up and down and— in and out . . ."

Her breath caught as he came closer and closer to her and his voice became softer and softer with just the faintest rasp to give away its emotional edge.

". . . winding in and around . . . binding, entwining . . ." His lips were not an inch from hers. "Licking, tasting . . . sucking . . ."

She was mesmerized by his eyes—fathomless, black as night, as unreadable as the sky—his eyes . . .

"Sucking . . . ?" she whispered in a breath.

"Sucking—the life out of a man who gets too curious," he said flatly, pushing himself away from her with such an abrupt movement that she almost fell backward.

It took a moment, and another, for his defection to register.

The snake! She met his eyes; they shimmered coolly, clearly, with absolute remorselessness, with neither a glimmer of kindness or any wish to protect her from her impulses.

Fine. She didn't want that anyway. She wanted his head, plain and simple. She wanted to enslave him in the very worst way— just as Nyreen had enslaved her father.

And that was all she wanted. To make him grovel. To wield such carnal power over him that he could not escape her. And he would beg if she ever left him.

She met that hard obsidian gaze without flinching. She would have him, whatever it meant, whatever she had to do, and she would start her campaign instantly . . . now—while her fiery anger fueled her resolve.

"Or breathe life into the man who dares . . . to be bold . . ." she whispered, lifting her chin just a little, offering him her mouth in a move that was daring in the extreme for her.

"Well, aren't you the brazen little piece—"

No, I'm not, but I'm going to be now. . . . She shifted her body so that she was sitting straight up with her knees bent and her bare feet on the ground.

"I see how it works, Mr. Rutledge. Men can be daring as they like, but the minute a woman asks for something—she's a 'brazen piece' . . ." She slanted a look up at him as she slid her hands slowly down the length of her legs to her feet.

He was watching; she could see his eyes following the movement of her fingers as she skimmed them over her limbs to encircle her bare ankles.

The power was there, she felt it; her whole body filled with the molten nectar of her new knowledge. It was all men ever wanted: willing women hiding behind coy protestations, and she had been watching Nyreen long enough to know exactly how *she* played that little game.

And big old Flint Rutledge wasn't immune to it, either. The heat from those darkling eyes positively scorched her skin.

She moved her hands downward to caress the instep of her foot. Yes, that was exactly right. There was that little glow behind that matte black of his eyes. She could see it, she could feel it.

"Nice bluff, sugar, but you're as virginal as the morning dew."

She stiffened instantly in anger. She would bend this man, she would. And she would do anything she had to. *Anything.*

She squashed her fury and lowered her blazing eyes so he could not read her determination.

"Am I, Mr. Rutledge? *Really?*" She moved her hands upward, toward the hem of her skirt. She pulled her skirt backward, up over her knees as far as it could go and just let it drape over her hips.

She was naked underneath. No confining drawers or petticoats for her. Not here, at Orinda, where she was to have played out a great love story with this man's brother, and where she had been forced to swallow the dust of disappointment.

But this might be better; this might be a whole lot better.

The hot air settled on her naked thighs like a drift of cotton.

She leaned back, bracing her trembling upper body against her shaking arms, and stretched out one long bare leg. She felt her excitement rising, a thing apart from her and indescribable in terms of anything she knew before.

Once again, she felt the potency of her body through the force of his response to her. He wanted her and through that desire, she wielded control.

This was what Nyreen understood, and this was what women were forbidden to understand.

What did she have to lose in this sultry Eden where no one watched and no one could tell?

They were alone; his face was stone-carved, unyielding with the strain of his wanting her. She sensed it. She felt it.

His resistance was like a glass wall, transparent, tempered, easy to shatter if she could only find his breaking point.

She shifted her body slightly and lifted her skirt just over the tempting curve of her buttock, and then tilted her challenging gaze upward so she could watch the muscle working in his cheek.

Yes, this was good.

"I am *sweltering*, Mr. Rutledge," she murmured. "It is positively scorching out here." She rested her hand against her naked hip and began playing with the material of the dress.

She was lying on her side now, with her legs and hip bare and the skirt of her dress draped just over the vee between her legs.

And she watched him, her gaze tight and taut against his, gauging how much it would take, how far she should push—avoiding the one telltale measure of his lust for her, which would mean her ultimate surrender.

"Isn't it, Mr. Rutledge?" she pulled the skirt upward slightly. "If I were back at Montelette, I could never get this comfortable. I used to sometimes take off my dress and just walk around stark naked . . ."

Nothing, still nothing. He was as still as the air, even with her dress inching up and up to reveal that one hidden place that no man had the right to see until his wedding day.

Not one sign of yielding—not one.

She gritted her teeth and pushed herself into a sitting position, and then rose up onto her knees.

"I'm so hot I think I just might do that little thing—"

He grabbed her ankle as she got to her feet. His hand was hot and dry and hard and his grip felt like it would compress all the blood right in her toes.

She thought her heart would leap right out of her throat. His anger, hot, molten, emotional, came at her like a tornado.

"Virgin bitch—you goddamned virgin bitch—you don't know what kind of fire you're playing with, sugar, and you're just lighting matches all over the place."

But she knew, yes she did; her body constricted at his touch, while her mouth opened to dare him yet again, in spite of the warning, in spite of his strength against the puny power of her femininity.

It was almost as if she couldn't stop herself now that she had started it.

"Or maybe I just know how to make a man's blood heat up," she murmured suggestively, even as she tried to quell her brief frisson of fear. "And I'm so hot. So let me go and let me get comfortable, Mr. Rutledge. No one invited you to stay."

"I beg to differ with you, sugar. You've been throwing invitations out since I met you. And you're just mad because I haven't taken them up."

"Why start now?" she said nastily, staring down into the fiery heat of his eyes. *Take that—Mr. Flint I-wouldn't-have-you-on-a-bet Rutledge. You'd have me now—I'd wager on that in a heartbeat.* But she wasn't so sure she was ready to have him.

"Oh no, sugar—I want some of that sweet heat you're offering."

His hand moved and she jumped. It felt like it was molded to her leg, moving upward and upward, under her skirt, to the naked back of her knee and then her thigh and then—she almost swooned from the feel of it gently squeezing the soft pillow of her buttock.

For the life of her, she could not move. The last thing she expected was that she would respond so potently. Her body felt molten, boneless, ready to slide right into his arms just from the hypnotic, forbidden feel of his long fingers caressing her naked leg.

How was this? She had thought it would take more—so much more, and he had turned the tables on her already . . .

And she felt like she could stand there and let him touch her like that forever. She wanted to sink into his knowing fingers and let him do whatever he wanted—

She could feel her breasts blossoming, her nipples tightening into twin taut peaks, easily visible against the thin fabric of her gown.

She wanted to spread her legs and offer him every treasure—

just because of the smooth, beguilingly arousing stroke of his knowing fingers.

And she wanted to run as far and as fast as she could from the shocking seduction of his expert caresses.

But still, she couldn't move.

Two hands now, sliding up and down the backs of her naked legs, up and down, skimming, feeling, cupping her buttocks underneath the wispy material of her dress—exploring her so intimately, so finely, she almost let herself sink into the oblivion of pleasure.

This . . . this—this was what he wanted, this—this surrender was all men wanted, the drive to feel, to caress, to possess—this conferred the power: her willingness to give herself over to this carnal feasting—this . . . !

"Sweet sugar," he murmured as he pulled her downward tightly to straddle his knees.

She felt it then—the root of his power, the hard part, the point of possession—it throbbed against her nakedness, contained and aroused; he wanted her.

"Kiss me, sugar."

Melting kisses, succulent and sweet, lasting only a moment— she remembered those kisses and he remembered them too—she felt him elongate under the spread of her legs.

Yes—a man was ruled by the thrust of his desire—she could feel it so plainly now; it was like a living thing, wanting her, trying to touch her, desperate to breach the barrier that separated it from her . . .

Power—the thing was to make him want her and never to succumb to the male potency of him.

But it wasn't working; it wasn't possible when he had hiked her skirt up over her buttocks and was hypnotically caressing them so that she could hardly think . . .

"Oh no—I wouldn't want to get you any hotter than you are already, Mr. Rutledge," she murmured, wriggling her behind away from his roving hands, which only put her more exactingly in his power.

He liked that; except that if he were courting her in the most proper way he would never be able to touch her anywhere—not anywhere—until the wedding night.

Men do like a willing woman—they just didn't like to marry them . . .

She didn't want to ride his seeking hands, but they were so persuasive, and the pleasure was so intense. When in her life would she have learned of this seduction of the flesh?

Never . . .

She hated him; she wanted to run. The thing had gotten totally out of hand, and she felt trapped in the fragile web of sensuality that she had spun.

A glistening web, sticky with resolutions, as intricate as lace, as indestructible as woven cane.

There was no escape—either from her own stupid intentions or from his awful determination.

His hands were so strong; they lifted her this way and that so that she could hide nothing from him. They worked in secret beneath the property of her dress, and they fondled and explored every naked inch of her—

. . . and she couldn't have stopped him, and ultimately, in spite of her rising panic and because of her burgeoning desire, she let him—

Until he grazed the lush cleft between her legs, seeking an entry—

"Now—you virgin bitch tease—*now*—I want your honey . . ."

Her body reared back.

He smiled, and it was not a nice smile. "Now we'll find out how *hot* you are, sugar. *Now* we come to that sweet treat every man covets . . ."

Now the secrets with which women hold the power over men—now . . .

Was she bold enough, angry enough, ravished enough to let him teach her the secret of a woman's strength . . . ?

"A virgin—with the heart of a Jezebel and the pouting smile of a bitch—you're a tease, sugar; you like to provoke a man till he's steamed enough to want you, and then you like to turn him face flat into the mud of the bayou . . . You'll give so much and nothing more, is that it, sugar? Just a little taste of that naked honey, just to whet the appetite? You hardly wine and dine on a man and then you're gone—"

Oh, yes, she thought avidly as he outlined the scene she desperately wanted to play, *oh yes, just like that and then I'm gone...*

"You've got that exactly right, Mr. Rutledge," she said coolly, wrenching herself away from his restraining hands with all the will and determination she could muster in the face of her duplicitous feelings. "I've had my fun ... for today."

She could see by his eyes how angry he was. But he wasn't going to force her. Flint Rutledge would never need to coerce anyone, least of all *her.*

"Bitch," he hissed, "virgin bitch—you're scared, honey; you've never had a man before—"

She hated him; right then, right there, she hated him because he understood the game perfectly. She wanted to kill him because he was absolutely right.

She lifted her skirts, swirling them around her legs as if she were dusting them off, pulling them higher and higher to remind him what she could give him—if she chose to. She was going to play this out to the bitter end.

"I've never had this man before, and I've had just about enough of him today," she taunted him; words were so easy—surrender was not. "Maybe another time, *sugar* ... maybe I'll show you what a real woman does when she wants a *man*—"

It sounded good—as if she knew; and she did know—she had the example of Nyreen the viper in her very own nest. She just wasn't quite ready to ... submit completely.

"Don't come looking for me, sugar. A Jezebel-bitch like you couldn't possibly fulfill my needs."

He gazed up at her smugly from his supine position and she wanted to grind her foot into his face.

Damn it—she should have ... she could have—

And then she thought of something better. She lifted her leg and planted one bare foot on his bulging manhood.

The hard part ... God, it was huge, bigger than she could feel when she had been pressed tightly against it.

She moved her foot, curling her toes around his sheathed

shaft, sliding it up and down the length of him, feeling every inch of him throbbing and pulsating beneath her naked foot.

Unbelievable—she gauged his reaction through her lowered eyelids. He wanted her; she felt the full exhilarating shift of power and she reveled in it.

There would be another time, another encounter, another chance. And then she would make him crawl to her.

And already she couldn't wait.

"No, I couldn't fulfill your needs, honey. I could just tell by the way you're laying so still and small—yes, call me Jezebel, Mr. Rutledge, call me a bitch—" She ground her foot down tightly against his hard heat then and stood over him like some triumphant warrior queen.

"And then you hope in your dreams that sometime when I'm in the mood, I'll give you another chance."

And with that, she boldly knelt on his chest, forced a hard harsh kiss on his mouth—and then she sprang up and was gone.

Chapter 5

She felt the power, the hard brazen insolent power of having bested him. She felt more than that: she felt the potency of her sex.

And she loved making him yield to it in spite of her qualms. She couldn't wait to try it again.

She rode the Boy hard and fast up through the fields of Montelette, in a fury of excitement.

Next time, next time she would not dissolve into a quivering mass of uncertainty when he touched her. Next time, she would know what to do, because now she knew what it felt like to be touched by a man.

Now she understood the swamping excitement that could override every consideration, every scruple; she would know how to use it now, and she would know how to control him.

And she wanted that so badly. The son of her father's worst enemy squeezed and manipulated like dough in her hands. Just like Nyreen handled her father.

Through his convulsive desire for her sex.

She wanted to comprehend how it worked, and already she had learned it wasn't enough to tease and tempt a man; a woman had to be prepared to play the game entirely through.

If she were going to make him beg and crawl, she had to be willing to reap the reward and she had to discount the cost.

And what would be the cost to her? A momentary pain, and hours of glory for the pleasure of making him bend to her will.

Wasn't that enough? Or was she leaping head first into the quicksand of her own anger and defeat?

She *needed* to see him again—she wanted to see him again right away to wipe away those telltale moments of hesitation that had given her away.

But that would be stupid, stupid, stupid. That was a virgin's way who was drunk on newfound knowledge, and she wanted to appear every inch the knowing temptress the next time she saw him.

No—the next time she sought him out . . .

She needed time, time to think and assess everything that had happened, everything he had said and every response she had given.

And she wanted to luxuriate in those new, molten feelings he had aroused; she wanted to understand them and above all, she wanted to use them.

They would give her the power—but only if she did not surrender to them.

She drew up on the rise above the fields of Montelette.

Damn, it was late; the field hands were trooping back through the cane to their houses.

Dinner would be waiting and she would be late—*and* she would have to change and make herself presentable.

She needed to slip into the stables and through the back door and up the servants' staircase if she were to even present herself within a reasonable period of time.

And all she wanted to do was lie in bed and *think*.

"Where is she? Where is she?"

Oh, God—Nyreen was shrieking at the top of her lungs. Dayne edged her way around the back staircase very carefully.

"Lucinda! "

"Yes'm—no'm—I ain't seen Miz Dayne. She ain't been nowhere in dis house fo' houahs . . ."

"You're lying!" *Slap!*

Dayne cringed.

"Where is she?"

"I ain't seen Miz Dayne since dis mawnin'."

Slap!

"You make me sick, always sticking up for her; always—no

one ever knows anything. No one ever wants to do anything. Well, we'll see—we'll see, Lucinda. We'll see who knows anything when I'm married to Mr. Harry. Get out of my sight, you hear me? *Get out of my sight!*"

"Yes'm . . ."

"*Shut up!*" Nyreen shrieked and Dayne heard the sound of scurrying footsteps and then Nyreen's deep body-trembling breaths as she attempted to control her temper.

And then her voice changed into a soft simpering coo.

"Harry darling—"

"Don't bother me with nonsense," Harry growled. "Come closer and closer—bother me with that, Nyreen, and you can have my attention anytime."

"I wish it could be. You could be doing anything you desired with me right now, Harry darling; you know that. But you arranged this dinner, my darling, and that insect of a daughter of yours cannot be found. And for all I know, she's listening to us right now. I feel so uncomfortable, Harry. We just have to wait, and I have to find the jade before our guest arrives."

She whirled away from him in a froth of petticoats and taffeta. "A kiss to you my darling. I hope our guest likes what he sees."

And then silence.

So he had done it, Dayne thought, inching her way into the hallway to make sure it was totally empty. She couldn't believe it. Harry had done it; he had invited someone to dinner to look her over.

And he was ready to sign the contract right now.

We will see about that.

It was a matter of changing her plans. She sauntered through the hallway around to the parlor. Her timing was perfect—she could just hear the crunch of wheels as a carriage pulled down the long tree-shaded drive to Montelette.

Her suitor would love the approach: the pristine white columns just barely visible below the hanging moss and then suddenly the house would burst into view, unencumbered by vegetation, its roof-line high and starkly pitched against the blue sky, and speaking of wealth and privilege and property and money.

Everything he might covet before he even met her.

"So there you are!"

Nyreen came flying up to her and pinched her arm. "God, look at you—well, you don't have time to change, Missy. Mr. Etienne Bonfils is due to arrive at any moment. No doubt he would like to see you exactly the way you are."

"No doubt," Dayne said dryly, wrenching her arm away from Nyreen's pincer-like fingers. "The truth is always best, especially up front."

Nyreen stared at her. "Are you even wearing petticoats? Bah—don't answer. Perhaps you need this lesson—or perhaps your father does, since he seems to think your mother raised you properly for some reason. Well, he'll see now, and then we'll get on with the business of finding your husband. Too bad Mr. Bonfils must be the sacrificial lamb. On the other hand—" she paused as the doorbell rang, "—he might like you well enough just as you are."

Dayne was caught: her father had appeared in the parlor doorway at the sound of the bell just as Nyreen threw open the door to admit her proper suitor, and one look at his face told her she had made the right choice at least.

But seeing his disgust reflected in his face, she knew exactly how she looked: like some common drab, her face flushed, her hair tousled, her dress hanging around her bare feet which were covered with bayou soil.

No amount of money could convince Mr. Bonfils to buy *this*— a woman who carried herself proudly in spite of the dirt and the improper dress and the knowing look in her eye.

The dinner was a disaster—just as Nyreen had intended, but she was in a fury that Mr. Bonfils didn't bite anyway: she wanted a suitor and fast, and Dayne just smiled at her across the table and noisily sipped her soup and watched Mr. Bonfils turn green with repugnance.

Nyreen could not rescue it—she did not know how, and Dayne, who did, was not going to help her. She let her father do the talking, because Harry knew all the right *male* things to say to bring Mr. Bonfils into the brotherhood of men who must indulge an unmanageable woman.

Mr. Bonfils understood that very well, but he was more taken with Nyreen and he even worked up the nerve to tell Harry, characterizing her as Harry's *properly* behaved daughter, and that he could become very interested in her.

"But Miss Nyreen is already spoken for," Harry said, treating the matter quite seriously.

"I am sorry to hear this. I thank you for your hospitality, Mr. Templeton. It has been quite an enlightening evening."

"I daresay," Harry said, saving his growing anger for the moment the door closed and Mr. Bonfils was out of sight and out of contention.

"*You,* young lady—"

"Father?" She was all innocence because she didn't care, and because she was very happy to have made a fool of Nyreen.

"You look like a whore—"

"I, Father? But I'm only copying Nyreen's good example," she said, her eyes wide with all innocence.

Harry's temper almost exploded; he wanted to smack her sassy mouth and he wanted to protect Nyreen. "Two weeks," he said ominously, clenching his fists so he wouldn't strike her. "Two weeks, Dayne, and we will have a suitor and you will be planning your wedding. And it will be someone whom all your tricks won't turn off, I'll tell you. So you just play your games—but be prepared. I will have my house to myself again—two weeks, young lady—no more, no less. Now go to your room . . ."

Her mouth working, her eyes sheered over with tears, Dayne turned away from him just so he wouldn't see how deeply his enmity affected her.

Two weeks—he was crazy; there weren't that many men in St. Foy and beyond who would be willing to marry *her.*

It was a bluff—it had to be . . .

And she wasn't going to let it deter her from her plans.

She mounted the staircase and then turned—and there was Nyreen, engulfed in her father's embrace, working the power with her pouty little voice and the press of her too desirable body against his.

Her resolve strengthened.

Whatever her father was planning to do, she still had two weeks to make Flint Rutledge bend to her will.

* * *

She simmered with a fine rage the rest of the evening and she didn't calm down until after she had had her bath and she was laying in her bed, wrapped in a thin robe which was light and gauzy as her afternoon dress.

And then she remembered; her body remembered the naked feel of a man's hands caressing her and the power of her sex.

Here was a place she could answer to no one and reign supreme. And this time, she would not let any virginal misgivings stop her.

She had to plan the next assault carefully. . . . She leapt off the bed and dashed into the hallway. "Lucinda! Lucinda!"

Lucinda came running. "What you want, Miz Dayne?"

"I need some help. I want to make some adjustments to my clothes."

She thought of it in an instant: tomorrow she would play lady of the manor with him, all buttoned up and properly dressed until—and if—she let him get any closer.

It would give her more control, more time to assess how the game was played.

She dressed very carefully the next day: her light unboned corset which now, because of Lucinda's handiwork, revealed, cupped, and thrust her naked breasts forward; and her most elegant drawers several years old and tight on her now, which were made of fine lawn and edged with lace at the waistband, knees, and at the slit between her legs.

She wore no chemise or petticoats over the steel hoop which Lucinda grudgingly fastened around her waist, and she wore a green satin swiss waist over which Lucinda poured a light yellow muslin skirt around which she fastened the matching tie.

"Wheah's yo' blouse you gonna weah wid dat?"

"No blouse today," Dayne said airily, admiring her bare shoulders and the green satin straps which made her skin look whiter. "I'll take a mantle—the pleated one there with the green braid—imagine how cool I'll be."

"You gonna be cooled right to yo' daddy's whip, you cah'yin' on like dis—"

"I won't tell if you won't. Besides, it makes so much better sense to wear as little as possible in this heat. I won't even tell anyone you dressed me this morning, Lucinda. Quick—go on now . . ."

"I'm gonna know . . ."

"Shhhh . . ."

Lucinda disappeared and Dayne turned toward the pier mirror, threw off the offending wrap and began tugging at the neckline of the dress.

God—the layers. Were she properly dressed, she would have been wearing a chemise under the corset, a corset cover over that, layers of petticoats, a blouse, the waist and the skirt and she probably would have fainted before she made it down the stairs.

This way—oh, this way, with her skin bared to the sultry heat . . . there—and her bosom straining enticingly against the confining green satin waist . . . it was perfect, and a wonder she had never thought of it before.

She picked up the mantle and threw it around her shoulders.

She felt the soaring power of her femininity—but it wouldn't hurt, she thought, to take a gun.

"So you're pretending to be the daughter of the house today," Nyreen said snidely as she watched Dayne come arrogantly down the stairs. "How convenient for you that your father has arranged still another dinner—Mr. Hanscombe from St. Alberville Parish—I collect you might know his name?"

Dayne paused, the rage in her just one breath away from being fanned into a full conflagration, complete with temper tantrum.

Everyone had heard of the Hanscombes of course. She shrugged. "I believe the name is familiar."

"Your father wanted me to forewarn you so that there would be no replay of yesterday's humiliating scene. You'll be dressed properly and you will appear on time—with dress, shoes, and hair in proper order."

"I wouldn't dream of doing anything else," Dayne said smartly and sidestepped Nyreen to open the front door.

"Your father won't put up with any more of your nonsense," Nyreen said warningly.

"Only from you, dear Nyreen," Dayne called back and slammed the door shut behind her before Nyreen could think of a rejoinder.

Harry crept out from the parlor.

"Excellent, my dear, excellent. She'll be on her best behavior tonight."

"Can you guarantee it?" Nyreen asked bitterly, pushing away his eager hands. "Can you promise me . . . ?"

"I can promise you something wonderful, my dear, now that we're alone; she'll be gone for an hour at least—maybe . . ." he murmured as he snuggled his face into her neck, "—even two . . ."

Nyreen hesitated. She had made enough fuss about Dayne already and she deliberately hadn't made any fuss over him for the last several days.

He was hungry. He was eager.

His hands were everywhere and she dodged them like a matador.

"Oh, darling Harry—still—not here, not here. I'd feel so much better—"

"Where?" he demanded roughly.

She smiled slightly, a cat smile full of knowledge and triumph. But Harry only saw that elusiveness he wanted to possess.

"In your office, darling Harry—in a moment: meet me there; I want to make very sure she's gone. Because if I'm certain she won't come, I'll feel very free to show you what it could be like—after Dayne is married and gone . . ."

She took the long road down to Orinda, driving a pony cart which had been her mode of transportation before her hair went up and her skirts went down.

And now her hair was back down and her bosom was decollette and instead of looking for adventure, she was looking for trouble.

And she knew it: the feeling went hand in hand with her unabated fury at the course her life was taking.

But a woman never had control over her life—*ever*.

How clearly she could see it now, and only because there was no mother to create the illusion that there were no rules and restrictions and that everything would be exactly as her daughter would want.

No doubt she would have perpetuated the lie for her own daughter—but now—oh now—there might be a farce of a wedding, but there would never be any children—unless she could wield this potent power she was just coming to understand with the man who would ultimately buy her.

Anyway—she didn't care—she *didn't* . . .

The excitement of both defying her father and provoking the enemy was like a drug.

She felt daring, reckless, sexual—in command.

She knew just what she was doing.

She was going to Orinda, with a gun in her pocket, dressed like a wanton, hoping to entice a man to ravish her so she could learn the secrets of using her sexual power before she married a man she didn't want.

Simple.

You could have just gotten a spell from Mama Dessie . . .

Except Nyreen doesn't work spells. I want that kind of power over this man. . . over every man, especially the one I am forced to marry . . .

It took twenty minutes to get to Orinda by slow-moving cart and another five to go down the driveway and to the barn.

It was falling to ruin just like everything else at Orinda, and its doors were open, almost as if someone were expecting her.

She drove the cart into the steamy darkness and then went behind the building to the water trough, which was shaded by trees and always full of clear cool rainwater. She filled the bucket that was always in the cart and took it back to her faithful mare.

She had removed the mantle a long time before, and she was sorely tempted to remove the unwieldy hoop, except that it would diminish the picture she wanted to present.

If he was here—*if* she wasn't crazy—

Maybe the heat was making her crazy . . .

After all, she was just standing in an old barn with the usual smells and rotting hay and harnesses and whips and gear hanging haphazardly from the beams.

She had no reason to think he might be here.

She moved to some hooks beside the door and fingered one of the whips. *A better motivator than a gun,* she thought—*if* he was here . . .

She took it down and snapped it into the air.

It made a sharp satisfying *crack,* almost as if it had broken the sultry air.

And she liked the feel of it—the woven handle was slightly frayed, and the lash itself was pliant, not stiff—but old and well-used.

She wrapped it around her wrist experimentally, liking the suppleness of the leather—and how it looked against her skin: primitive almost, sensual and strangely arousing.

Anything on bare skin—

Anything . . .

She tossed her gun into the cart and slowly walked out of the barn.

The heat hit her like the blast of a furnace; the sun poured on her bare shoulders and her head and overwhelmed her with instant lethargy.

She wanted to take off her clothes immediately; there had never been such heat; it came at her in waves, pushing at her as she made her way to the verandah at the back of the house.

No one could stand this heat; no one would even think to come to Orinda except someone like her with trouble on her mind.

She let herself into the rear hallway: the doors of Orinda were never locked.

It was cooler here, particularly because of the verandah, which surrounded the house on two levels; and there were very few windows open and so the heat did not penetrate the inner reaches of the house.

There were four rooms down here—the dining room, an office, a wine room, and a service room, as well as an interior staircase, which she mounted to get to the upper floor and the parlor where Mr. Flint Rutledge had made himself so comfortable in the days before he had returned to Bonneterre.

She was shocked to find there was still evidence of his occupation.

There were still some clothes there, and the bedding placed neatly by the parlor fireplace, a basket and a water jug—different things for a life different than the one he envisioned when she had come upon him that first day.

No rifle—he had learned that lesson. And the water jug was half full, which meant—what?

She opened one of the French windows and went out onto the gallery.

The air assaulted her again. It was *so* hot—almost without thinking, she began loosening the tie at her waist and slowly, slowly she unfastened the skirt and untaped her hoop and stepped out of it and just let the skirt fall to the floor. And then the little waist—a mere unhooking of the top and bottom fasteners and it was off and the air felt fresh and light against her naked, upthrust breasts.

She looked down at herself.

She was all in white, from her shoes to the remodeled corset and the only contrast was the faint dark line of her womanly hair against the straining opening in her drawers, the blush pink of her hard pointed nipples, and the leather lash wound around her wrist.

Now she was ready—*now* . . .

Mr. Hanscombe tonight . . .

Unwelcome thought. It dampened excitement like water on fire. *Did she really think bringing Flint Rutledge to heel would make Mr. Hanscombe more palatable?*

What a fool she was—

And then she saw him, bare-cheated and sweaty, sauntering out from the direction of the stables, and pouring a bucket of water over his head.

He instinctively looked up and he saw her, and she knew he wasn't surprised—that he had been expecting her, that he was there solely because he knew she would come—and in some way that perception angered her, as if her motives and her moves were obvious to him, and she could never catch him off-balance.

She stiffened her back and ran her fingers lightly over the cuff of leather around her wrist.

We'll see about that, she thought scornfully as she began walking slowly toward the staircase in the corner of the gallery. *We'll just see about that.*

"Well, well, well—if it isn't the virgin queen of Montelette. Did you lose something, Your Highness? Or would you like to?"

He stood twenty yards away from her, dripping with water and sarcasm, and she wanted to wipe the smug smile off of his face.

"Why no, Mr. Rutledge," she said just as kindly as she could manage through her heaving irritation and her inability to keep her eyes off of his hairy, naked chest. She would not let him intimidate her. She *wouldn't*.

"I haven't lost anything, including my composure, and the only thing I seem to have found is yet another slimy snake who is just aching to have his tongue shoved back down his throat."

"Oh sugar, *someone's* aching for my tongue all right—and I would just love to show you where . . ."

She felt her body twinge at the thought of *where*. It didn't help that his coal-hot gaze rested right on her breasts.

"I'm not in the least tempted, Mr. Rutledge."

"Aren't you?" he asked softly, insinuatingly.

The presumption of him! "Not at all, Mr. Rutledge," she said coolly. "Perhaps it is you—"

"Oh, absolutely," he interposed, cutting the ground right out from under her. "I'd love to get my hands on you again."

Her breath caught as he took a step closer. And she stood her ground: she had to—she had presented herself to him as ready and willing, and he knew it.

"You dressed to tease today, sugar. You know just what a man wants to see on a scorching day like today."

He took another step toward her.

"A man wants to see a woman coming to get what he can give her—offering just a little bit more this time—along with the memory of what she let him do before."

She was mesmerized by his voice, by her swamping feelings, by her body's hot memory of his caresses. Suddenly it was too easy to contemplate the ultimate surrender—because he had all the magic and all the power.

And she could only think of one last way to get back in control.

Her eyes rested insolently on the bulge between his legs—and her gaze kindled as she noted his reaction—oh yes, *yes*... this was the way: how stupid of her not to have known—

But now she did and she saw just how vulnerable that made him, and she made no move to stop him—yet—as he sought to master her.

Another step.

"You want what I can give you, sugar. You fancied yourself up to provoke me, like the Jezebel you are, and then you just stripped like you were offering everything to me. And now you're saying no?"

Another step.

"You couldn't wait for it ... you came for it ... you want it—"

He was two feet away from her, hypnotizing her with *his* power, his musky male power, and making it oh so easy for her to succumb.

And if she did—*if* she did ...

Her eyes flicked again to that rampant male part of him and distractedly she began unfurling the leather from around her wrist.

"You want it *now*—"

Crack!

She lashed out at him with a quick sharp snap of her wrist. "That's better, Mr. Snake Rutledge; I do think we have to whip you into shape."

"Well, well, well—the virgin bitch is just full of surprises," he murmured, not missing a beat.

"I came to cool off, Mr. Rutledge, nothing more, nothing less."

"Of course," he said agreeably.

"So you'll excuse me while Mr. Whip and I get comfortable. We'll just—pretend you're not here."

"Whatever you say, sugar-bitch," he said grimly.

Crack! She snapped the whip inches away from his body.

"You call me Miz sugar-bitch *ma'am,*" she said insolently and then she turned her back on him and sashayed—oh yes, it was the only word—she twitched her hips and minced her steps and hoped that his mouth was watering at the sight of her bottom undulating down toward the edge of the bayou.

Because she was remembering the feeling of her bottom undulating at the touch of his hands, and she was *not* remembering her agitation, and she would die before she admitted she wanted to feel him fondling her there again.

She lifted the hair off of the back of her neck, her body turned in profile just for him.

". . . God, Jezebel, you'd tempt a man to sin . . ."

He'd moved beside her, and his voice was soft in her ear, his hands, firm and quick already sliding down the silk of her drawers to feel for her willing flesh underneath.

She felt the heat of his body, the wet of his naked chest wedged against her back; the thrust of his spurting hard part—the mystery, the secret, the wonder . . .

"You couldn't stay away from this, not one day—could you?"

"*You* couldn't," she whispered, hesitating only one heart-stopping conscience-wrenching moment before she yielded to the feel of his oh-so-knowing fingers.

"You dressed for me . . ."

"Maybe someday if you're lucky, I'll undress for you—"

"You're almost there, sugar," he murmured as his one hand slipped around her waist and began moving upward toward her exposed breast.

Uh oh, uh oh—here was the moment—if he touched her, she would utterly lose control; she was almost there already, beguiled by his masterful hands.

And she couldn't—she just couldn't . . .

One moment of sanity before he caressed the one pointed tip—just one moment to wrest the tug of war back to her side . . .

"Ah!" She rapped his hand sharply with the whip handle. "I think not, Mr. Rutledge."

"Godalmighty—bitch . . ."

Good—he was hurting. Now what?

She smiled disdainfully. "Keep your distance, Mr. Rutledge." She flicked the whip at him. "We're going to do things my way now."

Her way? Her way? thought Flint. God, if she had her way, she would immobilize him.

Yes—get those lethal hands away from her. *Yes!*

"And just what the hell does that mean?"

She knew exactly what it meant as her heated restive gaze sought some way to control his roaming roving hands before they stroked the very juices from her.

"It means I can't trust you worth a damn," said Dayne, "and I'm just going to have to tie you up so I know exactly where your hands are at all times."

Yes, perfect. The tree . . . "So why don't you just sit right down there by that tree and wrap your arms around the trunk behind you—*do it, Mr. Rutledge*—" She flicked the whip again and it just grazed his shoulder blade.

He didn't see one opening where he could fight her for control of the whip. She was too damned good with it.

Grudgingly he sat and wondered how she came to be so damned good with it while she knelt beside him and twisted the supple lash of the whip tightly around his large wrists, and then she stood up and walked around so he could see her.

Oh Lord, this was wonderful, she thought. He was there and she was here and he couldn't do anything, but she could do whatever she wanted.

And more than anything, she wanted to make him crazy with wanting her. It was perfect: she could have him and she still would not have to submit.

"So much better," she murmured, bending over him so he got an enticing view of her taut-nippled breasts. "I do like being in control." She ran a conciliating hand down his perspiring chest and he flinched.

"Bitch," he spat. But his coal-hot gaze was fixed firmly on her brazen nipples.

"I love it when you call me that," she cooed, kneeling next to him and playing with the hair on his chest.

"I can't decide if you're innocent or stupid," he growled.

She brushed her fingers against his pebbly male nipples and he flinched again.

"I'm exactly what you called me," she murmured, working both of her hands now all over his sweaty hairy chest and loving the wet hard heat of it.

Down and down she moved her hands, her excitement growing. The feel of his hot muscular body lathered with his musky sweat, the burning sense of his eyes devouring her naked breasts as she rubbed her fingers over his hard nipples . . . just that, just that—the hard, the soft, the scent of sex between them—

And him, helpless in her hands . . .

She straddled his knees, her hands cupping his chest so that his nipples pressed flat against her palms.

"Bitch . . . I want you . . ."

"I know . . . I just love knowing that—"

"Yes, a bitch like you would."

She smiled—an enigmatic little smile and she thought he looked like he wanted to commit mayhem.

Good. It was just what she wanted.

She could feel him thick and tight and throbbing just between her legs, compressed equally in his fury and his desire.

"Sugar kisses, sugar," she whispered, leaning into him and offering her lips.

"Go to hell."

"Oh no, sugar, your kisses are heaven." And she slanted her mouth over his and delved for the hot wet sweetness inside.

He couldn't resist it: she wanted the hot wet taste of him. Her tongue begged for it. Her body settled tightly against his, demanding it.

Her hands felt and fondled him, enticing it. She could feel him, beneath her, elongating and pushing against the cloth barrier between them.

The feel of him both contained and explosive excited her. Her tongue grew wild with wanting. Her body arched into the kiss, her stone hard nipples two hot points against his chest.

Her body writhed as he prolonged the kiss; she rode him, her legs straddling his granite erection. Her hands went wild all over his body.

And then slowly, slowly she pulled away from him.

How perfect. How luscious.

And now—and now she wanted more.

"Delicious, sugar," she whispered, and moved herself so that her frantic hands could reach his straining manhood.

Now it was time for the hard part.

He made a muffled sound as she bared him to the sultry air and her torrid need.

She knew what to expect; she had seen him before.

But this—this close up—this shaft of pure male potency—all huge and thick and jutting upward proudly—moving as if it had a mind of its own . . .

The hard part—that kisses and play could turn into a monster or a lover . . .

But how—*how?*

She wanted to touch it, to feel the galvanic sense of its strength.

He watched her, his eyes coal-black and burning with some unnameable emotion.

She didn't back down; she challenged that gaze, she challenged his manhood.

She put out a tentative hand to touch it—and she found it was made of skin and muscle and a vigor all its own.

But the force of it—the strength—she slid her fingers lightly down the shaft, and he bit back a groan.

Interesting—with just a touch, he was butter in her hands? And what if she—?

She grasped it tightly and he shuddered.

Power. Power here, and not his—

Hers . . .

How lovely.

It was lovely; it was. There was something symmetrical and beautiful about the shape. It fit her hand perfectly.

It would fit her perfectly . . .

She looked up once again and met his scorching gaze.

He hated this; he hated her taking control. But most of all he hated not having the use of his hands.

She could see in his eyes exactly what he would do if he could only grab hold of her.

His anger aroused her; handling the most potent part of him aroused her.

She felt a sudden deep wet hunger for his kisses, and to press her innocent body against his nakedness.

She moved, catlike, to straddle his thighs, her body leaning forward to trap his ramrod manhood between her thighs and his stomach.

"Now—sugar—more kisses . . ." she murmured, undulating her hips still closer to the rock hard root of him.

But it was still not enough. She wanted to feel that nakedness against her; she wanted to own it.

She moved closer, hiking her body upward to insinuate her knees on either side of his hips, spreading her legs wider so that she could fit the long length of him precisely against her womanly core.

And there—and, yes—there—she could just feel the hardness against her thick bush of hair. She gyrated her hips still more tightly against him.

Now—now she could feel him, now—against the tender flesh of her velvet cleft as she rode him . . .

She couldn't get close enough to him; he was so hot and hard and his eyes glowed with a lambent light and he was so deliciously powerless and everything was hers for the taking.

There were feelings there—that was the most shocking thing; as she pressed and rubbed against his hot hard heat, she was swamped with sensation from her most guarded treasure.

"Oh sugar—so sweet," she whispered, riding the sensation, undulating her hips to capture the intense feeling of her soft naked femininity against the hard unforgiving rock of his manhood.

She hadn't expected it—she was utterly captivated by the mounding feelings between her legs that just kept heaping and heaping like thick clotted cream as she gyrated her hips against him.

And his eyes—that glowing knowing look in his eyes as he began the short tight thrust of his hips that made the thick ridged tip of him press up tightly against her velvet fold.

He knew what he was doing and what she was feeling and she didn't care—she wanted more and more; she wanted the air-whipped sensation to lengthen and tighten. She felt herself reaching for something, she didn't know what, just the fusion of the sensation, the release . . .

She climbed higher up against him so that her breasts were almost at the level of his mouth; he might just take one of her taut pointed nipples into his mouth . . .

The thought of it shot silver sensations through her veins.

Oh yes, sweet sugar . . . take it—take it . . .

She wanted to feel it, she was desperate to feel it; her body raced and rubbed against him, her breasts shook with the feverish pumping of her body.

So close . . . so close to what?

And she felt it—she didn't know what—a gathering of all the sensation, all the heat, all the hectic movement . . . she felt it—*it* . . .

And he leaned into her breasts and surrounded the one nipple with the sucking wet heat of his tongue—

And she fell right over the edge into a spiralling starburst of sensation that pulled her into an incandescent radiance like the undertow of the ocean.

Chapter 6

"It's time for me to go home, sugar. Walk me to the house."

She snapped the whip just to the right of his naked buttock and he moved—like a lion, angrily, resentfully, as full up of pleasure as she and not willing to admit it, and hating the weapon of her power.

But that was fine. She thought she had been extremely inventive about that: she had undressed him and tossed his clothes into the bayou, and only then did she untie him, and she had been crafty enough not to let him get the upper hand in any way.

"Problem, sugar?" she inquired sweetly when he stopped for a moment. God, didn't she just love the look of him naked and quiescent—nothing powerful there; he looked rather vulnerable in fact, and she could see he absolutely hated it, even more than he had despised her immobilizing his hands.

But she didn't mind that. She didn't mind anything he was angry about: she had gotten what she had come for. She had bested him: she had wielded the power and most of all, she had experienced the pleasure.

They stepped onto the verandah and she pointed him up the steps to where her clothes lay.

"Dress me, sugar."

His eyes positively flamed with fury.

"Hold out the hoop—I'll step into it—that's right, and no false moves because you know I can handle this thing—and that thing"—she motioned to his sleeping male root as she lifted her leg over the hoop—"that's right. Now—that green satin waist . . ."

She slipped her arms under the straps, and enjoyed the crisp sound of him snapping the hooks in place.

The skirt came next—and the one instant where she would not have her eyes on him or be able to retaliate if he tried something.

He was too quiet, damn it—

Stupid hoops—

No problem; he didn't look like he even wanted to try.

Why not?

And then the sash.

"Walk me down to the barn now—there's no one to see you, Mr. Rutledge, and I can be assured of the fact you won't jump into your clothes and come after me."

But the problem really was her mare was too slow.

She backed the cart out of the barn and mounted the driving perch.

And then he grabbed for her arm and almost toppled her to the ground.

"Not such a virgin after all, Jezebel. What an act—what a wonderful act."

Her temper immediately flared. "You'll be damned lucky if you ever get that much from me again, Mr. Rutledge. But I got such great pleasure out of wielding my whip—I might just decide to pay you another visit."

"Oh things will be a lot different if you do, Jezebel, because I'm going to teach you that the only one who has the whip hand around here is me."

She smiled insolently. "How defiant of you, Mr. Rutledge."

"I'm aching to give you the spanking you so richly deserve, you teasing bitch. Come around again and we'll see who will be disciplined next time."

And there was no doubt who he thought would be punishing whom; his lusty manhood had shot erect at the very thought of it.

Her glittering eyes narrowed and rested on the hard jutting tip of him.

"Oh yes, sugar—we'll see just who the hard master will be." She lifted the whip and circled it over her head—and *crack!* It snapped inches away from his male pride.

"Maybe that will hold you—until next time."

* * *

Mr. Hanscombe was as interesting as a lump of clay. Dayne couldn't keep her boredom hidden as the small talk ranged around the table, touched her, moved away again.

"Dayne, darling—you must be hot in that wrap," Nyreen kept saying.

"I'm fine, I'm fine."

"You're making me hot," Nyreen said, out of all patience with her languor and her apathy. "Zenona! Take Miss Dayne's wrap please."

"Don't do it," Dayne mouthed to the servant.

"Miz Dayne—"

Dayne looked up at her father's expectant and approving gaze. Well, that would change instantly.

She unhooked the wrap and let it slide from her bare shoulders, and then slanted a look up at her father and Nyreen, as she heard the sound of Mr. Hanscombe's jaw snapping shut.

"It's very cool," she offered into the shocked silence, although why Nyreen and her father should be shocked, she couldn't understand.

Mr. Hanscombe said nothing. But he was a gentleman, and gentlemen did not criticize ladies in their own homes. Oh, but he would have a tale to tell up and down the river ever after.

Nothing went right after that.

Mr. Hanscombe could not keep his piggy little eyes from her naked skin.

Nyreen was furious enough to flay her. And her father kept looking in every other direction but at her in order to avoid her blatant and mortifying show of skin.

The evening could not end fast enough, and it was at that moment that Harry Templeton understood that he did not have enough money to whitewash Dayne's iniquities and that more desperate measures were called for.

A rebel needs a rebel, he thought. Not everyone could be the courageous and proper lady like his Nyreen.

It was finally time for Mr. Hanscombe to take his leave and as Harry watched him drive off in relief, he knew finally exactly what he had to do.

* * *

Let him suffer, Dayne thought, lying naked in her bed the following morning after a sleep positively suffused with the pleasures of the day before.

Let him be begging to see me and then maybe—just maybe—I might think about . . .

But she was already thinking about it.

About how she would dress and what she would do—

"How stupid can you be?" Nyreen demanded, barging into her room and into her most private thoughts. "Do you really think Harry has no idea what you're trying to do?"

"Why no," Dayne said coolly, pulling the sheets around her bare body so that Nyreen wouldn't have cause to question that, too. "I expect he knows exactly what I'm trying to do. So he'll just have to do something else."

"Oh yes," Nyreen murmured. "Indeed he will. So you see, darling Dayne, he knows you better than you think he does." And she left as abruptly as she had come.

Which made Dayne very suspicious.

Immediately she called for Lucinda and her bath and a lightweight dress she could wear without the everlasting hoops which would only contain her and constrain her on a day when she wanted to luxuriate in her newfound awareness.

She couldn't walk a step without her body recreating the hard thrusting feel of him against her virgin nakedness.

And she was instantly wet with wanting more.

No!

. . . Oh yes. . . . She hadn't much time, after all. She had no time at all before someone else would be demanding her caresses.

She had to learn it all—and *fast.*

The naked awareness stayed with her, constant, arousing, a sentient feeling between her legs.

She went as far as the stables to visit the Boy.

Poor Boy. Nothing had been right for him, either, since Nyreen had come. Before then, there had been plans to race him in St. Francisville. She was going to train him and find someone to ride him, and her father had planned on some very serious betting.

But now . . .

Well—now—

No one cared about either of them.

She rubbed his nose and gave him a carrot, and let the fecund smell of the stable saturate her senses.

Ripe, rich, fertile, primitive . . . arousing—

Oh, she had come to the right place to indulge herself if she wanted to wallow in her luxuriant feelings.

With all the lovely leather gear just hanging there, working on her imagination.

. . . Imagine him harnessed, the gorgeous hard part of him thrust out between the leather bands, wrapped in leather, bound in leather, her engorged prisoner in leather unable to get away from any delicious manhandling she might dream up . . .

And she could just put him right where she wanted him . . .

So nice of Peter to teach her the elegancies of handling a whip—

She pulled one down and then another, feeling the suppleness of them, the potency of them.

And if he would look provoking all tethered in leather, how might she look?

The thought made her wet with anticipation.

She grabbed every leather thing she could find, and in a haze of carnal hunger, she took them all back to her room to play with.

"Don't touch me!"

"Nyreen, honey . . . I swear to you—"

"Oh, when I think—when I *think,* Harry—of all the lovely things we could be doing if only we had some privacy . . . it makes me ill the way Dayne is acting."

She looked up at him and moved slightly away from him to get ready to release her next salvo.

"Women have needs, too, Harry," she whispered. "And I wouldn't be caught dead in a compromising situation. And that's all I ever fear around here. That I might be showing you how much I want you, and that bitchy daughter of yours will walk in and catch us together. Look at me, Harry—"

She moved backward still farther and lifted her skirts.

"Sometimes . . . you know, I always have hope—and some-times—" she pulled it up still farther to reveal her bare legs, "—sometimes when I feel I need you so much I—do things no lady would ever do . . ."

The skirt went up higher. She was totally naked to her waist and she could see Harry almost salivating at the sight of her.

She dropped the skirts like a heavy curtain.

"But what if—"

Harry groaned. "Dear God, Nyreen, don't you think I know that? Don't you think I'm working on a plan? I can't stand another minute without you."

"But she's not locked up in a sickroom all day. And we agree that she's doing her best to turn off every eligible man who walks into this house. So what plan, Harry? What plan?"

Harry moved closer to her and put his arms around her narrow waist. "A subtle plan, my darling. One that will work, I guarantee you that. It will work or I'll risk losing you—that's how confident I am, Nyreen."

His hands began moving, lifting the skirt of her dress upward and upward in that breath of a space between them.

She could feel his protuberant sex nudging her as he hiked the skirt over her naked buttocks.

"*Harry!*" she protested with just the right note of censure. "She could—"

His groping fingers found their way between her legs.

"She won't. Damn. Nyreen. Just let me feel you—just let me . . . a little reward for my brilliant plan . . ."

She looked around cannily. "Behind the curtain, Harry. I just don't want her to see us—"

He shoved her behind the figured brocade curtain on one side of the floor to ceiling window and pushed her against the wall.

She helped him: she lifted her skirt and held it out of his way and, smiling her secretive cat smile to herself, she let him take all of her that he wanted.

It took all of her willpower to stay away from Orinda that day.

Instead, she took a knife and she hacked away at the leather and draped it all over her naked body, trying this erotic sheathing and that—twisting the strips around her arms, her neck, her ankles, her waist, her breasts, wrapping the long, handleless supple lash all around her body top to bottom and staring at the gloriously carnal reflection of herself in the pier mirror.

Oh yes—this . . .

Did she think it or did she want it? All she could feel was the pliant caress of the lash accentuating her voluptuous feelings.

All she saw was the tumble of her hair, the insolent look in her eyes, and her leather jewelry emphasizing the wanton nakedness of her body.

Let him wait—let him wait—we'll see who is stronger, whose need is more potent . . .

But even as she thought it, she felt the sheer arousing feeling of him pushing between her legs; she would never forget that sensation—never.

The headiness of the memory was a pleasure in itself.

She couldn't wait to experience it again—soon—tomorrow . . . she would conquer him again.

A bitching serpent in the garden and a man knew it, yet he stripped himself naked and invited the damn thing to take a huge bite . . .

And probably would do it again, he thought irascibly, as he shunted aside overgrown bushes and tamped down high-grown sun-baked grass on his way to Orinda.

Goddamn—a man just didn't leave himself open to a spoiled rich bitch getting under his skin—

Harry Templeton's daughter too—*shit . . .*

The kind of pampered belle you never let get the upper hand because she knew exactly how to crack the whip—and she had made sure he knew it—

But that was the last time—

This time . . .

He was hard as rock at the thought—this time . . .

He hacked his way through the overgrowth, walking today in-

stead of riding because he knew she would be there—this time—
and he wanted to take her in the sultry silence, Adam to her Eve,
alone with the secrets that only they could share.

The morning heat shimmered around him, rising up to gird
him in a sheen of perspiration.

He wiped a hot hand across his brow and then he ripped open
his damp shirt and fanned his dripping body.

This time—

He was absolutely sure she would not stay away. More than
that, with that fine-tuned bitch sense of hers, she knew he would
be there whenever she came—

And, more fool he, he had come to Orinda the day before,
hoping against bitch-belle hope she would be there to be taught a
lesson about defying him.

Bitch-belles were just aching to be subdued. He knew the type
precisely—he had run a thousand miles twenty years before to escape the constricting mores of a society that built its wealth on
the backs of blacks and got its patrimony from the wombs of its
belles while its slaves were concurrently birthing the master's ille-
gitimate children.

She was the epitome of everything he hated, and she was insolent and disdainful, *and* Harry Templeton's hellcat daughter to
boot.

God, he couldn't wait to pull her down from her pedestal,
down in the dirt, the mud, into the ripe rich scent of her arousal
and her surrender to him.

Yes. Under him, writhing, clawing, begging—

His dream—his fantasy . . .

Beyond his wildest imaginings—hot, waiting—wild with
wanting only him . . .

She had to take everything with her; she could not just walk
out of Montelette dressed in practically nothing, her body girdled
in leather.

The feeling of him rubbing against her moist feminine fold
stayed with her through the night and into the morning.

She wanted nothing to touch the swollen point of her arousal;
she slept naked that night, her wrists cuffed in leather to remind

her, as she tossed restlessly through the sweltering night, of forbidden pleasures to come.

And she could feel it; periodically her treacherous body stiffened with a gnawing arousal all its own, and she ached to feel a man's hard, straining erection sliding against the hot wet tender flesh of her.

She felt, the next morning, as if she could never get enough—of the feelings or the power or his sex.

And she didn't give a damn about the consequences; she *was* a bitch and she didn't want him to forget it.

And when Harry finally found some dupe to marry her, she would make him remember it, too.

She slipped out of bed.

She knew exactly what she wanted to take with her this morning, and exactly how she wanted to look when she encountered him again.

And she made him wait.

She thought it was only right that he should not be too sure that she would come.

She wanted him hot and hungry for her; she wanted to prolong her unbearable feeling of excitement.

Slowly she got ready; Lucinda helped her wash and found the missing pair of high heeled kid boots she wanted to wear.

Lucinda laid out stockings and underthings, a corset and petticoats, and she left them there; she could wear what she wanted in her own private eden, couldn't she?

And if the serpent penetrated her defenses today—she would finally know the secret of all forbidden pleasures.

But she wouldn't make it easy.

She carefully wound each leather strip into a ball and tucked them into a pouch which she would tie to her dress.

She wore a light afternoon dress of cotton with short sleeves and an unconstricted waistline over her aching nakedness.

The hem dragged because of the lack of a hoop and her boot-shod feet kept tripping over it, but she didn't care; she would shed it soon enough and she would get very, very comfortable.

She took her whip and she took a hat, to shield her face from the sun—and perhaps, initially, from him.

And she rode the Boy, who needed exercise, down the back roads to Orinda until they came to the overgrown track where she pulled him into a walk and began slowly and sensuously adorning herself with the long strips of the erotic leather lash.

Crack!

She stood on the upper gallery of Orinda and snapped the whip into the air and then again, down against the aging creaking floorboards.

Crack!

She looked like the embodiment of a wanton and she knew it, and she waited for the acknowledgement in his glittering eyes as he slowly sauntered out from the shade of the lower verandah where he had taken refuge from the heat—waiting . . . just waiting.

He shielded his eyes as he looked up at her and watched as she slowly unhooked her dress and let it fall to her boot-shod feet.

Christ . . .

She wore leather—leather cuffs around her wrists, a leather collar around her neck from which was appended two long strips that tied around her breasts in such a way that they were lifted and thrust forward, almost as if they were inviting a caress . . .

And she had tied another thin leather strip like a garter around her right thigh, just at the vee—just to direct his eyes to her lush feminine hair.

And then the boots—soft supple kidskin boots enveloping her naked feet; and the whip—the godalmighty whip that she handled like a goddamned lion tamer.

And maybe that was what she was . . .

And he, dressed in low-riding denims and nothing else, wringing with the musk of his sweat and the heat and the focused force of his unabating hunger.

She saw it all in an instant—the granite bulge, the burnished wetness matting his hairy chest, that immovable impassivity, except for the living heat of his eyes—but he wouldn't give her that, not this minute, not now.

She looked down at her mounded breasts and her nipples so stiff with anticipation.

She felt the weight of the leather on her neck and wrists, and the weight of her desire—heavy as ripening fruit.

"Come and get me, sugar," she growled, leaning over the gallery rail to give him a good, full view of her breasts.

"What if I don't, *sugar?*"

"Why, I'll just put on my little ole dress and go on back home and hope there's someone there who won't pretend to be immune to my charms."

Lord—had she really said that?

She almost thought she'd do it, too; she didn't think she could stand it another moment.

"Bitch," he hissed, as the image of her and some mealy-mouthed fop insinuated itself into his fantasy.

He moved slowly toward the gallery stairs, slowly, slowly to punish her for creating such a venal scenario when she knew she belonged to him.

She was standing with her naked hip propped against the gallery railing as he emerged from the stairwell.

"This is your lucky day, sugar," she cooed; men did seem to like cooing.

"How so, Jezebel? You made me wait two days, and then you threaten to give any other man you can find a taste of your naked charms—how does that make me lucky?"

She flicked the whip—a hairsbreadth away from his bare feet. "I didn't do it, did I, sugar? I'm here with you now, aren't I? So you deserve a little reward—but you have to put your big old hands behind your back, sugar—*now*—" Flick, *crack!* "Or should I tie you up again?"

Goddamn . . . he put his hands slowly behind his back.

She smiled, cat-like, elusive, at a secret only she knew, and she walked right up to him.

In her heels, she was tall enough so that he could graze her forehead with his mouth. He felt like smacking her instead.

She stood almost chest to chest with him, forcing him to look down on her luscious breasts with their succulent nipples.

She arched her back, and slowly and deliberately she cupped her breasts and leaned into his chest so that only her stone-hard nipples touched his sweaty skin.

And she stood that way, with just the stiff tips of her nipples pressing into the hard rock muscle of his hairy wet chest and his whole body jolted with the erotic feeling of those two taut peaks grazing his skin.

They were so long and pointy he could just see daylight between them, and the lengthening bulge of his already engorged sex.

He didn't know how he could keep his hands off of them.

"Don't do it, sugar," she whispered breathlessly. "Do you feel them?"

His eyes glittered—all the answer she needed.

She didn't move; she didn't move.

His body was soaked with heat and need, and she didn't move except to wriggle her nipples even more tightly against him.

Only her nipples. And those shimmering blue eyes that knew exactly what she was doing to him—to them—

God, the feel of him against the turgid points of her nipples, rock hard and soaked in sweat-lathered lust for her—

Another minute, another—she loved the feel of him against her nipples; she loved her nipples, so long and pointed and *hard* . . .

She broke the contact, suddenly, abruptly, deliberately and she smiled at him, the cat-smile, insolent, disdainful, as if she had felt nothing and she didn't give a damn about his aching coiling need.

She moved backward, so that he could look at her; she liked that part a lot—the way he looked at her, and the potency of her naked body.

A woman couldn't let herself care about a man, she thought deprecatingly. All she needed was to know how to manipulate him with her body.

And she could see in this man's eyes how very successfully she could do that.

"You like what you see, Mr. Rutledge?"

"A bitch in heat, sugar—"

She didn't like that one bit. "And you're a sniffing hound, Mr. Rutledge, with—one assumes—no discretion whatsoever—a typical rutting male . . ."

She turned her back on him then and flicked the whip over her shoulder so it just grazed the tempting crease between her buttocks.

She reached down and grasped the tip to pull the lash up tightly against her so it bisected her soft cushiony bottom.

She could almost feel his steaming anger touch her.

She looked over her shoulder. "Well, Mr. Rutledge?" she murmured provokingly.

He exploded.

Ten steps—maybe less—he grabbed her hot naked body ruthlessly and pulled her against him, all of her against all of him, and he held her squirming body against him with one arm, and he pinned her hands behind her with the other, and his mouth crashed against hers, overpowered her, took her, devoured her as he backed her down the gallery and up against one of the stained white columns.

"Bitch, bitch, bitch," he recited a litany against her lips between each brutal kiss. "You do that to me again and I'll take a whip to *you* . . ."

"I can't wait," she hissed, her body writhing against him, arousing him more, stoking her desire still more.

"Shut up—"

"Make me . . ."

He crushed her swollen willing lips.

"You need a good spanking."

"I can't wait to feel your hands on me, sugar."

"*Shit* . . ." He took her mouth again, hotly, violently, as if it were her body, as if he could do everything he was doing in her wet wild mouth to her wanton, wild body.

She could feel the craziness in him, and in herself.

She ground her hips wildly against that iron bar bulge; she pressed herself tightly against him; she let him ravage her with his kisses.

She wanted everything, *everything* . . . even her nakedness was not enough if he didn't do everything.

"Bitch, bitch, bitch—" he groaned. "Damn it, I don't want you—I *don't* want you . . ."

His aching words sent a throbbing terror through her and she wrenched away from him. Damn him, damn him, damn him—she wouldn't beg; the last thing she would do was beg.

She wanted to beg.

"Then let me go, sugar."

He stared down at her stormy blue eyes, and slowly he relinquished his hold on her.

They stood now body to body, every part of him touching every part of her, hot and wet and panting with need.

And if she couldn't make him want her again—what then? What power would she have then when even the potency of her naked body couldn't move him?

His sparking black gaze swept her lips, so kiss-swollen, so tempting still—

"*Goddamn*—" he muttered, and he swooped down again and entered her mouth as if he were entering her body.

She melted under him, her arms free now to circle his body, to reach for his shoulders, to hang onto him as if nothing else mattered.

His hands began an orgy of feeling her. Everywhere, every part of her he could reach, from thrall collar to her bulging breasts, downward and downward, his left hand fingering the leather strip around her thigh, and then both hands sleeking downward to cup her buttocks to lift her up high and tight against the rigid rock of his erection.

"What a luscious bitch you are," he murmured, as his fingers probed and explored her. "I wonder if you really are a virgin."

"Why don't you find out?" she whispered against his lips.

"You can be sure I plan to, Jezebel," he breathed as he stroked and fondled her into swooning submission, "just as soon as I teach you a little lesson in obedience—"

He pulled out of the kiss and turned her so fast, she hardly knew what happened except that he had seduced her into letting down her guard and now she stood face front to the column and he was immobilizing her hands with her whip.

"Now—Jezebel . . ."

His hands caressed her once again and she gave into the seductive stroking, arching herself into it and closing her eyes.

And then—*slap! slap!*

She felt the stinging heat against her buttocks, overriding the pleasure with a different kind of gratification.

Slap!

And once again: *slap!*

She would get him for this. She wriggled her buttocks against the sense of heat that enveloped them, almost as if she were inviting his discipline.

"And so who is your master, naked Jezebel?"

"I bow to your superior strength," she said tartly.

"You are still a virgin in the games men and women play," he murmured, slapping her briskly again.

"Oooo—if my hands were free—" she growled, pulling futilely against the rawhide tie.

He slapped her buttocks again.

"What would you do, naked Jezebel?"

"I'd stop you in a heartbeat," she vowed.

"How intriguing; I wonder how—tell me how—"

"I'd rather show you." She had to get away from the heat-washing spanking.

"Tell me—and I'll let you go. But if you don't—well, you know the punishment."

Damn him, damn him.

She licked her lips. "I would slide both my hands—" the words caught, and then she thought of the stinging feeling of his hand and she gamely went on, "right between your legs and I would feel and caress every inch of you until—until—"

She felt the bonds around her hands loosening.

"Do it, sugar . . ."

She blew out a breath and turned around.

He was standing there naked, holding her whip, waiting, wanting, his male root as hard as iron, long as a rake handle, and elemental and primitive as the bayou.

His jetty eyes held hers for one long moment.

And then she held out her hand and he walked to her and she slid it between his legs and found the taut source of his pride and began massaging and feeling it until he almost melted into her hand.

And she almost melted altogether.

"Lift your leg," he commanded. "The right one; I love the band . . . you know just how to do it, Jezebel—I swear I thought I dreamt you up—"

He knelt down on the floor in front of her.

"Your pleasure, Jezebel . . . this time," and he nozzled her between her legs. "Hold on, sugar . . ."

She held—she grabbed hold of the gallery railings the instant she felt the first jolt of his wet tongue against her nakedness—and he was pulling and sucking at her like—like—he thrust into her—into her inviolate feminine fold like he knew exactly where—

Exactly *what*—

. . . yes . . .

But it was too much, too much—and then—and then— in the wet, in the tangle of desire and femininity, he found the one burgeoning bud that made her whole body crackle—

"Oh my God, oh my God, oh my God . . ."

There were no other words, no other sensations possible . . . this was what she had yearned for, had dreamt about, had felt roiling around inside of her—the *needy* little nub of release . . .

And he knew it—how did he know it? He could positively enslave her with this—oh Lord, she couldn't succumb, she wouldn't succumb . . .

But he was sucking and lapping and her body was convulsing as the core pleasure swirled in her, sapped her will, focused on that one little pleasure point—one, one, one, wet and one and suddenly—explosively, unbelievably, shamelessly—*done* . . .

"Oh my God, oh my God, oh my God . . ." there were no words for this pleasure, this indescribable paroxysm of joyous release . . .

She sank onto the floor next to him—grabbed for him, felt herself lifted against him, the heat of him, the hardness of him, the need of him.

She reached out for him.

Gently, gently he lifted her and carried her into the parlor and laid her down on his makeshift bed.

"Just lie back, sugar—it'll take me just a minute—"

Just a minute, just a minute to straddle her hips and to fit himself between her mounded breasts, and another minute to slide himself back and forth against the erotic pillowing of them, once, twice, three times and again, and again—and then he stiffened, he pushed, he thrust frantically, intensely, primitively—and with one final sinuous surge, he came, spurting his seed across her chest and onto her heaving breasts.

She touched it wonderingly, and then rubbed it on her breasts and the taut peaks of her nipples.

"Perfect," he murmured, leaning over to kiss her. "Perfect—for this time."

Chapter 7

He lay beside her, one long leg thrown over the curve of her hip, pressing his ever elongating male hard part against her hot wet skin.

She felt flushed and satiated and still—still, she wanted more, still more, and she didn't want to move ever again.

His free hand roamed all over her, stroking her buttocks, her arm, her leg, pushing back the damp strands of hair against her forehead, avoiding—deliberately, she thought, the tempting mound of her breast—the one place she wanted to feel his touch.

It was so silent and so hot.

She closed her eyes and just lost herself in his roving fondling of her naked body.

His lips touched hers, once; his fingers parted and probed the enticing crease between her buttocks and went farther and farther between her legs to the soaking dew of her ripe femininity.

Yes there—she heaved a shuddering breath as she felt him stroking her there—already she felt aroused again; how could she be so excited again so soon?

She slipped her hand against his bare leg and up toward his hip, toward the pulsing power of his manhood which surged into virile life as he idly played with her body.

She closed her eyes—there was more, there had to be more or she couldn't be feeling like this, and he could not be so hot and hard and strong.

And she didn't want to see—she wanted to *feel*...

"Ah, Jezebel—" he breathed into her ear. "Perfect Jezebel, naked and willing in my arms, trading a little bit of punishment for a whole lot of pleasure . . . don't move, naked Jezebel, don't move . . ."

She could have sworn his ramrod maleness spurted even harder against the flat wet of her stomach.

And then she knew why.

His hand slid up to her breast and he began lightly moving his thumb across her turgid nipple at the same time he arched her closer to him to give him the perfect angle to caress her.

She felt like she was offering her breasts to him; her body swooned at the sensation of his thumb just moving back and forth, back and forth across the pebble hard point of her nipple.

It was almost unbearable; every inch of her body heightened with awareness at the pulsating pleasure point at the tip of her breast.

She wanted more—something more—and she didn't know what . . .

Pressure—she wanted—she needed pressure against that other pleasure point in the secret recesses of her body . . . she wanted—

His hand touched there suddenly and she strained herself upward to meet the carnal exploration of his fingers.

There, yes—there—oh there . . .

And then his heavenly tongue—all hot and wet and eager— just on the tip of her lush pointed nipple, poised to surround it with his lips—right there, right there—

She groaned as he simultaneously began rubbing and sucking the two engorged pleasure points.

And then—and then—the same thing, the same swoon of sensation like she was floating on molasses, deep and thick in the sticky liquid torrent of molasses, again—pulling at her, sucking at her—so sweet . . . so erotically unbelievably sweet and focused into that point, that one charged point . . .

It was coming, she could feel it coming, the blinding spiralling surrender to his hand and his tongue—it crept up on her suddenly, geysering up from nowhere, somewhere, from the heat of his mouth and his knowing finger, flowing through her body, a gush of sensation streaming through her body like a river and just as suddenly eddying away into ripples of sensation until there was nothing.

And only then did he stop, resting the heel of his hand on her pubic mound and relinquishing her wet turgid nipple.

The silence struck her, and the feel of his maleness strutting and straining against her.

They were so alone, as if they were Adam and Eve—the first ever to discover this pleasure . . .

She opened her eyes and met his glimmering jetty gaze.

"The best is yet to come, Jezebel."

"I can't wait," she whispered coyly.

"Virgin temptress—God . . . I can't keep my hands off of you—"

"I don't want you to," she breathed, pressing her lips against the crisp matted hair on his chest.

"You have gorgeous nipples," he murmured, running his hand across her breast. "Your naked body is made for a man's hands . . ."

Her body twinged at his words; even erotic words were potent, she thought; everything about the carnality between a man and a woman was potent.

But only if a woman were willing to give everything and hold back nothing.

She was willing—and he had not yet found surcease.

"My body is yours," she whispered.

He rolled onto her and then levered himself up on his hands and knees.

"You can say no now, sugar, and that will be the end of it . . ."

"I say yes," she whispered, feeling one little jolt of fear and guilt that it was so easy for her to do.

"You know what it means—"

"I think I know . . ." Did she know—did she really know anything? Like would it show on her face or her body? Could Nyreen tell, or her father, or the man who might marry her—?

And then she looked at him and she didn't care: this was his ultimate surrender, the thing she had set out to make him do—conquer her.

He lowered himself and brushed against her mound with his aching long length.

She shivered; he was *so* big . . .

And then she didn't know—or maybe she did—or maybe it was too late—

She felt him nudging between her legs in that magical place where all feeling emanated, where she was wet and wild with anticipation at what was to come . . .

He pushed, sliding easily just within her welcoming fold—and he stopped—

And she felt him, just there, the huge bulging tip of him surrounded by the soft woman-lips of her . . . yes—

Another push—and then the resistance—

But yes, he had expected it—and she had not—and it pained her that he knew more about her body than she.

"Bear with me, sugar," he whispered, grasping her thighs and running his hands upward to her buttocks and lifting her against the thrust of his erection.

Lifting her and lifting her, until she was forced to balance herself against his commanding hands . . . his hands, always his hands—

He pulled her still tighter against him and then he drove himself against the resistance in her and suddenly there was a tearing little pain, like somehow part of her had been thrashed away by the heaving motion of his body, and she moaned.

Instantly, his motion stopped.

"It's all over, sugar," he murmured, stroking her trembling thighs. "All over—nothing but the good part now, honey. Tell me when—tell me when; I won't move until you say when . . ."

The good part? The good part? What could be the good part of this achy little pain that felt like pinching fingers in the most intimate part of her body?

How stupid was she?

Nothing like before—*nothing* . . . except—except . . . the nudging feel of him between her legs, the sense of him pushing, faintly pushing against the pain, rotating his hips, grinding against her—pushing that much farther in and in and . . .

. . . in—

And suddenly so *in* that she caught her breath and forgot the pain at the sheer sense of him deep within her—in that place . . . the yearning place, the part of her that wanted more—how much more could she want than the whole towering length of him filling and filling her absolute aching center . . . ?

"I'm home, sugar . . ."

"You promised—" she whispered just a little breathlessly, and just as suddenly she had the feeling she wanted to escape him, just wiggle out from under this unexpected all-encompassing shameless carnal possession and run for her life.

"It's over now; there won't be any more pain, sugar."

Abruptly she realized that it was true: the pinching sensation had utterly dissipated, leaving that feeling of breath-catching melting of her body against the hard penetrating heat of him.

"Oh my God . . ." she breathed, "oh my God—"

It was enough—wasn't this much enough? But she knew it wasn't—not for him: he pulsed and throbbed within her with a life and a need of his own . . . the more, the more—

"You're melting all over me," he murmured, pressing her still more tightly against, coaxing her with attenuated little thrusts of his hips. "Come with me, sugar—"

Yes—

Her willing body acknowledged it, and the awed expression in her eyes, as he began his full bore possession of her—she didn't know, she was as innocent as the dawn, and she was, down to her kid boot-shod toes, utterly and totally *his* in her discovery of her power and her passion.

He braced himself on his hands so he could see every nuance of feeling on her mobile face. *Yes—that, and that and that—*he couldn't get enough of her.

He wanted to go on in her forever, his virile sex sheathed in her lush moist heat forever—

. . . and ever and ever—

—and ever . . .

He felt it—he tried to catch himself, pull himself from the point of pleasure so she could feel it, too—but he couldn't, he couldn't . . .

One look downward at her thrusting, taut-tipped breasts and he couldn't—

He drove into her wildly once, twice—his pleasure came in a spume of hot rich ejaculate, on and on and on, wringing him, wrenching him, drenching him until there was nothing more left for him to give . . . and he wanted to howl with a primitive conquering rage that it wasn't nearly enough and that he had come too soon.

And then he looked at her glittery eyes and felt the soft tentative rotation of her hips against his still-turgid sex, and he pushed himself tightly against her to give her his heat and his hardness, and he guided her hips, and pressed her firmly this way and that—and this—

And yes, he found once again that aching point that demanded the hard part of him in complement to it—and she felt the slide and rock of him against her frantic gyrations and she moaned and grasped his muscled arms to give herself purchase and heard his low-murmured words of encouragement—

"Spread your legs, sugar. Push tighter, push harder—come to me, honey, come—let go, let go—hot sugar—come to me—"

And she came—it came, bursting with a silvery slithering heat all over her body, different this time, no explosions, no geysers, just the slow shimmering iridescent slide of sensation from the center between her legs all up and down her body.

This, with him, with *that* . . .

. . . *yes*—

Now she knew.

Now she knew . . .

Afterward she felt—and she wondered if everybody felt—just a little ridiculous dressed up to play sensual games.

And yet, the costume still had the power to affect her; the minute she stood up, the minute her breasts settled into the confines of the slender leather strap that bound them upward and outward, she felt like Jezebel all over again.

And he—already—was imperiously erect.

"We could stay here all day, sugar."

She could be imperious, too. "I think not, Mr. Rutledge; I think we've done quite enough."

"What do you mean *quite* enough?"

She sent him a simmering, shimmering glance. "It was enough—for today."

"Goddamn—you little virgin bitch—you didn't know a

damned thing before today, and you had better show some gratitude that I took my time with you."

"The hell I will. Any man worth his salt, sugar—*if* he wanted me—and you wanted me—would have taken his time with me—I was worth it—*sugar* . . ."

"Maybe—just maybe . . . ungrateful bitch—"

"Save it, Mr. Rutledge. I'll give you this: I'm grateful that I know the power of my sex . . ." She stepped away from him almost daintily, "and the power of a man's desire. Most enlightening. And I think you could say I picked up the rest all by my little ole self."

She opened the parlor door and stepped out onto the gallery. In the far corner, where he had initiated her into the pleasures of her body, lay her whip.

Her back to him, she deliberately bent over to pick it up to give him yet another enticing view of her bottom.

"I'll be seeing you, sugar."

"Maybe—" he growled.

"You've got that right—maybe—if I feel like it—or it's raining—"

"Or you want something hot and hard between your legs, Jezebel, and you can't get it anywhere else . . ."

"Maybe that, too," she murmured, as she sashayed down the corner stairwell and out of his sight.

"Oh, you'll come," he muttered, leaning against the railing and watching her naked body disappear down the path to the barn. "Now that you know, Jezebel, nothing will stop you from coming."

Harry forced her to go up to St. Francisville to visit the Pipes family at La Broussard.

It was a master stroke really; if she were not in her own home, she could not—in good conscience and good manners—embarrass Harry.

And for the first time, she could make something of a good impression on an intended suitor.

His name was Tevis Pipes, and he was tall, dark, and distinguished looking in a heavy, thick-lipped kind of way.

Of course, now that she knew, she wondered about those lips and how they would feel against—

But they were so thick and wet and he invariably had a cigar clamped between them, and he treated her like a hothouse flower, his family having been an old friend of her mother's.

She was pleased to meet him. Less pleased to be there, but curious nonetheless of the way of things between a man and a woman, one who he surely thought to be an innocent but who now possessed all the secrets of Eve.

Lucinda had packed for her and had come on the trip to attend to her, so there was no way she could escape the ritual layers of femininity.

And the dresses: light as souffle under which both her temper and body were steaming.

The conversation: light as air with not a substantial word among her father, Mr. & Mrs. Pipes, and Tevis himself, who was supposed to be a man about town and a political up-and-comer.

He hadn't a cogent opinion in his head and he sat and stared at her as if she were some angel from heaven.

She wanted to tell him—she wanted to . . .

No, she didn't. She was a lady, she was playing a role; and if she were a Jezebel when she was at Orinda, then she was Maribel here—the good respectful little girl her mother had always wanted.

"She's behaving, Harry," Nyreen whispered gleefully behind the parlor curtains, where they cuddled and snuggled after everyone had turned in.

"Let's hope," Harry snarled, famished for the touch of her naked skin after three days of having to pretend to be her guardian and mentor.

"Oh God, Harry," she moaned, "does he want her?"

"I've convinced him and his parents to think about it; they would love a piece of Montelette—and I'd willingly give it to them just so I don't have to put my final plan into motion."

"Whatever you say, Harry," she panted.

"Whatever . . . " he groaned and then there was silence.

Dayne slipped away from the window where she had been hovering on the outside terrace.

Damn the man—damn him—final plans—pieces of Monte-lette . . .

It wasn't enough: everything she had learned—it wasn't enough. And it wouldn't prevent anything that Harry wanted to happen.

She had never known such a feeling of fury and helplessness.

The only good thing about a hoop, she thought, was that it kept Tevis Pipes very far away from her.

But he treated her like some kind of fragile flower anyway.

La Broussard was a stately mansion a half mile from the levee—too close, Mr. Pipes conceded jovially, when the river periodically overflowed.

But it was a house where he fully expected his son to return when and if he took a bride. Two ells had been added on to either side in order to provide privacy for a newlywed couple, and in the meantime it was occupied by the usual complement of guests passing through.

The hospitality was bountiful, although it was quite obvious that Tevis's mother expected a prospective bride to spend a great deal of time with *her* attending to the usual things that a married woman would, in company.

Nyreen of course was hampered by no such restrictions. But Harry had made it quite plain once again that Nyreen was already spoken for.

Dayne simmered with resentment even as she allowed Tevis to take her on languid little walks all over La Broussard and she half listened to his enthusiastic descriptions of the plans he had for the plantation once his father relinquished control.

Four days now, and no end in sight . . . with Lucinda overseeing her every move in her room, and Harry watching her like a hawk—she felt like a puppet, and Harry was pulling the strings:

"Oh yes, Tevis, that would be lovely."

"Oh no, Tevis, it's just a teeny bit too hot to go for a walk; I have to be careful of my complexion, you know."

"Oh, thank you, Mrs. Pipes. Lemonade—how lovely."

She almost gagged on the words.

"When are we going home, Father?"

"Oh my dear, aren't you enjoying yourself?"

She looked him straight in the eye. *"No."*

"We'll leave when or if Tevis makes some kind of declaration."

"I'm glad to know that, Father," she said caustically—and she was: now she could plot just how to alienate Tevis Pipes and have them leave La Broussard in disgrace.

Nights were the worst.

At night, her body was open, moist, yearning. At night, she couldn't quell the feelings, the insidious need, the furling desire that enveloped her.

Only at night, in the deep forbidden silence of the dark, could she give way to the longings she repressed by sheer willpower during the day.

She had to force Harry to take her back to Montelette. She couldn't stand the waiting and the wanting. She needed *him*—she needed to be what she really was, the jade who toyed with her lover and then welcomed him with open arms.

If that were true, the sly little voice within her countered, *if that were true, then Tevis Pipes would do just as well—wouldn't he?*

Wouldn't he?

She sat bolt upright in bed.

He would do; he *would* do. She would just apply Harry's philosophy to her newfound knowledge. Any man would do, and Tevis Pipes and his lavish plantation would do just as well as anyone.

And better than the outcast son of an impoverished family whose plantation was going to rack and ruin . . .

She dressed very carefully the following morning and minced her way downstairs properly layered in all the confining clothing Lucinda could find for her to wear.

Nyreen, Mrs. Pipes, Tevis, and Harry were already at the breakfast table as she entered.

"Do sit next to me," Tevis invited heartily and she smiled at him and sank languidly into the seat he offered.

"My dear—anything you could wish this morning—coffee, biscuits, ham, eggs, fruit . . ."

As if it were different any other morning since they had come . . .

She slanted a calculating glance at Tevis as she gave her plate to the major domo for service.

What was so bad about Tevis Pipes? He was solidly built; it could be said he liked his food—a lot; but his bulky frame was clothed in the finest tailoring money could buy. His bloodline was impeccable. His appearance of wealth was unassailable. His manners were faultless: he treated her like a princess and her father and Nyreen like valued members of the court. And his hospitality seemed limitless.

His face was too square and bluff to be handsome, and his lips were too thick, but his kisses could be wonderful. Maybe his pale eyes gleamed with that same knowing look as someone else she knew when he was in the throes of passion.

Could this man be passionate?

The major domo handed her her plate, heaped with ham and eggs and biscuits, and still another servant poured her a fresh cup of coffee.

"Oh my, this looks delicious," she murmured, shoving a fork into the fluffy eggs and lifting a bite to her mouth.

It was understood she would eat very little and protest that she wasn't hungry a lot, but she decided in that instant to test Tevis Pipes's mettle.

She dug into her food and gave every appearance of enjoying it while she wiped her place clean much to the dismay of her father and the shock of Tevis's mother.

"I like a lady with a good appetite," Tevis said gamely, smoothing over her animalistic gulping with true gentlemanly flair.

She batted her eyelashes at him. "I'm so glad, Tevis." She lifted her coffee cup to her lips. "And this coffee is so delicious. I declare, two or three cups of coffee in the morning starts things out just right."

They watched in a kind of horror as she kept them at the table, finishing off one cup after another until she had downed the third.

"You'all do make the *best* coffee here at La Broussard. Nyreen, dear, you must find out exactly the measurements so we can tell our cook . . ."

Nyreen's face flushed with fury. "Certainly, Dayne dear. What else would you like me to find out?"

Dayne's expression brightened. "Oh, I'd just love to know—" She stopped short at the dismayed expressions all around her. "But of course, that's for another time. Well, I'm just as stuffed as an old turkey hen after all that good food."

"Well, Miss Dayne, let me suggest you take a quiet little walk—"

"Dear Tevis! How nice of you to ask!" she cooed, interrupting what promised to be a pontificating little speech on the health benefits of walking after a heavy meal. "I would love to go for a walk with you."

Now he looked nonplussed, but good manners forbade him turning her down—and she knew it; he could not get out of escorting her gracefully and by the look on his face, he dearly wanted to try.

"Thank you, Tevis. I can barely move. A walk sounds delightful—down by the levee perhaps?"

"That will suit me very nicely," he said, somewhat stiffly this time, without his usual good humor, as he reluctantly took her arm.

They proceeded in silence for a while, and she could see that she had seriously discomfitted him.

Good—but not as much as I am about to . . .

"This is so nice here this time of the morning, Tevis; I can see why you love it so."

"Indeed I do, Miss Dayne—" He seemed as if he had been about to say more—and then he caught himself and went on, "indeed I do."

She wondered what he might have said—something about passing La Broussard on to the next generation probably, and if she had been the type of proper Southern girl she should have been, he would have been proposing marriage to her right now.

But she wasn't, and he wouldn't, and that was fine with her. And now it was time to put the icing on the cake.

"Tevis—" she began somewhat timidly.

"Yes, Miss Dayne?" His expression was stolid, unyielding. *Better and better . . .*

"Tevis—" Her voice was stronger this time, commanding, even.

He stopped and faced her. "Yes'?"

"Oh Tevis—" She threw her arms around him. "Tevis—kiss me . . . please kiss me. I've thought of nothing else night and day but your arms around me and your lips on mine. Please, please, please Tevis—"

"Miss Dayne—!"

He was so shocked.

She pulled him toward her as he simultaneously tried to remove her arms from around his neck.

"Please, Tevis—" Was that a little break in her voice? How opportune, how perfect—she sounded as if she really could not live without his kiss.

"Miss Dayne . . ."

"How can you refuse me?" she barrelled into his excuses. "I've been waiting days for the moment when we could be alone; surely a kiss between—friends—is not so shocking a thing?"

"Between—friends?" he said faintly.

"I'm longing to know your kiss, Tevis—" she murmured; oh, didn't she know just how to manipulate the man who wanted to be led? "A luscious little kiss to take back to Montelette with me—a secret between the two of us?"

"A secret?"

"A dear little secret," she whispered, "just between us. Don't you want to kiss me, Tevis?"

Dear God, was there ever a more recalcitrant man? Or was he thinking that the mother of his children would never, ever kiss him?

"Kiss me, Tevis," she begged, standing on her toes and reaching up to pull his mouth close to hers.

"Our secret?" he murmured, his lips almost touching hers.

"Forever," she swore, and brought his mouth heavily down on hers.

Fat, wet, thick, slippery, slimy, *inept* kisses—

Dear God—why, *why* did she even conceive of this stupid idea?

It was all she could do to keep herself receptive and she could not keep herself still for more than a minute before she pulled away and began fanning herself rapidly, just to give herself time to collect her wits and not blurt out the first offensive thing that came to her mind.

"Oh, oh—I am quite overcome," she murmured at last, because that was exactly what he would expect her to say.

But he was standing there looking like a thundercloud.

"And well you should be, you hussy," he snapped. "That was no innocent kiss, Miss Templeton. That was the kiss of—of—a woman who has had some experience . . ."

Dayne lowered her eyes. "Well . . . well, yes—I have been kissed a time or two, Tevis—but what difference does that make?"

But she knew it made all the difference in the world.

"We will go back to the house, Miss Templeton. I don't believe anything more needs to be said between us."

But much more was said between Harry and Mr. Pipes and in the end, in the indirect and polite way of the planter aristocrat, they were summarily asked to leave and thanked for their pleasant company.

And no, thank you, Tevis did not want to marry Miss Dayne Templeton, with or without Montelette.

Five days—six with the travel back to St. Foy—it seemed like a lifetime since she had been home.

Harry glowered the whole trip home. The little bitch had done something—he would bet his life on it, because prior to yesterday morning, he could have sworn that he and Mr. Pipes were going to be discussing marriage settlements within twenty-four hours.

So obviously his whore of a daughter had done something unspeakable to turn Tevis Pipes's interest into loathing.

Ah well—it didn't matter in the end—except for his frustration that he had wasted all this time and energy on something he had known from the beginning was probably not going to have a happy ending.

The two weeks he had promised Nyreen were nearly coming to a close.

But he had planned for that as well. Someone soon was going to make Dayne an offer she could not refuse.

There was nothing left at Orinda except the sultry scent of sex that permeated the parlor and hung in the air.

Only at Orinda—nowhere else could he find her, and she had not come for almost a week now, and he felt murderous.

He would have thought he would be the last one to be enslaved and entrapped by one brazen virginal Louisiana belle.

He would have thought he was too aware of the slinky, coiling, heat-logged sinkholes of the fog-shrouded bayou.

But a man didn't know where or when the dream would turn the reality; a man was never prepared when his every fantasy walked up and whipped him from behind.

He had immured himself on the frontier way too long; and he had exchanged one cloistered cell for yet another, with the same willingness to renounce all things carnal and mortal.

Only now he finally understood that he was the most carnal and mortal of men and that he coveted everything he had dreamt and everything that he had ever wanted.

Five days.

Five days without her.

Five days in the oozing fields of Bonneterre with the scent and the feel of her always on his hands and her pleasure indelibly imprinted on his body.

He would never forget it.

And he would never let her forget it, either.

Chapter 8

"You had your fun," Harry said the evening of the sixth day when they were finally back at Montelette and they were preparing to sit down for dinner. "Now you may start preparing for your wedding."

"What do you mean?" Dayne asked suspiciously.

They had travelled all night and into the following day as if they were being pursued by slave catchers. Harry had not said one word during the journey home, and Nyreen could only sit and simmer and wonder exactly what retribution he had planned for his intractable daughter, and how he was going to meet his deadline, which was mere days away.

"I meant what I said, young lady, but you apparently thought differently. Well, the end is near, and I'll see you settled suitably—" and he reached over and patted Nyreen's hand, "—and then I can finally get on with my life."

Nyreen smiled beatifically. "I can't wait," she mouthed, and he smiled back, and Dayne thought the two of them were just disgusting.

"Excuse me," she snapped, slamming her napkin on the table. "I've lost my appetite."

"I hope you have an appetite for marriage," Harry called after her as she fled the dining room.

Crass bastard, she thought vindictively as she paused at the foot of the stairs. Her own father!

She had been serious about deterring suitors—but she never in her heart of hearts thought he was so determined to get rid of her.

She hadn't believed him. She had really thought he would

back down when the two weeks expired and no one suitable had come up to scratch.

What power that Nyreen wielded!

She still couldn't believe it. Her father could not wait to get her out of his house and visit his obsessed sex on Nyreen.

Nyreen was perfect and she, Dayne, was not. Nyreen knew what she was doing, and now she herself possessed some of the secrets that bent a man to her will.

Yes . . . it was the only way. You played games, you enslaved them with the forbidden possession of your body, and in the end, you got what you wanted because they were so beguiled by your show of shameless desire for them.

She couldn't believe that Nyreen *wanted* her father: Nyreen wanted Montelette and everything that came with it—wealth, prestige, her father's reputation as a self-made man, the respect he was accorded, the power of being a plantation mistress—all those things—worth any price Nyreen had to pay.

And her father—the fool—had made it all too easy.

And Flint Rutledge, by his contemptuous dismissal of her, deserved to be enslaved and entrapped by his lust for her *forever.*

The thought of it filled her with an unconscionable desire to see him again—instantly.

But no—it was always better to make a man wait; it had been six days now—she was watching that little lesson right before her very eyes.

Seven days: he would be whipped up into a frenzy of wanting her.

And she didn't have that much more time to enjoy it.

It was the middle of the morning on the following day. Nyreen had awakened and come down to a leisurely breakfast all by herself because Harry had gone to the cane fields to confer with his overseer and take care of some business.

Zenona served the biscuits, gravy, and coffee with her usual impassive face, volunteering nothing, disliking everything, Nyreen thought, and she considered asking Harry to get rid of this one obdurate servant as a lesson to all the others that they must obey her—when she was the mistress of Montelette.

And *when* was the operative word.

God, she was feeling so itchy; so many things could go wrong, not the least of which was Harry's not finding a willing bridegroom.

And then there was the mysterious son, off on some godforsaken trip from which he could return at any minute.

The balance was so crucial here. She felt the devastating urge to shake Harry into submission, but she knew that she could not hurry him.

She could only feed him pieces of her experienced sexuality and make him more and more hungry to feast on the whole.

She felt like throwing dishes and glassware and having a genteel temper tantrum.

Only she was afraid it would get out of hand; there was just this untoward part of her that wanted to scream and throw fits and she had to consciously control it, and consciously battle with herself whether Harry—and Montelette—were worth it.

But of course they were. Every time she walked out onto the verandah and surveyed the fertile fields of Montelette, she saw dollar signs and comforts and trips and clothes from the best European dressmakers. Things she never could have afforded in a lifetime would soon be at her very feet by dint of her lightning acuity, which saw opportunities the way a gambler read cards.

And maybe she was a gambler at heart; this was too good for her, and she would allow nothing to get in the way, and she would take care of the little matter of the brother when the time came.

She settled herself in a caned rocker on the verandah and took up a piece of needlepoint that she always kept nearby.

It was a clever ploy, she thought; no one ever thought to look at it, and all she needed to do was keep punching the needle through the material to look as if she were the demure and well-brought-up ward of the house, concerned with nothing more than taking her rightful place when the time came.

Her fingers itched: that was a laugh. She was always constantly amused by the diverting myth of what she was supposed to be as opposed to what she really was.

It was merely a matter of attitude, she thought. You were

what you believed yourself to be. She had operated by that philosophy all of her life.

And Harry was the ultimate example of her bringing it to fruition.

As she thought about his gullibility, she heard his voice somewhere behind her.

"Goddamn, Nyreen—where is Dayne?"

Calmly and coolly she set aside the needlework and turned around to look at him.

"I have no idea. I thought she was upstairs."

"Hell no; Lucinda tells me she's been taking off somewhere every afternoon since before we went to St. Francisville."

She shook her head. "I know nothing about it."

"Hell. I wanted to give her a little taste of her future. Her intended has come to call."

He stepped forward and Nyreen suppressed an exclamation. Of course—just according to plan.

Harry clapped their visitor on the shoulder jovially. "Well, son, if I were you, I think I'd go find where my bride-to-be has got to."

She had thought it was going to be so easy. She would just dress herself—undress herself—and tiptoe down Bayou La-Touque to Orinda and there he would be and she would allow herself to capitulate in delicious, disdainful surrender.

So easy.

But her hands were shaking as she removed the erotic leather straps from the hiding place in her chifforobe, and her body flushed with a voluptuous heat as she held them—and remembered.

Oh yes, she remembered—the power, the enticement, the incitement—

His large, large hands . . . his large, large *hard part*—

Extraordinary part of a man—

She lifted her chin and examined herself in the mirror just as she had done a week before when she had returned from Orinda.

And it was the same: nothing was different. She bore no mark of Cain. There was no way to tell that she possessed knowledge any different than any other woman. There was no way to tell that she was not as innocent as when she had left Montelette that morning.

And now—there was only that hectic flush staining her cheeks and the knowing glitter in her eyes as she carefully wound one supple lash around her neck and down under her breasts.

She loved the immediate stream of erotic heat that washed over her as she tied the lash to lift and mound her breasts together. Instantly her nipples tightened and hardened; instantly, she felt the rush of wet to her center core.

She tied another lash around her hips with one long end cushioned between her buttocks and tied around her thigh just below the tangle of her erotic feminine hair.

And then what if she cut one lash up and tied the pieces around her bare ankles?

She felt her body stretching with carnal yearning at the thought of him stripping off her boots and finding the strips of leather encircling her naked feet.

Boots next, rising over her calf and tied down the front—uncomfortable? She thought not. A petticoat next to support the unstructured skirt of her walking suit and over that the prim and proper jacket with its striped sleeves, matching sleeve trim and lace collar. And a line of tiny buttons to undo to whet his desire to see her naked.

It was enough—too much even—she paced restlessly back and forth, playing with her leather thrall collar and finally wrapping a transparent black lace shawl around her neck to hide it.

And finally, her lovely long whip and she was ready, still trembling with that fine, thick sensual excitement.

She would take the Boy this morning into the bayou to make the ride, the anticipation short and sweet.

No one stopped her; no one questioned her. They never did because no one ever cared what she did or where she went.

The Boy was ready, straining at the bit as she saddled him and led him out behind and beyond the stable where no one could see her leaving.

She mounted him, tucking her skirts under her straddled legs, reveling in the taut feeling of the leather against her naked skin.

She thought she would explode with the tension.

It heightened everything, the sense of her femininity, the winding twining leather lashes that defined and emphasized her pleasure points; the feeling of sensual potency; the galvanizing rush to gratification . . .

And he would be there—he *would* . . .

She drove the Boy hard through the stagnant waters of the bayou, rushing, rushing, feeling her power, her vitality, her mastery—as potent a force in apposition to him as the thick water was to Boy's pounding hooves.

And just as suddenly, shockingly, Orinda came into view and she raced the Boy down the shoreline and up onto the lawn and far back into the trees where she dismounted, tethered him, and gave him water.

And then slowly she walked around the house, Eve in her garden of ecstasy, in thrall to the looming spectre of passion.

Silence reigned at Orinda—the thick matte silence compounded by the sultry heat, the saw of insects, and the heart-pounding throb of the blood coursing through her body in a rich vital excitement.

Soon—soon . . . She needed him, she wanted *him* to tame her body and penetrate her soul . . .

She was lost to him at the very moment she needed to be most in control . . .

No . . . no, that hadn't happened. She wouldn't let that happen. It was the pleasure, his mastery of her, her subjugation of him.

It was perfect just as it was.

She thrust open the door to the lower hallway of Orinda to the same impression of cool dankness and sultry ambience as before.

Slowly she walked up the inner staircase to the upper floor center hallway with the ripe scent of her own desire enveloping her senses.

The double door to the parlor was closed.

She pushed it open.

He lay there naked, sprawled on his bedroll before the fireplace, his male root thick and hard and lustfully jutting out toward her.

"Why hello, sugar-bitch, so nice of you to plan to come this morning. Strip off everything—*now*—and get your bitchy bottom over here—fast, or I swear to you I'll do it for you."

She stopped short and just looked at him, her whole body feeling breathless, almost boneless at the sight of him.

But never let him see it. "Will you, sugar?" she cooed—really, it was the only word for it. "Then why don't you?"

"And didn't you miss it?" he growled, leaping up in that instant and striding across the room in three steps. "Weren't you just waiting for the moment—" he reached for the tiny row of buttons on her jacket, noting abstractly the lush high set of her breasts, and in one angry tug, he tore it open to reveal her leather thrall collar and her naked breasts, her beautiful taut tipped quivering breasts and that galling knowing look in her eyes goading him and goading him until he yanked the sleeves down her arms to immobilize them.

She hadn't expected that; his explosiveness thrilled her—her helplessness aroused her. Her whip clattered to the floor and she didn't care.

He stood back to look at her and then he reached out both hands and began to deliberately thumb both hard pointed nipples.

She arched her back deliberately, pushing her breasts toward him as the molten sensation of streaming silver flooded her body.

"I love what you do to me," she whispered, shimmying her breasts more tightly against the carnal pressure of his thumbs.

"I know you do, sugar—" he muttered roughly and slanted his mouth over hers to take her lips in a violent kiss. "I know you . . . do—"

The onslaught of his mouth was sheer heaven; the spurting feelings flowing rampant through her at his masterful caresses threatened to fuse into something galvanic.

She could feel his towering sex thrusting futilely against her restricting skirt; she swallowed his fertile anger in his potent volcanic kisses.

And all at once he ceased his wet hot kisses and just reached down and ripped off her skirt.

"Well, well, well sugar-tongue. What have we here?"

She lifted her chin defiantly, horribly disappointed that he had left her nipples and her lips yearning for more. "Obviously nothing that appeals to you."

"I wouldn't be too sure about that, sugar," he murmured suggestively as he walked around her and eyed the intriguing placement of the leather strip girded around her hips and buttocks. "In fact, there's something about a woman's buttocks encased in leather that appeals to me a lot. It's almost as if you were begging . . ."

He grabbed hold of her suddenly, thrusting his arms around her, under her breasts, and lifting her off the floor—*"pleading, sugar, to be taught a lesson."*

"Oomph," she sputtered as he carried her over to the bedroll and, dropping to his knees, he laid her facedown on it.

"Just *begging,*" he murmured reprovingly, running his large hands over the firm curve of her buttocks and the supple leather that lay so provocatively against her enticing crease, "for the hand of your master—" he slapped her lightly, "to reprimand you," he slapped her again, "for your unspeakable absence," another slap, "when he expected you to be here—" slap, "to serve his needs." Slap.

"Are you clear on that, sugar-bitch? You plan to come every day for as long as I want you—" Slap.

He wasn't *hurting* her—but it was the humiliation of having to submit to his demands that enraged her.

"I'll come every day for as long as *I* want to," she shot back brazenly.

Slap.

She wriggled against the feeling, the flushy little feeling of excitement that started to expand within her.

"You're a piece, sugar. Give a bitch-belle a little power and she thinks she can tell everyone to go to hell. But I'm telling *you,* sugar—if you're not here every day, naked and waiting for me to manhandle you—if you're late or absent one minute past the time I expect to see you, you will never see *me* again. Now is that clear?"

He waited, running an arousing, exploratory finger all up and down the leather strip across her naked crease.

She shuddered. Never. Never. She wasn't sure she could stand it. She had to stand up to it.

"And what about if you're not here naked and hungry for me when I expect to see *you*, sugar?" she retorted insolently.

He slapped her again.

"Then you'll just have to wait," he growled.

She gritted her teeth. "Well, you're here and you're naked and hot for me and I can hardly wait, sugar."

She heard his erotic groan low in his throat, she felt him seize her under her stomach and cant her rosy buttocks upward toward him.

"You're damned right, sugar. You're here and I'm naked and so hard for you I can't wait to get my hands on you—"

She shuddered with excitement as she felt his hands spreading her legs and caressing her in this voluptuous new way and she shimmied against the probing of his fingers as he sought that welcoming fold—and instantly he replaced them with the hot, hard, forceful thrust of his manhood.

He drove himself in and in, deep within, until she totally sheathed his lusty sex in the wet hot heat of her sultry promise.

"Don't turn around, don't look, sugar. This is why you come; this is what you want—"

And it was, it was—and it was him, and the driving primitive male, hard part of him, a relentless force between her legs, pumping and pounding ferociously against her and deep within her body's hot velvet.

If she could bring him to this, helpless against the savage tide of his relentless desire; if she could make him threaten her because of his torrid need for her voluptuous sex; if she could play the wanton to his master—what power, and what harm.

And what danger when she just loved goading him and teasing him and just making him explode?

And soon—soon, even she, with his surging ravenous possession of her and his knowing probing fingers, she could feel the elusive spiral of feeling begin its torturous path from her womanly core upward and upward, almost as if it streamed upward to meet the essence of him to unite in a thread of pleasure that kept weaving and winding, whirling and skeining all throughout her body to a crescendo—a billowing cascade of sensation that hovered and hovered and suddenly peaked and splintered into an avalanche of pleasure.

She heard herself moaning deeply—"Oh, oh, oh, oh"—she couldn't contain herself, couldn't stop the vocal expression of what she was feeling . . .

He lurched against her, covering her with his body, driving into her with a rapacious violence, as if he could not get enough and he couldn't take any more, and the only thing left was just to stop.

Just the thought—just the hint of surcease in her lush hot honey—and he stiffened uncontrollably, beginning the final pumping press of his seed deep within her womb.

And when his wracking body ceased its endless spurting, he rolled over to one side, still hard and deep within her, and held her quivering body in the taut vibrating silence.

"Where were you?"

"I was unavoidably detained, sugar."

"By *whom?*"

She loved the menace in his musky voice, almost as if he were jealous; she hoped he was jealous, as he lay with his long, hairy leg possessively draped over hers and his towering manhood still stiff within her.

She wanted to make him crazy with jealousy so that he would always be waiting for her.

"No one important," she murmured dismissively, reaching back with her now freed hands and stroking his leg. *Someone horribly unimportant, sugar; a stupid slimy gentleman who might have wanted to marry me except you taught me how to kiss and he didn't like it one little bit . . .*

"Interesting. Detained by no one *important*—but someone who fed on your obvious charms for seven days. Seven days, sugar-tease, I waited for you. Think of it, while you were playing the bitch for some milksop, I was here naked, hot for you, bursting for you, and you were off squandering your kisses on some lily-livered whelp. Tell me, sugar, how *were* his kisses?"

She wanted to torment him into a rage for that, because he was so close to the mark and because she had to endure the seven days without *his* kisses and his hands caressing her.

"They were wet and *deep,*" she said throatily.

He made a growling sound. She felt him elongate deep inside her. "Did he feel your nipples?"

She wriggled against him. "I didn't *let* him—but he was so-o-o overpowering . . . " she answered coyly.

She felt him move, withdraw, and then a searing little smack against her buttocks.

"What a bitch you are," he snarled and he wrenched himself away from her and got up and walked across the room.

"Where were you?" he asked again.

She rolled lazily onto her back.

"It's none of your business, sugar."

"It's my business if you're not here when I want you."

"It was unavoidable, that is all you need to know."

"I want you here every day. *Every* day."

"I want you here, too," she murmured insinuatingly, curling into a sitting position and bracing herself against her outstretched arms so that her body arched upward toward him and her legs were invitingly spread.

He reacted instantly, his manhood stiffening to rock hard attention.

She smiled, that elusive, potent cat-smile and pushed herself upright.

"Well, sugar—" she murmured, pacing toward him slowly, her hips undulating, her breasts jutting forward enticingly.

She stopped an inch away from his aggressive erection, splayed her legs and lifted one foot to prop it against his iron muscled thigh.

"Why don't you strip off my boots so I can be as naked as you?" she purred, bracing her hands lightly on the leather lash that girded her hips.

He reached down and ran his large hand up the supple leather boot to the vee between her legs and then back again.

And then slowly he began untying her boot while she watched

through those glittering blue eyes with that knowing cat-smile hovering on her lips.

Slowly he eased the boot off of her bare foot to find the leather treasure wrapped there; he threw the boot across the room, still holding the heel of her naked foot in his large hot hand.

Slowly he lowered the flat of her foot until it was caressing the thick ridged tip of his granite manhood while his knowing fingers caressed the leather slave bracelet around her ankle.

She stroked the hot bulging tip of him with her naked toes. "You're bursting, sugar," she whispered, wriggling her big toe against the pearly drop that appeared at the luscious slit at the very probing tip of him.

"I'm hard for your rich hot honey."

"Let me slide my naked foot all the way down your gorgeous body, sugar, and just rest my leg right here, sugar, right on your hip so I can get closer and closer—"

She shifted herself, wrapping her naked leg around his waist and opening herself to his massive insatiable male possession.

He positioned himself to breach the lush veil of feminine hair, at the very outside of her creamy lips.

She felt the force of him gathering for one lightning drive deep into her honey-hot core—he possessed her with that one naked virile lunge, and he stood ensheathed in her, deep in her, filling her with every inch of the hot hard pulsating length of him.

"You need this, sugar."

"You want this, sugar."

"Tell me how it feels."

"Big and hard as a rock, sugar, just the way I like it," she murmured, winding her one arm around his neck, and giving him the wherewithal to cup her breast by holding his other arm and pressing it tightly against her.

"Kiss me, you tease."

She licked his lips. He covered her breast with his hot hand. She teased him with her tongue. When he came after her, she surrendered her lips, opening to the greedy wet of his demanding kisses.

He stroked her straining nipple.

And he hadn't moved a stroke within her.

"Oh sugar," she breathed against his lips. "You've got to . . ."

"I want to take you like this every day—"

She groaned and opened for his kiss.

"You were made for this, you were made for me," he whispered roughly, and delved again for her playful tongue.

She drank his kisses, hot, ravenous, succulent kisses.

"I made you a wanton, sugar; you belong to me."

"Yes-s-s," she sighed against the hard, biting press of his lips.

And still he hadn't moved, and all she could feel was the piston-hardness of him filling her center; she could not conceive of an emptiness in her anywhere when he was so thick and ram hard and deep within her.

She began to move against the long hot length of him, gyrating her hips in sharp little thrusts against that carnal hardness over and over again almost mindlessly as he thumbed her nipple and kissed her senseless.

It was so perfect; he was there and she could just rub and ride him, undulating her hips, shimmying against the building erotic tension in her nipple.

Oh God, her nipple—so much feeling—and between her legs as she massaged that masterly little point of pleasure against the thrusting maleness of him—yes . . .

And his kisses, long, leisurely, hot, wet kisses against the hot wet of her grinding and grinding toward the curlicue of pleasure in her nipple—

That just burgeoned outward and upward and without warning shattered, showering her with a radiant heat that suffused her entire body top to bottom, endlessly, endlessly . . . while he— flexed his hips into one massive thrust into her and he came against her lips—moaning—as he erupted into her in a long slow gush of ejaculation.

And together, they sank slowly to the floor.

"It's too much, too much," she murmured, as he pushed the damp hair away from her face.

She lay enfolded in his arms, her body wedged tightly against his sweaty chest.

"It's never too much, sugar. It's only never enough."

"I didn't know," she whispered, almost to herself.

"You know everything."

"Almost everything."

"Shhhh—"

It was so quiet, she could hear nothing but her own heaving breathing, she felt nothing but the sticky wet of her body against his and the creamy discharge between her legs, and she wanted nothing but to remain satiated and beside him forever.

Her body felt buoyant, unencumbered. Maybe she had slept—it seemed as if she suddenly jolted into consciousness from a lovely erotic dream; she could still feel the skeining desire streaming through her body, but he was not there.

The room was empty and the sun was low, banked behind the house as it was in late afternoon, and the scent of their sultry sex permeated the air.

Oh, she loved it; it was so potent, so heady that just the thought of it escalated her need, and to know he would always be waiting made her feverish to see him again that minute . . .

She rolled over onto her knees and stretched, as sinuous and silky as a cat. A cat who wanted to be petted and stroked and rubbed . . .

Where did this sensual hunger come from?

It was almost like it fed on itself, gratification of the senses walking hand in hand with a ravenous need.

And memory was a scary thing, conjuring up feelings and desires like living entities within her, recreating sight, scent, and sensation in a way that made her only yearn for more.

Such power.

Such pleasure.

And where was he when he had said he would always be waiting?

She got to her feet, one of which was still shod in a boot, and she walked to the French windows, opened one and went out onto the gallery.

From there she could see him down below, down at bayou's edge, so far away from her, she felt like screaming.

Maybe it was time to punish him for abandoning her.

She went back into the parlor, rooted around for her boot and pulled it on, and then located her whip, which she snapped experimentally into the air.

It sounded fine and commanding to her.

In moments, she was striding purposefully across the sun-parched lawn, and an instant later: *crack!*

She laid the lash down mere inches from his feet and he whipped around, startled, his eyes flaring with anger and his quiescent manhood jolting to instant lusty attention at the brazen sight of her.

"I'd say you're more than one minute late for me. I've been waiting for you, sugar, and you weren't there. You said you would always be naked and ready for me. You should be disciplined for disobeying." She snapped her wrist again and the lash cracked against the nearest tree.

He felt himself going rock rigid. "Oh no, sugar-bitch, you have it all wrong. You do the waiting and I do the punishing."

"I think not, sugar; who has the whip hand after all?" she asked sweetly, popping the lash out again and just snaking it against the slope of his hip.

He caught the tip of it and yanked it toward him, throwing her off-balance and catching her roughly against his chest.

"Tell me about it, Jezebel. Who has the whip hand now?" he murmured.

She felt furious that he could outwit her so easily. She moved her hands, groping for his ramrod sex, working her legs around him to try to trip him up.

He crushed her tighter.

"I'm hot and hungry for you, sugar."

"You're too late, *sugar;* those are the rules. You made them up yourself."

"Sugar-bitch. Fine, we'll play by your rules then." He dropped his arms and let her go. "See you later, sugar."

Damn him. She watched with mixed emotions as he strode off, turning his gorgeous towering erection toward her mockingly every couple of steps.

Who had the power?

How could he just walk away?

That was the thing she needed to understand—and she would not beg. She would *not*.

Resolutely, she turned and walked toward the barn.

"Waiting for you, sugar."

Oh God—he was there, laying on a bed of blanket covered hay, his rampaging manhood still bone hard with wanting her.

She walked over to him wordlessly and straddled him, positioning herself directly over his rooting tip, and then slowly she eased herself down onto him inch by granite inch.

"You're so *big,* sugar," she cooed as she settled into the nest of hair at his male root. "So hard for me."

"Bitch."

She smiled and shimmied herself more tightly against him. "I just want to sit here, sugar, and enjoy the hot fill of you inside me. Don't move. Don't move—ah, God, you're like a rock."

She felt him throbbing, the urge to thrust like a piston inside her. She felt the whole of her sheathing him, taking him deeply within her, so deep there wasn't room for anything else but this overwhelming carnal need.

He nuzzled her thrusting breasts, and then took one hard pointed nipple into his mouth while he caressed the other.

"Sugar-nipples," he murmured against the lush taste of it rolling on his tongue.

Her body spurted and she ground her hips downward.

"Sugar-tease," he breathed as he thumbed the other taut peak into a frenzy of feeling.

"Sugar-lips," as he moved his mouth upward to take her lips in a long voracious kiss.

Honey . . . honey all over him, from the feminine source of her; and movements—quick, subtle, grinding little gyrations as if she wanted their bodies to fuse and finally melt into the oblivion of pleasure.

"Ride me, sugar," he whispered, his hands grasping her hips and pulling her downward. "Like that—and like that—feel it, Jezebel. That's you. That's you . . ."

He slicked in a harsh breath as her body involuntarily began a crashing drive to culmination.

And then it was the two of them, heaving and thrusting and

gyrating with an almost animal need to possess; it was like nothing he had ever experienced, and it was perfect in its completion: they exploded simultaneously into the molten core of it, utterly surrendering to the underlying need that had nothing to do with their sensual games.

There was nothing more that was needed—ever again.

She lifted herself off of him slowly.

His darkling eyes followed her, his expression enigmatic.

"I'll expect to see you tomorrow."

She didn't refute him.

Deep in the dark recesses of the barn, a watcher smiled to himself. He had come to Orinda for a different purpose, having given up on his first intention, but this was like finding gold.

His eyes glittered at the sight of Dayne Templeton naked, and the solicitousness of her companion, enfolding her in something so she could make a pretense of being presentable.

The things one never would guess about the people one knew . . .

He was absolutely jubilant at his discovery.

Olivia Rutledge felt old. It was one thing to have Flint back at Bonneterre and taking charge, but it was quite another to be a mother and want to know the whereabouts of her child.

All she knew was that he left the house early and returned late and there was a lambent light in his usually inscrutable eyes.

Nothing had changed in twenty years—he told her nothing and she refused to ask.

"We'll have some crop this year," he said that night at dinner after having spent a long hot day somewhere away from her. "The fields abutting Montelette are gone but there's a fair amount that can be salvaged up and downstream, and some harvest from Orinda from all these years of self-seed. The strain may be even stronger because it hasn't been harvested, and I'm looking to cross-culture Bonneterre next year."

She didn't hear a word of it except *next year;* he was planning to stay on till next year.

"Ninety percent of the profit of this crop is going to pay off debt," Flint went on ruthlessly, "and fifty percent of that was incurred by Clay. By my reckoning, we've got seven more years of his folly to pay off on top of pulling some seed money to recondition the fields and expand production. And that's if he doesn't do anything stupid in New Orleans."

Olivia froze. But there was no going back now; Clay had already done it—he hadn't had any shame about turning to her for help, and out of guilt she had dug once again into the tattered pockets of Bonneterre to stave off still another debtor.

I fussed and kicked, he had written, *but deep in my heart I knew you were doing the right thing, turning Bonneterre back to him. What have I ever done to make you comfortable? All I give you is grief and here I am handing you still more, but with the firm faith that my brother can pull Bonneterre back up from its decline, I beseech you to help me just one more time . . .*

But she had learned, finally. She was going to exact a price: the deed to Orinda, and when that was safely and secretly delivered to her, she would hand Clay his check and wish him godspeed.

She had never been able to hold anything over him before; it was the most potent feeling—and it was almost instantly counteracted by her usual helplessness in the face of her older son's reticence.

His words just passed over her head; he had a paper and pen and he was listing figures, dozens of figures of projected production and reserves they could count on.

Well, she knew differently. A quarter of the reserves were going into Clay's bottomless pocket—but Flint didn't have to know that now. He didn't have to know it ever, if she could help it.

Just another thing she couldn't tell him.

And the thing she couldn't ask him: where he was spending his mysterious afternoons.

. . . not only his mysterious afternoons . . . but his days and nights, his heart and mind were full of Dayne Templeton.

She was so perfect in what she was—the brazen bitch-belle— and hiding behind the guise of the proper lady, a virgin no more.

He loved the contradiction and the irony of it.

And he lusted for the moment he could return to his Garden of

Eden and strip himself bare to the onslaught of this most inviolable desire.

He was waiting for her; she expected no less. She could never get away early enough, or easily, but it didn't matter any more.

He would be there and unspeakable pleasure would follow, and the sheer thought of it fueled her anticipation to a fever pitch.

What to wear for him today?

The collar, certainly. She could not imagine going without the feeling of her breasts lifted high and pointed for his pleasure alone.

But it was more than that—it was the feel of it to her, the thrall of leather around her neck, a sign of her own subjugation to her ever burgeoning sensuality, and the pure luxuriant sense of her own nakedness and its affect on him.

She watched herself as she wound the supple strips around her neck and under her breasts and fastened them there; immediately her nipples peaked into hard luscious points and she felt that hot streaming need course through her body.

Black stockings today, she thought, holding them up carefully and examining them for tears. Stockings that pulled all the way up to and gartered just at the vee between her legs.

And then the boots with their fragile little heels. And the leather cuffs around her wrists—it was enough.

Now she must cover her enticing body with a long dress with a high collar and hope she could escape Montelette without anyone questioning where she might be going.

All the subterfuge accelerated her excitement.

All the time it took to make her way through the clinging verdant undergrowth of Orinda until she finally passed through the gate of heaven and reached the house.

Up the steps slowly, so slowly, her desire rising in her like the wisps of early morning fog off of the bayou.

Preparing then before she entered the parlor, unbuttoning her dress to the waist, unfastening the kid boots, adjusting the stockings and the garters, loving the feel of being simultaneously dressed and naked; giving in to the sensual feel of her taut pointed nipples pushing against the opened bodice of her dress—

knowing he was inside that room and denying herself for another moment, another—still another as she grew shuddery with explosive need—and then she pushed in the door and stood poised in the doorframe.

He was waiting, lying naked, tense, pulsatingly huge, in front of the fireplace where he had laid a small fire over which he had a small kettle suspended on a hook.

She walked toward him slowly.

"Always late, Jezebel. You just love making me wait."

"I just love—" she nudged his iron bar of an erection with her foot, "—making you long."

He caught her foot and pulled off her boot. "You're right, Jezebel, I'm long all right—" He ran his large hand over her foot and under her dress and up the silk covered curve of her leg. "—I long for you naked under me—"

He pulled her downward so he could feel her further under the coy drape of her skirt. "Naked, Jezebel—I love the stockings; I'm going to strip them right off of you—"

She pulled away just as she felt his fingers probing for her vulnerable femininity. If he touched her, she would succumb right there, right then.

But she did so love their erotic games. She kicked off her other boot and slowly put one foot down on his granite erection and began stroking it with her silk-shrouded toes.

"Big talk, big man," she murmured throatily.

He pulled at the hem of her dress. "Bitchy Jezebel—you do like to play."

"So do you, sugar." Her toes nuzzled the taut sacs between his legs. "You're in a real playful mood."

"I'm in a mood to rip off your dress and take you right now, *sugar*—"

"Do it," she whispered, and as he eased himself to a sitting position, she threw her skirt over his head and isolated him, shrouding him with the feeling of her foot caressing his male root and the musky scent of her.

He inhaled the sweet, lush fragrance of her femininity, her want, her desire.

She felt him there between her legs, felt his hands grab onto her thighs, felt her foot slip away from his throbbing member so that she could balance herself as he took the first wet foray into her creamy coral core.

"Oh no, oh no—" he muttered, pulling her down more tightly against his mouth. "This is sugar—this is sweet—spread your legs, Jezebel—I'm going to feast—"

Oh no, oh no, oh no—she was so ready to accept his carnal kiss; her knees went weak, supported solely by the rock hard strength of his hands as he lowered her directly to receive his knowing and invasive tongue.

How did he know, how did he know, how did he know—she felt like a pagan princess dancing a fertility rite as her body drove into the thrusting pleasure of his tongue.

He knew, he knew—oh God, he knew—he found the bursting bud at her point of pleasure and he knew—he knew what to do— what to do . . .

She wanted to strip herself naked so that nothing would impede the unimaginable pleasure of his sucking and licking her— she wanted to see him that way between her legs, her body arched against his unbelievably facile tongue as it stroked and coaxed her to the moment of supreme surrender, another male root to pleasure her.

She thought it—and she felt the twinge, as if her body reverberated with the visual image of it and its pure possession of her.

He found her again; she almost screamed with the sheer naked joy of what she was feeling—the point of pleasure building and expanding and his tongue magically, deliciously following her every movement and taking her exactly where she wanted to be taken.

She wanted nothing between them, nothing, and she tore wildly at her dress, pushing it away from his head, tearing it off of her body and just tossing it—just throwing it away.

And then she burst, exploding into his wildly sucking mouth at the very instant she wanted to feel that inward drawing movement against her pleasure point—and she came and she came, and she thought she would never come again.

"Don't move . . ."

She whispered, she breathed—she was balanced against his

mouth and she could feel it against her juice-soaked feminine hair and she felt like she was on some luxuriant cloud and she never wanted to move ever again.

"So you're satiated and I'm starving," he murmured after many long minutes of stroking her stockinged legs and her buttocks and bringing her down from her pleasure haven.

She considered for a moment and she felt her pulses leaping at the thought of his throbbing hard part just lusting to possess her.

"I'm hungry, too, sugar," she whispered and she began slowly lowering herself and feeling for him as his hands guided her with agonizing deliberateness to his surging member.

And then she was there—and there and so very *there* as she lowered herself, soft to hard, hard to soft, onto his rigid flexing manhood.

Breathless as he filled her to completion. And sitting high on his lap and face to face, with her tight taut nipples practically in his mouth, begging for his kisses.

She arched against him, laving the curvy pillowing mounds of her breasts, loving how the thrust of them tempted him, loving the long hard thrust of him.

His tongue flicked the pointed tip of one breast and she shuddered.

"Sugar-tease—" His mouth surrounded her nipple and she ground her hips downward in response so that she was pressing more tightly against him.

And then it was just the flagrant pressure of his gentle sucking and the hot hard sense of him sheathed in her, and the gentle rock of body against him—just that, nothing more—

—that—nothing more . . .

. . . and then the spangling streaming gush of sensation totally apart from her pleasure point, inundating her, submerging her, drowning her in an ocean of hot iridescent color . . .

And he—he thrust himself upward once, twice—a beat as he felt himself giving, three times—with her hard hot nipple deep in his mouth—and he toppled into a spew of release, so long and powerful that it wrung every last drop of seed from him and still it kept coming and coming, twining streamers of pure pleasure over every inch of his body.

And after, she curled against him, seeking the sustenance of sleep, her body wet and languorous, and already ripe with anticipation for the pleasures to come.

She kept him in constant turmoil. He was always hot and hard and ready for her, his body in a permanent state of arousal because of her; there was no rest for him.

He was ready for her now; he felt as if his hard length was reaching for her, commanding her.

He wanted to wake her and take her, and then explore every forbidden crevice of sensuality as if it had never been discovered before.

But there was time—time for that, time for the redolent pleasures to come this afternoon—and time again for more tomorrow.

He swung the little cauldron back over the banked fire and stirred it with the tin spoon he had laid on the hearth.

There was nothing like a bitchy virgin who thought she was wielding some power.

He stirred the pot, lifted the spoon, and gauged the thick substance coating and dripping off of it.

Almost . . .

She stirred.

"Easy, sugar," he murmured, swinging the pot off of the heat.

God, he didn't know if he loved it better when she was wrapped up in leather or black silk. He stroked the long line of her silk encased leg, imagining stripping off her stockings inch by languid inch.

She stretched, curving her body upward and outward, her arms raised over her head.

And then she felt him grab and pin her hands and she opened her eyes to meet his.

"I'm hard and hungry for you, sugar," he murmured, his mouth slanting over hers. "I need those sugar kisses—" and he claimed her instantly, without giving her time to think.

She opened to him willingly, taking his tongue, sucking it, playing with it, raining little kisses all over it, answering his inundating need with the rising force of her own.

She groaned, bucking against his holding her immobilized, and whispered against the hard sensual line of his lips, "I need to feel you."

"Need to feel what, sugar?"

"How hard you are, how ready for me—"

"Right there, sugar, practically pushing you out the door . . ."

He moved over her and put the hard heat of him between them, ramming it tightly against her thick bush of feminine hair.

"Yes . . ." she breathed, inviting his kisses again.

And he kissed her, slowly, languidly, arousing her, provoking her, and, relinquishing her hands, moving finally downward to her thrall-collared neck, to her shoulders, to her goading breasts, and downward still to the lean line of her hip and her luscious silk-shrouded legs.

Here—oh here . . .

He paused and licked a line from her hip to her lush feminine hair and then left a trail of hot wetness from her pulsating vee to the top of her stocking, digging his tongue deeply into the garter-wrapped edge of it and pushing it downward.

And then his hands, working off the garter and sliding the stocking off of her leg with tormenting care.

And his mouth, nipping and sucking every inch of her skin right to her very toes.

And there, he pushed apart her legs, slid his tongue up the underside of her bare limb until he reached the hot welcoming fold between her legs; there, he paused for a deep arousing carnal kiss before proceeding to the other leg, working his way down with his hands and his tongue until he had stripped off the other stocking.

And then, finally then, when she was all spread and creamy with need, he came to her, lifting himself over her, and laying his carnal weight just where she wanted to feel it, and the lush pressure of his mouth over hers.

Lifting her hands again high over her head.

Pinning them.

Tying them together with the soft sensual silk of her stockings . . . softly, softly . . . his mouth working against hers all the while—

He moved and all his hot weight and his hot kisses seemed to vanish in the blink of an eye.

She waited, tremulous with longing.

He reached for the little cauldron that was hanging by the curious little fire and he moved it toward him and lifted out a long spoon and lifted it to his mouth.

It was perfect: just past meltingly hot and not quite cool.

He dug into the pot again and this time brought the spoon over toward her, lifting it high and tilting it so that the thick sticky syrup dribbled down onto her mound.

Oh my God—hot—not so hot . . . wet—oh my God—

The second spoonful made a path up her stomach toward her straining breasts.

Ohhhhhh . . .

And the third coated her tight nipples.

"And now"—he breathed, setting aside the spoon— "now . . ."

She could never have conceived of such a now—the hot sticky syrup absorbed instantly into her thick thatch of feminine hair and dried around her nipples like a coat of armor—and then his mouth, his insanely insatiable mouth coming at her, sucking and lapping the syrup from her hair, from the creamy lips of her throbbing fold, from every inch of her between her legs—

And still he was not finished—

From her belly—he licked the twining, winding path of glutinous sugar syrup all the way up her body to the sugar stiffened peaks of her quivering breasts.

He nuzzled them, tonguing the dried edges of the syrup.

"Sugar nipples," he murmured, mounting her on her breath-catching gasp of pleasure.

And then he was over her, his hot and hard manhood the only part of him touching her, probing her, parting his way with soft, soft strokes into the cream of her desire.

He pushed, and he pushed, one torrid inch at a time, in and in and still farther in until he was wholly sheathed within her and balancing himself on his outstretched arms.

"Tell me what you want," he commanded.

. . . want, want . . . ? She had what she wanted—him, naked

and throbbing deeply inside her—what she wanted, what did she want, what . . . ?

"That again—" she breathed.

"What again?"

"That—that name—that sugar name . . ."

"Sugar-bitch?"

She groaned. "No-o-o . . ."

"Sugar-tease . . . ?"

"No . . ."

He ducked his head and sucked at the dried syrup around her nipples.

"Oh, oh, oh—" He was thick and deep within her and his mouth was so magical on her skin, touching, kissing, drawing his tongue across her sensitized breast.

She was never going to last—

"Sugar—sugar . . . "—he came closer and closer to one stiffened peak—"sugar-nipples . . ." his mouth closed over it—and squeezed . . .

And her whole body heaved, bursting with explosive pleasure and she bore down on him hard—harder, grinding and grinding into him to extract the last possible glittery sensation from her shuddering culmination.

It was the end: she had died—and all that remained was the relentless pumping of his body against hers on and on and on until he stiffened and fell headlong into a long, wracking, body-drenching completion.

And then there was nothing but the heat, the buoyant contentment between them, the faint crackle of the fizzling fire—and the watcher beyond the louvered French windows rubbing his hands together and contemplating a firecracker of a union with the unexpected little tart in the room beyond.

Chapter 9

"So there you are," Harry boomed as Dayne made her way downstairs, dressed properly now, her hair rolled up in a chignon at the nape of her neck, her body light with the release of sensual tension.

"Father," she said coolly.

"So glad you decided to favor us with your presence. I don't suppose you'd care to tell me where you were all afternoon?"

"No, I wouldn't."

"Too bad, young lady. You could have helped with the wedding announcements."

Her head shot up. "*What?*"

"Nyreen and I have been sending out your wedding invitations. Are you hungry, Dayne? Zenona's about to serve dinner. The wedding's Sunday, by the way, down at the church."

"*What?*" She felt instantly disoriented, as if she had walked into someone else's wild nightmare. "What wedding—what invitations? What are you talking about?"

"Why, the two weeks' time in which I was going to find you a husband. And I have, and he's here, and he's agreed to the terms, the date, and the time—and I'm glad to say, he's staying with us until the nuptials. Come in to the dining room, Dayne—" he motioned to the door, the threatening note in his voice deepening. "The thing is done and there's nothing you can do to stop it now."

"I could run away," she shot back.

"I wouldn't try it, young lady. I'd have them hunting you like a runaway slave, and you sure as hell wouldn't like that. And as I see it, there's only one thing you could sell that would support you in the manner to which you're accustomed. I really think it would be much easier if you gave in and accepted your bridegroom."

"Who is it?" she asked stonily.

"Someone who's perfect for you, daughter—and someone apparently you've gotten to know quite well behind my back—ah, Clay my boy—I trust the champagne is suitable? Excellent. Nyreen, my dear, ring for a glass for Dayne. We have much to celebrate tonight!"

"*Traitor,*" she hissed over the thin rim of her champagne flute.

"Ah Dayne—come on, it's just what you wanted, after all," Clay said in his most conciliating way.

"I changed my mind."

I'll bet you did, he thought virulently, regarding her speculatively. *You got a taste of a rutting stallion and you're about to be married to a wild boar—it couldn't be more fitting: Flint gets the plantation, and charming old Clay gets the girl. Perfect.*

"Too late, honey. I need the money real bad, and your daddy's throwing it around in big generous chunks for the dauntless suitor who will take his wild daughter to wife. It's nothing more than you wanted anyway, so what is your problem?"

"The problem is," Dayne spat, reining in her temper with heroic effort, "my daddy's buying you—and I don't want you."

She turned on her heel, but he grabbed her arm.

"Mighty picky, Dayne Templeton, when there isn't a man from here to St. Francisville who'd come within a hundred miles of Montelette because of you. You'd be an old maid, if it wasn't for me—"

"How magnanimous! I'd rather die on the shelf."

"You'll die when you seat yourself on my shelf, *cherie*—"

God—God! She slapped him—once, and when that wasn't enough, once again.

"You have nothing that interests me, Clay."

"Nor you me, *cherie*—and you never had," he said vindictively as he rubbed his cheek. "Besides, money is a lot hotter next to a man's skin than a cold bitch like you."

"Fine—I'll tell Father to pay you off and we'll call it quits."

"He's never going to call it quits, *cherie*—he wants to stoke that little bitch's stove, and he's not going to let anything stand in his way. Sorry to tell you, Dayne—this is it—you and me, and you had better not stand in my way."

"Oh my dear—I'll plough your way to New Orleans as long as you stay there."

"Well, I'll plough you and my path to the city's pleasures and I'll have your daddy's money to boot," Clay retorted. "Like it or not, *cherie*, it's a man's world and they've already forgiven me for my father's death. Think of it—the linking of two great bayou families—when next Sunday rolls around—I'll be the golden-haired boy once again and not even my sainted brother can over-shadow me then."

He lifted his flute. "A toast, Dayne. A toast. To good times on your father's bounty, and a good roll with you before my real life begins . . . no? Little bitch. Well, to my happy life at any rate. I'm going to enjoy this marriage immense—*shit*—sonuva . . . what the hell—you're a sore loser, Dayne, and you just poured champagne on a hundred dollar suit. I bet Harry will pay to replace it—what do you think—don't go away, Dayne, we have lots to talk about, lots to plan in our new life together . . ."

A nightmare.

An utter, complete nightmare.

She flew into Harry in a fury.

"You're going to buy that pretty-boy murderer?"

"Nothing was ever proved."

"Stinking men—you all stick together. I'll kill him before I'll let him touch me."

"They'd haul your ass to hell, daughter. You might as well give up and make the best of it—it's settled."

"I'll kill you," she hissed. "How could you do this to me?"

"I'm not doing anything, young woman. I thought you'd be as pleased as punch. I had it on good authority that you and young Clay had a kind of hankering for each other."

"He killed it."

"Well, he's a goddamn Lazarus then, because he's about to resurrect it. I suggest you go along with it, Dayne. After Sunday, there's no place for you here."

"Can you keep your piston in check that long?" she muttered bitterly.

"Goddamn, girl. I expected *gratitude*. What a foolish old man I am . . ."

"You're a fool all right—and you're old, and you're tripping over your lust for a whore who covets exactly what you're handing over to Clay—and her pockets are every bit as deep as his. She'd just as soon kill you as sleep with you, but you don't give a damn about that—" she swallowed her tears.

"Or about me—as long as you get that taste of young flesh. Well I'll tell you, Father, it won't get you up any farther or faster but you will have to take that fall. And by that time, it will be too late—and I will never, ever forgive you as long as I live—"

And she turned away from him, her back ramrod straight, her shoulders squared, and she walked out of that room without looking back.

A minute later Nyreen slipped in.

"Is she gone?"

"Three more days, my darling."

"And then they'll be in New Orleans, and Montelette will be all ours."

"It's all ours now, my darling."

"I know, I know—"

"Feel free, my darling."

"Soon," she whispered, wrapping her arms around his neck. "Oh—oh so soon . . ."

He wheeled around in his chair and pulled her onto his lap. He loved the feel of her whole body snuggling tightly against him.

And she was perfectly willing to give him that much. But she had just spent a violent half-hour in Clay Rutledge's bed, and she wasn't nearly ready for anything else.

She thought it was excellent that Dayne was marrying a randy young stud; delighted he was as amoral as she, and she was thrilled he liked a short quick encounter anytime, anywhere.

She was counting on him visiting his family often, both the

Templetons and the Rutledges, and being the most solicitous of sons-in-law.

The prospect appealed to her immensely: periodic afternoon gratification here and in New Orleans.

She would be going to New Orleans often to spend Harry's lovely money—the hundreds of thousands he would not be giving to Clay as a bribe to marry Dayne.

She let Harry's heavy hands stroke her into her lovely daydream.

Everything was going just right.

> *Dear Mother,*
> *I didn't need the money after all. I'm going to marry Dayne Templeton and her father has made a generous settlement. You are invited to the wedding which is to be held this Sunday, at the Little Church in St. Foy starting at noon. Friends and family are being notified. I hope you'll attend; it is such short notice because I have pressing business in New Orleans and we've decided to forego the usual formalities.*

Oh my God, oh my God—Olivia crumpled the note and threw it across the room.

Harry's daughter—and her son. If there were a god in heaven, he had to be laughing. Dayne Templeton, her daughter-in-law . . .

How would she tell Flint?

She didn't come.

He couldn't believe it. After everything, after the games and the agreements and the incredible spending of passion, she didn't come, and his fury grew in direct proportion to the number of hours he had allowed himself to wait.

But that was not even the whole.

That Friday, he waited, and he felt like a fool. Women like Dayne Templeton had been raised from the cradle to be belle-bitches; it was in their natures, in the very fiber of their being.

He didn't know why he had expected anything less—of her . . .

And so he didn't wait long; and he didn't expect to play games. But he didn't have any hope: Eve had tasted the fruit of passion and there was no other end to the story—she possessed the power of her sex and no man could hold her.

Saturday he returned from hoeing down the canebrake, having nearly exhausted himself with the backbreaking work that could have been done as well by the field hands.

Olivia distractedly summoned Praxine to bring Mr. Flint a drink and then with some bravado sank into a nearby chair.

She had decided she had to tell him this: this marriage changed everything—and it meant Orinda was possibly lost to them forever.

But worse than that, it was *Harry's* daughter—

She couldn't believe it and she didn't know how she was going to bear it.

She watched him gulp down the drink like a drunken sailor and request a pitcherful more.

"I have to talk to you."

She didn't even feel like he was listening. And that was all of a piece as well; he was the one who always went his own way, just as he was doing now, and her only hope was he would be as infuriated as she and somehow take some action.

But what action—*what* did she hope he would do?

"Talk."

You couldn't get more succinct than that.

Her hands shook as she removed Clay's crumpled note from her skirt pocket and hesitatingly tossed it onto his lap.

"What's this?"

She was so tempted to say the obvious, but she kept her mouth shut as he smoothed out the paper and began reading.

"*Good goddamn . . . shit—*"

Oh God—she could feel his fury fomenting.

"*Son of a bitch . . . that goddamn good for nothing son of a bitch—*"

"Flint—"

"Shit—how the hell did he . . . never mind. Damn it, damn it, damn it—"

"Harry will settle money on him," Olivia interposed at his first gasp for breath, "and you know what that will mean. But worse than that, Flint—worse than that is—you know it will be Rutledge money."

"*What?!* What the hell—" He felt fit to kill; he would strangle Clay with his bare hands before the son of a bitch put one licentious finger on Dayne Templeton.

And now his mother—

He took a thick, deep breath and clamped down on his rage. "What's this about, Mother?"

"You have to do something. You just have to do something. I will not have my son married to the daughter of that thief. And if Clay gets his hands on that dowry money—dear God—Clay goes through money like a shark through water, you know that. . . . He *cannot* marry Harry Templeton's daughter."

"It seems as if he can," Flint interposed calmly, when his every emotion was flaming out of control.

"I hate him. I hate that Harry Templeton. You know why . . . because he hatched up that scheme all those years ago to steal from my family when I turned down his offer of marriage."

He knew the story. And he had heard her same anguished rhetorical question all the years he was growing up—

"Where did he get the money to buy Montelette, I ask you, when he was counting on marrying me to fund his life as a gentleman farmer?"

And he knew what Olivia believed: that Harry was so furious when she accepted Verne's proposal that he deliberately set out to court her maid Celie behind her back, promising he would buy her freedom and take her up North.

And that Harry had coaxed Celie into helping him finance their flight by suggesting that her mistress's jewelry was easily turned into cash and that she'd never miss one little diamond or sapphire.

"Harry has been living off the Rutledge jewels ever since and he's just going to hand over the proceeds to Clay, and I can't bear it—"

And Harry had done what every man in his position would

have done with someone like Celie after he had used her to get what he wanted—he had abandoned her. And he left her with child.

A year after that—as Olivia had told it so many times that it had become family lore—after she and Flint's father had wed, Celie had given birth and it was obvious the jewels were irrevocably gone, Harry had come back to St. Foy a wealthy man just waiting for the opportunity to throw it in Olivia's face.

"And no one to this day could prove anything," Olivia said bitterly. "And Harry was always fabulously successful—"

And there was a wealth of history in those words: Harry and Flint's father had always been in a death-grip competition, in which Verne always lost.

It was the genesis of the feud; they never spoke—they battled on the playing field of production and success: of which upstart would come out ahead.

They had been crazy, the two of them, and Flint had never been certain that his father wasn't the crazier of the two.

Or maybe it was Olivia who had always been certain that Celie had not given over all the jewels to Harry, but had cannily hid some away for herself.

But Celie had died soon after in an accident, and Olivia had never been able to find out the truth. And that was long after Celie had torched her room to hide the evidence of the theft.

But Olivia had always believed that Celie's daughter knew the secret of the hidden cache and she had used it to lure Clay and her husband.

Miss Queen Meline, she called her, as Meline sassed and sashayed her very pregnant way around Bonneterre, threatening to reveal who was the father.

He knew all about the fresh-mouthed Meline whose one act of capitulation had cost the life of his father to avenge her honor.

He understood everything, even as Olivia recounted her grievances all over again and he nodded in the appropriate places while giving vent to his own rage.

"I always swore I would die before I would let Harry get his hands on Bonneterre—but I could see it coming. Clay going through his birthright like a spooked race horse; his father killed in a stupid act of male honor; Lydia crazy in love with Peter Templeton—just because she knows she can never have him and to spite me—

"And now this—Harry will hand over to Clay what is rightfully mine—and isn't that a fitting dowry for Dayne Templeton?" she added bitterly. "Harry wins again."

She stood up suddenly in a movement of blazing fury. "I can't believe this—Harry wins again. He will take over Bonneterre and bury us both."

She made a futile gesture of helplessness and sank back down into her chair.

"I've looked for the remaining jewels all these years," she added wearily. "Oh, there's nothing to find. I looked everywhere; I even lowered myself to search Celie's cabin. There is only heartbreak and anguish ahead if Clay marries Dayne Templeton. You've got to do something—"

He was so silent for so long; she couldn't tell what he was thinking, or if he had even heard a word she had said.

She felt the draining emotion of impotence. Clay would marry Dayne and go off to New Orleans and Harry would send his field crew to Bonneterre and bury over the fields and that would be the end of the Rutledge reign as the premier plantation family in St. Foy Parish.

Dear God—

And Orinda, her own beloved Orinda—gone, gone—Clay would ransom it for yet another game of cards . . .

Poor Dayne, poor unsuspecting girl—

"Son—you have to do something. Clay cannot marry Dayne Templeton . . ."

He heard her vaguely in the back of his mind.

But he had known from the moment he read the putative invitation that Clay was not going to marry her as well as he had known the elegant solution that would avenge his mother and recover what was rightfully hers.

And after all that, he would have Dayne Templeton as well—as neat a dovetail as a man in a rage could ever want.

* * *

And so she had walked straight from paradise into hell, and once again the thing was out of her control.

Only this time she had no way to vent her fury.

And she had only two alternatives: marry Clay or abandon everything.

Both drastic and both inconceivable.

Nor could she beg the help of Mr. Flint *I-wouldn't-have-her-on-a-bet* Rutledge.

He was waiting for her, even now . . . She couldn't let herself even imagine that—because tomorrow she would turn up on his doorstep as his sister-in-law.

And he hadn't needed to do anything—she would be a member of his family and as available as a house servant.

The irony of it was rather appalling.

In the morning, she would don her wedding dress and proceed by carriage into St. Foy Village to the little church her family had always attended.

Clay would await her there, delightedly contemplating the terms of the settlement—which were absolutely disheartening.

Her father had promised to pay an income to them on the provision that Clay kept her in New Orleans, and away from him, Nyreen, and Montelette. The discretionary use of the funds was in Clay's hands, and she knew already that meant they would be living fashionably and expensively and that he would not let being married cramp his style.

She closed her eyes in despair. There was just nothing she could do that didn't mean leaving Montelette forever.

And that meant handing everything over to Nyreen, and she would die before she did that.

Nyreen could not win. Her father was an unforgivable besotted fool, but when he was gone, Montelette would remain—not Nyreen, not Clay, and not the old feud.

Just Montelette, fertile and timeless—the house and the land.

And if it meant putting up with this marriage to ensure her patrimony, she would do it; and once they were wed, she would think of some way to make it work—for her.

She reluctantly donned the dress now ivory with age, its layers of lace and file crochet seeming to glow against the satin under-skirt and bodice. It was a simple dress, depending on the cut and the extravagance of its lace against satin and skin for its effect, and with it she wore a wreath of white flowers entwined in her hair from which was appended a tulle veil.

She carried a matching bouquet and she took the smallest, slowest steps possible in her white kid boots so she could delay things as long as possible.

Only Lucinda would not allow it, as Dayne twisted and turned in front of her bedroom mirror and wished this were a wedding for love or dynasty or some reason for which she could be reasonably content.

"You is beautiful, Miz Dayne. Miz Maribel be watching from heav'n proud fo' yo' choice and happy fo' yo' new life."

If only she were . . .

Lucinda peered out the window. "De cahriage done come . . ."

"Thank you, Lucinda—"

She picked up the delicate lace hem and made her way to the door.

"Ev'rthing gonna be fine, Miz Dayne. Mama Dessie be cookin' away fo' de breakfust and ev'rthing gonna be just how you want."

Not everything . . .

"I appreciate that, Lucinda."

She paced slowly out of her bedroom door. They would stay on at Montelette one night, and then Clay had strict orders to hustle her to New Orleans first thing in the morning.

It was going to be a mockery of a wedding to be acted out as though it had some meaning.

And she didn't know how she could salvage it.

I can only save myself, she thought mordantly, but she couldn't get away from the fact that, in the end, she had had no choices whatsoever.

She was astonished to find the church was full. It was a small church to be sure but it was right on the main street of St. Foy, right near the general store, so of course there must have been great word-of-mouth and no small curiosity factor.

Because of Clay's name, of course, and it being linked with a family whom everyone knew had existed side by side in enmity for years.

Her heart started pounding erratically.

Clay was nowhere to be seen; the hall was preternaturally quiet except for the undertone of conversation which was so low it was almost as if no one wanted to be caught speculating on the nature of this mysterious and embarrassingly sudden union.

She saw neighbors from here and there and a swarm of townspeople whom she did not know but who had paid the event the compliment of dressing up to suit the occasion.

And she saw Olivia Rutledge, imperious in her perfect posture and black lace trimmed afternoon dress.

Oh God, this is really going to happen . . .

The altar was draped in white and festooned with flowers. Someone else, perhaps the minister's wife, was taking this travesty seriously enough to make it seem like it was real, and she felt the prick of tears behind her eyes.

She wished it were real.

"There you are." Harry, in a frock coat and lavender trousers. "Well—you do me proud, Dayne. You have the look of your mother as she was twenty-five years ago."

Her tears and self-pity evaporated instantly.

"You cannot sway me with comparisons and compliments," she said tartly, utterly unmoved by the soft look on his face.

"Well—" Harry said, slightly discomfitted and choosing to ignore her prickly response. "I'll just go see if the minister is ready. Clay is with him, you know, and Nyreen is here, ready to stand as your attendant."

"If she comes one foot near me, I will trip her," Dayne said tightly. "And then you'll have a public spectacle—which I don't think you want, given your unfatherly feelings toward . . . us both."

"It's a good match," Harry said defensively.

"It gives you a foot in the door to Bonneterre and it gets me out of the way," Dayne contradicted. "And don't delude yourself that I am doing this for you. I am doing this for reasons you will never understand, and I intend to be vindicated in the end, even if I have to kill someone to do it."

"That's no way to talk on your wedding day," Harry said chastisingly, making a show of straightening his tie. He took out his watch. "Ah—I see it's almost time to begin. Let me fetch the minister and your bridegroom."

He motioned over her shoulder and withdrew just as Nyreen appeared, dressed in a gown of brocaded ivory satin, which, with her dark complexion and long, shiny black hair, made her look even more exotic than usual.

"Congratulations, Dayne. What a beautiful dress."

"Congratulations to you, too, Nyreen. A beautiful conquest."

And I thought I could figure out just how you did it, but there wasn't a foolish old man in the vicinity on whom I could ply my newfound knowledge—

Nyreen's expression tightened with anger.

"I won't miss that insolent mouth, I'll tell you."

"I daresay you won't miss me at all, Nyreen, but who knows what the future may hold."

Nyreen smiled nastily and Dayne neatly slid in the verbal knife.

"But you obviously know what your future will hold."

Nyreen's smile faded and her mouth opened to retort, but she stopped short, staring at the door.

Harry limped in, his frock coat rumpled, his tie askew and his trousers slightly the worse for wear.

Simultaneously, from the front of the church, the minister rang a melodious hand bell and sonorously announced, "We will begin."

Immediately, from the loft above, the organist launched into the wedding march and before Nyreen could either say a word or ask a question, Harry pushed her ahead through the entrance to the chapel.

Nyreen tripped, righted herself, and began the bridal procession, walking down the aisle before Dayne could reach out and pull her back.

Harry took Dayne's arm. She wrenched it away. "I will *not* be hauled down the aisle by you. We will walk side by side."

She resentfully took her place next to him as they waited for Clay to appear beside Nyreen at the altar, and she cast him a curious glance from under her veil.

He looked like he had been in a fight.

Clay stepped into the chapel from the side door and moved slowly next to Nyreen.

The organist played a crescendo to announce the coming of the bride, and she hesitated a long, futile moment and then resigned, she began the long, torturous path down the aisle with Harry by her side.

She didn't know the faces: she saw only Olivia Rutledge's stony expression, and a sea of color—and Clay's curiously red face and tight morning dress.

She stepped away from her father and beside him and looked expectantly at the minister.

There was a long, strained moment of silence as the minister waited, which only heightened the tension.

She felt Clay step closer to her. She saw the minister nod and heard him say again, "We will begin."

He rifled the pages of the service and began in the time-honored way, "Dearly beloved—"

She felt the tears spill out from her eyes.

Not too late, not too late; she could just turn and walk back up that aisle and choose the wanton life her father had predicted for her. What could be worse than this?

She took a deep breath, took a half-step around and felt a hand surreptitiously take hers in a hard meaningful grasp: her father, aiming to stop her once and for all—

She turned violently to warn him to let her go—but it wasn't her father; he stood a half dozen paces behind her, his face white and resigned.

It was Flint Rutledge, and he was standing beside her at the altar, his hand hard and tight on her wrist, and Clay was nowhere visibly around.

Chapter 10

She wanted to run—just push him away and knock him down and run.

No one should ever have had to face those hellishly burning jetty eyes in front of a minister—

"Dearly Beloved—"

His grip was like iron on her wrist.

"We are gathered—"

"Don't try it—"

His voice was like iron, underscoring the minister's gentle words, barely a breath in her heat-washed ears.

"—united in holy matrimony—"

"If you run, I'll leave you at the mercy of Clay—"

God, what a threat—the dissolute Rutledge or the Rutledge who had decamped and might well do it again . . .

She wrenched her arm away and turned her head resolutely toward the minister, her chin up, her shoulders squared.

"—which is no more than you deserve—"

Dear Lord, he was so angry but he made the most appealing bridegroom—so tall and so dark with those inscrutable coal black eyes, and that body all tucked and straining against the formal morning coat and dove gray trousers . . .

Not like Clay—not like Clay in the least . . .

But *his* wife? *His?*

She could not be more *his* than she was already. But she could feel, with every passing word of the service, the dissolution of her power.

She had made him bend in the final awful ultimate way, and she had no doubt he would make her pay and pay and pay.

"Do you—" the minister droned and Flint said firmly, "I do."

"And do you, Dayne Rouleaux Templeton, take—"

She heard the words as if they were in a dream. *It was really happening—*

She bit her lips and looked up at Flint's glowering expression. *You had better not back down now . . .*

"I—I do," she said finally, faintly, and then she girded herself and said it again with strength and conviction. "I *do.*"

The congregation let out its collective breath and the minister beamed.

". . . pronounce you husband and wife—ladies and gentlemen, may I present Mr. and Mrs. Flint Rutledge—"

Flint grasped her unwilling hand and forced her to turn and face the assemblage to their polite applause.

"Mr. and Mrs. Rutledge invite you to a breakfast reception at Montelette Plantation," the minister continued. "I believe there are carriages waiting for those who do not have transportation. The festivities will begin in an hour—"

The organist struck the keys in a majestic chord and launched into the recessional.

"You can't—" Dayne hissed under the music as they paced their way back up the aisle.

"I can and I did, Jezebel. I've avenged my father and banished the villain, and at the very least I expect some gratitude."

The minister awaited them in the vestibule.

"This way." He indicated a door off to the right side where, in his office, they were to sign their names on the marriage certificate.

Dayne's hand wavered—it was so official—so irrevocable . . .

"God bless you," the minister murmured.

"You'll join us at Montelette," Flint said, shaking his hand.

"As soon as may be," the minister said gratefully, as he added his name to the certificate.

Flint took Dayne by the elbow and marched her back into the vestibule and pulled her through the open door into the sunlight.

A dozen carriages from both Bonneterre and Montelette

waited in line at the curb—along with the milling, gossiping assemblage.

Dayne stopped short at the sight of Olivia Rutledge who awaited them right outside the door.

"My dear—" Olivia stepped up to Dayne and took her hands firmly in her own and said in ringing tones loud enough for everyone to hear, "Welcome to the family."

She met Dayne's skeptical gaze frankly and forthrightly. "I welcome you as my daughter-in-law."

And then she took Flint's hands. "I never expected . . ." she murmured, "It's the last thing I expected. Is it—I . . ." Her words stuck in her throat, but still, she was Olivia Rutledge, the crowd was watching—and listening—and she could do no less than maintain civilities and appearances.

"I'm very happy for you," she finished, forcing the warmth into her voice for everyone to hear.

"Thank you, Mother. It was the right thing to do," said Flint.

"Yes, yes—I see that," she said distractedly. "I cannot go to Montelette."

"No one expects you to. There is enough talk already, and Harry disappeared the moment the ceremony was over. You sent Praxine and Tull over to Montelette?"

"The minute you told me to. I will see you later—at Bonneterre."

He allowed her dry, rasping kiss only because everyone was watching and nobody could understand how it got turned around that one brother was supposed to marry Harry Templeton's girl, and somehow it got to be the other.

But—in the spirit of the thing, it didn't matter: there was transportation to Montelette, which was some forty-five minutes' drive down the bayou road and the prospect of food and a party to look forward to.

They waited politely until old Mrs. Rutledge's carriage was out of sight, and then they cheered as the bridegroom helped the bride into their carriage, and even long after the dust had settled.

She stood on the upper gallery of Montelette and watched as the carriages arrived; the only thing she had removed was her veil and Lucinda had gone to put her flowers in water so at least for today they would not wilt.

Outside below her, the servants had arranged long tables in the shape of a U right on the front lawn and had covered them with pristine white tablecloths and had scattered snowy flowers and orange blossoms across the virgin surfaces.

Even as she watched, an unfamiliar black woman, whom she assumed was Praxine, was laying out silverware at one end of the tables, and behind her, a stately black man wheeled out a cart loaded with dishes which he then carefully placed nearby the silver. Zenona followed a moment later with a tray of glasses and napkins, and then each of them returned to the house.

The guests, such as they were, had just begun to arrive, and she thought their dazzled expressions as they debarked the carriages was amusing and a little sad.

Flint appeared beside her.

"You might wish to change out of your gown."

She shook her head. "I have only one dress and one nightgown. Father shipped everything else to New Orleans."

"You won't need anything else," Flint murmured, and she felt a wave of heat suffuse her body.

This man was now her husband; she could not see him as the man who had pleasured her body so unimaginably two days before.

This was the man who wouldn't have her on a bet. This was the man over whom she imagined she had some measure of control.

She had no control over anything—not her wedding, not him, not even her life—if she'd gone into the church to marry one man and had come out with another.

She kept her eyes on the scene below as a parade of servants began laying out the food that Mama Dessie so meticulously prepared.

Maybe Mama Dessie put a spell in the wedding cake.

Maybe she was going crazy: she was standing on the balcony of Montelette with the man who two days ago had sucked the very vitals out of her and had sworn he wouldn't have her.

And somewhere, between Bayou LaTouque and New Orleans,

Clay Rutledge was cursing his bad luck and his brother's superior fortune: Flint Rutledge had wrested away Bonneterre and now he had taken the woman that Harry had paid him to marry.

How provident; Flint was obviously a man of destiny.

She looked up finally into her husband's inscrutable jetty gaze, and she wondered just how much he had beaten out of Harry.

Instantly, as though he could read her mind and the suspicion there, he grasped her arm and pulled her against him with a kind of restrained violence.

"You bitch. You godalmighty ungrateful little bitch—Miss high-and-mighty Jezebel—but it's all of a piece—you've never been anything else—and I might just be God's biggest fool. Hell—" he thrust her away from him. "Come when you're ready, Jezebel. You always do."

Nyreen was not happy and she didn't understand why. She prowled the rooms of Montelette as the servants scurried to and fro at the direction of the stately Bonneterre butler, Tull, and she felt the awful pressure of having made some kind of stupid miscalculation, only she couldn't figure out what it was.

"Nyreen—pssst—"

She heard the whisper, coming out of the under-stair closet and she edged her way over to it casually and opened the door as if she were looking for something.

"Clay, you fool, what are you doing here?"

"I gambled and lost, *bébé*—I need you . . . *now*—"

"Are you crazy? Harry could walk in at any moment—"

"I don't care. That son of a bitch brother of mine took everything—everything except you . . ."

"Harry let him," she murmured, feeling herself rising to a keen edge of excitement. "Harry." She slipped into the little closet that was barely big enough to contain the both of them.

But Clay was not as bulky and large as Harry; Clay was slender and aristocratic, and the only part of him that was bulky was the part that counted most.

"Cocky of you to just walk in here and hide in the closet," she whispered, reaching for him.

"I'm cockier than ten men put together."

"Cockier than one man I know," she breathed as she quickly and expertly undressed him. "Oh God—oh you are—" she gasped as she lifted her skirt, and he proved it. ". . . you . . . are—"

That little interlude took all of five minutes, and then she chased him from the house.

"You'd be a fool to stay here. If Harry catches you—he's still fuming at the high-handed way your brother just up and forced him to change his plans. You have to go, you hear me?"

Grumbling, he went, slipping out the rear entrance as guests swarmed across the front lawn and into the house, gaping at its sheer size and ostentatious opulence.

Still, she felt restless. What good was Clay to her now except as a diversion in New Orleans—if he could still afford to stay in New Orleans now that he could not count on receiving that stipend from Harry.

Nothing—*nothing* was going right.

Harry was sniffing after her like a boar in heat. He *was* a bore. The only thing interesting about him was his money and his huge hot hands. The rest she had made up: a figment of her imagination like the erotic stories she invented to entice him with every encounter.

Bah—so be it—she had made this bed and though she hadn't even rumpled the sheets, she was already dissatisfied.

It was the money. And the leading him on that had lent such spice to her months at Montelette. And now one obstacle had been removed and there was nothing to prevent her rutting union with Harry.

Ah well, she had had worse . . . and surely better the moment Clay stepped into the picture.

But still she felt that nagging discontent, as if everything she had pushed for and worked for was meaningless now that it had been attained.

Yet how could that be? Montelette was everything she had dreamed of; and Harry was positively swimming in more money than she could spend in ten years and as intoxicated with her as a man could be.

She could command anything, just anything.

Except what she really wanted.

Only she didn't know what it was.

Not yet, at any rate. Perhaps the seduction of Harry was the first step in her voyage of discovery.

She heard a door slam high above her and then Flint Rutledge came storming down the stairs and out the dining room door.

She stared after him, feeling the instant start of desire sweep through her.

And then she understood why she was feeling such deep-rooted disquiet: it was because Dayne, who was supposed to have been punished, had gotten the prince, and she—the heroine—was doomed to wind up with the frog.

All the carriages had arrived and Dayne reluctantly made her way down to the lawn from the upper gallery to greet the guests.

From somewhere behind her, she heard the lilting strains of a violin, a surprising sound over the still-hushed tones of conversation around her.

Or maybe the surprise was that Flint must have arranged that because no one in her family would have.

And as she walked across the lawn, carefully lifting the fragile skirt of her gown, Tull came out of the house wheeling the tea cart once again, this time bearing three beautifully decorated white frosted cakes.

My wedding cake—I hadn't even thought about a wedding cake—or any of the little rituals of a bride, she thought mordantly. And so here were the cakes, and Mama Dessie beaming from the dining room door, and Tull, with his elegant posture, arranging the trays among the orange blossoms in the center of the table.

And Flint, watching her from among a crowd of well-wishers, his heated gaze scorching her already burning skin.

She lifted her chin and walked with great precision across the intervening space between them to join him under what looked like a trellis—something that had to have been put together within the last few hours because she had never seen its like on Montelette.

Guests were already lining up to his left as she took her place beside him; she didn't know many of them and yet they were so kind and graceful in a situation that smacked of outright artifice that she felt at once grateful to them and her husband for again preserving a semblance of reality against a situation that could have become a farce.

But her marriage was not a farce: it was real—the words she had spoken were real, and now Flint, angry as he was with her, had made the very real attempt to make the event everything it should have been.

Whereas Harry would have shunted her off into her room and had a couple of cigars with Clay and discussed with him some kind of timetable to keep her far away from Montelette and his unholy desire for Nyreen.

She was gratified to see that Nyreen was not looking any too happy herself as she walked among the guests as a good hostess ought to and made a show of seeing to their comfort.

The well-wishers took such delight in this unconventional marriage that Dayne could not help smiling and shaking their hands warmly as each and every one wished them health and wealth and godspeed.

And Flint was so good with them. They knew him not—though they might have remembered him from years before—and she would have supposed that all his rough years on the frontier would have made him less mannered than he was.

But to a man and woman, the parish guests were very taken with him. There was a warmth about him to which everyone responded: he had lived among them someplace else—a common man laboring in common circumstances and he had not been known as a plantation owner's son.

He had been himself, laboring by dint of his own strength and desire and he understood them as they passed by, shaking his hand and giving many kind benedictions, and somehow everyone knew this.

They were equally generous with her—and she felt somehow that she did not deserve that—that all her years immured on Montelette as the daughter of a prosperous landowner had made her more oblivious to people and less than kind herself.

But no one, curiosity-seeker or friend, judged her, and at the end of the exhausting round of handshakes, smiles, and good wishes, she began to feel as if this were the ending to her wedding reception that she had always conceived of.

Above them, behind them, somewhere on the gallery, the music kept on playing, underscoring her feelings.

And then Harry made his appearance, and she wondered whether this had been a condition of his settlement with Flint.

Flint took her arm and led her around to the center of the head table, directly behind the beautiful cakes.

"It is time for your father to make the toast."

"The toast—? Harry—?" she said faintly.

But Harry was beside them already, with Tull at his heels bearing the champagne bucket and a glass.

"Ah!" Harry boomed as Tull opened the bottle and poured with great finesse and elegance into the flute. "Champagne . . ." He took the foaming glass and turned to the guests.

"I give you my daughter, ladies and gentlemen, and her new husband, Mr. Flint Rutledge of Bonneterre Plantation—neighbors and now—a dynasty united!"

"Hear, hear," the guests murmured as Harry took a healthy drink from the flute just as the servants began passing among the guests with trays full of champagne for them to salute the next toast.

Tull then poured two flutes for Dayne and Flint, and Flint lifted his and turned to look deeply into Dayne's somewhat bedazzled eyes.

"To the union of the unexpected—and the much desired," he proposed, winding his arm around hers so that she would be sipping from his flute and he from hers.

"Hear, hear!" the guests exclaimed and everyone then drank.

"We will now cut the wedding cake," Flint said, "and we invite everyone to partake."

Tull handed him the cake knife, one of Olivia's heirlooms, which had been brought from Bonneterre, and held the cut-glass pitcher of water as he doused the knife blade in it and then inserted it into the larger of the three cakes.

These two slices were specifically for the bride and groom, and when those slices were set aside on two delicate china plates, Mama Dessie came forward and took that cake away to be packed and preserved for the future, and Tull began the careful cutting of the two remaining cakes.

Once again, Flint fed her, popping a rich piece of white frosted fruitcake between her lips. And she fed him, letting her fingers linger lightly on the hard firm line of his lips—as if it were real . . . as if it were everything she had ever wanted.

And maybe, she thought, as she and Flint began handing the slices of cake to the guests, just maybe it was.

Nyreen was hiding. It really was nothing more, nothing less. She just could not face Harry right now and she knew he was going to come after her at any moment.

She felt sick and stupid with her ignorance and too-quick decisions that had made her lose out on something that might have been quite wonderful.

She could have made Harry treat her like a daughter of the house, and she might have met Flint Rutledge first and it could have been her wedding that they were celebrating.

She cursed her foolishness, her cupidity and her stupidity.

She wanted Flint Rutledge with a fury that was almost galling. His brother Clay was nothing next to him.

She didn't know what she was going to do.

Or even if it was worth considering murder.

After all, there was all of Harry's lovely money—and she knew the Rutledges didn't have any, and all because of Clay.

So that was one thing.

But the man! That tall, dark, mesmerizing man—nothing effete or aristocratic there—he was all man and proportioned to fit; she had sized him up in a minute when he hadn't been looking at her.

How was she ever going to settle in and marry Harry when that man was as close as a fifteen minute drive in a carriage?

Well, she could . . . That was exactly what she had been planning to do about Clay . . .

But this was different. This was so different. This was a man she could want for herself—forever—and now that simpering little bitch had him, and she didn't know quite what she was going to do about it—yet . . .

Who would have thought that St. Foy was just bursting to the seams with such beautiful men?

"Nyreen! *Nyreen?*"

Damn—Harry! She looked around wildly for a place to hide.

"Where's my darling girl? Come to me, Nyreen—come now—the thing is almost done. They'll be gone in an hour, maybe two, and I want you—Nyreen . . ."

She took a deep exasperated breath and moved out into his line of vision.

"Harry darling . . ." She *was* sincere—she had had so many years of practice. She was an actress—she always had been, in those rough little mining towns she and her mother had frequented; she had learned very early how to make a man a pauper and treat him like a king.

This was no different, and it had come about just as she and her mother had planned, and all out of the pure chance of meeting Harry's brother and her mother's exquisite skill at making him fall in love with her.

Dear mother—she wondered as she walked into Harry's embrace just where her mother was and what success her hydra-handed stepdaddy had had out west.

But she only wondered for a moment. The plan had always been that her mother would go and she would stay and between the two of them, they would suck the Templeton men dry.

And she was that close to success and she couldn't imagine, as Harry began to fondle her, why she was even thinking of throwing the whole thing away because of some gorgeous, impoverished man like Flint Rutledge.

It would be stupid beyond belief.

Dayne would be gone in a matter of hours. Harry could be manipulated in bed and out; and, soon enough, her mother would join her and by then she would have gotten enough out of Harry to set them up for a lifetime.

She smiled to herself as Harry began taking those caressing little liberties and whispering in her ear, hoping against hope that she would fulfill all her promises to him, and take off all her clothes the minute Dayne left Montelette and let him finally have the freedom of her luscious, naked body.

*   *   *

They rejoined the guests after she allowed Harry fifteen minutes of fondling her behind the closed doors of the parlor.

By then the crowd had thinned—Flint had arranged for the carriages to return the guests to town—and those remaining were on the verge of overstepping the bounds of good manners.

Flint looked pointedly at his watch several times and drank probably more champagne than he should have, but by then he didn't care.

The reception had gone off without any hitches and with a semblance of taste thanks to Tull and Praxine and the long-vaunted wine cellar at Bonneterre from which he and Tull had dredged up enough wine and champagne to celebrate his nuptials.

It was enough, and it was unspeakable to him that Harry had merely wished to get rid of Dayne with no ceremony whatsoever and that it was Mama Dessie and Lucinda who had cared enough to make the cakes and gather the decorations and set up the tables.

He did want Harry to pay for his follies. The time would come, he would see to it. Harry would pay and pay, and he would never know that his restitution covered Olivia's cache of heirloom jewels and that the ransom was his daughter.

The porcine prig—displaying that whore of his as though she were fine porcelain and every bit as good as his own daughter—and cherished in a way that Dayne had never been.

He couldn't wait to get Dayne out of there.

He found her in the kitchen, talking to Mama Dessie.

"Oh now," Mama Dessie was saying, "whut de bullfrog know 'bout de lookin' glass? Didn't 'spect Mast' Harry to be thinkin' 'bout weddin' cakes and all; wasn't nuthin' to do, Miz Dayne, and I just gone and done it. You got to tie yo' kerchief to fit yo' head, and dat's what we gone and did and don' need no gratitude fo' dat, chile."

Dayne smiled faintly and patted her shoulder. "Well, I'm grateful anyway."

"No problem, chile. Look here—yo' man done come . . . umm umm, Miz Dayne—don' look lak dat—you don' know nuthin'

bout de taste of de jelly till you opens de jar. And you is goin' wid
yo' man on a Sunday, so you is never gonna leave him—" She
gave Dayne a little push toward Flint as he came into the room.
"Go on, girl—you cain't marry de man two times nohow—"

"It's time to get ready to leave," Flint said curtly.

"So soon—" Dayne turned and looked back at Mama Dessie,
who nodded at her helpfully.

"Go on now, Miz Dayne."

Flint held out his hand to her and she took it reluctantly.
"Good-bye, Mama Dessie."

"I see you soon," Mama Dessie said with absolute certainty
and she watched with guarded eyes as they exited the kitchen.

She turned back to her pots and cauldrons, and her potions
and spells. "Real, real soon . . ."

The sun had moved to the side of the house and the lawn was
now bathed in shade.

Already everything had been cleared away except the tables
and at the moment, two field hands were dismantling the trellis,
which they would put on a wagon and cart over to Bonneterre.

There was an air of peacefulness about the place, a calm, a
stillness as if the very atmosphere were replete from the celebra-
tion there.

Flint felt it strongly as he inhaled the bouquet of a final glass
of wine and he waited for Dayne to change her dress so they
could make their final departure as quickly as was polite.

Although he didn't feel in the least like being polite to Harry
Templeton . . .

. . . who just then was beseeching Nyreen to change her lovely
brocade dress to something more comfortable—something that
didn't require corsets and stays and miles of petticoats . . . something she could easily slip out of once they were finally alone together.

She was so bored by his usual importuning that she was just
staring out the window and not even listening to him.

". . . Harry—there's another carriage coming down the drive—"
Well, she had to say something to distract him even though it was

probably just another guest who was either rudely late or who had forgotten something.

"Nyreen, darling, I beg you—"

She did like that, his begging her—it opened so many delicious possibilities.

"Harry, I beg of you—don't put me in a compromising position with Flint Rutledge sitting on your front verandah and someone's having the bad taste to be arriving two hours after the event. Can't we just take care of the newlyweds first? I promise, I swear everything will be just the way you want it when everyone is finally gone—"

Well, she had to—she just had to: Harry was just not going to stop pleading with her, and there was this stupid carriage pulling up, and the absolutely disturbing presence of Flint Rutledge practically outside their window.

And Dayne—God, she was never going to get rid of Dayne . . . Dayne Rutledge—dear God . . .

. . . *pretty dress, that—Harry had better buy me something just like it to make up for all his nagging* . . .

Anyway, it was probably the carriage that had come to take Dayne and Flint back to Bonneterre.

"Come, Harry, we have to be civilized and say good-bye to your only daughter. After that, my darling, we'll unleash the roaring lion—"

She led him out of the house, and he came grumbling after her onto the verandah.

The carriage had stopped just at the bend of the driveway before it curved to pass in front of the house.

"That was perfect timing, Dayne," Nyreen said. "This must be your driver."

They all watched as the driver dismounted, but instead of coming to the verandah steps to escort Dayne and Flint to the carriage, he went around to the far side and opened the carriage door.

A man stepped out who was tall and slender and well-dressed, as they could see just from his dove gray trousers, which were visible from beneath the carriage body.

He stood for a moment, still in the shadow of the carriage, almost as if he were staring at the surroundings and then finally satisfied, he began pacing his way toward them with a slow deliberation that almost set Nyreen's teeth on edge.

And then he came into view—a man so elegant and sure and handsome that she thought she might just throw herself at him and beg him for mercy.

Vaguely she heard Dayne's suppressed little shriek—"Oh my God—oh, oh—"

And Harry's vibrant curse: *"Shit,"* almost as if the newcomer had deliberately chosen to visit at this of all times just because it would spoil his fun.

And then Dayne again, her voice raw with excitement: "It's Peter—it's Peter . . . Oh, thank God—Peter's home!"

No one could have stopped her: she took off from the verandah and raced in a most unlady-like way across the lawn and straight into the arms of the god.

Nyreen seethed; one more thing—it was just one more thing she could and would hold against Dayne Templeton Rutledge— one more thing that Dayne had taken from her, and it didn't matter one bit that Dayne was not even aware of it.

God, she hated her: she had the right to be hugged and held tightly by that most gorgeous of men, and she, Nyreen, had to contain herself and wait and sit, simmering with envy until *Dayne* was ready to let him come up to the verandah to meet the others.

Oh, she was clever, Dayne was, hugging him like that and looking at Nyreen as if she could divine all of her secret desires.

And then finally, finally Peter, so tall, so indomitably male, wrapped his arm around Dayne's waist and steered her back toward the others.

Definitely a man with manners and sensibility, Nyreen thought as she looked up into his sparkling blue eyes and he took her hands in his.

Hello darling—I definitely do not want to be your stepmama . . .

And in that lightning moment of recognition and understanding, she jettisoned every single plan she had made since before coming to Montelette three years ago.

Chapter 11

Irrevocable. The thing was done . . .

But . . . if she had only been able to persuade her father to wait just another day, Peter would have returned and she never would have had to walk down the aisle.

And now he was at Montelette, spoiling all of Nyreen's plans and she was Mrs. Flint Rutledge, mistress of Bonneterre—whatever *that* meant—forever.

She sat across from Olivia on the upper gallery of the house and watched as the evening light settled over the bayou as delicately as a silk shawl.

She had nothing to say to Olivia so there was a tenuous and uneasy silence between them that was underscored by the chittering sounds of nature.

"Are you thirsty, my dear?"

Olivia's voice, cracking slightly in the blue moody silence.

"Why yes—" all politeness; this was her mother-in-law after all.

Olivia picked up a little silver bell on the table beside her.

Praxine appeared instantly at the melodious ringing with a tray in her hands.

"Miz Rutledge." She bent over Dayne respectfully and Dayne took a tall glass of lemonade from the tray.

"Miz Olivia?"

Olivia motioned to her to set the tray on the table beside her and Praxine withdrew.

Dayne sipped and watched the opalescent twilight descend.

Olivia picked up a glass and looked at it as if it were a crystal ball and she could tell the future in its depths.

"Clay has gone back to New Orleans," she said finally.

Dayne had nothing to say to that. Clay ought never to have been lured back by Harry and placed in the untenable position of being forced to marry her.

And yet she had wanted him, and weeks before, she had sneaked up to Bonneterre past this very gallery to beg him to marry her.

And he had said no to her and yes to Harry, and she felt a residual fury building up in her that whatever Harry had offered was a lot more potent than she herself.

If only Peter had . . .

No—too late for that . . .

The Peter who had returned home was as much a stranger as a familiar face. He had grown up and taken on the brittle veneer of a world traveller. He had seen everything, gone everywhere, and, if she were reading the message beneath his descriptive words, he hadn't wanted to return.

The money had run out; and the implication had always been that he would return and take his rightful place beside Harry at Montelette.

And he looked as if Montelette were the last place he would ever want to be.

Nor was there anything she could tell him that he did not immediately perceive.

"Maybe I can blackmail him into paying for another year in Europe," he had murmured in her ear as he hugged her good-bye, and he had meant it.

She just hated that she had to leave him when she had so much to tell him.

But all he had wanted to do was visit Maribel's grave and then unpack and unwind from the exigencies of travel.

They walked up to the small family plot together to look at the fragile grave of their mother, and Dayne could not tell him that Harry had been chasing after Nyreen while their mother lay dying.

"She was comfortable at the end," she murmured, kneeling to pull away some weeds from the blanket of flowers that were always blooming over the grave. "She was content knowing you were doing what you most wanted to do, and I had the Boy and Father—well, Father had Montelette. She loved Montelette. She never regretted marrying an upstart and coming to St. Foy, and she was all consideration, even when she was so ill, and she agreed Father should take his brother's daughter to live with us while his brother and wife went west. She never counted the cost. And neither did Father."

"Kind altruistic Father," Peter said, lifting his elegant head and staring back toward the house. "He's going to marry her?"

She looked shocked; he sent her a skeptical look as if to say anyone would have inferred it, and she answered curtly, "Yes."

"So he got rid of you . . ."

That had hurt; it was so obvious. "Yes."

"And now I'm come back to spoil his fun. I wonder what the chit will do now?"

"This chit has to go home with Flint Rutledge, Peter dear."

He helped her up. "Don't you want him?"

"I wanted Clay—before. And then Father wanted me out of the way very badly, and it didn't matter who. How do I know if I want him?" she added bitterly.

But his question struck at her forcibly because she knew the answer: she wanted him when she could wield the power.

But now . . . now, she thought as she sipped the luke-warm lemonade and stared out at the darkness surrounding Bonneterre, there was no power at all: it was trussed up and bound by legalities and dowries and things that had nothing to do with her wants or needs.

She was a piece of chattel and her father had been forced to change the terms of the bill of sale, but he had gotten the better of the bargain anyway.

And in the end, she had no power at all.

Her wedding night.

She had changed her wedding dress at Montelette, and had folded her nightgown and toiletries into a traveling case and worn her one and only other dress which she now removed and hung carefully in the chifforobe in her bedroom at Bonneterre. *Her* bedroom—the bedroom of the mistress of Bonneterre. It was spacious, a corner room with windows on two sides and one ominous connecting door between it and her husband's bedroom.

Yes, her husband . . . husband, husband, husband—her mind could not shift over and put the label on the man who had been her willing lover for the past two weeks.

Husband . . .

He had bought her.

Harry might have set the terms, but Flint Rutledge had bought her as surely as if she were a slave.

She was no longer a mistress, and yet she was.

He would put her on a pedestal and go off and find his comforts elsewhere.

It was the way things were done.

Husbands of the planter class did not make messy, wet, steamy love to their wives. They kept mistresses in New Orleans for that, women who were bound by none of the restrictions and enjoyed all of the pleasure.

The pleasure . . .

Endless, full-bodied pleasure—at *his* hands, oh God, *his* . . .

She stared at herself in the pier glass mirror by the chifforobe.

And where was Jezebel now?

She was in her bedroom at Bonneterre, dressed in her corset, chemise, drawers, stockings, and petticoats—and her constricting gold wedding band—just like any good plantation wife.

No naked passion-soaked bodies here.

No sign of her *husband* as she sat with Olivia in the long, difficult, desolate silence of the early evening.

And no husband waiting all naked and hungry for her.

She had crossed some line the moment that gold band had crossed her finger, and it was as if the wild desire in her heart had somehow been exorcised.

She had to get used to being alone—and virginal and pure once more.

* * *

"*Nyreen!* Dammit—let me in! Nyreen!"

"Go away, Harry—stop making a fool of yourself."

"Dammit—" He pounded on her door more violently until she had no choice but to open it, unless she wanted both of them to look like errant fools.

"What? *What?*"

"You know what," Harry growled, his eyes almost bulging out at the sight of her in her thin silk gown under which he just knew she was wearing nothing. "Just let me in."

"Harry—" She pushed at him futilely. "Harry, dear—"

"You promised, Nyreen—you goddamned promised. Today was it—today *our* life together would begin—"

She shrugged and turned away from him and he shut the door emphatically behind him.

"Yes I did, but I didn't expect we were going to have a permanent houseguest after the fact."

"He's off in his own wing, Nyreen. He won't bother us; he doesn't suspect a thing . . ."

Naive Harry; Peter Templeton knew exactly what was going on—she had seen it in the quick assessing gaze he had given her and his father—and he thought the less of his father for it, too.

But she wouldn't tell that to Harry. Harry would believe whatever he wanted to believe—and he certainly would not believe her.

"Dear Harry," she murmured, schooling her expression and turning to face him. "Don't you think I too am longing for you? Men just don't understand the nature of the constraints placed upon women. You can go rut wherever and whenever you like and no one would think the less of you because of it. But I—I—"

"You are a rutting whore, and you're not going to put me off again," Harry interrupted petulantly. "All those promises, Nyreen—for *what?* For me—or for my money?"

She recognized his mood instantly and shifted into an aggressive stance. "I want *you*—how could you ever doubt that? Or don't you count all the things I've done for you so far? You're being stupid, Harry, ruled by your urges rather than your good sense. Your son sleeps a hallway away and you think I can just prance around the house naked to satisfy your lust, and you have no consideration of the fact that he might walk in his sleep; he might see me, and he might want me too . . ."

That forbidden image precipitated the desired response.

"*No!*" Harry roared. Christ—it had never occurred to him—his mannered son having lusty urges . . . but how could a man help it with Nyreen around? God, what if he saw her? What if he *forced* himself on her?

Nyreen smiled, that elusive little self-satisfied smile; Harry was selfish, and she had always been aware that she could count on that, and she knew it the way she knew everything else—by dint of her experience with men.

So she knew that the image of her and Peter would keep him chained by her side and his demands that she fulfill her erotic promises would diminish so long as Peter remained with them.

That suited her very well, particularly because she loved the idea of her and Peter together—that young handsome man and all six feet of his firm delicious flesh—nothing like Harry, nothing.

"So you see—" she shrugged.

"I have to have you."

"Of course you do, my darling. I want that, too. I just can't fulfill your fantasy of me running around the house naked." She paused for effect. "Yet."

"Naked where?" Harry growled, locking the door.

She turned her back to him. "All the delicious places we've discovered where we can—rut to our hearts' content," she said silkily, letting the thin robe slide down her shoulders.

She turned to face him, the robe totally open, knowing that just the sight of her naked body would enslave him.

She hadn't allowed him to see her fully naked very often—it was infinitely more arousing that way—but he deserved a reward this evening for giving her what she wanted: the time and space to seduce his son.

"Come Harry," she beckoned, allowing the robe to slide off of her arms and into a froth of material around her bare feet. "Come—"

He ripped off his clothes, he picked her up and carried her to the bed and there, expertly, manipulatively, and deliberately, she made sure that she would continue to get her way.

His wife—
He prowled the grounds of Bonneterre like a caged animal seeking some connection between the sleek tigress whose naked body he had ravished and the prim and pure Miss Dayne Templeton whom he had virtually forced to become his wife and who now awaited him in the mistress's bedroom above.

Mistress one way or the other—and Olivia had been avenged: Montelette was now in Bonneterre's fold. And if Harry thought any differently, he would learn soon enough that it was not Clay he was dealing with.

He had taken the first step. Dayne Templeton Rutledge was just a complication along the way, a means to an end . . . a convenience—

And now—a wife . . .
With everything that entailed.
His wife.

The tigress tamed. Jezebel in ashes and sackcloth repenting of her sins. What else could a wife do? Wives didn't roll naked and sweaty with their husbands dressed in leather thrall collars and nothing else.

Wives didn't sneak out to secret places to tempt a man to lust and sin.

You got children with a wife and then went off and took your pleasure elsewhere . . . and left your wife to manage so that you could taste freedom once again.

He knew how it was done: his own father had lived a lusty enough life between the slaves of Bonneterre and his octoroon mistress in the city. Money was a great leveler and Verne had poured it out openhandedly like wine everyplace but on Bonneterre.

And when he had started with Celie, Flint had walked out and left him with the useless profligate Clay who had blown away his stupid profligate life over yet another slave woman.

So he had come full circle; Bonneterre was his, as it always should have been, Clay was gone, and he had taken the daughter of Verne's worst enemy as his wife.

It was perfect, so perfect.

Except that Harry Templeton was expecting to ride rough-shod over *him* and take over Bonneterre—and Harry had no idea that things were going to be entirely different . . .

But that was a thought for another day.

Tonight he wanted his wife—his *wife* . . .

He wanted . . .

He turned abruptly on his heel and started back to the house.

He didn't know which Dayne Templeton he thought he would find in the mistress's bedroom of Bonneterre.

As he eased open the door between the bedrooms, he saw her standing in front of the pier mirror dressed in the constricting feminine underthings that were such a nuisance, and he came joltingly alive with such rampant a need for her that he was certain she could sense it.

He moved into the room until she could see him in the mirror behind her, beyond the bed, in her sight and just out of reach—just as she appeared to him.

His wife . . .

He had bought her pound of flesh to secure his birthright and he had the instant feeling that she knew it.

And that neither of them had thought beyond getting through the ceremony and getting rid of Clay.

And that everything had changed.

She didn't turn; she met his inscrutable jetty eyes in the mirror.

The silence stretched out, thick, full of portent, a wall between them that she wasn't willing to breach.

Jezebel could not live within the cotton wool confines of Bonneterre.

She had no power here. She had a husband and a new life and somewhere she must make a place for herself, despite her clamoring body, despite her resentment that she had been sold into bondage, despite him.

"Well—*husband* . . ." she said dampeningly and then the words came out—words she had never intended to say—or maybe she did, she would never know; maybe all she wanted to do was regain the sweet sensual power that was so heady.

Or maybe she just wanted him and didn't want to consider the ramifications of that.

Whatever it was, she reached over, took her brush, slowly and deliberately let down her hair and began brushing it, all the while watching him in the mirror as she took long, sweeping strokes and shook her hair free over her shoulders.

And she said, "I *thought* you said you would always be naked and waiting for me. I didn't suppose there were restrictions on where or who or what . . . but—" she stopped brushing and turned finally to face him, "I guess there are. You obviously can't be lusting for your *wife*—as opposed to—" she began walking toward him slowly until she was finally face to face with him, ". . . oh, that little trollop with the whip and leather thrall collar down at Orinda.

"Well, *husband*—I'll tell you what . . . why don't you . . ." she pushed at him with both hands, "just go to *her*—" she pushed him again, "and see if she's down there," another push, "waiting for *you*—all warm and willing and ready . . ." another push—

But he wasn't moving, and the light in his burning coal-dark eyes was getting deeper and deeper with his growing anger.

"Go find your *ghost*, sugar"—push—"and sleep with *her* on your wedding—"

He exploded; his palm silenced her, roughly covering her mouth, and he simultaneously grabbed her hands and pulled her tightly against him.

"You talk too much, sugar," he murmured against her ear, his voice laced with his unremitting frustration. "And you have goddamned nothing to say. So here's the thing: I expect my *wife* to be waiting for *me*—all hot and heaving and ready for anything— even if I have to strip her naked and lock her up to make her do it . . ."

"Youp wmptnt," she protested behind his huge hand.

"Wouldn't I, sugar? Hell, yes—I own you now—I can do whatever I want with you—and I know exactly what I want to do with you—"

His hand came away from her mouth to the front of her chemise where he held her hands.

"Don't move, sugar—"

Both hands—both, before she could make a move to get around him and away from him, both his hands hooked into the bodice of her chemise and *pulled* . . . She shrieked as the delicate material ripped and he yanked her underthings ruthlessly off of her and tossed them out to the adjoining bedroom behind him.

Everything: her shoes, her stockings, her drawers mercilessly dragged off of her as she beat at him, swore at him, screamed at him.

But she wouldn't beg him. She wouldn't—ever.

She stood before him, naked and defiant, her expression mutinous and her treacherous nipples, already taut with excitement, betraying her.

"Well, sugar—now I'm your *naked* wife, and I don't see you keeping your part of the bargain."

"Well, *sugar*—the reason is I'm going down to Orinda to my *ghost* lover and I'm leaving you locked in here to repent of your sins. Then maybe you'll be a little more hospitable to your *husband*—and forget about everything else."

"I won't forget I'm in bondage to *you*," she spat.

"I should hope not, sugar. That's just where I want you. Naked and in subjugation to me." He backed out of the room, closing the door slowly so that she would understand the full import of his anger.

"That is what I bought when I married you. Pleasant dreams, sugar," he murmured as he pulled the door closed and locked it from the outside.

She stared at it for a moment disbelievingly. He hadn't—he wouldn't—

She grabbed the doorknob and turned it—nothing; she pounded on the door furiously for a full fifteen minutes, hoping against hope that Olivia would hear her and send Praxine—but nothing.

She stormed furiously to the hallway door and pushed and pulled and banged at it.

God, he really meant it. *Really.*

It was as if the bedrooms existed in a little world by themselves and no one dared come up and no one dared interfere.

And so she was locked in her room on her wedding night like the veriest child—naked and alone and hot and thirsting for revenge.

She wrapped herself in her flimsy nightgown and huddled on the bed.

Naked for him indeed—he'll be lucky if I even stay here one more day. I'll just tell Peter and he'll figure out a way around this ridiculous marriage. I will never get married ever again. I can get more by being a Jezebel than I can by signing a marriage certificate. No other woman alive would be alone in her bed on her wedding night . . . I hate him—I hate him—I hate him . . .

Mistress Jezebel—or Mistress of Bonneterre—why, *why* did she have to choose?

But she could have wound up with the ridiculous Mr. Bonfils—or the awful Mr. Hanscombe . . .

Oh? And was she to kiss Mr. Rutledge's feet and thank him for saving her from *that?*

She shuddered with anger—because the end result was and would have been that any and all of them wanted her solely because of Montelette, nothing more, nothing less.

But if she had the power of Jezebel, they would have wanted her only for herself.

She slept—she did, utterly unaware of anything by the time her dreams claimed her, but she had the feeling that sometime during the night she had heard the rasping of a key in one of the two doors . . . or maybe she had wanted it so badly, she had dreamt it, she didn't know which.

She was slow to awaken and by then a tray had been brought and left at the foot of her bed.

And she was hungry; she was amazed at how hungry—she scrambled across the bed and pulled the covers off of the dish of eggs and ham and stuffed a biscuit into her mouth as she was pouring the coffee.

Morning.

The sun slanted through the windows and pooled on the floor in front of the bed.

A slight breeze wafted in through the muslin curtains and the open shutters—opened by Praxine when she had delivered the tray?

She bounced off of the bed and went to the windows, which overlooked the front of the house and the fog-rising wisps coming off the bayou.

Morning. Everything looked a little brighter, a little more possible. The coffee was excellent and still steaming hot, the biscuit warm and tender, butter melting in her mouth.

She poured another cup of coffee and pulled an upholstered chair over to the window so she could look out.

She felt better—things would get better.

Flint was, in all likelihood, out in the field; Olivia was probably still asleep. It was early yet, the time of day she had most liked at Montelette.

She could eat, wash, and dress, and perhaps learn her way around Bonneterre—

Lord, she was hungry. She ate every bit of the food and drank most of the coffee. She watched the sun come up in increments, burning away the fingers of mist that caressed the water.

She felt ready for anything.

She set down her cup and opened the chifforobe.

The cupboard was bare—her one and only dress had been removed stealthily sometime during the morning—or the night—and she felt the full fury of her impotence sweep over her like a tide.

She reached for the coffee cup and hurled it against the empty interior of the chifforobe—*crash!*

A plate next—*crash!*

The coffeepot next—*crash!*—spattering drops of coffee all over the floor and the inside of the closet.

The tray—

But just as she picked it up to heave it, she heard the faint rasp of a key in a lock, and she slowly lowered her arms, and moved suspiciously toward the connecting door between the bedrooms.

She could hear nothing.

She tucked the tray under her arm and reached for the door-knob—paused—thought the better of it and stepped back.

He ought to come get me, she thought angrily, wavering between wanting to stay exactly where he had put her, and trying to make an escape through his bedroom where the door to the hall-way quite obviously would *not* be locked.

She bit her lip and felt again the full force of her own fragility. It wasn't possible that Olivia had unlocked that door. But there was only one way to find out.

She took the doorknob resolutely in hand, turned it and pushed open the door.

He was laying on the bed naked and waiting for her. "Good morning, *wife,*" he said lazily, tucking his arms behind his head so that she could get a good full view of the line of his elegant torso and his rampant erection. "If you throw that tray, you will be in big trouble."

"You are already big trouble," she retorted irritatedly, moving toward his hallway door. "I wouldn't dream of imposing on you further."

"Isn't that funny, sugar? I've been dreaming all night myself . . ."

"I can't imagine what about," she interposed icily.

He rolled over on his side to look at her, noting that her stormy eyes followed the movement of his body, the rock hard thrust of *him.*

"Sure you can, sugar."

Her body twinged at the soft insinuating note in his voice and because she couldn't keep her eyes off of the torrid naked force of him.

"Don't talk nonsense, Mr. Rutledge," she said ruthlessly, "I've become a plantation wife. What do I know about such things? I've been sheltered and protected all my life."

"Oh yes, wife, you're a regular doyenne of the domestic circle. Someone taught you real well how to please a man—and your husband expects you'll do everything you can to gratify him . . ."

"Oh—I think not, husband. I believe a plantation wife has

other . . . tasks which keep her more diligently occupied." She edged toward the hallway door. "So if you'll ex—"

He pounced on her like a lion, seizing the thin stuff of her nightgown and pulling her back toward the bed with one mighty yank that tore the material.

The tray clattered to the floor as she felt his hot hands grasp her bare skin and his strength pull her backward onto the bed with him.

"A plantation wife has been raised to do her duty," he murmured seductively as he straddled her writhing body and tore off what remained of her nightgown.

"Do her duty? Do her duty? Get you sons so you can find some New Orleans trollop on whom you can visit your lust? Oh no—*husband*—not me, not me. You got Montelette but there won't be . . . sons—get them with a mistress if you must—"

"I have a mistress," he growled, wrestling her ruthlessly underneath him and pinning her with the full flat weight of his body.

"Oh no, oh no—you have a *wife*," she panted, pushing at his broad hairy chest and bucking her hips futilely against the arousing nakedness of his driving hard part.

"I have . . ." he lowered his head and slanted his mouth so that he could reach hers, "a Jezebel to warm my bed and a mistress . . ."—he licked her lips—"to excite me . . ." He inserted his tongue between her lips and began rimming the soft inner recesses of her mouth.

She made a small resentful sound at the back of her throat as she felt the rich wet tip of his tongue penetrate, and then her treacherous body almost seemed to liquefy against the shocking contrast of his rock hard manhood with the lush wet touch of his tongue.

Her mouth opened to him, and her hands fisted against his chest, as if she couldn't decide whether to keep pounding him or if she wanted to resist touching him.

She didn't know which; his kisses propelled her into a thick resonant erotic dream where all she was aware of was the soft, undulating curves of her body pressing against the hard, unrelenting nakedness of his.

Fragile—she felt so fragile against his strength and the driving power of his granite manhood. She felt like a wife, duty-bound to submit, and honor-bound to suppress every lustful feeling.

She felt caught between her burgeoning desire and her feeling of betrayal.

But her body betrayed her in the worst way: her body wanted his kisses and caresses and her body responded while her mind drowned in excuses and ploys to avoid his ultimate possession.

Well then—let him, let him; I don't have to respond—I can do my duty like any good wife . . .

And it would serve him right, too—if he expected the Jezebel in his bed and got the virgin wife instead . . .

It would be perfect—just perfect.

She felt him lift her and spread her legs to prepare her for his delicious probing of her feminine fold and she had to suppress a moan as she felt him crown her entrance and begin the soft hard slide deep within her satin sheath.

Inch by long, hard, pulsating inch he pushed and stopped and pushed and stopped until she thought she would go out of her mind with the pure delirium of wanting his throbbing granite manhood fully and finally possessing her.

And then he was there, deep and hot and male and *there* and she couldn't conceive of anything else—ever.

He took possession of her lips, her mouth, his large hands framing her face and lifting her chin to give him deeper access to her mouth and tongue.

And he stayed this way, in full wet possession of her, until she thought she would scream with wanting him.

But when he began the slow sensuous drive toward completion, she felt herself resisting the pleasure, tamping down on it as would the dutiful wife—just to show him . . . just . . . !

. . . Just refusing to meet the torrid undulation of his hips as he coaxed her and teased her—

. . . Just stiffening her lips and refusing to tumble headlong into his lush wet kisses—

. . . Just keeping her straining body and itching hands still, so still against the flagrant male drive of him as he tried to entice a response from her—

... Just—as limp as she could make her body and as weary as she could make her expression as he drove into her like a piston, his growing annoyance with her fueling his possession into a moment of violent frustration.

"Damn it, damn it, damn it—"

And suddenly his body heaved into a galvanic lunge, almost as if he had been pushed unwillingly over the edge and into his long, spuming, wrenching release.

And then there was silence, a recriminating bone-chilling silence, and he stared straight into her triumphant blue eyes with a fulminating anger that was so touchy, she knew she had better not say one single word.

"Such an obedient, conscientious, *accommodating* wife," he growled, his hands pressing angrily against the sides of her face. "So compliant, so submissive—and such a goddamned little cheat . . ."

It was the last thing she expected to hear.

"*What?* What?" She squirmed against his hot, wet weight. "You bastard—you . . . ham-handed scheming bastard—what did you expect of a *wife?*—you marry me for my money, you lock me up, you steal my clothes—you make me into a possession—well, husband, I'm determined to play that role to the hilt: possessions don't have feelings and they can't play games or manage plantations. They're inanimate, objects you can buy, sell, and display.

"And here I am, yours to parade around as you will. Think of me as a rag doll with arms and legs and a body you can pose any which way you desire—husband—a thing to do with whatever you want . . ."

Oh God—she heard the low growl in his throat as she finished her harangue, and she thought for sure he might just hit her: his eyes were like burning coals, searing her with the intensity of his anger as without ceremony, he levered himself off of her.

"A thing? A rag doll?" he hissed. "We'll see about that, Jezebel—"

And he pushed apart her trembling legs and sought her hot, wet feminine fold so drenched with the juice of his reluctant release.

"No—no . . ." she moaned as his fingers found her throbbing center.

"Oh no? But a rag doll can't talk; a puppet can't have opinions or make demands. A possession can't—groan with pleasure . . ." and she made an involuntary noise in the back of her throat and spread her legs still farther apart.

"You were made to be a mistress, Jezebel—made for me, and I have you now, irrevocably . . . mine," he whispered, as he felt her body respond to his expert handling. "Mine, sugar—mine . . ."

Oh, he kept saying it and saying it, and still, she felt her own anger and her own need mixing up into the pulsating thrust of her hips against his agile, knowing fingers—until the sensation was like a big, thick bubble welling up within her, pushing its boundary, its limits, stretching to the utmost until that ultimate explosive burst of pure crackling pleasure—edgy, jagged pleasure, piercing and bright blue, like sunlight off of glass.

And his—irrevocably, forever his.

She knew it, she felt it, and she would die before she would ever admit it—to him.

Chapter 12

He left her alone and locked in her room, this time without any clothes at all since her nightgown was now in shreds and there was no trace of her one good dress.

But surely her father would arrange to have her trunk sent back from New Orleans. It was only a matter of time.

And meantime, Olivia would probably inquire after her, and perhaps Peter might come to visit so that soon, very soon, Flint Rutledge would feel so embarrassed by the fact she had no clothes, he would remedy the situation.

A husband ought to buy his wife some clothes anyway, she thought righteously as she pulled back the cover on her bed and yanked out the top sheet.

Even a *kept* woman deserved some privacy.

A sheet made a very nice dress, she thought, as she folded it and twisted it this way and that and finally tied it together over one shoulder. It covered the body right to the feet without all the contraptions and paraphernalia that a woman was required to wear, and it was comfortable and lightweight, too.

She pulled up her chair to the window since that was about as close as she was going to get to being outside for now, and she amused herself by listening to the sounds of the heat-drugged afternoon and resolutely not thinking about her husband.

There was nothing more to think about—in all, he would always have his way, no matter what she wanted, and she was going to make it as hard as possible for him.

And the rest—well, the rest was the rest, and she wished she could have an afternoon with Peter to hear how he was faring after a day at home and what he thought and what he planned to do.

She would send him a note—she would ask for the Boy so that she could continue working with him on Bonneterre, and she would plan to race him at St. Francisville in the fall.

Surely Peter would still be here in the fall . . . ?

Praxine brought her lunch, entering the room with the aid of Tull, who waited sternly in the hallway as she set the tray down and withdrew.

It was unbelievable: her husband was going to keep her in this room like some unrepentant child who needed excessive punishment.

Her husband . . .

She lifted the cover from a basket of fresh baked biscuits and a small bowl of soup. Soup to nourish and sustain, hot soup, reminiscent of a morning's lesson in humility.

Bread and water for the prisoner—nothing more, nothing less.

She wanted to throw it in his face.

Instead, she finished every last drop.

He came to her in the afternoon, hot and sweaty from the fields, tearing off his clothes as he entered the room.

"I see my compliant wife awaits me," he said caustically, reaching for the sheet and pulling it away from her tingling body. "An obedient wife doesn't hide herself from her husband. You are meant to always be ready and waiting for my return, just as I am always naked and hungry for you."

And he was—not even his rough workclothes could hide the force of his straining erection. It leapt out at her, naked and powerful, hot with desire, reaching out to bury itself in the hot moist center of her.

He carried her to the bed with no preliminary whatsoever, but still she was ready for him, aroused by his uncomplicated and raw need for her, and his thrusting savage possession of her.

She didn't think; she didn't know that she too could want the quick driving culmination that left them both breathless and pulse-poundingly angry and needing more.

She didn't know she would love the sweat-scented feel of his body, muscular with the morning's work, sticky against hers, aroused from his ardor rather than satiated by his lust.

But there was so much she did not know.

"A submissive wife will wait for me here, like this, in bed with no thought on her mind but when her husband will return to possess her again. And he in turn will think of her luscious naked body in all readiness to take him the moment he walks back in that door; he lives for the moment, wife, and he thrives in a state of hot, aroused readiness all day knowing that his naked and willing wife awaits him when he returns."

She felt her breath catch, and her body, already in turmoil from her culmination and the picture his brazen words painted, stretched languidly, as if she were deliberately enticing him to stay.

Oh but she was a wanton; her body knew every undulating inviting move to arouse a man—he was half dressed, in his mind halfway out the door, and her hips moved, grinding against the soft covers when they should have been grinding against his granite hardness, and he spurted to life once again.

She was the embodiment of Jezebel, the temptress, still an innocent, born a wanton, her body perfect, sugar perfect, and made for him.

And he could see in her languorous eyes that once was not enough and that she was aroused by the sight of him, too.

Deliberately he finished dressing, and then ran his large, hot hand down the whole length of her naked yearning body.

And then, just as deliberately, he left her, locking the door pointedly behind him.

For a long time, she lay in bed, her body fluid with yearning, the heat of the room and the scent of her sex enfolding her like the sheerest of silk cloths.

This was what it was like to be a slave to the senses: to revel in her naked body, in what it could feel, what temptation it could invite, and what havoc it could wreak with the man who wanted her.

This was power, his sequestering her so no one else could see her or have her but himself.

And he wanted no barriers between him and his erotic desire for her; he hungered for her naked body every minute of every day and he wanted no impediments to his carnal possession of her.

He wanted her hot with longing for his touch, naked and needing only what he could give her.

Alone and away from everyone, she did not need to clothe herself; her very nakedness was arousing, the more so because she could concentrate her thoughts on him and the moment he would come to her.

Her body recreated the pleasure of the moment in and of itself as if it had a separate life from her. His kisses, his erotic handling of her, his luxurious kisses, his hard driving possession of her, her wild voluptuous need for him . . .

Her body streamed with readiness to take him, every granite inch of him . . .

Such power—

Jezebel power . . .

Power she thought she had lost when he had married her . . . or could he have wanted to marry Jezebel?

She ran her hands down her sleek, heat-sticky body.

He wanted this part of her only for himself, a slave to his explosive desire for her.

And what did she want?

She wanted what the Jezebel in her wanted: him naked in her bed right then, lusting for her.

And she knew exactly what she wanted to do—

She wanted—

The door opened—

He stood there, naked and bursting for her, his glittering eyes feasting on the sight of her on the bed, her body ripe with need for him.

She turned in her erotic restlessness and saw him; her eyes narrowed and she smiled, an elusive little smile that said she knew everything, and that she had known he couldn't stay away.

And she was just as he had pictured she would be: her naked body hot with excitement and hunger, her thoughts centered solely on him and his sex and the moment he would return to claim her.

He closed the door behind him.

The air was thick with tension and luxurious yearning.

She didn't want to move: she wanted to just look at him.

And he didn't want to move—he wanted just to look at her and prolong this erotic union forever.

She knew it: she couldn't keep her eyes off of his forceful manhood. She stretched languidly, spreading her legs, reveling in her nakedness, inviting his carnal possession.

He felt himself spurting with erotic need, but he didn't move.

She squirmed under his heated gaze, her body dancing with enticement, her nipples stiff with longing.

He still did not move.

She ran her hands over her nakedness, feeling what he would have felt were he caressing her as he should have been, and she could see the visible effect on his rigid still-lengthening member and still he did not move.

"Husband—" her voice was throaty with desire. "—you are quite obviously hard and you look *very* ready . . ."

"Not hard enough, wife, not nearly ready—not yet . . ."

She made a strangled sound.

"And I will look at your naked body as long as I want to, wife—"

"I—"

Power . . .

Her naked body was power—he could not get enough of her . . . yes—

She rolled her hips and arched her back. Yes—he was not yet ready for her and he was hard as a rock.

She felt perfect for him—her sinuous body, her tautly pointed nipples, the erotic shape of her breasts, the enticing mound of feminine hair waiting for him to breach its secrets once again— yes . . .

If he could not get enough of her erotic femininity—such power she would have . . .

"Husband, you are so wonderfully hard—"

"I've been hard every minute since I left you," he growled. "All day long, all night, just hard and wanting you. After I left you, the thought of you naked and waiting made me hot and hard all over again ..."

"I love the thought that I do that to you—" she whispered, stretching out her hand. *Such power ... such wonderful, erotic power*—"Do you know what you do to me?"

"Why don't you tell me ... wife ... ?"

"I want you inside me right now. I want to feel you, every inch of you; I want to be naked and ready for you all the time. ... Every time I think about you, I want you; my body needs the hot, hard feel of you inside me day and night. Let me come to you— let me ..."

Power—she was Jezebel, a creature of naked body ... she moved off of the bed toward him, tantalizing him with her undulating hips, until she stood a breath away from his kiss, his manhood a hot iron bar between them, her hard pointed nipples grazing his hairy chest.

"Let me—" she whispered, her voice trembling with suppressed excitement to be this close—this wet with wild longing ...

"Let me," he breathed, and she felt his large hands on her shoulders as she lifted her eager mouth for his kisses.

His hands on her shoulders, moving down her chest toward her swelling breasts and her tender nipples, downward to thumb the thrusting peaks as she surrendered to the wet, lush pressure of his mouth; downward, to surround her waist and caress her hips; downward once again to stroke and grasp the firm pillows of her buttocks.

And then he lifted her and she bent her knees against the rock hard flat of his hips and wound her arms around him as he shifted her until he could probe for her.

Slowly and deliberately he lowered her inch by throbbing inch until she finally and fully enveloped him.

"Do you want this?" he growled as he backed her up against a wall so he could have purchase to move.

"I love this," she hissed against his lips. "I feel every rock hard inch of you and I want it."

He devoured her sassy mouth with hard kisses.

"Do you want this?" He thrust into her still harder, tighter so that there was not a breath of air between their straining wet bodies.

"I want you any way you want to come to me," she whispered, inviting his lips again.

"Jezebel," he murmured, taking her in firm methodic strokes as he held her buttocks and drove his need against the solid backing of the wall.

"Jezebel loves your kisses," she whispered and opened her mouth for his wet, grinding possession of it.

It was another kind of heaven: his lush kisses, his hard hands pumping her buttocks as he drove into her like a piston, and the hot ravishing kisses that enslaved her.

She felt his hands all over her bottom, feeling, stroking, probing and she wanted to reach down and feel what he was feeling and know what he knew.

He was pushing her downward onto him so that every stroke she felt a sensual collision with his male root and she felt him totally and intensely deep within.

Every stroke—his hands, the wall, the heat, the knowledge that he would want her all over again, even with the satiation of this need—

His rhythm shifted and he drove into her with a pulse-pounding rhythm, hard, urgent, one endless motion that was the whole of her world as he took and took her and the slippery, sliding glass mountain she climbed just splintered into a thousand fragments of pleasure all over her body.

And he came a moment after, that long, wrenching release that felt as if she were wringing every last drop out of his body.

And then he carried her to the bed, with her head buried in his shoulder and her legs still wrapped around him, and still sheathed in her moist hot center, he lay down with her, his weight all on top of her, and relished the pure carnal pleasure of having possessed her.

She awakened slowly, becoming slowly aware that she was lying on her stomach, her fingers buried in the thick, crisp hair of his male root.

He was next to her, his huge right hand cupping her buttocks—no, stroking her buttocks lightly, slipping his fingers now and again into the erotic crease and downward to rub lightly against her nether lips as though he were begging entrance.

She turned her head which was buried in her pillow to look at him.

He was sprawled out hugely next to her, his recalcitrant manhood standing stiff and tall, moving almost as if it were bowing to a show of appreciation.

And his hand was moving, moving, moving, titillating her, arousing completely from her buoyant rest.

Jezebel was so easily seduced.

She wriggled her hips, inviting his further exploration, and he accommodated her with those long, masterful fingers that knew just where she wanted to feel their erotic probing.

Just there—and there—

She felt that telltale twinge of arousing excitement . . . there— she moaned in encouragement—and there . . . as his fingers slipped into her velvet fold to the moist, hot core of her.

Hot and ready—as his expert fingers explored her most secret place—ready for him, ready—canting her lower torso upward to give him easier play; so ready . . .

"I can't keep my hands off of you . . ."

It was a breath in her ear, erotic and telling all at the same time.

"I don't want you to . . ." she whispered and his fingers slipped deeper into her hot, velvet sheath.

He kept them there as he levered himself upward to straddle her from behind.

"I want you now—"

"Are you hot for me?" Jezebel, wielding her power, a little coy, and definitely all-knowing.

"Too hot for you . . ."

"Are you hard for me?"

He growled and nudged her.

"I need to feel how hard . . ." she whispered, and he shuddered at her words, and holding her hips tightly, he thrust himself mightily within her welcoming fold.

And he didn't stop; it was as if he were an engine, driving and driving against the soft moist enveloping heat of her, holding her buttocks, guiding her, commanding her, covering her with the heat of his body and the drenching wet of his muscular possession of her.

Everything was feeling: she couldn't see him, couldn't touch him, could only revel in the sensation of this new reverse manner, all her feelings centered on him, on his forceful coupling with her as he drove relentlessly to completion.

Musk and magic—scent and sensation—were all she felt, all she knew as he surged against her, plumbing the depths of her desire and making her his once again.

And then tendrils of feeling were eddying outward from her womanly core and foaming suddenly soft against hard, breaking suddenly, fragile and wet against hard, hard rock, and then pulling away slowly, slowly as the rock remained and remained . . .

And then he drove deeply into her, and he was shattered by a violent shuddering spending of his seed, wet and filling within her.

And she slowly, slowly eased her body downward so that the whole of his lathered body covered her and he was still deeply within her, and in this way, once again, they fell asleep.

Nyreen was angry: clearly Harry did not know when to stay out of the way, and every time she saw her way clear to approach Peter—big, elegant, handsome Peter—Harry invariably interfered.

The problem was, Peter seemed immune to her charms, and she was so frustrated she had taken to dressing more provocatively in order to entice some kind of reaction from him.

But instead it was Harry who was reacting, and all he ever wanted to do was carry her upstairs for an afternoon of pleasure.

Everything was going well, as Harry thought it should: Peter was riding out every day with Bastien and taking an interest in the management of Montelette, which left Harry endless free time to pursue *her* and make her keep her promises.

Well, she didn't *want* to keep her promises to him. She wanted to make more and exciting promises to Peter and his god-like young body. She wanted to sneak into his bedroom at night and force him to take her.

She wanted Harry out of the way and she wanted Peter to ask her to marry him.

She just didn't know what she was going to do, as the first week of his return passed, and he had still not looked at her the way every man looked at her when she sashayed into view.

She wanted to teach Peter a lesson, and she wanted him grovelling at her feet, and she was feeling intensely restless and unable to think clearly.

If only her mother were here—

The advent of Peter changed everything, just everything.

And she couldn't decide whether it would be better to marry Harry first and then somehow get rid of him, or to get rid of him and seduce Peter.

Either scenario had its pitfalls, not the least of which was Peter's disinterest in her.

Which made the idea of marrying Harry seem more attractive, because then she would be related by marriage and he would *have* to deal with her.

Oh, but marrying Harry . . . and living in the same house with that delicious, young male flesh . . . that would be so hard—and there was no guarantee Peter would stay on after.

Not unless she could seduce him and make him her slave . . .

And then suddenly he was there, as if she had conjured him up with her lascivious thoughts, tall and elegantly turned out, even first thing in the morning.

"Good morning, Peter," she just managed to say with some touchy reserve as she gathered her scattered wits about her. "Your father is out in the field this morning. I expect you'll be joining him?"

He poured himself a cup of coffee. "I'm taking the Boy over to Bonneterre—which my father should have thought of doing days ago. He hasn't been exercised or cared for since that travesty of a wedding and he is Dayne's and she should continue his training. Did you say something, Nyreen?"

She had said nothing, she had choked on the beignet she had

popped into her mouth because she could not get away from Dayne.

Every time she turned around it was Dayne, Dayne, Dayne—Dayne had gotten Clay; Dayne had gotten the pariah prince of Bonneterre; Dayne was adored by Peter; and Dayne somehow had won . . . and Nyreen still couldn't figure out quite how.

She watched with mixed emotions as Peter finished his coffee, having declined to eat anything more, and went off toward the stables to get the Boy ready.

"Is he gone yet?"

She jumped. "Damn it Harry—you scared the life out of me!"

"I was just waiting for him to go—is he gone yet? I figure he'll be there more than a few hours. Dayne will be sure to make him stay and listen to her little tale of woe—and you and I will have all that lovely time to do exactly what we want."

A feeling of dread washed over her. How, *how* could she keep up the pretense with Harry when it was Peter that she wanted?

She girded herself and played for time, stroking his face gently. "Aren't you the sly one, my darling? Who *really* suggested taking the Boy to Bonneterre?"

"Who do you think? He'll be gone for hours. Even that sot-faced Olivia wouldn't be ill-mannered enough to send him off the minute he got there. And that will give us time, my darling Nyreen, so much time . . ."

She let him kiss her with his thick, sloppy lips and she murmured against them coyly, "Time for what, Harry dear?"

"Time for some of the things you promised me, Nyreen," he muttered, taking her mouth again in a hard, ruthless kiss. "Things I've been dreaming of . . ."

"Haven't I?" she cooed, pulling him down more tightly against her. "Haven't I wanted the very same things, Harry darling? I'm so hungry for your kisses . . . let's not waste time talking, my darling . . ."

Let's not waste time so I can get this over with as quickly as possible . . .

And she sought him this time, flicking into his mouth like a snake, eager and dangerous both, until he moaned for mercy.

"You know what I want, Nyreen."

She sucked at his lower lip. "Are you sure there is time?"

"I'm sure."

"It will be like a foretaste of our life together," Nyreen whispered. "Go, Harry—come back in ten minutes, and I will be waiting for you, just like I promised—go . . ."

"Swear it—"

"Childish, Harry."

"I feel like a child."

"When you return, you will feel like a man. Now go—"

Olivia came down to greet the young man who looked so much like Dayne it was almost breathtaking.

The same blue eyes, the same cast of features but so much more masculine on him, the same thick blond hair. And Harry's male body—more beautifully knit together, tall and elegant, and very, very sure of himself.

"Do join me for breakfast, Mr. Templeton—"

"Peter, please."

"Of course, and I am Olivia." She motioned him to a chair beside the small table that Tull had set up on the upper gallery, to which he was now bringing a second chair, followed by Praxine with more food and a cup for him.

"There! This is much more pleasant—do you take breakfast outside at Montelette—Peter?" God, his expression was so like Harry when Harry was young that her hand trembled as she poured the coffee.

He nodded and sipped, not wanting to speak, wanting to assess this woman who for so long, with her family, had been considered his father's greatest enemy.

"Of course we haven't seen much of my son and new daughter-in-law—" she continued delicately. "Not having had a wedding trip . . ." she let her voice trail off. "Well, they've been rather to themselves for the past week; in a separate wing so that it's much as if they were actually away . . ."

She stopped short; there was just no diplomatic way to put it; and if Flint thought she did not know what was going on, well—she was scandalized enough that she hadn't seen him for days and that all meals were delivered by Praxine to his room—and half of them weren't even eaten.

"I don't feel as if I should interrupt them," she said finally which was about as descriptive as she cared to get.

"No, of course not. But the Boy—"

"I'm sure she'll be so happy," Olivia murmured, relieved to be off the subject of just what was occupying her son and his wife for the past week. "Tell me about your plans now—Peter—I trust you'll be staying on in St. Foy?"

"I haven't decided," he said noncommittally, but he had decided a long time before he had returned home. He was going back to Paris and there was nothing Harry could do to keep him immured in this godawful bayou.

"Wise not to make hasty decisions," Olivia murmured, and wondered just how she was going to keep the conversation going until the polite limit of an hour had been reached.

"Have some biscuits, Peter. Tell me, how has Harry been since the wedding?"

She didn't want to know—but she bent her head and listened carefully, courteously, and with every evidence of the greatest interest.

Harry was in a tearing hurry to return to the house. The moment was at hand—Nyreen's total capitulation to him, the embodiment of his every fantasy.

He slowed his steps as he came up the gallery steps and into the front door.

"Nyreen! Nyreen darling—where are you?"

His voice echoed off of the high-ceilinged parlor and he felt a wallop of fear that she might have just gone and left him.

"Nyreen!" His voice sounded desperate, even to him. Damn it, damn it, damn it—it was his house, his money, his control of this homeless and heartless bitch whose parents had abandoned her. "Nyreen!"

"Don't shout, Harry," she said huskily behind him. "I'm here and I'm waiting just for you."

He whirled.

Oh God—she was, she was waiting every bit as naked as in his dreams, standing in the doorway between the parlors, her hand on her hip, just waiting . . .

"Nyreen," he breathed.

She walked into the room toward him and he thought he would die to possess those firm breasts and that dark sinuous body.

"Nyreen."

"Let me sit on your lap, Harry," she whispered, and he sank weak-kneed into the nearest chair and she mounted him, straddling his legs, cupping his face, and leaning into a deep, dark, soul-seeping kiss.

"I want you," he muttered, his hands working desperately at his clothes. "I want you . . . on the floor—*now* . . ."

"Whatever you want, Harry darling," she agreed, slipping off of him in that same sinuous movement and sliding down onto the floor. "Come to me, Harry—I've been waiting for you . . ."

He fell on the floor—he fell on her and shoved his way into her willing body—a moment as fertile as his dreams—

While she lay beneath him, easily accommodating him, in a scene no different than a hundred others she had played out with other desperate men in godforsaken towns from Texas to Nevada.

She was so good at what she did: a moan here, a pat there, a grab, a thrust—with that cat-smile surfacing now and again as he whispered into her ear everything he wanted to do to her—everything . . .

"Do it, do it," she whispered, encouraging his hard pounding. There would be a moment—and she knew just when it was—that she would stiffen and tumble into the throes of a wondrous culmination.

But he wasn't ready yet—and so neither was she; she didn't mind his hot, sweaty body all over her as he pumped and pumped away, immersed in his dreams, and seeking that gushing surcease.

"Oh Harry," she whispered in his ear, "oh Harry—" she really didn't need to do more; he didn't need any more than that, just her moans and groans and the certainty that she wanted him, *this* for years to come.

Not hardly.

But allowing him the dream, when she was in full control, was easy. It was like coasting in a wagon down a small hill—always with the element of danger unless you had the steerage in your hand—just like that: Harry pumping and Nyreen coasting because it was going to take him so long—too long—to slake his need.

And then she heard the door slam and footsteps and she looked up into Peter's furious eyes, and she knew exactly what he saw: her dusky body entwined with his father's, her eyes clear and knowing exactly what she was doing as his father drove one last time into her and ejaculated in a loud, coruscating groan of satisfaction.

And then he was gone, and she felt glad—glad he had seen her naked and wound around his father's aged hips, so that he would be so jealous he would lure her away from Harry any way he could.

And on that impossible fantasy, she felt her body stiffen of its own volition and the sizzling hot pleasure dance along every willing inch of her.

"So—*Monsieur* Clay—let us see those cards."

Clay froze. The speaker, duVallet, knew him too well, had been his nemesis for years, and one to whom he always, always lost.

He threw down the cards resentfully. "I'm strapped, duVallet. You'll have to take a note—or the deed to Orinda."

"Ohhhh, I think not, my good friend Clay. It is time to pay the piper. And the piper does not wish to be saddled with a moldering old plantation that has no productivity, or a worthless note for money you cannot raise. Spare me this time—it is ever so: you always lose and you always come away indebted to me. And you gamble recklessly, with no regard to your circumstances. It is offensive, *Monsieur* Clay, and it is dishonorable. And so, me, I ask you—how will you pay this debt of honor this time?"

Clay felt a rush of horror. It was the first time ever that duVallet refused to take his note or the deed.

There was nothing else—nothing—

Except his life.

And duVallet had no compunction about demanding an eye for an eye, especially when wealthy planter families were involved.

But everyone in New Orleans was aware that his brother had returned and stolen his money tree out from under him.

He had been counting on the settlement to see him through—and after, on Harry's generosity and his goatish desire for the inestimable Nyreen and his yearning to be left alone to rut with her.

All of that would have been on his plate if only his brother had not interfered.

He had funded this game on those expectations, and duVallet had let him, knowing full well what had been the end result.

"Well, *mon ami?* Is there nothing?" duVallet asked patiently—too patiently—because he already knew the answer.

"I—" Clay croaked. "I don't know. I won't know until I go back to Bonneterre. There might be something there—if my brother has been as efficient as he claims he is. He might have already salvaged enough to advance me something."

"From a harvest already mortgaged three growing seasons ahead? *Dieu, Monsieur* Clay, you take me for a fool."

"My brother is a lot smarter than I am," Clay retorted. "Maybe he's a miracle worker, too. And anyway, there's always my mother . . ."

"Ah yes—the long-suffering Olivia. I am aware of everything, *Monsieur* Clay. There is nothing of your financial situation I do not know."

He felt like a dead man—he was a dead man.

"You have to let me try," he said finally, hoping he didn't sound like he was begging. But there was nothing, he knew it and duVallet knew it.

Nevertheless, duVallet was a man of some sensibility; he knew a man had to try. And he knew, too, that *Monsieur* Clay could not run far or fast enough to elude his men when he was ready to collect his final payment.

"As you say, *Monsieur*—a man has to try. Two weeks then, *mon ami*—two weeks for you to cajole the money from your brother or your mother or some source that will open for you like the Red Sea. Two weeks, *Monsieur*—and a generous two weeks at that." He snapped his fingers and the bodyguards who were his constant companions made their way outside to assure his safety in passing.

Two weeks.

He was going to die—and he wondered why, if that were the truth of it, he didn't just stay in New Orleans and gamble his life away.

But he didn't. He spent the night with an expensive whore whom he could not afford to pay, and in the morning, he had a lavish breakfast at the hotel, rented a buggy, and in a leisurely fashion, which was meant to imply he had no worries or cares whatsoever, he began the trip back to Bonneterre.

Nyreen could hear them fighting all the way up in her bedroom.

"I cannot stay in this house with that slut for another moment—" Peter's voice raised in righteous anger. "God—you were like a rutting boar—you should have seen yourself . . . you should have seen her eyes . . ."

"Damn you for looking!" Harry shouted. "I'm going to marry her, damn you, so shut your smutty mouth. You're my son, not my judge, and I won't have you maligning Nyreen."

"No need," Peter sneered. "Anyone can see what she is—"

"Damned right—she's an innocent, upstanding woman, and I'm going to give her my name."

"She's a scheming whore and everyone knows it."

A noise—a thump, as if Harry had pushed his son up against the wall.

"You say that again, son—"

"She's a scheming whore; and if I'd have her, she'd be in my bedroom tonight."

Crack! Harry slapped him.

"You're right, son—you can't stay in this house another minute. Get your stuff—get out . . ."

Oh God—she felt a fierce panic as Harry shouted the words and instantly she flew out her bedroom door and down the gallery steps.

"Harry—Harry . . . don't, don't, don't—don't be rash don't—"

She forced herself between the two of them as they stood panting with fury, eyeing each other as if they were moving in for the kill.

"Harry darling, don't let your anger force you to do something you'll regret . . . Harry—listen to me . . . what will everybody say?"

"I hear you," Harry said flatly. "Very well—let him stay . . . until he finds somewhere else to go—without my money. You're too good, Nyreen, after what he called you. Too forgiving."

"He's your son, Harry. I couldn't stand to be the cause of your sending him away."

Harry looked at Peter, and Peter stared back hard and unforgiving, resenting her standing there so pious and pretentious and so knowing, like a sly cat.

"He's sending himself away," Harry said remorselessly. "Two weeks, boy—that's all the time you've got. No matter what—you're gone." Then Harry turned and stamped away.

Peter put the full blast of his anger on Nyreen. "You bitch. You had better stay away from me; I'll kill you sooner than kiss you."

"I'll take you up on that," Nyreen purred, and Peter turned on his heel and stalked away. She watched him, her pent-up desire pouring through her like a waterfall. "Oh, will I ever take you up on that."

It had been a week—she *thought* it had been a week—a week immersed in such erotic excitement that nothing else seemed important or possible.

He would not, could not let her go. He wanted nothing inhibiting or impeding her nakedness and he wanted her available at all times.

He never tired of looking at her, and she found she loved displaying herself to him to entice him—Jezebel, wielding her power to the hilt.

Everything about her aroused him; he could spend languid hours just kissing her and never touching her, and he would surge into a rock hard erection just from that.

Or she would sit on his lap, facing forward so that her thighs became the soft moist sheath for his jutting manhood poking up between them, and she could press herself against his rigid sex, and arch herself against him so that he could have her mouth and play with her hot, hard nipples while she stroked the underside of his towering shaft.

She loved this deliciously erotic position: she could both ride him and play with him, and he could fondle her nakedness and whisper in her ear as he stroked her thrusting breasts.

"Your nipples are such hard delicious points," he would whisper, squeezing them gently and sending a lightning bolt of pleasure through her body. "I love feeling them, I love sucking them—I don't want them ever to be covered up and out of my sight," and she would groan with the pure delight of his aching need of them.

"You just want to keep me locked up and naked for the rest of my life," she would murmur, "and thinking about this." And she would slide her hands all over him, squeezing him and undulating against the towering thickness of him.

And their words and caresses would finally take them on the long, slow, luxurious climb to the peak of pleasure, mutual, overriding, as draining and satisfying as any of their voluptuous joinings.

And after, in two hours or three, in the heightened sensual ambiance of the room, their passion would blaze out of control once again.

It was like being a harem of one, except that she understood that she possessed the most potent power of all: his uncontrollable desire for her.

And she knew—she just knew—that they could not remain in this fantasy realm forever. And that when he finally unlocked the door, Jezebel would reign supreme.

It came sooner than she expected—later on that evening, after an early dinner that neither of them really ate, and another delicious hour exploring the limits of their sensuality, they heard an imperious knocking at his bedroom door.

"Flint! Open up. Do you hear me? Open up!"

Olivia's voice, totally unexpected and shocking, the tone of her voice so urgent that it could only be that something terrible had happened.

He leapt out of bed and through the connecting door.

"A moment, Olivia—" as he rummaged for something to pull on over his naked body before he pulled open the hallway door. "What is it?"

She took in his rumpled hair, unshaven chin, and bare chest disapprovingly.

"It's time to come back to the real world, Flint. Clay has come home, thoughtfully bringing Miss Dayne's trunk with him. I'll expect you both downstairs in an hour because I cannot face him alone. Do you hear me? Clay has come home—he ran out of money in New Orleans and he has nowhere else to go . . ."

Chapter 13

It had not quite been the homecoming he had envisioned.

Flint had slammed down the stairs like an avenging devil, barely dressed, hardly shaven, his expression remorseless.

"What the hell are you doing here?"

No civility, but what could you expect of a man who had foraged in the wilderness for twenty years? His brother had no conception of the notion that appearances were paramount and must always be preserved.

He himself was above all that certainly, and he moved forward, his hand extended, his expression benign while his mother watched in abject disbelief.

"And good evening to you, brother mine."

Flint brushed his hand away. "What do you want?"

"A vacation in the country, of course," he said lightly. "I assure you, I have no hard feelings."

"It's more likely you have no hard currency and you want to finagle some out of my hard work," Flint said stringently. "Forget it, Clay. Your mother is not in charge any more. And your charm is totally lost on me."

Damn . . . Clay schooled his expression not to show his frustration and mounting anger.

"I brought Dayne's trunk."

"I'll give you a tip—but I know it won't cover your expenses."

"You are being inexcusably rude."

"You are irredeemably selfish."

They stared at each other, toe to toe, almost head to head—as different as brothers could be side by side and nose to nose.

Clay felt it; Flint dismissed it as he was already dismissing Clay and his feckless concerns from his mind.

Clay felt like striking out—it was patently unfair for his brother to have such an advantage when he was the newcomer on the scene.

He had tried—but he had always hated getting his hands filthy, and Verne hadn't believed in overseers, and after, there was never enough money.

"A family doesn't turn its sons away," he said righteously. "Even after a hiatus of twenty years—let alone twenty days."

"Go to hell," Flint growled. "You're not going to live off of my sweat, brother, and you can count on it."

"Now Flint—" Olivia tried to make her tenuous presence known. She couldn't have them fighting. She couldn't have anyone overhearing that Clay was not welcome in his family home, even though she was aware that he would ruthlessly try to charm some money out of her.

Surely she was strong enough to resist.

"Let him stay," she said somewhat imperiously. "After all, he was thoughtful enough to bring Dayne's things to her . . ."

And it was, in fact, more considerate than he had been in years. And maybe, just a small part of her was scared that he was running from something he could not escape. She couldn't bear the thought of that.

Her son was her son, no matter what he had done.

"I wouldn't call it thoughtful," Flint said disparagingly. "Call it a diversionary tactic until he aims the big gun and holds us hostage because he's hard-pressed to raise cash. You don't fool me, Clay; you're hardheaded and when you're desperate enough, you'll run faster than a hound after a fox. And then you'll move in for the kill."

He wheeled around to face Olivia. "Let him stay—but don't say you weren't fully and properly warned."

In some respects, Clay thought the next morning, it was very nice being home. He had no responsibilities whatsoever, he was waited on hand and foot, and Olivia was sensibly staying out of his way so he did not need to listen to lectures.

And Flint was predictably getting his hands dirty working in the fields. He could see the improvement already and he was quite in awe of his brother's single-mindedness—in all respects.

And he had shrugged off Flint's little tirade as merely bad temper brought on by excessive *work*.

And then there was Dayne—mistress Dayne with her kiss-swollen lips and her voluptuous air of satisfaction.

Mistress Dayne, who could have been his and whom he wanted desperately to bring to her knees for having allowed Harry to renege on their marriage agreement.

He was a little shocked he felt so vindictive about it. And he resented that she acted like nothing had happened. Like it hadn't changed *his* life completely.

But he wasn't going to think about that—for at least one day while he got acclimated to the slower, more aggravating pace of life at Bonneterre.

God, it was boring.

And it would have been perfect if he had married Dayne and gone off to New Orleans to spend Harry's money; he couldn't have invented a better life for himself, and he still didn't understand why it had all fallen apart.

It was Flint's fault of course.

God, to compete with such a formidable older brother who could both cut the ground out from under you with your mother and forcibly steal away the woman you were promised to marry—and then to have *her,* damn the bitch, come out looking so erotically sated a week later—well, he knew all about the lascivious goings-on at Orinda before his brother had precipitately taken Miss Dayne away from him.

And there was no reason to suppose he couldn't use that knowledge to his advantage now that he was back on Bonneterre and fighting for his life.

Everything was a matter of degree. He had no qualms about upsetting his mother by his return; it was easy to act as if nothing had happened before he left. It was the way of things: one pretended not to remember things that were uppermost in one's mind.

Olivia would never forget—and neither would he, because he

would never have come to this pass if his brother had not returned, and in all probability he would have married Miss Dayne properly and legitimately and Harry would have dumped all kinds of money into his hands to maintain Bonneterre—and *him*.

And who could have known that the prim and proper Dayne Templeton would have such a flair for erotic and lewd little games?

It was the only thing he regretted—that he hadn't known and he hadn't taken her offer when she had made it.

He could have shown her delightfully nasty little games, all kinds of games that he especially liked to play.

He thought, as he watched her approach the next morning, that maybe—just maybe—it wasn't too late; there was no one safer or more needy than a married woman who loved to play the wanton.

It was a matter of handling it right, without recriminations or blame, without telegraphing his own violent need to settle his monetary affairs, and covertly, without his brother's knowledge.

After all, who had been the first to breach her virgin mouth? And the first to touch her virgin body?

He had some rights after all. And he could be an excellent actor when he wanted to be: he had been acting all of his life.

He watched appreciatively as she saw him, paused as if she would turn in a different direction, and then exert her usual good manners to confront him head on.

"Good morning, Clay." Her voice was subdued, even reserved as she came close to him. "A hot morning, wouldn't you say?"

"No hotter than most," he said, shrugging. "As hot as the secret of the night, perhaps," he added pleasantly, noting with pleasure that his little jab found its mark as her eyes darkened and she hesitated again.

"Please join me. My mother seems to be indisposed today."

And of course he made it impossible for her to refuse. She sat down tentatively in the chair opposite him, looking around her as if she had never seen the dining room gallery before.

Or else looking everywhere but at him.

"Well . . ." she said helplessly because she didn't have a single word to say to him and she thought it was out of bounds of all good taste that he should show up here after he had been beaten out of both his inheritance and his prospective bride.

"Exactly," he said practically. "Look, Dayne, let's not try to pretend things didn't happen. I don't want my presence here to make you uncomfortable. I'm not holding any grudges. I don't say I don't wish things had been different, but you know me—all my life circumstances of one sort or another have dogged me and I've always landed on my feet. Who am I to quarrel with Harry's reasons for wanting to marry you off, or my brother's reasons for interfering?"

He had her attention, in the most oblique way; he could see she was listening by the alert tilt of her head, but she still wasn't looking at him—still didn't want to look at him—because . . . because why? She couldn't bear to remember all that had been between them?

He hoped so. God, did he hope so: it was such a deliciously wicked thought, especially now that he knew what she was capable of.

And didn't he harbor even more ill-will against his brother because of it?

But Miss Dayne wasn't biting—or perhaps she was thinking— the silence between them became protracted, as if she were fighting not to ask the obvious question.

But her curiosity would win out—he was a betting man—he was sure of it.

"What do you mean, your brother's reasons for interfering?" she said reluctantly.

"Why do you suppose?" he asked, his tone offhanded, almost disinterested.

She retreated again, not wanting to answer, really wanting to say *because he couldn't bear to have another man touch his Jezebel,* but how could she say that to Clay when she didn't want to know whether it were true or not.

It was true for her, and that was all she needed to know— Or was it?

It was so easy to forget about hateful Harry in the throes of her own unbridled passion.

So of course there was more—there had to be more . . .

She didn't want to know it . . .

"I don't suppose you know what happened that day, do you?" Clay continued, his tone now almost kindly, paternal.

"I don't have to know," she said sharply. "The result would have been the same—Harry wanted me out of the way."

Clay ignored her. "We had signed all the papers and the minister was preparing the registry and in he marches, Mr. High-and-Mighty Rutledge the First, and he takes every last paper and rips it to shreds—shreds, I tell you, so that nothing can be validated and everything has to be done all over again. And he hauls me outside and he tells me quite plainly that he will kill me if I go through with this marriage, and then he gives me the thrashing of my life—never in all my years have I experienced such humiliation—and when your father tries to come to my rescue, he takes him on as well.

"And when he is done, and we are beaten, our manhood crushed under his boots, he dictates the terms of our surrender: he has a valid license, the minister will change the papers, there will be no monetary settlement, damn his eyes, and he will have sole control and management of Bonneterre just as before and your father will have no shared interest in it whatsoever; he will require no cash infusion and no indebtedness to Harry.

"There isn't much your father can do or say: my brother is handily removing you from his home and needs no incentive—which is exactly what Harry wants anyway—"

"Well there—" she interrupted testily. "Isn't that enough? And what can you be insinuating?"

"And Harry will have no control over anything," Clay continued as if she hadn't spoken. "But that isn't like your father—is it, Dayne—to make that kind of bargain and not get something for himself in return?"

She hated him then, just hated his smug smile and cocky words, hated him for walking back onto Bonneterre and dirtying up the circumstances of her wedding still more.

He had the power now—he could see he was upsetting her and he was reveling in it. He hadn't changed one bit and she couldn't imagine she had ever wanted him.

She had to get control; she stood up abruptly. "You haven't

heard a word I said, Clay. Listen hard: I really don't want to know what you're implying. You can keep your nasty little innuendos to yourself. I'm not going to help you and I'm not going to see you any more than I can help it."

She shoved her chair into the table in an angry violent little movement.

"Tell you what, Clay—you must have had some contract with my father. Maybe there was a dissolution clause. Maybe you can get him to pay a penalty and that would solve all your problems."

"Bitch," he said pleasantly, covering his anger. Damn and damn—he almost had her—almost . . . she was just a little too smart—smart-assed and smart-mouthed.

But he wasn't done with her yet.

He watched her sashay into the house—Mistress of Bonneterre, he thought. How well the role suited her, in all of its guises.

So he had come after her . . .

The mistress in her was pleased, insolently sure of her power, aroused even by the thought of his taking what he wanted just as he had taken her on his terms all week long.

She didn't want to think about it any more than that. He had come for her—she had bent him to her will—and she had not been helpless, in spite of Harry and his unholy lust for Nyreen.

She wanted Flint, right there, right then, but he had gone up to supervise the work crew chopping and carting wood to the sugarhouse.

And there was nowhere to go to escape the insidious presence of Clay except to her room where, that morning, for the first time in a week, she had had to put on clothes.

He had dressed her—kneeling naked before her to slide on her white silk stockings as she caressed his unruly manhood with her one bare foot, Jezebel to the core, exposed and moist and wanting him.

On the chair that morning, he had taken her, with her naked body canted slightly upward, her stockinged legs wrapped firmly around his hips, and him kneeling in obeisance to her lush sex— it had been perfect, perfect . . .

God, she wished Clay had never come!

She shouldn't have talked to him; she should not have allowed him to plant doubts in her.

Flint had come for her—wrested possession of her away from *them,* and saved her from a life of unending misery with Clay.

It was enough . . .

She raced up the steps.

It was more than enough . . .

She threw open the hallway door to her room and stopped short.

He was standing by the window, naked, waiting for her.

"Close the door, Jezebel," he commanded harshly, and she shut it behind her with a definitive slam, her insolent gaze raking over his naked body. "Get over here."

She got—walking slowly and deliberately undulating her hips until she was directly in front of him, an erection's width away.

"I can't stand to see you talking to another man."

"Your brother has nothing I want."

"Show me."

"How can I—I've got on all these clothes." She was so sure of her power.

He reached out and ripped open her bodice and pulled until the entire front of her dress tore apart. "Now you don't," he said, pulling the fragile material away from her body and leaving her standing before him wearing only her stockings and kid boots.

She moved forward a step and straddled his erection so that he was cradled between her thighs and against the lush secrets of her feminine hair.

"Now I have you," she murmured, brushing her stiff nipples against his chest. "What are you going to do about it?"

"I'm going to make you beg for me."

She arched her back and shimmied her nipples against him so that his rough hair excited the tender tips.

"Why don't you do it then," she whispered, reaching behind her to grasp the firm ridged tip of him. "Or maybe I'll make you beg for me . . ."

But as they taunted and teased each other, she felt as if there were a thread of desperation running through their frenzied drive

to completion—as if there really were a serpent in their garden—
and his name was Clay.

So late at night—it was sultry, steaming, with no moon in
sight, only the dank heat of the bayou that soaked into the bones.

He had forgotten; it was so easy to forget things in New
Orleans—there were so many ways to dull the memories and
such a sense of unreality once he was away from the humid heat
and the mossy tendrils that could choke a man.

A man didn't need to be bound up with the land. A man
needed to be able to do anything he wanted to do, and to have all
the women he could handle—then a man was free.

Except if a man was dead—as he would be, if he couldn't
come up with duVallet's money.

It was a conundrum: how did a man pay a debt with money he
didn't have?

Why, with his word of honor and his family name; he was
Clay Rutledge and his word and his family name ought to have
been enough.

With anyone else it would have been. Not duVallet, the ring-
master of the New Orleans circus that dealt in gambling, drinking, and prostitution.

If he had been smart, he would have joined duVallet years ago—
but a Rutledge couldn't get his elegant fingers dirty. And besides,
there had been more interesting temptations at Bonneterre, and
they had cost him nothing.

Up to a point.

God, the worst thing about being back on Bonneterre were the
memories and the recriminating eyes of that uppity major domo,
Tull.

His mother hadn't come down to speak with him, either. And
Mistress Dayne had avoided him all day and his brother had been
out somewhere in the field getting sweaty and dirtying his hands.

But at least he'd had the chance to plant his nasty little notion
in the fertile field of Miss Dayne Templeton's mind.

One success to be chalked up on his side.

He lit a cigar, one of the many of his indulgences he brought with him from New Orleans, liking the little glow on the end of it—a beacon to lady luck, inviting her to hone in on him.

And it was so peaceful here on the lower gallery of Bonneterre where he sat.

For the first time in weeks, he could relax, knowing there would not be a knock on the door signifying duVallet was after him once again.

A man needed some time to relax from his troubles, and a man needed a good cigar and maybe that was all he could hope for before duVallet finally caught up with him.

He stubbed out his cigar and tossed it over the railing of the gallery.

The air was so still, it felt as if there were secrets everywhere.

"Mistuh Clay—"

A soft voice, a secret, wafting out of the silence, darkness cloaking darkness.

"Mistuh Clay—"

"I hear you," he whispered.

"How come you ain't come to see me, Mist' Clay?"

"Meline—damn it—you know I just got back."

"I knows you got big trouble, Mist' Clay and dat we done talked 'bout gettin' some powuh—but you ain't interested 'cause you ain't been to see me to . . . talk—"

Shit—he moved into the shadows, toward the voice. God, she must be big as a house by now and looking to get him crazy—just as she always had done.

Shit—he should have let his father have her; she had caused no end of goddamned trouble and she wasn't about to stop.

"Shhh—Meline—shhhh . . ."

" 'Member my secret, Mistuh Clay?"

He wracked his brain trying to think what she could be talking about.

"Fo' you lef' las' time, Mistuh Clay, we done talked 'bout whut my mama done tole me—y'all get some smarts in N'Awlins, Mistuh Clay? You ready to take some powuh in yo' hands and make somethin' wif it—fo' yo'self and fo' Meline? Y'all come find Meline when you ready, Mistuh Clay—I c'n see you ain't never given no thought to whut Meline got to say . . ."

And she was gone—drifting into the black night like a wraith—leaving him grasping at the implications that sounded familiar, so familiar . . .

A secret . . . power—uppity house servant—hadn't she importuned him in exactly the same way minutes before he had left New Orleans . . .

Something about her mother . . . ?

Whut my mama done tole me . . .

He could almost hear her mouthing the words as he brushed her away and cursed himself for being a fool because his first thought had been *the jewels*.

The story on which Olivia had weaned them. Missing jewels, taken from her by Celie, given to Harry Templeton in the hopes Harry would take her up North to freedom.

And Olivia's wholehearted belief that the canny Celie had saved a stash for herself just in case Harry hadn't lived up to his promises.

And when he abandoned her and came home with his Creole bride, she had hidden the jewels and passed on the secret to one person—Miss Queen Meline, her daughter, seducer of Olivia's husband and her son, catalyst for murder—

By God, the little bitch owed them the truth—even if it turned out the jewels did not exist and Harry had gotten them all.

But what . . . oh, delectable thought . . . what if they still did?

What if there were one little diamond left from one little ring that Harry might have overlooked or that Celie had saved for herself?

What if there were *more* . . . ?

Did he dare believe . . . ?

Did he even dare pursue Meline once again to find out the truth?

Was it desperation—or lady luck tipping the scales in his favor once again?

He didn't know . . . he didn't know—but he was very willing to grasp at every last possibility . . .

Nyreen could not sleep. It had been a day, two, three, since Harry's altercation with Peter, and every day Peter left Montelette in the morning and returned at night and she could not stand not seeing him all those many hours.

She *needed* to see him.

She needed *him*.

Nevertheless, she welcomed Harry to her bed like the good courtesan that she was, and she moaned and groaned as he pummeled his weight against her and murmured his need and his desire for her.

What more could someone like her want? She had done it—she had enslaved Harry Templeton and brought him to the point of marrying her by her sheer animal sexuality.

Except no one told her about Peter.

God, Peter . . .

She thought she would die if she didn't have Peter—she had to keep him on Montelette, she just had to. And she had to get rid of Harry somehow—

But her mind wouldn't proceed any further than that because there was no way to get rid of Harry short of killing him.

She just could not bear to think about that. She wanted Peter and the days were ticking away too fast, and soon he would be gone.

Harry was snoring, in a deep sleep of depletion because she had made sure that he would be exhausted by the time he was finished with her.

She touched him. He did not stir.

She swung her long legs out of bed, and reached first for her silk robe, which she draped loosely around her shoulders, then for a candlestick before stealthily sneaking out of the room.

Down the hall now—not even thinking about what she was going to do, but acting on pure animal instinct—carefully lighting the candle, compelled by her need of him and the scent of him locked deep in her memory—she made her way to Peter's bedroom.

The door—a formidable obstacle.

She reached out a trembling hand and tried the knob.

Unlocked.

She smiled a cat-smile of triumph. He thought he was so alone, so isolated from everyone else—

She edged her way into the room.

She would look—she had just come to look . . .

He was sprawled out sideways on the walnut-framed bed, his arms and bare legs going every which way, a sheet wrapped around his torso.

Her breath caught. If his legs were bare—and his hairy, hairy chest—what of the rest of him . . . *what*—?

She shielded the light as she walked around the bed.

God, he was beautiful, just beautiful, his body more muscular than she could have imagined under all those impossible clothes.

She had to see him.

She felt her body shiver with a tingling excitement and she set down the candle carefully so it gave off indirect light.

Then she let the sleeves of her robe slip from her shoulders as she approached the bed.

She had never been more excited about a man in her life.

She kneeled on the bed and pulled the sheet gently, patiently, loving the streaming, screaming need in her to see him, to have him, loving each little impediment to her achieving it because it increased her lust to have him.

The sheet came away in her hands—and he was all there, as thick and thrusting and rigid as a piston.

Her throat felt tight with tension. It was as if he had been waiting for her.

As if he had been secretly wanting her. As if he were dreaming of his ultimate possession of her.

She prodded him lightly to make him turn onto his back.

Perfect—she felt as if she could just devour him—she ran her fingers lightly down his furred chest to his male root . . .

Iron . . .

She climbed carefully onto the bed and straddled him.

God, he was a sound sleeper—

All the easier to place herself exactly where she wanted to be—at the probing tip of his tumescence—

She was wet enough for both of them; slowly she lowered herself downward and downward, loving the slick slide of his lusty staff as it came deeper and deeper within her.

She felt him spurt—and then he woke up with a start.

"—What the goddamned hell—?"

She leaned over and savagely took his mouth—and almost died from the sheer pleasure of the feel of his firm lips and the dry, hot wet of his tongue.

"Don't move—" she breathed against his mouth. "You don't have to do anything . . ."

"Damned right—you whore—get the hell off of me—!"

"Oh, I think not, lover . . . I think you like me here just fine . . ." she purred, and captured his mouth once again.

She was a goddamned tiger, pushing him and pulling him, pumping him and devouring him until he couldn't stop, didn't want to stop, needed her turbulent possession of him—just like that—churning, tumultuous, insatiable, ravenous—a thousand words, a thundering waterfall of sensation and him, drowning, drowning under her expert and ferocious possession.

"I know you want me," she whispered, pulling brazenly at his lower lip. "You've been looking at me, lover, and remembering my naked body underneath another man, and wondering how it would feel, knowing you could make it better—couldn't you, lover?"

"Bitch—trollop—whore . . ."

"I love you, too, lover," she cooed and delved into his mouth once again.

And then the ending came—the whirling, swirling gathering of his power and his might for the one great thrust of pleasure deep into her wanton soul.

"Nice, lover," she murmured, still riding him, stroking him, playing with him.

More than nice, more than anything—ever—for her . . .

"So virile," she whispered, "so powerful . . ." *Iron*—ramming into her pulsating core.

"Bitch—" but there was no heat behind it, none at all.

"You can't leave me now," she murmured, sliding expertly away from his still-heated possession of her.

She walked to the door, bending to pick up her silk robe and to give him a good view of her rounded buttocks.

She slipped her arms into the robe and turned to him to show him her provocative body, half clothed, half naked, and that which was revealed was exactly what he wanted to see: her ripe taut, tilted breasts and the bushy triangle that hid all of her feminine secrets.

"I'll be back tomorrow night, lover. You'd better be waiting."

Olivia had not given one single thought as to how Clay would fit into the newly knit fabric of Bonneterre.

It almost looked as if he expected to eat and sleep and laze around and nothing more.

And she thought it was unconscionable, but she didn't know what to do about it. Avoiding him didn't work, either, because she was so consumed with curiosity about what he was doing she could barely stand it.

So when she came down to dinner the next night, and everyone was forced to linger, to Flint's intense displeasure, she knew that preserving appearances didn't solve anything.

She had nothing, not her sons, not her husband, not even the grieving of his death in a way that could comfort her.

She had a wastrel son and a competent one and somehow one had gotten himself married to the intended of the other, and Clay was still in trouble and Flint was as distant as ever and deliberately immured with his bride, and she didn't know what she could do to stem her feeling of helplessness.

The only thing that conferred power was money. If she had money, she could travel, she could hire workers for Bonneterre, she could control her sons—both of them.

But everything was gone except the house, the harvest and useless Orinda, and whether Flint could save any of it was debatable.

She wasn't sure she had that much faith in anything—except the existence of her jewels.

She had lived on that fable forever, surreptitiously searching every inch of Bonneterre for one little sparkle, one little ring that could save her and her son from the ignominy of poverty.

But she hadn't known then that it was Clay who was impoverished.

Still, she hadn't stopped searching, not even till this day—late at night, early in the morning, even dirtying her hands by sneaking down and rooting among Meline's possessions, going over and over the same ground she had searched for the last twenty years, hoping against hope to see—this time—the one thing she had missed all those other times.

"Meline . . . pssst—Meline—"

She came creeping out of her cabin, her body trembling at the success of her attempt to lure him.

"Well, lookit here," she murmured, "here come Mistuh Clay finally cottonin' on to whut I been sayin' and wantin' to know de secrets. Well, well, well—"

"Meline—damn it—"

Oh, the anger in the master's voice—she knew all about the anger and where it got her. Master Clay wasn't going to be doing any sweet talking tonight. Master Clay wanted what he wanted—but then—so did she.

And she was a lot more hard-headed than her mama. "Shhh—Mistuh Clay, shhhhh. Ain't no used t' gettin' riled—I ain't so stupid like mama—I want my freedom papers fo' I tell you somethin' . . . 'cause I got de secret and you need to get de powuh. You give me my powuh, and den you has it, too. Don't hafta come wif me; don't hafta do nuthin'—just get dem papers, and I give you de secret and I be gone—whut you say to dat, Mistuh Clay?"

"You want papers?" he whispered in disbelief.

"I want *de* papers, ones dat get me an' de chile no'th to freedom, Mistuh Clay—and den we talk. Think you kin do dat, Mistuh Clay—fo' all dem jewels whut my mama tole me where to look?"

God, it was like she knew his inmost weaknesses—maybe she did, because the parentage of the child was still a question to be determined. Him or his father. One or the other and the whole of St. Foy was just aching to know.

How hard would it be then to get her some papers and sneak her and her stomach off of Bonneterre and out of his life forever?

One little trip to New Orleans would take care of it—an investment in his future with which he could solve every last one of his problems—even though he had to sneak back into town to accomplish it.

"You'll get your papers," he said grudgingly. "Now you have to give something."

"I give enuf, Mistuh Clay—I give you my mama tole me where and whut and I been knowin' all dis time and cain't do nuthin' 'bout it. Now I can, and you gonna help and we both gonna get whut we want."

"Swear to me, Meline—"

"Now why I gonna lie 'bout dat, Mistuh Clay? She done took de jewels just like Miss Olivia said, and she give dem to Mistuh Harry—except she kep' a bunch just fo' herself supposin' Mistuh Harry be lyin'. And wasn't he just? Ain't nuthin' you don' know anyhow."

He was thinking the same thing. The story was so like what Olivia had imagined, he could almost envision Meline eavesdropping on one of her many tellings of it and embroidering it to suit her purposes.

But a desperate man had to believe in desperate measures. A secret long-lost treasure trove of jewels was his only hope now.

He wheeled away from her without answering and disappeared into the night.

Peter didn't say one word to her as he walked out the door the following morning, and Nyreen felt fit to kill.

As if it were nothing—as if she were nothing!

Or she was exactly what he had named her . . .

She bit her lip in anger as she watched him ride off, knowing he would be gone all day, aware that Harry was hovering somewhere in the house waiting for the moment he could be alone with her.

She couldn't believe Peter could just walk out and leave her with Harry—Harry with his expectations and his old man's hunger for her nubile young body . . .

Damn it, damn it, damn it—mother darling, I just know you never foresaw this complication when we hatched this plan. Now what do I do? What? What?

But she knew what she was going to do: she was going to humor Harry, she was going to strip for him and spread her legs for him, and all the while keep her mind on Peter and what was to come tonight.

Flint had sent her to their room as if she were a child, and Dayne felt resentful that he had even chastised her.

"You owe no duty to my mother," he told her furiously. "Your only duty is to me—when dinner is done, my obedient wife excuses herself immediately and goes upstairs to strip off her clothes and wait for me."

"Oh? You don't excuse yourself and come upstairs immediately and strip off your clothes and wait for me?" she retorted insolently.

He hadn't answered that one; he had just turned on his heel and walked away—and fully expected her to comply with his demands.

And so she had done it—gone submissively upstairs to their room and taken off her clothes—and then, damn him, he had made her wait for him.

She could not decide whether he was being cruel or clever.

The waiting was torturous after a day without his caresses; her body felt like a quivering bowstring, at a fever pitch to be touched, streaming with the need to be possessed, and yearning to see him naked and taut with wanting her.

She felt her body unfurling like a petal, moist and delicate and ready for him.

But still he did not come and she took her voluptuous yearning to their bed and nurtured it until she fell asleep.

And when he came, he was naked and hard for her and she was not ready for him.

"Oh no, Jezebel—oh no . . ." he breathed, as he climbed into the bed beside her and lay down facing her.

He was full to bursting with his need for her, and he slowly inserted his throbbing manhood into the soft cushion between her thighs, and simultaneously inserted his tongue into her mouth.

It was a possession without possession, without movement and without release—just the sweet treat of feeling his stiff mus-

cular flesh against hers and his hot tongue penetrating the wet recesses of her mouth.

Just that . . . just—

She came slowly awake, stretching her lush body around the
hard heat of him between her thighs, squeezing him and undulating against him before she fully realized that his nakedness was
the iron between her legs and his hot demanding tongue was the
wet heat in her mouth.

Softly she came awake against his tongue, meeting his urgent
penetration of her mouth. Quickly she came awake to the urgency of his need, lifting her leg and bracing it on his hip so he
could achieve full hard complete penetration of her moist haven.

And they lay that way, mouth to mouth, body to body, her hot
juices drenching him with her own need, her mouth eager and hot
with her desire.

He didn't move; he didn't move. There was something about
maintaining that utter stillness that heightened everything.

She could feel the tension in his muscles and the unremitting
throb of his passion.

He filled her both ways, with the hard thrusting heat of his
maleness, and the wet thrusting heat of his tongue.

Her body shuddered at the thought of it, a trickling little
feathering of pleasure taking root in her very vitals.

He didn't move; he didn't move—what strength of will it took
for him not to lunge and plunge to his own drenching release.

She felt the strain of it and the wonder of his willpower; she
felt her body giving to his hot, hard possession of her; without a
stroke, without a movement, he filled her and pleasured her and
she felt it deep down to her feminine core.

And it twinged and the pleasure came in a vast, engulfing
wave that merged her into his skin, into his need.

One movement then, one shimmy of his hips as he thrust and
the wave took him, too, catching him in the undertow and
pulling him deep into sensual oblivion.

It was deep, deep into the night. A kerosene lamp was burning
in a corner of the bedroom and he was wide awake and looking
at her.

She was lying in bed, her arms up over her head so that her body arched forward to display her breasts.

And as always, he was rock hard and ready for her and unmoving in his desire to just look his fill of her.

Revenge was sweet, he thought. He had come to her as an adversary and now he did not know how he could ever let her go.

In this private haven, there was nothing between them; they were as newly made as if they had just been created.

He did not have to think about debts and droughts and overseers and undergrowth; he did not have to consider motives and machinations, or dreams and decisions.

All he needed was Dayne, his mistress, his Jezebel—his own Eve in life.

She was in a state of high tension already, her body stretching in that luxurious inviting way, in response to his ever-stiffening erection.

Now the delicious waiting game would begin again, enhancing the desire, heightening their voluptuous need.

He was sitting reclined in the roomy upholstered chair by the window, his thrusting manhood a tower of granite; she was lying on the bed, stretching and undulating her hips like a sleek cat trying to provoke him and tempt him with the erotic shimmying of her body.

But he wasn't ready to possess her yet. He wanted her to look her fill of his rampaging manhood, to remember the naked feel of him possessing her and pleasuring her.

"Are you hot for me, Jezebel?"

"As hot as you are for me, sugar," she whispered breathlessly. "Come here."

Her body was liquid, molten, slithering slowly and confidently over to where he reclined like a pasha.

She reached out and stroked the underside of his throbbing shaft. "So hard, sugar, so hot," she whispered. "So ready."

"Not ready enough. Not nearly hard enough. Make me ready, Jezebel."

She felt a shiver of anticipation. His glittering eyes caressed her naked body; she felt them like a touch. All she had to do was stand there and let him look until he was ready to explode.

But she wanted his kisses; she wanted his fingers expertly playing with her teasing, taut nipples; she wanted to feel his hot, bare skin on hers.

She wanted him to explode—*now*—and she knew just how to incite him.

She knelt down between his knees as if she were bowing to the focused force of his masculinity, and she arched her back so that the hard pointed tip of one nipple rested on the thick ridged tip of his shaft.

And then she rubbed it against him, moving her shoulders and chest, her eyes never leaving his as they changed into burning coals of desire.

She felt him tense; a tiny drop of his pleasure appeared on the very tip of his shaft; she felt him resisting and she felt him give—explosively as he wrenched himself away from her and pushed her down onto the floor and mounted her.

"You know just how to make me hot, Jezebel," he growled and she spread her legs to welcome his ravishing push into the hot velvet of her. "But that's what a Jezebel does best—"

Her mouth stopped him; her luscious tongue seduced him. She wanted no words, no games, just his wet, hard pumping possession.

Time stopped. His stamina was endless.

She didn't want to come; he didn't want to stop.

She filled his mouth as he filled her body and they rocked and goaded each other with a primitive need to conquer.

And then he slowed his violent thrusting and she could feel his effort to maintain his control.

He shifted, so that she could bear down on him and he began a slow languorous stroking that made her body melt against him in surrender.

Supple and slow, her culmination came, spiraling upward from her lush center and skating downward again to meet with his twisting geyser of completion as his lathered body gave in to its wracking volatile need.

She lay cuddled in his lap, her bottom nestled against his slumbering member as he reclined in the soft cushion of the chair.

He had slept as the lamplight flickered and the steamy, sultry darkness enfolded them in its embrace, and now he was awake again, tormentingly aware of her body pressed against him.

He could not help himself; his hands moved, sliding all over her, feeling her nakedness, freely and gently probing and exploring all of her soft compliant body as he held her.

Softly she awakened to a dawning sensation of voluptuousness as she felt the erotic movement of his hands.

She lifted her lips to him, begging for his kiss. His arm wrapped around her, pulling her tightly to him, and his tongue filled her mouth, drowning her in wet satin.

His hand slid between her legs, seeking her crown of feminine hair, pausing there to stroke and provoke, prolonging the moment he would seek deeper.

She moaned and arched herself against him, writhing tightly against his stiff length and spreading her legs in invitation.

His free hand draped over her shoulder to caress her taut nipple.

He never broke the kiss as he shifted her body so that she was straddling the length of his shaft; her hungry undulating body pressed down on him, begging for his tormenting fingers to find their way home.

She writhed against him, spreading her legs wider, deepening her hot kisses, offering him both hard-rippled breasts.

He kept stroking and kissing her, stretching out the moment of possession, driving her wild with his kisses and caresses.

"Now," she whispered against his lips, breaking the kiss for one fraught moment.

His questing fingers paused in their erotic stroking.

Her body moved frantically against him as she took his mouth in a hard, wet, demanding kiss.

Not another word between them—just the honey of her need and his hard penetration—now—his fingers breached her velvet fold and her body stiffened and then bore down on him, hard, hard.

Her kisses were hard, and she demanded the hard squeeze of his fingers on her nipples; her hands grasped his hard thrusting manhood and she stroked and pumped him for all she was worth.

He couldn't handle her wild tumultuous body; she wanted his fingers deeper and deeper—he was drowning in creamy coral—her hands were sliding all over the hard-ridged tip of him—her nipples stiffened into ripe peaks of pleasure as her body wriggled and writhed seeking his probing fingers even deeper—two of them, three—more—she couldn't get enough, of his fingers, his ravenous kisses, his fondling her nipples, the hard, thrusting heat of him in her frantic hands—

And then he broke the kiss to seek her luscious nipple; his mouth closed around its stiff peak and she moaned as waves of crackling heat enveloped her—flowing onto her hands as his violent climax joined with her own.

Chapter 14

Olivia had had a sleepless night. She had absolutely no doubt that Clay was in trouble and he was looking for both a way to get out and hide out while he tried to cajole some money from her—or from someplace else—and she didn't care to think what that resource might be.

So she was shocked when he announced that he would be going to New Orleans, and more than a little happy that his insidious presence would be removed from the premises for the better part of the day.

But there was no question: he would never have come home to be of help. He never ever had wanted to stick his hands in the soil and pull the growth from the land.

And that was the difference: Flint had been out in the fields every day before this precipitous marriage, helping with the weeding and thrashing of the cane, and digging new drainage ditches and seeing to the cutting of the wood for the boiling up of the harvested cane in the fall.

All the minute spring and summer tasks that Clay had never cared to give a thought to.

So she couldn't worry about Clay; she couldn't do a thing about the money, except the useless futile searching she had been engaged in for the past twenty years.

And now there was the problem of Lydia, her fractious daughter who doted on Clay and was his ally in all things. Lydia was planning to come back to Bonneterre for the few weeks before she was to go back to school.

She had the letter right in her hand as Flint joined her for breakfast and she waved it in his face.

"Lydia is coming home."

"Yes?" He couldn't think about his spoiled little sister whom he hadn't seen since she was a baby.

"Not directly, of course; she'll be spending two weeks with Augusta Rushton at Valloire—almost home, of course. I've written to tell her the news of your marriage, which I know will thrill her, given her feelings about Peter Templeton."

"Of which I am not aware," Flint said dryly, reminding her that she was dealing in specifics of which he could have no knowledge. "Nor do I care to be."

Olivia cleared her throat. "I beg your pardon. She's been in love with Peter Templeton all of her life—unrequited love, of course, which has grown by leaps and bounds into almost an obsession. She has been living for the news of his return from Europe, and though I don't wish to be the first to tell her, she must be made aware that there are changes here."

"What does she do in the normal course of events?"

"The same—school until early summer, then visits with friends in other parishes, and then she goes up to the academy in St. Francisville for one more year come July. But I wouldn't put it past her to come running home when she hears about Peter."

"How have you afforded her schooling up to now?"

"The usual way, of course. She must have finishing, Flint; it's absolutely necessary before she seeks a husband."

But he knew nothing about these feminine necessaries.

And he couldn't care anything about a sister he barely knew.

"Will there be money this year—do you think?" Olivia asked tentatively.

"How can there be when every damn penny is mortgaged against Clay's excesses—?"

Olivia looked away. "Of course—"

"You indulged him outrageously and now you can see the end result: he has no conscience about foisting himself on Bonneterre again—and you know it's because his creditors are after him yet again. But damn it—" Flint stood up abruptly and towered over her so that, for one moment, she shrank back against her chair, "—damn it, I will win and I will wrest a fortune from this soil and none of it will pay for his follies."

He stalked off, and Olivia watched him go with mixed feelings. He who had been the rebel was now her strength; and he who had been her golden child was now the weak link . . .

But if she could redeem herself—and him . . . if what she believed were really true—

Dear Lord, she had to find that cache of jewels—it was now more imperative than ever.

He had been waiting, he had—in spite of all his protestations and all the vile names he had called her, Peter Templeton had been naked in his bed that night when Nyreen came to him again.

She hadn't any doubt; he could no more deny her than any man she had ever wanted.

And she had left him, panting and begging for more as the sun rose, and she had slipped back into her place beside Harry with scarcely a ripple in his deep sleep.

And then she had time to luxuriate in the thought of Peter's firm lathered flesh, and how much she enjoyed sinking down onto him inch by inch in the soft glowing candlelight.

He had the body of a god and the stamina of a goat.

She wanted him forever and now she had to consider what she must do next.

She would do anything to keep him at Montelette.

Anything . . .

She had never ever expected this splendorous sensual side to her compulsory marriage, Dayne thought dreamily. It was almost as if fate had taken a hand to punish her father by mating her with a man who was perfect for her.

Perfect—she touched her swollen lips—she could almost not bear to leave their room, but Flint was long gone, reluctantly headed to duties in the field.

When she came down to the dining room, no one was there.

She ate a perfunctory breakfast, waving away waffles with cane syrup and accepting the biscuits and cafe au lait.

And then it was time to see to the Boy.

She heard him as she entered the stable, and the low, rich tones of someone cajoling him as he moved restively in his stall.

"Miz Rutledge . . ." the voice was respectful, familiar as she came into view—she remembered him from the time she had come seeking Clay.

That had been so long ago it felt like years had passed since.

"Agus, ma'am," he introduced himself.

"How is he today?"

"Needs exercisin', ma'am."

"Then you may saddle him up, Agus, and I'll take him out."

"Yes'm."

The Boy indicated his approval as she patted his nose and fed him a carrot, and wondered again how Peter had spirited him out from under her father's nose and why he hadn't made a return visit since that day.

That day—it had been . . . what? All of two or three days ago?

Time was meaningless when her days were measured by such different parameters.

But it was good to get out. Both she and the Boy needed to get acclimated to Bonneterre.

She veered off toward the sugarhouse and the cane fields, by-passing the track to the slave cabins.

The work of cultivation had only just begun: everywhere field hands were hoeing in and peeling off weeds and dead leaves from the immature plants.

Another gang was beating through the rows, looking for insects—ants, lice, borers—and rats.

Somewhere in their midst, she would find Flint, overseer and master of them all.

Master of her—

Hundreds of acres in spindly, broad-leaved plants, immature now, siphoning off sun and moisture and nutrients from the lime and magnesium-rich soil, a sight she had seen every day of her life at Montelette, taking on new significance here because it was all accomplished by dint of one man's toil and against the enormous odds of his brother's neglect.

Even she knew of the desolation of Bonneterre under Clay's

indifferent stewardship; hadn't he complained of the many incompetent overseers hired and fired in the course of a growing season?

And what had he left but debts and destruction?

No wonder in the end he had become so eager to marry her. What must her father have offered him?

Which begged the question that Clay had only hinted at—what had Flint been paid?

Oh dear God—she hadn't wanted to think about that—not ever. It didn't matter—it couldn't, in the face of their inexorable, mutual seduction.

Clay had said Flint hadn't accepted anything from her father. Nothing. He had come for her; he must have—but that would give Harry nothing in return and she could not believe, as she looked out over the verdant fronds of cane, that there was nothing Harry had wanted when he had coveted Bonneterre all his adult life.

Harry wanted control, Clay had said—and she had refused to listen to the rest.

How could she believe anything he said? He had lost everything in yet another gamble turned bad.

She knew what he was; she had always known—he was danger and risk and rebellion, everything her mother would have wanted her to resist, and the ultimate altar on which Harry would have sacrificed her.

Why *had* Flint stepped in and married her?

She felt dislocated suddenly; she was surrounded by everything she knew and yet she knew nothing.

She had allowed herself to be immured in Flint's sensual, sexual world, a slave to an uncontrollable, voluptuous lust for him.

If he came to her right now and demanded she lay down with him in the cane field, she would do it—she knew it; even the thought of it sparked an uncontrollable reaction in her very vitals.

She would do it—Mistress of Bonneterre—she might never be free, unless she discovered some unpalatable truth.

What could be the truth of why Flint Rutledge had overpowered her father and his brother to willingly join with her for the rest of his life?

How different the story was when one came out of the fog of carnality and into the sunlight of plain hard facts.

It was time to pay her father a visit, time to talk to Peter, and time to see whether all of Harry's vicious little ploys to get rid of her had been rewarded in fact.

And most of all, it was time to find out the truth.

The truth—the truth—what was the truth?

From his mount, perched on that memorable little rise that separated Montelette from the fields of Bonneterre, Flint watched the inexorable march of his workers going about their tasks.

What was the truth? He was born for the land. He hated the system and the line of men in bondage to him whose whole life was devoted to make him richer.

And he would be richer. In the barren and desolated fields he had found gold: ratoons of second growth cane miraculously seeded from the previous season's dried and wasted cut, which had never been cleared.

Bless Clay for squandering his energy on his self-centered pursuits, and curse him for creating a labor force less willing to work because they were so used to his profligate ways.

But Flint had dealt with it—slowly, in between his arrival and his marriage to Dayne, he had instituted incentives, laid away the whip, and worked shoulder to shoulder with his field hands doing the most menial of tasks, from weeding the new growth to scouring away must and rust from the tender stalks.

There were gardens now, behind the slave cabins and planted nearby the kitchen door by Praxine, all let go to waste by Clay's indifference.

And he had plans for the dairy and to breed horses—race horses, from the get of Dayne's Boy . . .

He could see the future stretching beyond the limits of Bonneterre to Orinda, and making it productive again. And beyond Orinda, expanding westward, taking his interests back to Montana—packaging, shipping, and selling cane syrup and molasses, all produced and refined on Bonneterre . . .

It was possible, anything was possible.

He felt like he had the world at his command. He had Bonneterre and he had Dayne and her sweet, savage surrender.

And if Clay got in his way, he would mow him down like a scythe mercilessly cutting cane, and with no remorse whatsoever.

It seemed to Dayne that something should have changed for the week that she had been cloistered at Bonneterre, but in truth everything seemed no different.

She took the track through fields and up the rise where she had first encountered Flint so that no one would see the Mistress of Bonneterre riding like a common worker.

And she entered the fields of Montelette just as the overseer Bastien was shepherding a gang of field hands to a new location on the back forty.

"Miz Dayne." He was courteous as ever, and just a little feral and she had never liked him and did not feel safe within a mile of his presence let alone three feet.

"*Monsieur* Bastien."

The crew stood aside as she passed, the imperious daughter of the house—she could be nothing else, no matter who she married or where she went to live.

Ahead of her about a mile stood Montelette, its roofline cutting into the blue, sun-baked sky, as timeless as a dream.

She snapped the reins and urged the Boy forward at a canter, and pulled up as she approached the outer buildings of Montelette, the sugar mill, the dairy house, the overseer's house, her father's office, the garconniere, and all the tall, thick, beautiful trees that shaded every part of the grounds except the house itself.

There was activity in the dairy house, the stables, and in the vegetable garden and beyond.

Everything moved with precision and efficiency and always had.

In truth, her father had had nothing to do with running Montelette, and he had always spent time running after things to suit himself.

She dismounted near a stand of pecan trees, which Harry had

never harvested, and picked her way over the fallen shells to the house.

It was quiet as death at the house.

She climbed the gallery stairs to the upper level and hesitated a moment before the entry hall door.

It was so hot, so still. If she hadn't seen the servants and field hands at work, she would never have been able to tell there was any life on Montelette.

She pushed open the hallway door and stepped into the house.

It was cool in the hallway, which was buffeted by a surround of rooms—the parlor to her right, a reception room across, a sitting room and bedroom to the back, next to the rear stairwell.

She pushed open the parlor door—"Father?"

No answer. She went to each room successively, calling him, calling Nyreen, and got no answer.

She felt her determination rise; he had to be here—and she was going to find him, no matter what he was doing.

She ran down to the ground floor where there were more bedrooms, a service room, and the dining room.

She found them there, Nyreen lying naked on the long, polished mahogany table, her father bare and burly and brutally pumping his lust into her very willing body.

"Goddamn to hell—!" Harry had finished and wiped himself with the discarded tablecloth before pulling on his trousers and boots and even thinking about going after Dayne.

She hadn't gone very far: she was pacing in a murderous rage around the front lawn, and he felt no different than the day she had burst into his office and caught him with Nyreen.

He felt guilty, as if he had no right to covet and possess the body of such a glorious creature as Nyreen, and one who wanted him every bit as much as he wanted her.

Damn it, a man should not have to feel guilty because he wanted a hot little body writhing under him. And those nipples: those dusky nipples that he had feasted on for hours—

Shit—he was too easily aroused by the voluptuous charms of Nyreen, who was perched mockingly on the table, still naked, with his juices flowing out of her and onto the antique finish of the table.

God, he wanted her again; he could not go out and face his daughter with a bulge in his pants.

"Would you get up and get dressed, damn it."

She reached out a hand and stroked his protuberant bulge. "Darling Harry—you just can't stop. I'm such a lucky woman."

"You're everything I've ever dreamed of," Harry said gruffly.

Nyreen smiled her elusive cat-smile. *Any whore is everything you ever dreamed of, you stupid old man.*

"You're probably right, my darling; I really can't run around naked when your daughter is here." She hopped down from the table and stepped toe to toe with him. "But just think—" she rubbed her nipples against the rough meager hair on his chest, "—I can have the fun of getting undressed for you all over again."

He made a sound deep in his throat as she slipped out of his grasp and disappeared into the service room and up the back staircase.

He touched the wet that stained the dining room table. He could never eat here again without thinking about the taste of her—and he had better stop thinking those lustful thoughts if he wanted to face Dayne with any kind of equanimity.

Still—his erection would not quit, and he could see that she was getting angrier and angrier and he finally tucked himself down, and went out to confront her.

"Well, my dear—"

"Well, dear father—caught in the act again . . ." she said stonily.

"Snooped and spied on, you mean, by a daughter who doesn't know her place and when she's put there, doesn't know enough to stay there."

"Put there? Put there? Don't you mean bought, sold, signed, sealed, and delivered there?"

Harry shrugged. "Whatever. You're not my problem anymore, Dayne, so tell me what the hell you're doing here sticking your nose in places it doesn't belong?"

"I think it's more like you're sticking something in places it doesn't belong," she said snidely. "You haven't stopped; you can't see what a snake she is, and you haven't even married her."

"That will come," Harry said stiffly. "Is that what you wanted to know? I'm going to marry her. And I promise I won't ask you to be the maid of honor."

"How nice of you to spare me when you had no compunction about it at my mockery of a wedding." She whirled on him. "Nor did you have any conscience about bribing Clay Rutledge to marry me—so tell me, father—what did you barter with Flint to get him to consummate the deal?"

She felt him pulling back; the air between them changed and became charged with something indefinable, and something that told her that her instinct was right.

"Well—"

"He was going to marry you, no matter what."

"You were desperate at that point, if he had beaten up Clay and was ready to take you on."

"Well," Harry said, shrugging. "You know that much already—there wasn't anything he wanted from me."

"Something you wanted from him then?"

He snorted. "I'm related to Bonneterre through the marriage; what more could I want?"

"More than relativity, Father—even I know that . . ."

"But I wasn't in any position of strength, my dear daughter. I wanted you married and off of Montelette, and I must say, he has not made good on his promise to keep you away."

She shook her head; it sounded right—Harry was desperate, Clay was out of contention, and Flint was determined, so he had taken her with no bargains or barters attached—simple—just what she would have wanted . . . and what she had hoped to hear.

And then her attention pricked up as she caught the meaning of what he had said. "What do you mean—his promise?"

"This is ridiculous, young lady; if you want to know the terms—go ask him."

"I'm asking you. There *are* terms then—he didn't just marry me out of hand; he's not a white knight, is he—Father? Or is it that no man is pure? What were the terms, Father? What did *he* demand in order to go through with the ceremony?"

Harry turned away from her. "Montelette."

"*What?*"

"Oh, your husband is not a selfish man, Dayne; in fact, he's eminently fair. I made out the will right there, and the good minister witnessed it—two copies of it, since your husband wouldn't trust me not to alter it. It's irrevocable: Montelette is to be equally divided between you and Peter on my death."

"What?! What sense does that make? That doesn't give him Montelette."

Harry looked at her for a long moment, and she saw defeat in his eyes, in his posture. "It gives him all he wants and needs—it brings Montelette back to his family. And I never meant to tell you that. Never."

She felt stricken, consumed by things she knew nothing about. There was a reason—there had to be.

"Why?" she whispered. "Why?"

"He believed a stupid old story that Olivia told him about how I got the money to buy Montelette. And I tell you now, Dayne, it's not true and it never happened. Now you get off of Montelette, and you go ask that bastard husband of yours just what Olivia's pretty little story is."

She moved her mouth to make some kind of retort but no words came out. So many thoughts tumbled through her mind, not the least of which was that Nyreen was utterly cut out of a widow's portion, if he married her and if she survived him.

"I will," she said finally, clamping down on her anger at all the betrayals. "I will."

Flint had come all right—to collect her legacy and tote it up in the column to Bonneterre's assets.

She wouldn't forget that—she wouldn't.

And now she could walk away from her father with no remorse whatsoever. He was a stupid, foolish old man who had betrayed her mother and his daughter for the taut young body of a whore.

She wouldn't forgive him for that—ever—or for selling her to Flint for his own little pound of flesh.

Nyreen was consumed by a pounding, killing rage. She lurked behind one of the thick columns just outside the dining room, listening, listening, wrapped like a wraith in a tablecloth, and hearing all her plans destroyed in the space of a minute.

All the planning and finagling, from the moment she and her mother had met Harry's feckless brother and decided he was an easy mark and an entree to better things because of his wealthy Southern brother, until they had come east to deliver her to Montelette, her sole purpose had been to reinvent herself as a young innocent who could seduce and lure Harry into marriage and provide her—and her mother—with a comfortable inheritance.

How many years? Two years, three?

She felt a heaving nausea at the wasted time and all the hours she had put into enticing Harry and letting Harry take his little liberties and teach her—*teach* her? Ha!—the ways of a woman, ways she had known from her childhood when she had been sold for a night to a party of gentlemen who preferred their virgins young, prepubescent young.

There wasn't anything Harry could teach *her;* she had been looking forward to educating him—long after the ink on the church registry was dry.

She felt like throwing something.

But she couldn't give in to emotions. When one depended on luck to run one's life, one had to be adaptable and ready to turn on a dime when circumstances defeated the purpose.

She had always played her hand like that, and her time at Montelette had been the longest she had spent anywhere in her whole life.

And now it was time to retrench.

She edged away from the column and slipped into the shadows of the lower hallway and the rear stair.

She was a quarter of the way up, on the little landing at the curve of the stairwell, when she heard the noisy stomp of boots behind her, and then Peter Templeton appeared—and stopped short, his expression reflecting his contempt.

She had taught him nothing, she thought irritatedly, and he had just taught her something: there was always a way—and he didn't know it yet but he was going to be it.

"Hello lover," she purred, as she surreptitiously worked the tablecloth free and let it slip to her feet.

She met his eyes with her cool cat-smile and then her gaze swept downward between his legs and her smile deepened.

She moved down a step, two, until she was just above him and could brush him with her body and look him in the gorgeous stormy blue of his eyes.

"Why don't we just take advantage of this moment," she murmured, slanting her mouth over his and sliding one hand down to work his erection free.

She didn't even let him revile her. She captured his mouth and took him expertly in her hand in the space of a breath, and she positioned him and mounted him by pushing him against the wall and slipping one leg around his hips.

"I just love how you say hello," she whispered, when he was fully sheathed and she was wound around him like a cobra.

"You vile bitch," he growled. "Whore. Slut. Harlot . . ."

"Does it make you feel good, lover?" she purred, beginning her own movement by pushing her foot against the cold wall. "Call me what you want—you are hot for me and I like variety . . ."

"Variety hell—" he snarled. "You probably just came from my rutty old father—"

"How right you are, lover—on the dining room table—a regular feast—"

He made a sound like a wounded animal deep in his throat, and he turned violently so that her back was against the wall and he could ram and jam himself into her to block out the picture of that lustful old boar tasting her and poking her into submission two rooms down the hall.

She pressed herself against him, and gave herself to his young feverish flesh. He was good, he was hot, he was a yard hard with no sign of stopping.

Gorgeous young flesh—hers for the taking if she handled it in just the right way . . .

What an unexpected bonus that Flint Rutledge had interfered; she almost felt like offering him a reward.

The thought of him pumping his lust into her willing body

made her gasp with pleasure; two gorgeous men, on tenterhooks for her—she would manipulate them into it—somehow; she was just the bitch to do it.

She groaned as Peter heaved one last time and spent his angry seed deep within her core.

Chapter 15

She had never, ever been in control of anything. Not her life, not her fate, not her seduction of Flint Rutledge—*nothing*...
Ever.

She whirled away from her father in a fury. *Let him die, let him die tomorrow—I will never, ever set foot on Montelette again*...

She couldn't wait to get away—she raced the Boy down the track and into the fields, thundering past the workers, past row upon row of stalks with their overhanging green fronds brushing her hair, her shoulders, her tears as the Boy took his head and galloped away from Montelette forever.

And she didn't stop until she reached the dividing rise between the fields where she blindly pulled him into a jerking, panting halt and slid off his back into a sobbing and incoherent form at his feet.

It wasn't fair—it just wasn't fair. Her whole life, her whole, whole life, she had had to do what everyone else wanted her to do; she had never had any freedom, ever—even when she had been at her most rebellious—what freedom?

What price?

The price of giving her father *his* freedom—freedom from the sickroom, freedom to pursue his lustful urges—all at her expense—*hers*—

Her life had been upended and no one had cared—and now the end result of her exercise in exerting control had come to its logical and futile end: Flint Rutledge had wanted Montelette all along—and he hadn't wanted *her.*

And she had been his willing dupe.

She felt stupid, gauche—victimized, by both her father and the man she called her husband.

She felt as if her heart would break.

The Boy nudged her.

She had cried herself to sleep, lying on the grassy rise, emptying her soul into the limbo between her two lives, and as she came slowly awake, she felt depleted and spent and she felt as if she could never be filled up again.

She rolled over and bumped into the Boy's front hooves; she mentally shook herself and eased her body into a sitting position.

It was obviously very late afternoon—and it was steaming hot and eerily silent.

She heard not a single sound; there wasn't a breath of air. It was as if she had been reborn into her own little world.

A world in which she could maintain some modicum of control—

A world in which she would make demands and hold people accountable—

A world in which she would not be a sacrificial lamb ever again.

She felt at one, removed from everything, disengaged and unemotional.

She wanted answers and she wanted retribution.

The kind of things a well-bred Louisiana belle did not *demand;* the kind of things best left to a brazen vixen—a Jezebel . . . like herself.

She had packed everything away at Montelette, thinking she was leaving all that behind to marry Clay.

Simple enough to equip herself once again.

She rode the Boy slowly and thoughtfully through the tenderly blooming fields of Bonneterre and around to the stables.

Of course, there would be Agus to contend with, but a Jezebel wouldn't wonder in the least what he would think of her unusual request for some leather. And if he did wonder about it—well, it was none of his business anyway.

She dismounted as she entered the yard, and walked the Boy into the stable.

Agus came immediately to take him from her and she handed over the reins and watched them walk away.

She took a casual look around until they had turned the corner toward the Boy's stall, and then she made her choices from the gear suspended along the doorwall and walked boldly out of the building testing the heft and the crack of the whip she had selected.

It was very nice . . . powerfully nice.

She coiled it up under her arm and snapped the second whip she had taken. That one was a little lighter, a little faster, a little less businesslike.

The lash was supple, flexible . . . perfect for dressing to suit the occasion.

It was time—it was more than time. And the Jezebel in her knew just how to get results.

It was unnaturally still and quiet. No one was around except Tull who was always there, hovering, silent as a ghost, his face impassive, the expression in his eyes impenetrable.

She passed him by with a brief nod and he withdrew as she mounted the steps.

The house felt empty, devoid of any kind of life and she wondered whether it had always been like this and in what kind of barren surroundings Flint had grown up.

And then she stopped herself; that was inviting trouble, to evoke sympathy for the cool and calculating Mr. Flint *I-wouldn't-have-her-on-a-bet* Rutledge who got her by resorting to manipulation and blackmail instead . . .

And who knew whether he had even planned it all along, from the very moment he had first stepped foot on Montelette at Harry's behest—

Oh God—that made it worse—much worse—

She felt her anger boiling up and a scorching need to take some kind of action and get some kind of explanation.

She didn't know how she was going to contain herself until evening when Flint finally returned from the fields.

But she would, she would; she had a host of little Jezebel chores to do, like finding a knife with which to cut the lash on the lightweight whip. And she wanted to bathe and wash away all vestiges of her anguish.

And she wanted to plan very carefully just how she was going to vilify Mr. Flint Rutledge the moment he walked through that door.

He could not, could *not* keep his mind on work and away from the memory of his morning with Dayne.

It was impossible to forget, improbable that he wanted her all over again with a savage need that overrode everything and was utterly outside of his control.

It just *was,* and it crept up on him at odd times, times even when he wasn't thinking of her or their erotic coupling; times when he was thinking about the future, when he was immersed in his dream—the times when he felt her most inside him.

He had come back to Bonneterre for a reckoning and he had found restitution: Bonneterre now belonged to him, and he had gotten reparation for Olivia.

Everything he had hoped, everything he had envisioned, and some things he could never have planned.

Dayne—he could not have predicted her; in his wildest dreams, he could never have imagined her.

And in his life, he never could have conceived he might marry her.

And never let her go . . .

Never.

Go to her now—go . . .

He fought his rampant need, he battled his lust, he clamped down on his unruly manhood—and he lost.

He was at the front door of Bonneterre within five minutes and racing past Tull and up the steps, the thump of his boots echoing oddly in the sultry silence.

Into his room, off with his shirt—the door between their rooms was closed—she was there naked, her body, her sex, her need slumbering in the steaming heat.

Mine . . .

His feeling of possessiveness utterly overwhelmed him.

Mine—forever . . .

He pulled off his clothes, his hunger for her so all-consuming that he was ready to explode before he even saw her.

He threw open the door.

Crack!

The slash of her whip stopped him in his tracks.

"—the hell!"

Crack!

"Don't take another step."

"*Shit*—" He took an experimental step forward—and she snapped the lash within two inches of his thrusting erection.

And she looked like she was enjoying it, too. She looked like the embodiment of Jezebel, decked out in her thrall collar with the ties beneath her breasts that lifted them enticingly and supple strips tied around her wrists; there was one erotically placed around her right thigh, just at the juncture between her legs. And she wore the heeled kid boots—and she looked as if she wanted to grind them right into his face.

Crack! "Not another step, sugar."

"Goddamn—I want my wife—"

"Your wife doesn't feel like coming out to play, sugar. And I would just love to whack off a strip of your hide—so maybe you better tuck your big old plaything away."

"I know just where I want to stuff it, *sugar*—and didn't you make real sure that I couldn't keep my eyes away?"

"Indeed I did," she said insolently, the whip poised in her hand as she watched his mind veer from bewilderment to pure male cunning.

"I want you to look and look and look—" She moved the whip from her shoulder downward to brush her mounded uplifted breasts, grazing one taut nipple, and then purposefully pulling it downward over her flat belly and into the thick bush of her feminine hair so that her thighs supported the handle of it and the lash protruded upward and outward and dangled to the floor. "—you traitorous bastard—because you'll never ever have it again—"

He thought he would just ejaculate right there out of frustration and anger. She was merciless, contemptuous—she meant it, and he had never wanted her more.

He took another step forward. "Why don't you explain that, Jezebel?"

Crack—Her hands were like lightning, caressing the lash one moment and wielding it with ferocity the next.

"You son of a bitch—you know just what I'm talking about. This marriage; your blackmail. This Jezebel is not a piece of chattel to be bartered for a stupid vendetta between your family and mine. Don't move, sugar; I will take you down in a heartbeat and render you useless—which to my mind is exacting payment for your betrayal. Care to settle the debt?"

"I'd like to settle deep in you, Jezebel, and we'll work things out—nice and slow and easy . . ."

Crack!

She caught him that time, a little tingling crick on his thigh—close, deliciously close.

"Oh, I definitely am looking forward to *verbal* intercourse with you, sugar—and we'll get nice and vulgar—just like your reasons for marrying me."

"Goddamnit, Jezebel—"

Crack! The lash pricked him—again just grazing his thigh.

"Tell me," she said silkily, stroking the supple leather, "tell me about Montelette and just how my father got the money to buy it—and what that has to do with Olivia Rutledge. And then maybe I can let things ride . . ."

Shit . . . he rubbed his leg tentatively. Who the hell had gotten to her about his settlement with Harry? And that stupid old story about the legend of the jewels?

Crack! Teasing him against his opposite thigh.

"Harry told me, sugar—he just left out the *painful* details. So if you would be so kind . . . ?"

He met her insolent gaze and girded himself; his erection had not diminished, nor his ravenous excitement to possess her, and the only gratification she wanted was the answer to her questions.

He was willing—very willing, on all counts.

"There's not that much to tell, Jezebel. Olivia believes that when she consented to marry my father, Harry became involved with her personal house servant, a woman named Celie, and convinced her to steal the Flint family jewels. Harry promised he would take her North to freedom, but instead he took the jewelry and he abandoned Celie, and months later, he turned up in St. Foy with the deed to Montelette."

"He could have gotten the money anywhere," Dayne interrupted irritatedly as she impatiently slapped the whip against the side of the nearby bed. "He could have won it gambling. He could have come into an inheritance. He could have—"

"He could have, he could have, he could have—it's more likely he didn't. Celie torched the room to cover up the thefts, and Olivia believes very strongly that she did not give over all of the jewelry to Harry—through some sense of self-preservation . . ."

"Or knowing how all men lie—"

"And that she hid it somewhere on Bonneterre . . ."

A fortune in jewelry—here? Her ears pricked up at that. *If she believed the story—if . . . It was so far-fetched; it meant Harry was every bit as much a thief and liar as she had come to know. It meant her life had been built on a foundation of lies—Harry's wealth, their family's status—and anything he had ever done to augment that meant nothing, absolutely nothing . . .*

"But the prime fact remains that Harry came into a source of a powerful lot of money in very little time, and he chose to settle obscenely close to the woman who had rejected him. You decide his reasons, Jezebel—I believe my mother, and that is why Montelette is back in my family now instead of Bonneterre being hostage to yours."

"This can't be true."

"It is as true as Celie's word—she died soon after; she fell down the steps—but she had a daughter who was told the story, who told it to others . . . it can't be dismissed—and it can't be proven. I had an opportunity to take what was mine—and I took it—"

"You *used* it—you manipulated *me* . . ."

"I think not, Jezebel. You loved every minute of it. And what your father did and how it affected my mother is no business of ours—"

"Except insofar as you can use it as a lever to add another asset to the plus side of Bonneterre's profit column."

"Goddamn, Jezebel—"

Crack! A nerve-wracking skim at his knees.

She wanted to punish him, to make him hurt, to make him feel her anguish and her pain.

"And what am I, sugar? Surplus? Excess? Overage? Gain? Loss?—"

He leapt on her then, before she could lift her arm and wield the whip and he toppled her down on the bed, and pinned her squirming form under him.

"I call this overabundance," he murmured, nuzzling her breasts, his surging body just ramming up against her. "I call this put together, joined and coupled—and nothing in the past or our present can prevent it—it is, Jezebel, and we are . . . Your body doesn't deny it, even if you do."

"My body is stupid and a slave to pleasure," she panted as she writhed beneath the heat and the strength of his body.

Nothing had changed, nothing—she had no power—no power in her hands, no power to resist him. Her power was corrupted—sold for the touch of his hot tongue against her taut nipple, her anguish reduced to an equation which was quantified by his inevitable possession of her.

It could not be—it was too much, even for her and her sticky, hot body liquefying beneath him.

She felt the give of him as he began his earnest seduction of her breasts, and she took the moment—she heaved against him, stunning him so that he rolled off her and she gained purchase to crawl onto her knees across the bed, her whip still in hand.

"It isn't that easy, sugar," she whispered. "You have some culpability here. You weren't some white knight rescuing a damsel in distress—"

"Not hardly," he said dryly, sitting back on his haunches so that his lusty manhood was like a magnet between them.

She reached out the length of the whip and caressed the underside of his shaft. "You got what you wanted, sugar, and yet you expect me to roll over and spread my legs. Isn't that just like a man?"

He grasped the whip and held it tightly. "How do you know what I wanted, *sugar?*"

"What does any man want but land, money, sons, and power?"

"And what did I get, Jezebel?"

"More than you bargained for . . ."

"Isn't that the truth—?" he murmured, tugging at the whip. "And what did you get?"

She gave the whip handle one mighty yank, jerking it out of his hands and back into her power, and then she gave him a long measuring look.

"Betrayal, sugar—out and out betrayal."

The hot sultry night descended like a suffocating woollen blanket.

Nyreen lay in bed next to Harry, her mind far afield from his gropings and mumblings.

"Let's set the wedding date, my darling," he panted, as he fondled her breasts, her belly, and forged his way still lower. "We must set a date, Nyreen. I need to know"—as he penetrated her slick hot velvet core—"you'll always be mine . . ."

She drew in a sharp breath as she parted her legs more fully; his hands were so big—he was so earnest, and every once in a while, hurtful. But then a little pain added a zest to the proceedings—when it was perpetrated by some slick young body instead of Harry.

A date—God, how could she keep her mind on the stupidity of a wedding date when he was upstairs, all hot and lathered with waiting for her?

"Whatever you want, Harry," she muttered, trying to work up some enthusiasm for the old goat without resenting the fact he had literally disowned her before even marrying her.

But her feelings about that had already gotten in the way—everything had just slithered into oblivion with his betrayal and she didn't even have the energy to pretend.

"Harry—it's so hot . . ."

"Ahhhh—Nyreen—"

That importuning voice she hated so much.

"I'm so hot," she pouted, knowing full well he would volunteer to take the burden from her if she would only accommodate him.

"Just—just . . . let me, my darling. Just—let me."

"Oh—all right . . ."

Oh goddamn, damn, damn . . .

He mounted her in a frenzy of need and pumped away for several minutes and then shot his seed and rolled off of her.

"You're so perfect, my darling."

"Go to sleep, Harry . . ."

Tonight has to be the night—I have to get him out of my life soon—now . . .

"The date—?"

"We'll talk tomorrow," Nyreen told him coldly and turned away from him and his possessive hands.

I've got to get away from him—I've got to, got to—

She didn't know how—

Maybe she did—

What if he caught her and Peter together?

No—that was suicidal. . . . He would kill her—he would kill Peter . . .

Only if Peter didn't get to him first—

Thrilling thought . . . did he hate Harry enough, did he despise her enough to kill for her?

She sucked in her breath.

It was an utterly staggering thought.

How? *How?*

She would have to devise a way to get him to follow her—and she would have to be prepared to deal with his rage.

How? *How?*

She didn't care—she just didn't care; whatever she did, she had nothing to lose.

She lay next to his heaving, snoring flaccid form and continued plotting and planning deep into the night.

"Get out of my room!"

She was on her knees, her legs splayed, across the bed from him, slapping the whip against the mattress, readying to flay him with more than words; it was just incomprehensible—her father's chicanery.

And yet look at how ruthlessly he had gone about disencumbering himself of responsibility for her; he would have married her off in a heartbeat to the first taker, and traded off half of Montelette in the process—just to get what he wanted.

What else might he have done thirty or more years before—unknown, impoverished, and rejected out of hand by the wealthy family of Olivia Flint?

"Get out of my room!" Her voice was deadly calm. "I'll kill you if you don't get out in one minute."

She lifted her arm and snapped the lash high in the air. "Weapons *do* confer power, sugar; men have known that for hundreds of years . . ."

She cracked the whip again, this time just to one side of where he crouched opposite her on the bed.

"I don't feel like being sabotaged by sex today, sugar. Move it on out—!" *Crack!*

"Sure," he said sarcastically, leaping off the bed one second before the lash landed where he had been kneeling, "so why are you dressed for it?"

"Because I felt like it, that's why. I don't call this dressed for sex; I call it dressed like *me*—now get *out!*"

He backed out slowly, cautiously—she was in a state and she watched him with those glittering, knowing eyes in the charged silence between them as his nakedness began to seem superfluous and his manhood got tired of waiting and retreated.

She slammed the door behind him, a sound of infinite finality—his wife—

He had come to her in a moment of triumph and got sucked into her rage at his perfidy.

And yet there hadn't been any other way—because Clay would not have been alive to have her.

He threw himself on his bed, naked and soaked with sweat, the heat sticking to him like bolls of cotton, thready and impossible to brush away.

Like his thoughts of Jezebel—naked and wallowing in her pain in her bed in the next room.

* * *

The promise of unbridled pleasure finally pulled her from the bed.

Peter was waiting; she was longing to couple with him.

She shook Harry and shook him; God, he was hard to awaken. She didn't want him fully conscious—just barely, enough so that she could whisper in his ear:

"She's with Peter; she went naked to Peter's room."

He sputtered and shook his head—"Hunhh?"

"Naked to Peter," she whispered again, her lips close to his ear and then she slipped into the hallway, not even bothering to put on a robe.

He was waiting, boiling with equal parts of heat, anger, and need.

"Bitch—get over here . . ."

His naked body was slick and lathered with sweat as he lay sprawled out on his bed in the guttering light of a small, unobtrusive candle.

His strong large hand reached out and grasped her arm as she came to him, and he wrenched her down next to him.

"Did he do it to you tonight?"

"What do you think, lover?"

She climbed over him and spread her legs and let him feel her.

"You whore; you go from bed to bed and you love it."

"You love it," she whispered, brushing her nipples against his chest.

He grasped her hips and pushed her down onto his probing tumescence—and down—he felt it and she felt it—the lush accommodation of her body into her textured heat, made ready by the lunging moistness of his father's seed.

He hated it; he wanted to punish her for giving to the old man. He wanted to devour her whore's body so she would never want anyone else ever again.

"What if he finds us?" she whispered close to his mouth.

"I'd kill him," he grunted in concert with his long, plunging strokes. "I'd bloody kill him. I hate him. I hate you . . ."

"I know it. I know it . . . ahhh, I know it—" And she hadn't miscalculated—he would do it, she had triumphed—she listened for Harry's footstep on the gallery stair.

Harry awakened suddenly, explosively into the seething heat of the early morning.

He could barely make himself move, so lethargic did he feel from the stultifying heat, and his first attempt at trying to turn over ended with him flopping back against the pillows in resignation.

The heat was a block buster; a man just didn't want to challenge it. It was easier to give in to it—it and the simmering sensuality of his own Nyreen.

He reached out his hand—and touched the sheet.

Nyreen!

She was gone—!

His heart started pounding painfully. Where? Why?

To relieve herself—yes . . . of course—the heat made a man crazy—

The naked promise of a woman like Nyreen made a man insane.

She would be back—soon and he would exert his proprietary rights: he needed her *then* and she was his for the taking.

He waited, with patience . . . with fear—and finally with growing anger.

It didn't take a woman that long to relieve herself—

He eased himself up and swung his legs over the bed.

He was naked and throbbing with need. Where the hell was Nyreen? She had promised to be there for him—any way he wanted her.

And she had been—every fantasy that he could have invented, she had been.

And now? In the slithering heat of the night—where was she?

She went to Peter—naked with Peter . . .

The insidious little thought wormed its way into his consciousness.

Naked with Peter. . .

NOOO-O-O-O!

He roared, he beat his chest—he felt his body contracting with a kind of murderous desire—

"Noooo!" The pain suffused his body, his mind, his heart—
"*Nyreen!*"

She was his, wholly promised to him and possessed by him as
if they had already said their vows.

She couldn't . . .

She hadn't—

He had to see . . .

Because she wouldn't be there—she wouldn't betray him like
that.

But still, the little voice whispered evilly in his mind: *naked
with Peter, she went to Peter, naked with Peter . . .* and he howled
with the pain, as he pulled on his pants and foraged for a candle,
and finally, trembling with anger, made his way toward Peter's
room.

It was so dark—

A man could imagine a hundred sounds in the dark. The stillness on the bayou was accompanied by a thousand buzzing insects. The heat hung over him like a thick brocade curtain,
stifling, a wall impeding his every move.

A whishing sound, a huff, a step?

Even he couldn't be sure it wasn't his shadow and his own feet
as he stepped cautiously ahead, down the gallery and on toward
Peter's room.

A click—a hiss . . . a whuffing against the floorboards—

He was almost there, almost . . .

She wouldn't—

He stepped into the room, which was dark as a tomb, and he
held the candle up high over Peter's bed—

And she was there, huddled next to Peter's naked body, her
hand possessively covering his engorged member—brazen, shameless—a harlot and seducer of innocents . . .

He screamed his pain, he roared—

Peter jerked awake and reached under his pillow, but Harry
was already out the door.

He jumped off the bed and raced after him.

A gunshot reverberated in the death-still night and then the
sound of something irrevocable and heavy hitting the ground
below.

Chapter 16

She had to get it straight in her mind—all the permutations that had led to this moment of her lying naked in a bed at Bonneterre plantation, married to the son of the man her father had most despised, while that father prepared to unite himself with his brother's whorish stepdaughter, who was young enough to be his child.

How? *How?*

Slowly she unwrapped the ornaments of Jezebel from her body and laid them aside. Pieces of leather. Power in proximity to skin and in the wielding of a weapon. Supple lengths of leather that belonged in a barn and not a lady's bedroom.

But she was no lady . . . not anymore: she was a pawn in a game that—if she believed her *husband*—had begun years before she was ever born.

When Harry Templeton wanted to take a step up in the world and vied with his nemesis, Verne Rutledge, for the hand of a woman who had something to offer besides her body.

That was perfectly comprehensible: Harry would have been the riskier choice because there was in him the element of the confidence man and perhaps Flint's father had been slower, steadier, kinder—or maybe Olivia herself had been too overbearing, domineering, bitchy, and needed a man she could boss around.

And Harry was hardly that.

So she had accepted Verne Rutledge's proposal—a man, like Harry, with no prospects. But she had been a woman of some means, enough so that her family could provide for the construction and the purchase of the lands adjoining, which became Bonneterre.

This she knew from Harry, from her childhood when he talked so bitterly of Verne Rutledge as his rival and his enemy.

Harry had counted on marrying Olivia and acquiring all the assets her family could provide.

Had he? Would he? Like he counted on marrying Dayne off and "acquiring" Nyreen? As an asset for his aging virility? Or a trophy for *her* covetous greed?

How must he have felt when Olivia turned him down and turned to his hated rival?

Murderous? Betrayed? Vindictive?

Envious that Verne would get everything and he would get *nothing?*

Jealous enough to hatch such an insidious and devious plot to get his hands on that which might have become his to begin with?

Was he that spiteful and malevolent—to use someone as helpless as a servant as a means to attain his ends?

Her heart started pounding painfully.

She could not only imagine it, she could *see* it, almost as if it were a play being performed before her eyes.

Her father and an illiterate slave—him coercing and offering her hope, and she believing because she wanted to that her "mistus" would never bewail the loss of one little diamond . . .

And all because of that, and because Celie might—*might*— have been canny enough not to take her father's words at face value—just because of that, Flint Rutledge had beaten up Clay, blackmailed her desperate father, and taken her as his wife.

And her father said it was a petty little story and it wasn't true—and he challenged her to demand that Flint tell her because he was sure Flint would not.

Dear Flint—more canny and manipulative than Harry ever had been—waiting for his chance, she would wager, from the very moment he had accosted her on the rise, knowing who she was in all probability, and just waiting, waiting, waiting, patient as a lion and as ready to pounce.

And so now Montelette was hers—half hers—when she had

expected the whole to be dumped unceremoniously into Nyreen's naked lap, and she herself was left with a treacherous husband and a legend of missing jewels that her father might or might not have instigated the theft of—and nothing to salvage her pride or her honor.

Lydia arrived the following morning; Olivia saw the dust from the carriage long before it rounded the driveway in front of the house from her early morning seat on the upper gallery where she was drinking a cup of tea.

"Damn," she murmured, setting aside the fragile bone china cup. "Damn."

She stood up and walked to the railing as the carriage ground to a halt in front of the steps.

And there was Lydia, pinch-faced and bone-thin as ever—her fashionable clothes making not one bit of difference in either her appearance or her personality.

Lydia stood up in the carriage and faced her mother's tired, worn, disapproving face for one long moment.

"Mama?" she acknowledged, and then she allowed the driver to help her down, and she waved Agus, who had magically appeared from the stables, over to the boot where her luggage was stored.

By that time, Olivia had managed to get down the stairs and onto the lower verandah.

"Lydia, my dear—" What could she say? Lydia was her daughter, but it was borne upon her again that she did not like her at all.

"It seems like ages since I was here last," Lydia said brightly, "and now Clay is back and my mysterious missing big brother—*how* old was I when he disappeared?"

"Young enough not to remember," Olivia said. *Or suffer,* she thought mordantly. And how she had suffered, and cried.

And now it was like he had never gone and Clay and Lydia were the strangers—and they had been closer to her heart.

"Come—your room is ready, you'll want to freshen up before you meet Flint—and his wife."

Lydia brushed aside her hand. "I don't care about that—I want to see Peter."

Olivia sighed heavily. "My dear—Peter? *Now?*"

"I've waited *years*," Lydia said petulantly. "It's the only reason I came home. I don't care about nasty old Flint and his stupid old wife."

"He married Peter's sister," Olivia said mildly, and she had the gratification of seeing her daughter's thin pursed lips form a stunned, "Ooooh."

Well, she hadn't told her in her letter—and she didn't know why, except perhaps she had maliciously envisioned this moment, which was both hurtful and exciting to Lydia.

It meant she didn't have to sneak around to try to see Peter. It meant all things were possible with Peter.

And it meant her rotten, sneaking, unknown big brother had beaten her to the punch, and she hated him instantly.

"Oh, well—" she said finally, huffily. "That does make a difference, doesn't it? Dayne, am I correct? She and Clay were carrying on something fierce last year. I heard about it from Augusta, of course . . ."

Ah, a little of her own back: Mama didn't know about that—but she knew so little about Clay anyway.

"Where is Clay?"

"I don't know," Olivia admitted warily. "He'll be back—soon. They ran him out of New Orleans, you know, and he really has no place else to go."

"Except the understanding and welcoming arms of his mama," Lydia interposed nastily. "Well—isn't that nice—we're all home together, Mama, for the first time in twenty years."

"Pssstt—Lydia . . . !"

She whirled. "Who's there?"

"Shhh . . ." Clay edged around the corner of the garconniere.

"Oh—brother mine—! Oh, darlin'—Oh Clay—!"

She threw herself into his arms and he held her tightly, yet somewhat gingerly.

"Why are you hiding? Does Mama know you're home?"

"Am I ten years old, for God's sake. Damn—nothing ever changes around here . . ."

"Oh sure it does, brother; for one thing, you aren't running things anymore."

Clay looked at her sharply. He couldn't tell if she were being nasty or sympathetic; her pale gaze gleamed with some feral emotion as though both of them were locked in a secret.

"I *have* to see Peter," she said suddenly, urgently. "I was going to sneak out—Mama thinks I'm upstairs resting . . . resting!—when the most important moment of my life is at hand!"

"Hey, hey—no rush, baby sister," Clay said with just a little malice. Time for payback, absolutely.

"He's probably not going anywhere for a while. Harry's got big plans to marry this sweet young thing who's been living with them, and she is hot to go with whoever's ready to shoot off—hey—don't get upset; I'm sure Peter's as pure as refined sugar when it comes to women, and saving his hankerings all for you."

She wrenched her arm away. "You bastard. You son of a bitch—nothing's changed, *nothing!* You're still as vicious as ever."

"And you'll protect me till you die, sweet one. We love each other too much, don't we?"

"I love Peter. I would die for Peter."

"Peter's not dying for you," Clay pointed out maliciously.

"He hasn't seen me all grown up. And now Harry can't stand in the way—since Dayne married big brother, I mean. There's no more feud. There's nothing to stand in our way."

"There is no *our* way," Clay said cautiously. "Peter Templeton hardly knows you're alive."

"That's not true: remember the time at Valloire, when he pulled me out of the water and made such a fuss over me, and he never cared that Daddy was watching and looked fit to kill? Daddy hated it that Peter was so brave that day and Daddy didn't know how to be. I fell in love with Peter that day, and I know he had some feelings for me.

"I used to see him the same way you used to see Dayne—at church and social events. And he was just as gentlemanly and courteous, with that little gleam in his eye—as if he were trying to

tell me something else, and he couldn't because of Daddy and because of his papa. So I know, Clay Rutledge, and don't you dare
to try tell me different . . ."

"I wouldn't dream of it," Clay said, throwing up his hands.
He knew futility when he saw it. Lydia had been living a murky
romantic dream for these past seven or eight years, and he wasn't
going to be the one to give her the eye-opening dose of reality.

It wouldn't require much—just a polite introduction to the
oozingly sensual Nyreen—he had to smile thinking of it, feeling a
rush of warmth in his groin and a kind of latent anticipation . . .
and he said coaxingly, "Don't barrel on over there, Lydia—I'll
take you, if you really want to go—you know—a neighborly visit,
so you don't appear to be too forward. You know how gentlemen
hate a brazen woman."

"Do you know—I am tired to hell of what *gentlemen* like; it's
always at variance with what they actually *do* and somehow the
brazen women always seem to get the attention. Do you know,
Clay, I learned that lesson this summer at Valloire: ask for what
you want, because if you wait for a gentleman to make an offer,
he'll hand himself over on a silver salver to the 'lady' who gets the
most attention. Well—I want Peter's attention, and I aim to get it.
Now—are you coming or—"

She stopped short as she saw a figure round the corner of the
house, waving at them.

"Damn, it's that nuisance, Sudie May—Mama gave her over
to me for my personal maid and she's been on top of me every
minute—"

"Miz Lydie—Miz Lydie—" the maid panted, slowing to a
walk when Lydia remained where she was, "I been lookin' all
ovuh fo' you—an' dey been lookin' fo' Mistuh Clay, too. Yo'
mama want you down de house—Mistuh Peter from Montelette
done come, and dey is waitin' fo' y'all to come."

They entered the parlor at the very moment Dayne came in
from the hallway; it was like a play, perfectly staged.

There was Peter, by the fireplace, looking exactly as Lydia remembered him, tall and elegant, with his blond hair somewhat
rumpled, and his lean face impassive, waiting—

For her?

And then there was Mama, seated on a small sofa beside the fireplace, her hands betraying her agitation, her expression otherwise calm.

Across the room, by the windows, there was a creature: slender, full of herself, her long hair barely styled into any kind of fashion, her dress the height of elegance and yet with a certain brazen disregard of it—in the neckline, perhaps, or the way it hugged her figure just a little too daringly—

Lydia was green with envy instantly, of the Creature's dress, manner, her sangfroid, her insolent eyes that were fixed on some attraction out the front window that only she could see.

And then there was Dayne Templeton Rutledge—her mind rolled all the syllables around mockingly, angrily; the Templeton who had crossed the line and infiltrated her home and taken her mother's place as Mistress of Bonneterre.

She was dressed simply, in a dark blue dress that reflected the stormy color of her haunted blue eyes. She didn't look elegant— or anything else except breathtakingly beautiful—Peter's counterpart, with all his grace and elegance and a steely reserve all her own.

Dayne glided across the parlor to put her arms around him and kiss him, and Lydia seethed with jealousy that she had the right to touch him, and she, Lydia, did not.

"Peter, dear—"

He put up his hand. "We're waiting for your husband."

"I'm here," Flint said from the hallway, and Lydia looked up curiously as he entered the room.

Big . . . intractable . . . older, so much older than I thought . . . Impressions flicked into her mind like whiplashes—fast, stinging, immutable.

He doesn't look like me, she thought smugly, settling back again. *He looks like a hired hand.*

"Well, now—" Olivia said, "we're all here, and you are looking extremely distressed, Peter. What's wrong? Has something happened?"

Peter looked around at the assemblage, his eyes resting for one speculative moment on Lydia Rutledge, and then focusing on Flint on whose shoulders he was about to shift his burden.

There was no other way to say it but bluntly: "Harry had a fatal accident last night."

Olivia's hands went to her throat; Dayne sank onto the sofa beside her, brushing off Flint's hand.

"How?" she asked, and her voice was steady and unclouded with emotion.

"He was shot at close range. He was on the upper gallery . . ." Peter paused a moment trying to think how to make it sound logical when nothing about it was, "for some reason. We think he was attacked as he was going down or coming up the stairs. We found him at the base of the staircase on the lower gallery, and there was nothing we could do to save him."

"Oh my God," Olivia murmured. "Dear God. Harry—gone—"

A lifetime of hate and plots and vengeance—gone. "Who—?"

Peter shook his head.

"But there was no one else there," Dayne said suddenly, "except you—and Nyreen."

"And the everlasting house servants," Nyreen put in, her soft musky voice cutting like a knife through the shock in the room.

"Oh God, it's true, it's true," Lydia whispered emotionally, undercutting Nyreen, distracting everyone's attention from the Creature. "They were talking about it at Valloire—how the servants at Penellen just rose up and murdered their master and mistress and went on a rampage and burned down the house . . ."

There was a gaping silence.

"Or it may have been a stranger, a marauder who was looking to steal something, and took my father's life instead," Peter said when he had gathered his wits after the reaction to Lydia's little melodrama had subsided.

"It *must* have been a thief—an accident," Olivia said, easing herself upward to go to Peter. "My dear boy—I'm so sorry."

"I've called the minister; we want to lay him out and bury him tomorrow—late in the afternoon, next to mother. Dayne?"

"That will be fine," she said.

"Will you come?"

"I swore I'd never go back," she said fiercely.

"For me?"

She hesitated just for a moment. "Only for you," she whispered. "I'll come—tonight—"

"I'll come, too," Olivia said.

"And I," Lydia put in, eyeing the Creature—wondering about the Creature.

Olivia tugged on the bellpull and Tull appeared.

"Order the carriage, Tull—please. Let me think: we'll need food and drink. Clay—Flint—tomorrow early, we'll need to mark out the gravesite. Agus can help and Junior, and that noxious overseer of Harry's—that should be enough . . ."

She was like a battalion commander rallying her troops, familiar with death and its rituals and letting nothing get in the way of preserving appearances.

No one would say she faltered when her daughter-in-law needed her help. Dayne looked about ready to collapse from the sheer weight of emotion, and her own daughter about ready to crow as she led them down the gallery steps and they piled into the carriages to go to Montelette.

"Well now, Mistuh Clay, whut you got fo' me?"

Clay started as he heard her voice—*that* voice—the voice that would haunt him forever: Meline, taunting him and trying his patience.

He had had moments in New Orleans when he believed her story was nothing but voodoo hocus-pocus—a fairy tale conjured out of nothing to invest Celie with some power when she had lost all hope.

And now Meline dangled it, like a carrot in front of a mule, knowing in desperation, he would do her bidding. And because there was too much between them—a fact that was becoming increasingly obvious every day.

"I have the papers," he said, patting his coat pocket. "And what have you got for me?"

"Aww, Mistuh Clay, now I ain't so gullible as my mama—you know dat; you got somethin' fo' me, I got somethin' fo' you—we be doin' a tradin' of powuh—tonight, Mistuh Clay, fo' Mistuh Harry's hant come get you—you come see Meline tonight."

"Damn it—"

"Oh no, Mistuh Clay—tonight—" she bared her teeth. "I know whut you wanna do, and I be tellin' you—*tonight* you gonna find out de secret and de powuh. In dat same place, Mistuh Clay—I know you didn't never fo'get."

She slipped away like a shadow almost before he could reach out and grab for her.

God, there were ways to handle uppity servants who tried to intimidate you . . . He wished he were certain and sure that Celie's legacy didn't exist.

He would show that Meline—she couldn't push him around like that and get away with it. Just because he had slept with her—just because he had shot his father over who had the right to her . . .

Damn her, damn her—he hoped Harry came back and haunted her. Maybe Harry knew—now—what Celie had done with all the jewels all those many years ago.

"You lookin' peaked, girl," Mama Dessie said as Dayne wandered into her big stone kitchen and aimlessly walked around the room touching things. "They ain't nuthin' you got to do: Miz Olivia and Mistuh Flint done took care of ev'thin', jes' like wif yo' weddin'."

Dayne bit her lip. She had no tears. She felt nothing. She felt like she had been gone for years and it had only been—what?—a day.

"Wasn't no good here, Miz Dayne. I done heard de owls callin' just befo' Mistuh Harry got de sickness—sickness of lust, like dat woman done put a spell. Ain't nuthin' good wif dat woman. Nuthin'," Mama Dessie said emphatically, pushing Dayne over to a chair. "I gonna make some tea fo' you, Miz Dayne. Special tea. You gonna feel bettuh, and Mistuh Harry gonna rest easy now 'cause he don't got to deal wif dat wicked woman."

She put up her kettle, and then dug into a canister for a table-spoonful of spices and herbs.

"I put a spell fo' you, Miz Dayne, give you protection from dat woman . . ." She bustled into her pantry and came out a moment later with what looked like a small primitively made doll and handed it to Dayne.

"I make fo' you. Protection from dat woman. Got asafoetida, got honeysuckle, got garlic, onion, mustard, got parsley an' pepper an' rice an' sage—got a little Spanish moss in dere an' some groun' up turnip—gonna take of you, Miz Dayne. Gonna do."

She took the object tentatively in her hand just as the teakettle emitted an eerie shriek.

She jumped at the sound and dropped the poppet. The thing was chilling, macabre. It couldn't have powers; how could it have powers?

She bent to pick it up.

"Ummm, ummm. Watuh boilin' . . . Good—good." Mama Dessie took the kettle and poured it over the mound of herbs she had heaped in the cup. "Smell dat now, Miz Dayne. Breave dat deep inside yo' soul . . ."

Dayne clutched the doll and bent her face over the steaming infusion and inhaled.

"Got anise an' clove, cinnamon an' honeysuckle. Gonna taste good, make yo' own self be calm, be able to face whut gonna happen. You feel, Miz Dayne? Deep, deep it go—deep into yo' body, into yo' min'. Dat woman cain't touch dere nohow."

She took a second cup and a strainer, and poured the first cup's contents through the strainer.

"Now—fo' you—" She handed the cup to Dayne and bustled about the kitchen again, ordering her helpers as Dayne slowly sipped the tea.

Immediately the warmth spread all throughout her body; she felt calm, centered, less shattered and frenetic.

"Mama Dessie take care of you," the old woman said, patting her shoulder and then squeezing gently so that a different path of warmth rushed through her veins.

Magic, that.

"Cain't leave Montelette nohow—but I been makin' spells, takin' care, Miz Dayne. Don' you fret none, I ain't gonna let dat wicked woman hurt you. I promise, Miz Dayne—I promise . . ."

* * *

She had never been to Montelette, and Lydia prowled the house with an avid curiosity that bordered on rudeness.

Of course she omitted the dining room—Harry's body was laid out there and the door was closed.

And upstairs, Peter and the Creature, Olivia and the minister were discussing arrangements.

She hated the Creature. The Creature was like a witch with mysterious powers who had first leached onto Harry Templeton and now was quite obviously after his son.

Of course, no one else saw it but her.

She wandered upstairs to the parlor once again where Peter was writing out death notices which would be delivered up and down Bayou LaTouque by Magnus, a young slave with energy and intelligence.

"Mama Dessie's taking care of the food; I'll send Praxine and Tull to help in the morning, and we'll measure out the plot tonight, so that will be taken care of as well," Olivia was saying.

"And, of course, Nyreen—we'll want to send word to your mother so that she can come for you."

"Will we?" Nyreen murmured witheringly.

"My dear—you can't stay here *now;* it's just not possible."

Thank you, Mother, Lydia breathed, from her hiding place just outside the parlor door.

"Of course, you're right," Nyreen said finally, rather ungraciously, Lydia thought.

"In fact, I really should insist you come home with us tonight," Olivia went on, ignoring the fact that Nyreen visibly stiffened and that her smoldering gaze shot immediately to Peter—who said nothing to defend her.

They are all the same, Nyreen thought virulently. *Everything for appearances; nothing in truth.*

"Tomorrow," Nyreen said smoothly. "Tomorrow—I really want to be with Harry tonight. I—I owe him so much. He took me in, he treated me like one of the family, he made me feel so welcome and so at home—"

She looked at Peter again and smiled her elusive cat-smile.

"And Peter—we've only just met but he's like the brother I never had."

"Of course, my dear," Olivia agreed, moved by Nyreen's sincerity. "Of course. And Lucinda is there, and Zenona, and Mama Dessie who is so particular."

"Oh yes," Nyreen said blandly, "I just love Mama Dessie . . ."

"Well there—it's perfectly acceptable. I'll just speak to Zenona. Now—has anyone seen Dayne?"

"Perfectly acceptable," Nyreen murmured and brushed by Peter as she followed Olivia out the door, "to *me*."

It was another steaming night; the darkness simmered over Bonneterre, hovering, the denseness in the air almost a living thing.

You couldn't move. You couldn't think. You just wanted to divest yourself of anything extraneous and give yourself up to the thick heat in the air and hope that sleep would eventually come.

Flint turned restively in his bed, broken by the sight of Harry's body—a life now futile, cut short, and in vain. Not immortal, not indestructible, but still able to wreak havoc on other people's lives—even in death.

Untouchable—his life, his father's, Dayne's—his sister—his *sister*—where had she come from with her covetous eyes and envious soul?

And Dayne—as lost as he felt without her supportive hate of Harry to fuel her days—

And Montelette, now eerily half hers, a prophecy in the making and now truer than bones while all of Harry's deceits and deceptions had died with him.

He grieved—for the death of Harry, and the birth of the life between himself and Dayne, but most of all, for his own father, whose death had forged an inconceivable chain.

Dayne lay in her bed, feeling drugged with the heat and soporific with the scent of spices from the protection doll that Mama Dessie had given her.

"You war' it under yo' dress if you can," Mama Dessie told

her. "You tie it 'round yo' waist under yo' dress when you know dat woman comin', you hear?"

She held it in her hand, marveling at its precise shape and the fact that its features were blank and its arms and legs stiff as sticks.

Soft puffy little doll, exuding penance and peace.

Yet she felt the nagging nick of restiveness, as if she didn't want to give in to somnolent oblivion.

Harry was gone, and she couldn't quite believe it.

She eased herself out of bed and went to stand at the window to stare sightless at the blank dark night.

Dark—dark—

He knew his way around Bonneterre like a blind person and still he felt a shiver of uncertainty as he made his way down the steps and on to the grounds.

Barely any light to suffuse the heat-charged air: a mere sliver of a moon, its bright light diffused as if it had been smeared by God's hand.

He felt lucky—in the same way that he did when he was riding high in a card game: the stakes astronomical, his life on the line.

His life was now in the hands of an uppity house servant who thought a little too much of herself . . .

Yet still—still—she wasn't so smart, so cunning that she could keep taunting him with this delusion and think that she could produce nothing after he had fallen for it.

No—there was something to it. And it was the answer to everything; it was the requiem for his father and for what she had done to them, and it was right and proper that she both held the secret and was about to relinquish it.

"Mistuh Clay—"

There was her voice, soft as a breath.

"Meline . . ."

"De papers?"

"I have them."

"How I know dey got whut you say dey got?"

"I want what you have."

"Always did," she muttered, remaining sequestered in the darkness and unsure still how much to trust him.

"Meline—I am serious, I am not playing games. I want nothing more than to give you what you want in exchange for the jewelry. It's as simple as that."

"Ain't nuthin' so easy, Mistuh Clay. You give me de paper."

"And then what?"

"Den I give you somethin' to think 'bout and I gonna check yo' papers . . ."

"Check out *how?*" he demanded, instantly suspicious. "Are you telling me someone can read? Damn it—are you?"

"I be checkin' it out my way, Mistuh Clay, and you ain't gonna be checkin' me out 'cause dey ain't gonna be no trade nohow if you do."

"No—*no*—I won't accept those terms. You take the paper and you tell me the hiding place and we go our separate ways."

She snorted. "Think I'm some kind of chile, Mistuh Clay? Easy, like my mama? Oh no, oh no—I got mo' brains, mo' gumption and I ain't in love wif you, Mistuh Clay; you cain't sweet-talk me nohow."

He felt his rage boiling up, his frustration was intense, and the idea that this slut of a servant possessed this kind of power over him was ludicrous.

Insane.

He was insane for putting himself in this position, and he felt an overriding need to get a grip on his temper.

He managed—just barely. He had only a week to produce some money. He needed to play out this slim threat, no matter what.

"Give me something to think about, you said," he reminded her icily.

"Give me de paper, Mistuh Clay."

Her hand shot out—he felt it on his sleeve—he felt enslaved by it, brought to his knees by a lowly house servant who was no better than she should be.

He slowly took the paper out of his breast pocket and grazed her fingertips with it.

She grasped at it, her fingers crushing the edge of the paper—

but he wouldn't let go and he tugged on it lightly so she understood he still maintained possession of it.

"Think I'm some kind of child?" he sneered. "Pull the paper and I promise you, the whole thing will rip to shreds and you'll have nothing. Tell me what I want to know—and the paper is yours."

She pulled and she heard the least little ominous ripping sound. Mistuh Clay was smart—too smart for her—always had been, too.

But she was just like her mama—she had put something aside and he wasn't going to get the whole.

If he could figure out the clue.

"Mama said—she said:

> 'don' look in no cane
> don' look in no well
> don' look de fields
> don' look to sell
> powuh come sweet
> dip in yo' hand
> taste on dat sweetness
> straight from de land
> come to de table
> take yo' place
> reach fo' tomorruh
> straight in yo' face . . .'

"Dat be it, Mistuh Clay."

"That's *it?*" he demanded disbelievingly. "What's *it,* you stupid girl? That's a stupid work chant—that's *nothing,*" he growled as he pulled on the coveted piece of paper instead of her lying, cheating neck.

"Damn it, you hear me, Meline—I want to know *where* and you don't leave until I do—"

His anger spewed up again, and the more he pulled on her precious paper, the more she relinquished her hold. She couldn't take the chance that he would rip it to shreds—she just couldn't.

He felt like ripping her to shreds.

"Meline—"

"I don' know nuthin' more, Mistuh Clay; she done teached me dat when I was a chile—how I gonna remember some fool hidin' place fo' all my life? Whut you thinkin'?"

"I'm thinking you're a liar, a user, a tease, just like your mother," he growled, nipping the paper away and throwing it into the darkness.

"Mistuh Clay!" Her cry was anguished, full of fear.

It gratified him—he grabbed her neck and pushed her to the ground.

Chapter 17

Nyreen awakened slowly, basking in the pleasure of being in Peter's bed and the certainty that he would not, could not leave Montelette now.

He appeared in the doorway, already properly attired for a funeral. "You'd better get dressed; they'll all arrive in another half hour."

"Still time, lover," she coaxed him.

"Not St. Foy time," he said ruthlessly. "They do everything on time to a fault—especially marriages and funerals. Don't let Olivia find you here."

He left her there unceremoniously to do what she would on the heels of that lesson in manners, and grudgingly she swung her legs over the side of the bed and tried to decide what to do next.

She didn't really want to get dressed, she wanted to stay naked and couple with Peter all day long.

But when she finally wandered downstairs to her room, she found that Lucinda had already prepared her bath and laid out the proper clothes.

"Dey comin' ten o'clock, Miz Nyreen—you ain't got much time."

"Thank you," she said curtly, stepping into the tub with her usual lack of modesty and aware that it shocked Lucinda, "I've already been given a lesson in what that means. Hand me the soap, will you? And the wash cloth?"

Lucinda wasn't used to watching any mistress scrub herself, but Nyreen waved off all her offers of help.

"Just towel me down and help me figure out how to dress as

quickly as possible—" *And get rid of all those old fools so that I can seduce Peter all over again.*

She came downstairs just as the beginning of a continuing parade of carriages rumbled up the drive.

The dining room door was open and Harry's body was within, dressed now, and surrounded by candles. He was laid in the lower half of a plain pine box, which had been knocked together by Bastien and the plantation carpenter, and the table was draped with a fine cloth beneath and an elegant rug and *prie-dieu* in front.

She turned away abruptly.

Yesterday, the night before—hadn't seemed real. Peter had killed for her, had wanted her so badly that he had destroyed his father for her.

It was enough, enough.

And then, as neighbors began to tiptoe into the room, crowding her, reverently stepping forward one by one to pay homage to Harry, it seemed like too little.

They buried Harry in the little cemetery where he would be side by side with Maribel.

The minister spoke, hailing Harry as a devoted father and brilliant businessman, a valued friend, a long-standing resident on the bayou.

No talk of weddings and blackmail. Nothing about beatings and barter.

Harry became in death the wealthy upstanding citizen he had always wanted to be in life.

No one but she would know any differently, Dayne thought. She and Nyreen would always know the truth and the secret: Harry had fallen for a scheming slut and had done anything in his power to have her.

His sins had caught up with him, but it was not the retribution Dayne would have wished.

Even Peter was dry-eyed while others sobbed and wailed. And Flint's expression was hard as stone, and she couldn't tell at all what he was thinking.

Afterward, after Harry's body had been interred, the funeral guests went back to the main house where Mama Dessie had laid out the post-funeral breakfast.

Then she had to suffer through an interminable feast of memory about Harry for one hour, two—she had to smile and thank everyone and by that time she *was* close to tears.

But Mama Dessie was close by.

"You got de powuh?" Mama Dessie demanded in a whisper as she made Dayne take a cup of tea—protection tea.

She nodded; she hadn't dared walk onto Montelette without it—Mama Dessie would have known.

"She bad, dat woman, she wicked; look at her face, Miz Dayne; she waitin' and watchin' and who know whut-all. Too dark to see whut—it dere like ghosts—"

Dayne shuddered. "Mama Dessie—"

"Didn't have no ghosts when yo' mama was alive," Mama Dessie said in dire tones. "Wasn't nuthin' worrisome den."

"Thank you, Mama Dessie."

What could she say? There was nothing worrisome then—only the repercussions of a deed long done and a secret left unspoken.

Montelette was hers—hers and Peter's now, and in honor she ought to sign her share over to Olivia.

Or to Flint—wasn't that why he had married her? Maybe he had had a hand in speeding things up . . .

Oh dear God—no . . . no—

Her heart started pounding unmercifully at the thought.

No . . .

She would die.

Not on top of everything else.

She moved like a ghost through the line of people who had come to pay their respects to Harry, thanking them, accepting their kind condolences, wishing them well in return.

And then she saw Nyreen, hanging back by the verandah stairs.

Nyreen had killed her father, as surely as if she had fired the bullet—Nyreen's selfishness, her greed, her eye on the prize—as if Harry had been some kind of trophy. Wealthy planter and young nubile trollop—oh yes, he had been a prize indeed.

She felt the tears finally pricking her eyes, and she was suddenly, shockingly swamped in a wave of grief so deep, so unremitting, she just sank to her knees where she was, and let herself cry.

"I don't feel right about it," Olivia said stringently once they were back at Bonneterre and relaxing in the parlor. "Letting that woman stay on at Montelette—after the reading of the will—there was nothing, nothing for her, and her mother and Harry's brother must be notified to come take her away. As soon as possible. I am so put out by the fact she would not take my good advice. Nothing good can come of her being alone on Montelette with Peter."

Lydia could not have agreed with her mother more. And worse, she had so few days in which to accomplish her goal of getting Peter's attention.

He had to have been prostrate with grief, yet he had held up nobly, never letting anyone see the depth of it.

Not like Dayne, who had just cried like a baby suddenly, inexplicably and embarrassingly in the middle of everything.

Both her brother and Peter had rushed to her side, like she was fragile or something—but it was Flint who had taken her away, back to Bonneterre and the comfort of her room.

They were up there still, and what Peter and that Creature were doing together now, she did not care to imagine.

Except that her mind was running off in forty-five different directions, and all of them involved scenes with the Creature and her beloved Peter.

"Clay, you are so quiet."

"Am I, Olivia?" he said. "A man died . . ." *And a woman, and a baby was born unexpectedly . . .*

And he had handled it, he had handled it all and he had taken the baby straight to Mama Dessie in the dead of the night—he was no fool—and he had left it there without a clue.

Mama Dessie had magic, she would bless the child spawned of his or his father's seed, and she would care for it, too, and never ask where it had come from. And Peter would not know the difference, one child from another when he had been away for so long.

And the other—well, the other—with her poems and lies while all the while she bore on her person the evidence of her treachery—hers and her mother's both—the other had deserved what she had gotten: her voice stilled after all these years, and the legend proved to be no lie.

He had searched her, before he had pushed her body into the bayou, and he had found it—simple, stark, shining, stunning— one small gem of a quality that could only have been bought for his mother's dowry.

A prize the little bitch had saved for herself, meant to be converted to cash if she had ever gotten a mile beyond the bayou . . . and he had meant to see that she wouldn't.

And maybe that was all of her mother's legacy—the only thing Celie had taken for herself, probably because she was entranced with the sparkle, the shine, the clarity of it—one small faceted diamond, nestling in her rough slave hands and the ultimate symbol of freedom.

For him now instead of her. For his debts—for his sins?

He was so quiet, basking in the triumph of overcoming the odds. He was a gambler; he knew the probabilities.

He could leave tomorrow . . . and all the evidence would float away.

"Clay? Clay?"

Olivia again, intrusive, annoying, everlastingly there.

"If you'll excuse me, mother?"

Olivia snapped back in frustration. "Certainly, son," and he left her with no ceremony whatsoever with Lydia fast on his heels.

And then she was alone, with her memories, her thoughts and her regrets, a woman suddenly old, whose time, with the passing of her former suitor, had finally gone.

"I do love your delicious body," Nyreen whispered, edging her finger down Peter's chest and down still farther until it disappeared into the crisp nest of hair between his legs.

"You love my delicious inheritance," Peter said rudely, pushing her hand away.

"Indeed I do, but what fun is it to share it with someone else—especially your sister, who already has a plantation—by marriage, at any rate."

He knew the answer to that of course: he would run Montelette—*if* he wanted to stay at Montelette, and he and Dayne would come to some arrangement about her share, and that would be the end of it.

"I mean—what if it were *all* yours?" Nyreen asked daringly, her fingers moving upward to stroke him tantalizingly.

"Christ, I'd run for the nearest coach going out of town. Why the hell would I want it to be all mine?"

"Because your father was rich and he made a very good living out of growing and milling sugar. And so could you, lover."

Rich, Peter thought, and stagnant. Rotting on the bayou in this stultifying heat and having to import almost everything except food.

It made no sense to him; it never had.

But he wasn't going to tell that to Nyreen while her fingers were making voluptuous circles around and around the taut sacs between his legs.

When she was there, when she did that, he wanted nothing more than to stay at Montelette forever.

Lydia didn't know where Clay had disappeared to, but she knew exactly where she was going: back to Montelette to find Peter.

There was always some old nag in the barn she could take out for a ride, and it was easy to convince Agus she needed a breathing spell away from all the talk of death and mourning.

He gave her an ambling old mare, and she went off down the track and toward Montelette; and when she was out of sight of Bonneterre, she kicked the mare into a tremulous trot until, twenty minutes later, she came to the gates of Montelette.

Here was the driveway that, not three hours before, had been crowded with carriages of mourners.

Now it was empty, desolated, as empty and desolated as she knew Peter was feeling.

That Creature could have no sympathy to offer to Peter. She was too self-absorbed, too remote. Icy.

Whereas she, Lydia, was a cauldron, seething with heat and laving warmth to give to Peter.

He had been waiting for it, too, she was sure of it.

A man like Peter, so gentlemanly and refined, could see right through the likes of the Creature.

And he would want someone from a background and station similar to her own.

She was a grown woman now, ready for marriage.

Maybe she would ask Mama Dessie to give her a spell so that Peter would love her. Everyone knew about Mama Dessie's spells: Praxine talked about her all the time. And people sent from miles around to have Mama Dessie do up a concoction for them.

She dismounted right in front of the house. She wasn't shy, and she didn't care what anyone would think. She was a caring and concerned neighbor who had come to see Peter in his hour of need.

She shuddered as she passed by the windows of the dining room. She couldn't bring herself to enter the house on this level and so she slowly climbed the outside steps to the upper gallery.

Here, every room opened off of the gallery and there were two side wings, also opening onto the gallery, containing more bedrooms.

But she wasn't looking for bedrooms—she was looking for Peter.

And there was no one else around.

She heard a sudden gurgle of laughter and she wheeled around toward the direction of the sound.

She crept down the gallery knowing full well what she was going to find: the Creature and Peter together, naked, joined, and rocking violently together in the throes of illicit pleasure.

Dayne needed to think; she couldn't think. Harry was gone and it made no sense to her that no one knew exactly how he had died.

But she didn't want to speculate on who or why or how because that led her into murky waters she did not want to explore.

And it made her feel less in control than before.

She felt absolutely nothing about anything; it was as though she were dead inside, too, and the union between her and Flint, and the Jezebel part of her had never lived.

Flint knew it, too. He wouldn't have thought Harry's demise would affect her like this; she hated Harry for what he had done to her.

And now it was as if Harry in death had achieved a kind of sainthood that he had not had in life.

And Flint didn't quite know how to bring back the glowing sensual creature he had taken as his wife.

"You'll need to talk to Peter," he commented the next morning as they went down to breakfast together.

"Will I? Why? And why should you care?" she snapped. "Or are you counting on my inheritance now for some reason I don't know about?"

And did you kill Harry to get it?

The thought swooped in like the tide, resisting all of her efforts to push it back. Montelette was half hers, and now—half his.

If only there were a way to give him back what her father had extorted—without the cost of losing Montelette . . .

How clever he had been, her husband.

Husband.

The word sat oddly in her mind.

Husband.

Her father had been a thief, a husband, a seducer.

What would her husband become?

A seducer, a thief, a husband.

How much were they different under the skin?

She couldn't keep thinking this way, she couldn't. There would be nothing—if she truly believed that all Flint had meant to do was steal Montelette away from her family and use her as the means to do it.

But still—he would not have married her otherwise . . . would he?

Her head felt like it was going to burst.

Ultimately, she could not face the morning listening to Lydia's inconsequential chatter or face Olivia's sympathetic eyes.

She took the Boy and went down the bayou road toward Orinda—silent, crumbling, secretive Orinda—she could be alone there as she always had been, even when she had been waiting for Clay.

The way seemed both familiar and strange.

It had been perhaps two months since her first fateful encounter with Flint Rutledge, and it was even more curious to remember how anxious she had been to see Clay.

She couldn't remember her feelings for Clay any longer. He was a cipher, a portent of evil, a willing conspirator with her father—he would have sold off her share of Montelette in a heartbeat and taken the money and run.

She dismounted at the barn, tied up the Boy and meandered aimlessly down toward the house and the sunburnt front lawn.

There was such an air of desolation that the past two months seemed like they had never happened.

Orinda was silent, wrapped in the dense heat, and calmed by the lull of lapping water a hundred yards beyond.

The sun bore into her skin, seeping the energy from her soul.

She couldn't run away, not even here where there were so many memories; they didn't wash away the questions and the uncertainties.

Someone had been desperate enough to attack her father. For Montelette—or for some other reason?

Nyreen? Had Harry told her of his unholy bargain with Flint and had she, expecting more than a widow's portion, decided to end the charade and . . . and—

Oh God—seduce Peter instead?

Melodrama, she chided herself, pure melodrama . . . except that she was certain Nyreen was capable of it. Hadn't Nyreen gotten rid of her?

She was close to the edge of the water now, and she looked down into its murky surface—

. . . *beautiful to look at from afar, and dirty as sin under the surface . . .*

Nyreen.

And then, just then, something heaved against her—something violent and angry—and she toppled over into the water, flailing, sputtering, floundering in the water, beating at the air because nothing was there.

No—not *nothing . . .*

Something *was* there, something soft and bulky, sopping and immobile.

Frantically she pushed her soaking hair out of her eyes and hesitated a long moment.

There was no one on shore—no one in the bushes—and yet a phantom someone had deliberately given her a mighty shove into the bayou . . .

She felt a chill that had nothing to do with being immersed in the water. Someone had pushed her . . .

She waded slowly toward the object she had seen as she came up for air.

No, not an object.

Something floating. Colorful—

A dress—skin, dark skin . . .

Oh God, a leg . . .

She screamed—she turned, she fell, and she picked herself up frantically, splashing her face full of rancorous water as she stumbled onto the shore.

A body—oh God—a body . . .

She turned and ran, her drenched skirts pulling against the weight of her body, slowing her down.

She had to get help—she had to get away; she could still feel the thrust of the push on her back. And she couldn't look at the water; the body bobbed there as if it were just waiting for discovery.

Thank God for the Boy—she would be back at Bonneterre in no time and get help for that poor drowned soul—

She was out of breath as she dragged herself up to the barn and stopped short as she comprehended the worst thing of all: the Boy was gone. Untethered and either let go or ridden away . . . and she would have to walk to Bonneterre if she were to get there at all.

*   *   *

She was going to die—she really thought she was going to die—it took hours, just hours to make her way back to Bonneterre, and she was exhausted when she got there, as much from emotion as the physical exertion of the walk.

And then the telling: trying to convince Flint that she had seen what she had seen and that someone had pushed her and that the Boy was missing.

Olivia thought she was crazy, touched by the sun.

"Nothing better to do than go wandering off down to Orinda—of all places?" she asked nastily. "No sewing to supervise or stores to lay in? I could think of a dozen chores to occupy you if you're so bored after only a couple of weeks."

"Someone *pushed* me," Dayne said, "and there's a body in the bayou and we can't leave it there."

But Flint would not let her come when he and Agus and Junior went to retrieve it and brought it back wrapped tenderly in pure white—now soaked—cotton.

"It's Meline."

"Dear Lord—" Olivia then, utterly shocked and disbelieving. "But who—?"

"The person perhaps who shot my father?" Dayne suggested testily.

"Nonsense. A thief, nothing more. But this—this—"

"We put her in her cabin; Praxine is attending to her. She says the baby was born." He let the horrible significance of that sink in.

"We have to notify the authorities," he added unflinchingly. "After that, we'll bury her next to Celie . . ."

And that will be the end of that.

"We have to look for the Boy," Dayne said into the tense, strung-out silence.

"The Boy will turn up," Flint said; he wanted to say more— she looked so haggard, so wrung out—so furious. But there wasn't much they could do—not this day. They had to look for Meline's baby.

"The Boy might never turn up," she countered, still containing the unreasonable little nub of anger that all his energy would be directed toward Meline—who didn't need his help—as opposed to his wife, who did.

"We'll do it one thing at a time," he said calmly. "Meline first—we search for the baby, and hope to hell we can find it—or some reason why."

"You tell Miz Olivia she got to send fo' Mama Dessie," Praxine said to Dayne. "Dis bad—dis got badness attached to it, and Mama Dessie got to do some cleansing of de spirits fo' we lay Meline to rest."

"I'll tell her," Dayne said respectfully. She had had several hours and now she felt less shock and more fear. Someone had deliberately gone after Meline and left her that horrible way.

"And de chile—ain't no chile, Miz Dayne. Don' know whut happen wif de chile. Was born. Ain' no chile."

"They didn't find the child," Dayne said, shuddering, the memory of the search incised in her memory like a steel engraving.

"Got to know 'bout de chile. Chile belong to Bonneterre, to Meline's people."

"I understand. Maybe Mama Dessie will have some answers," Dayne said. "I'll go tell Miz Olivia."

"Done laid her out in de cabin. She don' look so good."

"I know."

"Was bettuh you foun' her, Miz Dayne."

"I understand."

She left Praxine in the kitchen and went to find Olivia. She was sitting with Lydia who was unusually quiet.

"They want Mama Dessie to come."

"Nonsense," Olivia snapped. "What can she do?"

"It's what your people *think* she can do that's important."

"I never held with that," Olivia said sharply. "I don't believe in giving in to superstitious nonsense."

Dayne gave her a hard look. She didn't know anything about this woman who was her mother-in-law—who even might have been her own mother, had fate taken a different turn.

She wondered for a moment whether Olivia hated her and held her accountable for the sins of her father.

She wondered how Olivia had treated her people; and underscoring that thought was a distant rhythmic chant of grief that even infiltrated the big house.

Flint was out in the field, gathering his laborers in early to prepare for Meline's funeral.

It was a time of waiting after it had been determined that someone had deliberately taken Meline's life after she delivered her child.

It was shocking; among the house servants there was outrage manifested by muttering and covert hostility.

Olivia did not understand her people. Mama Dessie had to come, for the comfort of her people and to put a spell on bad spirits.

It made perfect sense to her.

She turned from the window where she had been staring at the trees that dotted the front lawn.

She was the Mistress of Bonneterre.

She would send for Mama Dessie herself.

They stood in the field behind the row of slave houses where Meline had lived and Mama Dessie demarcated a circle and instructed the men to bring back wood for a fire while she made the incantations.

"I despise this," Olivia said grimly from her vantage point on the far side of the upper gallery which overlooked the cabins. "I hate it that your *wife* took it upon herself to—"

"My *wife* is Mistress of Bonneterre," Flint said, shading his eyes toward the cabins where the workers had formed a circle around Mama Dessie and someone had lit a small fire. "And she's with Mama Dessie, as she should be."

Olivia fell silent. *I never thought . . . it never occurred to me in the weeks before or after that wedding that she would step into my shoes and that Flint would let her . . .*

She felt an awful moment of isolation as if she had been cut adrift from everything that she had ever known.

The death of Meline closed the chapter on that book: there was no long-lost cache of her jewelry—Meline would have taken it out and flaunted it long ago.

Olivia had lived on such hope that if she couldn't find it, Meline would somehow torment her with it as she had taunted her about everything else.

But instead, right before her very eyes, her past was dying and everything that had fueled her existence at Bonneterre was as evanescent as the smoke rising in the distance and dissipating into thin air.

There was nothing left—Harry gone, now Meline, and Montelette belonged in part to Dayne . . . Flint had done exactly what he had set out to do and what Clay could not: avenge her past and bring Bonneterre back to life.

But Clay had gone, had left mysteriously once again—this time late at night—and no one had seen him since.

And now she had to contend with Flint's support of his *wife*—his wife—she shook her head. A month ago, two months ago, he hadn't had one thought on his mind about taking a wife or making a life at Bonneterre.

How quickly things changed; how obsolete one became in the breath of one moment.

"Mama Dessie makes up a packet of basil, clover, asafoetida, hyssop, lemon verbena, thyme, vervain, bay, mint, cumin . . . herbs that are believed to have some magical properties," Flint said into the simmering silence.

"Mama Dessie knows. She's looking to exorcise bad spirits on account of the way Meline died, and to purify Meline's soul."

"Mumbo jumbo," Olivia muttered.

"She's very powerful," Flint said, ignoring her, but he had always ignored her and she knew it. "Everyone believes in her magic. She will tie up the herbs and chant over them and when the time is just right, she will throw them into the fire and cast out the spirits so Meline can rest in peace."

"You know so much about—why don't you go join them in their heathen rituals."

"I was planning to," he said coolly. "I just didn't want to leave you alone."

But I am alone, she thought futilely, and it was like a cry that she had to suppress deep inside her or the emotion of it would deflate her altogether and she would shrivel into nothingness.

She watched, her back steely straight, as Flint left her and made for the cabins.

Twilight was lowering, and the mist of smoke from the fire grew more intense—so intense she felt as if she could feel the very heat of it right on her very own balcony.

This wasn't the way things ought to go, she thought. Her son should be by her side, and her daughter-in-law, too, and her very own daughter, who was out somewhere—probably right in the middle of that restive crowd with its pagan beliefs and its ability to shift on the moment and become something more threatening.

She turned her back on it and walked away the very moment Mama Dessie tossed the packet of purification into the air and into the flames.

The very moment when Dayne, who had been just outside the circle where Mama Dessie had set up her altar, had moved closer for the ultimate moment of the ritual.

The instant of the magic, when once again she felt that violent angry shove at her back and she went pitching forward toward the fire.

Their hands pulled her back—their hands which were never to touch their mistress on pain of death—their hands brought her back from the edge of the flames.

"Oh God, oh God, oh God—" she was frantic—her hem had caught, and she and they were stamping at the flaring flames that licked at her feet. "Oh God—"

She felt like fainting; she felt like screaming . . .

"Dey gone, mistus," somebody said. "Dey out, dey gone."

"Oh God—" Would she ever forget the whump of those hands hitting her and then the helplessness of falling toward the fire . . .

"Oh God—"

"Lemme th'ough, lemme th'ough—"

Mama Dessie—she heard her; she felt her large warm hands. "You weahin' de protection—you weahin' it?" she asked urgently.

"Yes," Dayne whispered, "I'm wearing it."

"Good, good, good—good—de spirits be watchin' you; couldn't

nobody hurt you, Miz Dayne. You got de powuh on yo' side . . . and yo' mistuh comin' to watch ovuh you."

"Flint . . ." she murmured faintly.

He grabbed her. "Mama Dessie . . ."

"She fine—I made a spell and she wuz weahin' it and she fine. Now we got to continue wif de purifyin'; got to start all over again, now, and banish dem evil spirits . . ."

And she did, patiently, slowly, with great reverence she chose from her containers of herbs and sifted each one into her packet, defining each, reassuring her audience that Meline's spirit would be cleansed and the evildoers who had murdered her and tried to harm Miz Dayne would be punished.

And then she threw the packet into the air once again chanting her incantations, and the packet fell into the flames and exploded into a great blue light against the twilight, and it was as if it were a sign from above.

Mama Dessie folded her hands over her chest and nodded her head. "And now—" she said emphatically, "we is finished."

Chapter 18

Two deaths—two accidents . . .

She couldn't get it out of her mind.

Somehow related?

With Harry's death, she inherited. But Meline—why would anyone want to murder Meline?

Celie's daughter . . . who maybe knew her mother's secrets—

But no, she would have been so young—too young to know what any of that meant.

Yet someone had strangled her and taken her newborn baby. It made no sense.

And someone had tried to . . . to what? Kill Dayne? Drown her in the bayou? Push her into the flames?

Could she have died?

And then who inherited?

She shuddered.

She had known that answer all along—from the moment Harry died so mysteriously, inexplicably, incomprehensibly.

Someone had pulled that trigger and freed her inheritance for the taking.

And now someone was after her.

And in the dark of the night, in this house with its interconnecting doors and secrets, it wasn't too hard to guess who.

"It is time to begin the work of winter," Olivia said the next morning as Dayne joined her and Lydia for breakfast. "And you, too, my dear girl. Somehow I don't think they teach practicalities at this fancy school of yours."

"Mama . . ." Lydia protested. "I have better things to do than—"

"If you do, I haven't seen you doing them," Olivia said tartly. "You'll come with us this morning. I promise you that your future husband will be mightily impressed with how knowledgeable you are."

She cast a faintly dubious look at Dayne. "As will of course my son."

Dayne bristled at Olivia's tone. "I'm fairly well acquainted with my household duties, Olivia," she said, reining in her anger. "You have only to show me where you keep the stores and Praxine and I will take care of the rest."

Olivia sniffed. The nerve of her! Dismissing her like a servant, telling her that her services were no longer needed.

Mistress of Bonneterre—arrogant, shameless daughter of a bastard . . . She still hadn't come to terms with the idea that this marriage had been the sole and only way to save Bonneterre from Harry and from Clay.

Yet it was done, and now it seemed like a futile gesture on the heels of Harry's death. She would have shot him herself if she could have prevented Flint's marriage and saved Bonneterre.

"Well—here is the storeroom—everything is intact: Clay brought back the staples in March, and it's almost time to begin canning. Let me see—the materials are over here; we ordered them last year, and you'll find Sudie May and Deecy are excellent at cutting patterns and sewing."

She turned to Lydia. "You see, my dear, when you are mistress of a great plantation, you have a great many responsibilities besides caring for your husband. So many things go under your purview—everything from dispensing the stores to putting up hams. Oh, I don't say your servants won't help you, but there is much more to housekeeping than ever you would guess."

"I don't want to guess," Lydia said peevishly. "Why can't I just have fun now and think about it when I get married?"

"Alas, it's too true: this *is* your time to have fun and the rest should come later."

And besides, Lydia thought resentfully, *Peter would never ex-*

pect me to dirty my hands doing all these silly chores. That was why there were slaves and house servants.

It was almost eerie standing opposite Dayne and having her mother recount these things and Dayne looking so much like Peter except for her hair and her dress that Lydia felt like fainting.

"So my dear, why don't we both leave Dayne to her chores and go have a cup of tea? Dayne, do join us when you've finished here?"

Nicely nasty once again, prising up each little nerve ending, for what purpose Dayne could not fathom.

The old witch had won. She and her son had decided to get their revenge and they had done it—in spades—and she didn't even have the sense to recognize that relinquishing her duties was a further victory for her.

But she, Dayne, had to keep busy: she had too much pressing on her mind. The Boy had not yet come back and Flint was adamant about the futility of searching for him.

"He'll come back—or someone will find him." He was sure of it, so sure; everyone knew the Boy.

Unless, she thought suddenly, mordantly, Flint had stolen the Boy from her himself.

One little diamond. One precious, flawless, perfectly cut little diamond, and all his troubles were over and he walked away from the stunned duVallet with money in his pocket.

"My dear Clay—I'm utterly astonished. Every dollar and on time. Your inventiveness amazes me. Your code of honor, your adherence to your word impresses me."

Yet he counted every last dollar—twice while Clay stood there, itching to throw the money in his face.

"My friends, *Monsieur* Clay has come through. His debt is cleared; his word is his bond, and so I will let it be known that *Monsieur* Clay is reliable, dependable, and solvent—at least of this moment, eh?"

"As you say," Clay murmured, squirming. The book was clear and open once again for his perusal: duVallet said so and duVallet's word was his bond as well.

Already he could feel his luck turning. A little game some-where, tonight, and he might turn one hundred beautiful free and clear dollars into a thousand.

"My friend, you have entree where you will. I give you my customary word of caution. Don't get carried away. Don't try to double your luck. Do not let me see you darken my doorway again with such a burden as the one you have just discharged. And, my dear friend, do think once more about coming to work for me. If you can keep your gambling lust and your debts under control—why, I can use a smart man like you—eh?"

The money burned a hole in his pocket. He was in New Orleans, city of fast women and fast money, and with all his re-sources, he could have the city at his feet.

Dinner at Antoine's first, to savor his victory over his most re-spected foe, to savor his life, even if it had come at the cost of an-other.

But she was dispensable—and he was not.

He began feeling heady with a kind of power as the evening wore on.

Luck—he felt it breathing in his ear, soft, seductive, beckoning him like a siren, as tantalizing as any woman.

A round of cards—or two or three—there was enough in his wallet to finance that for the first time in years. He had a cushion, leeway to make a mistake, misread an opponent, discard a dicey hand.

For the first time, lady luck whispered provocatively, *you will be in control . . .*

Yes—that was the thing: he had been in control from the mo-ment he had forced the truth from that little bitch's body. He had been in control.

And so now it was time to test that luck, time to take his windfall and parlay those lucky dollars into the fortune he should have always had.

Nyreen was tired.

Tired of life on Montelette, tired of the suffocating heat, tired of waiting, tired of coaxing, and especially tired of the waffling indecision of the only man she had ever wanted in her whole life.

"Lover, you are *boring* me to tears."

"I'm boring myself," Peter muttered, turning over on his side after yet another rampaging violent bout of sex with Nyreen and her insatiable body.

"What are you going to do about Montelette?"

"I'll decide that after your mother gets here."

Damn, damn, and damn—her mother, for God's sake, as if she were some protected and pampered little brat like that Lydia Rutledge.

Or was that what he really wanted?

He couldn't make a decision because he looked at her as a willing body and not the kind of woman he would ask to marry him.

Like he was a king or God or something.

Shit—his blood was just as dirty as hers, only Harry had somehow cleaned it up by buying this stupid plantation and making himself into the sugar king of St. Foy.

Only that whole thing would be going to seed pretty soon if lover didn't get off of his butt and look into just what Mr. Bastien was doing in the fields with those huge high stalks and those gangs of field hands that he kept busy somehow doing something during the day.

Damn it—did she have to do *everything*? And *think* of everything?

She was aching to say something, and she pushed it back just in time as she was struck with one telling realization: she really was Peter's whore, and that was how he thought of her—nothing more. And maybe something less.

It was such a stunning perception that she felt breathless with fury at the obviousness of it.

He would never marry his whore. He would keep her like a quadroon—maybe even in New Orleans—and he would lavish her with sex, money, and possessions but he would never take her to wife—only to bed.

If Harry had not betrayed her, Harry would have married her and lived happily ever after, and she could have tended to his needs with one hand and no heart and still satisfied *him*.

But this son of a bitch—

She had to bring him to the point—and fast. Everything she had tried thus far had yielded no results, and she could see that his interest in staying at Montelette was quickly fading.

"Maybe *I* shouldn't be here when my mother gets here," she suggested coyly, looking for some way to perk up his jaded sensibilities.

"Where the hell else would you be?"

"Well—" she wriggled her body upright and propped a couple of pillows behind her back—"Olivia Rutledge has been quite scorching in her disapproval of my staying here with you alone. My own dear mother would be shocked . . ."

"Would she?" he muttered thickly. "Does she know what a little whore you are? Could she imagine you were sleeping with two men at once and loving every minute of it?"

"It excites you, doesn't it?" she whispered. "Tell me you didn't harden at the thought of it. Tell me you wouldn't get an erection like a house if I found another lover and you had to share me with him . . ."

"Jesus . . . !"

She pulled away from him abruptly and swung out of bed. "I'm leaving."

"*What?*"

She smiled, that elusive cat-smile, and calmly rooted around for her robe and slipped her arms into it and folded it across her naked body.

"It was a nice ride, lover."

"Shit—get back here, you bitch."

"Bye-bye, lover. Enjoy your dreams."

She was out the door before he could stop her, before his befuddled brain understood what she meant to do.

He caught her just outside her bedroom door and threw her onto her bed and ripped off her robe.

"You're going nowhere, bitch, and you know it," he growled before he penetrated the moist feminine heat of her.

"Don't be too sure, lover," she murmured, thrusting her body eagerly against his.

Oh, she could die for this—that hard young body pouring sweat all in aid of pleasuring her like some rutting bull.

He could die for this: he would get it nowhere else, and it was time he understood he had gotten too much and she wanted something in return.

She pushed him off of her, sound asleep and a dead, wrung-out weight. She pulled herself out of bed and over to her closet.

She had to be fast, she had to be quick. A dress, some under-things; she hardly had anything anyway, a straw bonnet to protect her from the sun—

Damn, she should have learned how to ride—or at least drive a gig.

No, someone would take her. There had to be someone who did the driving.

She stuffed everything into a small bag.

Olivia Rutledge was right; one dealt with the realities of the situation. If it was proper behavior and a lady that Peter wanted, then she would give him proper behavior and the most ladylike of ladies.

And in the meantime, he would learn what he was missing— and what he could not live without.

It rained.

The heat was unremitting, the sky an ominous gray, and then the clouds opened up, and it poured.

Olivia hated rainy days.

Lydia sat sulking by the window.

Flint was out in Verne's office working on accounts.

And the new Mistress of Bonneterre was down in the kitchen with Praxine picking through fruit and boiling up jars—like she enjoyed it or something.

Rainy days were the worst: nothing ever happened on a rainy day, and Olivia never could find anything to occupy her a whole long day—not even a book—and then the heat was too suffocating to even try to do anything else.

But the rain was good for the crop and lack of it was the one thing Flint had worried about.

So it rained.

And during the rain, it was hard for Olivia to avoid thoughts of the previous weeks—and how the threats, the secrets, the return of her children—all of them—had crystallized into this one domestic moment where everything was suddenly and beautifully meshed into place, and she was all at once the outsider.

Down in the kitchen, Dayne listened to the thundering rain while her berry stained hands sorted through the fruits and vegetables with barely any cogent thought to what she was doing.

It was busy work to occupy an idle mind that was creating the most fantastic scenes of murder, vengeance, and death.

It was almost impossible to comprehend.

Her *husband* wanted her share of Montelette so badly . . . that he had blackmailed her father to get it, married her for her inheritance, murdered Harry to precipitate her coming into her legacy, tried twice to injure her and possibly kill her, too—and had stolen her horse to show her who now had the power.

It was *not* her Jezebel self, for all her whips and threats.

She felt frozen and stiff with impotent fear. How could she fight him?

Nothing could be proved.

Harry's death was an accident; the one witness to her husband's coercion would never tell. The two incidents involving her had to be her imagination—she had slipped on the bank of the bayou, had stepped too close to the purifying fire.

The Boy had been spooked off by the scent of death.

And she was overwrought and needed more rest.

Damn and damn.

She felt that thready little pain weaving its way into her consciousness. Every time she tried to parse out some logical explanation of the events of the last several weeks, she felt the pain.

There was no explanation, there was no logic.

Harry had been murdered and she was in danger—she felt it, she believed it with all her heart—and there was only one person who wanted what now was hers, and that was Flint.

She stepped to the stove to throw a bowlful of berries into a boiling pot, and then turned away to set aside the bowl on a nearby table.

"*Miz Dayne!*—"

She heard Praxine's shrieking warning as though it came from far away, her mind operating on some level all its own.

"Miz DAYNE! ..."

She was moving even as Praxine screamed her name again, moving sideways as the great steaming cauldron of boiling berry juice toppled over onto its side, sending a blue flame flaring, and the scalding hot juice spilling onto the floor, an inch away from having fallen wholly onto her.

An accident—it had to have been an accident: her hand must have caught the edge, or something ...

But her hand wasn't burned; she hadn't felt dragged down by any unusual weight ...

"Don' worry none 'bout dem berries," Praxine said because she didn't know what else to say. Her mistress's lower torso had almost been boiled to bits—one more inch, one more second where she stood still—and the doctor would have been there and Miz Dayne been salved and bandaged up to a faretheewell. "I clean dem up."

"Thank you, Praxine." Her voice was shaky; her limbs felt watery. "I think—I'll go upstairs for a while."

"Yes'm."

She made her way slowly to the kitchen door, removing her splotched apron as she went and leaving it on one of the work tables before she exited.

She grabbed hold of the banister of the service staircase.

Oh my God, oh my God ...

It had happened again—another accident, another carelessness, something else imaginary on her part.

Her secret, hers—unless Praxine told someone. She would have to caution Praxine not to tell anyone.

Not anyone.

She forced herself to take the first painful step up.

She had to stop him.

Stop *him:* the man who had seduced her with his kisses and turned her into Jezebel, who had shown her that surrender was the most powerful weapon of all—

Him ...

And all he had wanted was Montelette.

And all she wanted was her life.

She had nothing to barter. If he removed her and succeeded to ownership of her share of Montelette, he would have no trouble at all with Peter. Peter had no feeling at all for Montelette; he would sell out to Flint in a heartbeat and probably on any terms Flint cared to name.

And if something nasty happened to her, who would question it? Look at how Harry's death had been glossed over and buried with his corpse. And now she was having accidents all over the place.

A careless moment and she too would be gone—and no one would question it because she had been so distraught and thoughtless since Harry's death—

Oh God—she could see the whole thing, she could even hear them talking, making the excuses, counting all the money . . .

She forced herself to take another step up, and another. For all she knew, Flint was waiting for her, helpful and kind and ready to push her down the steps while looking as if he were the most so-licitous husband in the world.

She was scared to death of what awaited her at the top of those stairs.

She heard a noise, a scraping noise and then a step, and she let out a moan.

And then a voice floated down to her—distorted by her terror and her fear.

"Dayne—Dayne?"

Oh God—Flint . . . *Flint*—coming from where? And how did he know it was she down there?—standing and waiting threaten-ingly for her at the top of the steps.

She turned—she ran—back through the kitchen and out the rear door, into the rain and the soul-sapping heat.

And then she didn't know where else to run. The rain was coming in sheets, almost as solid as a wall.

Far off she heard the rumbling of wheels and the frightened neigh of a horse pushed beyond endurance.

A carriage—someone arriving? In this torrent? But still—a way to escape? Could she?

She groped her way through the mud and the blinding rain toward the front of the house, toward the sounds—the protesting horse—the grating of metal on shell as the carriage came to a halt—hoofbeats, and the wild braying acknowledgement of freedom as something came at her through the torrential curtain of the storm—

The Boy! Dear Lord—the Boy! Dancing and prancing with his wild free run, oblivious to rain and restraints, coming at her like the figment of her imagination—and she couldn't catch him, couldn't stop him—

He raced wildly down the track toward the stable and disappeared from sight beyond the thick fall of rain and fog that obscured everything and invested it with the amorphous quality of a dream.

She was drenched, and frozen between terror and joy and wondering how she could move another step beyond where she was.

The verandah was just visible ahead of her, but she couldn't bring herself to take refuge there.

She felt disoriented, threatened by any contact with the house and everyone within.

But she was absolutely soaked through; she couldn't think in this morass of mud and saturating water.

She stumbled across the remaining several yards and into the shelter of the verandah and sagged against the closest of the supporting columns.

Here, for one pulse-pounding moment, she felt safe. But her heart was thundering wildly, her dread escalating with the intensity of the storm.

She wanted to hide.

She needed to hide so she could think. She couldn't think with the storm raging a foot beyond the verandah and the threat of death hovering over her head like a sword.

Flint—*Flint* . . .

She shoved her streaming wet hair out of her face.

She could leave him—but to go where and do what? She couldn't go back to Montelette—it was the first, most obvious place anyone would look.

And she had no money—not of her own, at any rate.

So her choices were limited: stay and die—or leave and die, because surely a woman alone would die on the streets.

No choice at all.

None. Out of her control, just as everything else had been for all of her life.

She couldn't stay anywhere near the house.

And she couldn't get any more soaked through than she was, so she thought the next best thing would be to see if the Boy had really found his way home and at least she would be *doing* something instead of standing there and giving in to her panic and every tall tale her imagination could conjure up.

She headed into the squall in the general direction of the stables, her saturated skirt dragging and impeding her with the weight of the water and mud, so that it took her fifteen minutes at least to cross the back lawn and find the track to the stables and barn.

And then she had to slide open the heavy weight of the door, which alerted Agus that someone had come. He rose up before her, faintly menacing and then abjectly apologetic.

"Miz Rutledge—what you doin' out in this storm?"

Good question—no good answer; the pampered mistress should be tucked cozy and safe in the confines of the big house in weather like this.

Her best defense was to slough off the question and immediately distract him.

"I saw the Boy."

"No ma'am—you didn't. He ain't come back."

"I saw him," she insisted, but for one disorienting moment, she thought that perhaps she *had* imagined it. "He's on Bonneterre—wherever he is; he came this close to me—" she measured off the distance.

"I ain't seen 'im, Miz Rutledge. And I know you grievin' him."

"I know I saw him."

"I b'lieve you, ma'am. I go lookin' when de weather calm down some."

She didn't know what else to say, and she knew she ought not stay there with him, either.

She made a move to leave.

"Cain't go back in dat storm, ma'am."

"I—"

"No need. You be safe here. Mama Dessie say—we got to watch out fo' de mistus."

Her eyes flickered. Mama Dessie? What did that mean?

She stared at the pouring rain through the open door. It felt like a year since she had discovered Meline's body—a month since Mama Dessie had purified her possessions and freed her soul.

Only yesterday.

Only a day since Meline had been carried from her small house on the edge of the avenue of cabins and down to the old little cemetery next to the bayou.

Only a day . . .

And then Mama Dessie had gone to the house with sachets of herbs to cleanse the house and banish the evil spirits and bad feelings, but everyone knew no one would go near Meline's house again for a long, long time.

A long, long time—

She felt a clamoring in her head.

Who would look for her there?

For a long long time . . .

She turned, and without a word of explanation to Agus, she bolted from the stable and disappeared into the fog and rain.

So the Creature had come finally, with her lying eyes and snaky ways to insinuate herself into Mama's good graces, and Lydia wanted to scream with frustration.

There she stood, dripping water, after—what? almost two weeks—suddenly realizing the error of her ways.

"Of course you were right," she was saying. "Absolutely right, Olivia. I never should have stayed on at Montelette alone with Peter, and I hope I may take you up on your offer to stay here."

And what could Mama say? She couldn't be outright rude; she had never withdrawn the invitation, and so far as Lydia knew, she hadn't yet tried to get in touch with the Creature's mother because that would be rank interference.

So she was stuck: she had to offer hospitality whether she wanted to or not.

Olivia smiled stiffly and said, "Of course you may. You did the right thing, Nyreen."

Oh, I know I did . . .

"You're so kind," Nyreen murmured. "I'm so grateful."

But she didn't sound grateful at all—she sounded smug, and more than that, triumphant.

Olivia rang for Tull. "Miss Nyreen will be staying with us for a few days—prepare a room please and send Sudie May to get her bags and show her where she may change and rest before dinner. There now—you had a lot of courage braving this storm."

"The house was so empty—just me—Peter was off somewhere—I felt so alone, so isolated just depending on him and the servants—no, it's time for me to make other arrangements, and I promise I won't trespass on your hospitality any longer than it's necessary."

Sudie May came flying into the room.

"Upstairs ready, Miz Olivia."

"Excellent. Show our guest the way then."

Nyreen followed her out, that elusive cat-smile playing all over her mouth.

Lydia watched her go, skepticism etched in the sharp frown on her face.

"I hate her."

"We will do what is right," Olivia said.

The only thing right is that she is not with Peter now, Lydia thought, which meant they weren't doing those ugly naked things together that had made her want to retch.

It would work out, she thought. She had fought and planned too hard and too long. She had to have him.

It had to work out.

It *had* to.

* * *

Rain—
Coming on the heels of his disastrous and unprecedented bad
luck at gaming the night before—
His aching head—
Jinxed . . .
duVallet had come and gone—already.

*Not smart, Monsieur Clay. Not at all. All those lovely dollars
and all that good will—you tossed it away like a piece of tissue
paper into the river. Poof! It disappears just as if the water had
had the power to melt it away.*

*You are not a stupid man, Monsieur Clay. And in point of
fact, I was stunned when you repaid your debt and had the great
good sense not to take the money and try to augment it. No, so
sensibly you retained some dollars and managed to get yourself in
worse debt than before.*

*Tch, tch, tch. Now what will you do, I wonder, my good
friend? So much money. So little time. Two weeks, my dear
friend—two very generous weeks. I hope your source will be generous once again, eh?*

His source? His *source?* One tiny beautifully cut diamond
pitched into the maw of his sickness.

He would never stop, he knew it—not even if he made the big
stake—because then he would want to see if he could do it again
. . . and again.

But he could never do it again if he were dead. Or maimed so
badly he could never move again.

And now he was losing a day because of the rain; he never
went anywhere in the rain because it was so messy, so *wet.*

He rolled over in his bed and moaned.

Two weeks, two weeks—he wondered what was so magical
about two weeks . . .

He closed his eyes against his pounding headache.

He didn't know what he was going to do—there was no more
Meline to taunt him . . . only the stupid little rhyme she had learned
as a child—and the perfect little diamond that now seemed like
every bit as much a fantasy as the legend of his mother's missing
jewels.

He could hardly remember the rhyme. He could barely remember his name.

Meline could tell him nothing now.

Who would save him?

He had to get out of New Orleans; he had to go—where? he wasn't even solvent enough, or coherent enough to think clearly.

He would go back to Bonneterre . . . He could always go back to Bonneterre.

He could—

He could just keep looking . . .

He had two weeks and the worst credit and collateral of any man in New Orleans. Orinda was a dead issue, unproductive, moldering away, barely worth the ground it was built on.

Of course, Olivia didn't know that, and he wouldn't hesitate to use it—but only as a last resort, because his paragon of a big brother would see right through that ruse.

But meantime—he could keep looking.

If there had been one diamond, there must have been more—one little diamond was enough for Meline, for her to carry and feel it brought her luck perhaps, to give her hope that he would fulfill his promise and she could, ultimately, try for freedom.

Too bad she had to tease him with that stupid rhyme—what the hell had been the words?

Jesus.

He couldn't afford to waste one day.

He dragged himself slowly out of bed and began preparations to leave for Bonneterre—even in the rain.

Chapter 19

The rain didn't stop and Dayne did not appear and Flint slammed through the house in a fury as uncontrollable as the storm.

"She was in the kitchen," Olivia said for the hundredth time. "She and Praxine—the kettles—the fruit—for heaven's sake, Flint, I've told you already . . ."

"Why did she turn and run?"

"I don't know; how could I know?"

"Hell—"

"And Praxine said a kettle of boiling water tumbled over and almost scalded her? And then she just disappeared? How is this possible? Of course she's upstairs, or with Nyreen perhaps—?"

"Not the hell likely," Flint growled, staring out into the teeming rain. Good for the crops, dire for anything else that might get caught in it.

Hell—she could have slipped in the mud and be laying out there somewhere, as helpless as Meline had been and at the mercy of the very same force—

He couldn't—he wouldn't think of it.

Goddamn . . .

He should have forced the issue between them long before this. He had been too lenient with a woman he already knew liked to play rough.

No fragile flower, she; no one was more inflexible, more obdurate. She wouldn't have run, either, in spite of the circumstances.

She felt their connection every bit as intensely as he; she would not have decamped.

He had left it too long, had betrayed her too hard—she had had nowhere else to go from there—

But she had gone somewhere . . .

The rain was interminable. It was impossible to tell the time of day except that finally the sky darkened and his futile search took on a kind of frenzy.

What if she were out there?

There was absolutely nothing missing from her room: she hadn't planned to leave—she couldn't have—and yet she was nowhere in the house and she could only be out there . . .

Alone and terrified?

Frantic for help?

He would have searched the grounds hours before—but there was nowhere to go in that mud sodden mess—

He felt his whole body constrict with helplessness.

Damn it, damn it, damn it—Dayne . . . !

"Someone's coming," Olivia said suddenly.

He heard it, too—the faint rumbling in the distant darkness, wheels on shell, crackling up the long driveway.

"She wouldn't be in a carriage . . ." Flint said, almost giving in to his feeling of futility.

"Maybe she got lost. Maybe someone down the bayou rescued her—" Olivia suggested, knowing that wasn't very likely, either. She herself wasn't feeling much pain that Dayne had gone missing.

But watching Flint's agony was almost unbearable.

Footsteps, on the stairs.

The door flung open and a shadow beyond it, too large and bulky for it to be Dayne.

"Well? Well? Is anyone home? Anyone care to even welcome me home?" Clay demanded lightly as he threw off his wet dripping cape and stepped into the room.

Peter awoke alone in his bed with the thunderous sound of the rain rapping on the roof.

Now where the hell was she?

He pushed himself out of bed and padded down the hallway, his body aggravatingly ready to take her on again.

God, she was merciless. Absolute hell.

And he had no compunction about taking advantage of all that she offered.

He had even been titillated by her amoral attitude about his father—and a little envious the old goat had still been a randy old stud.

And he felt like a damned rutting ram, so where the hell was she?

She was nowhere, and he felt frustration that she had inconvenienced him like this.

Where the damned hell was she?

No one in her room—just that scent, musky, overwhelming, arousing, the embodiment of her.

He felt himself aroused to new heights just inhaling it.

Shit—the bitch . . . how the hell did she expect him to expend his lust if she weren't here?

No wonder the old man had chased after her. There was nothing damned else to do in this place.

He had spent a week ramming his frustration and his need into her hot, willing body—

And the moment he especially wanted her, she had up and gone—

Goddamnit, goddamnit—

What the hell did she expect?

If a whore offered herself and asked no payment, a man would take everything she had and charge her for the pleasure.

He would have thought she would have known that.

Or maybe she had other ideas on her mind.

God, a piece of trash like that—who would spread her legs for his old man and then come dripping wet with the old goat's juices to be thumped by him—?

She would want him to *marry* her?

A goddamn joke . . .

If he even *wanted* a wife, he would look among the planter elite, find some simpering little ninny who would bow and kowtow to his every whim and run his house while he ran amuck in New Orleans.

Every man knew that; he could swear his daddy even raised

him with those expectations. He could remember the old man disappearing in town for months at a time, and Mama calm and distraught both, and never letting them see or hear anything that might defile him in their eyes.

God, he got harder just thinking about it.

He would never enslave himself to some little bitch like Nyreen who had expectations, who wanted his fidelity and would go off and seduce every man in sight if he got out of line.

Stupid woman.

Insatiable whore.

He supposed he ought to go find her. He supposed he would stay hard and hopping until he found her and spent his lust in her body.

She was good for one thing at least, and as long as he stayed on Montelette, he didn't mind at all the thought of her remaining there for *his* convenience—and not her own.

He would look first at Bonneterre—Olivia would invite him to stay in all probability, and if she were there, he would decide right on sight how to deal with her and her treacherous body . . .

It was a very small wooden cabin, room for one—maybe two, no more, and it had about it an air of desolation as though the occupant had been long, long gone, and not just a couple of days.

Just inside the door, to the right, there was a bed, a dresser, and a washstand. To the left, there was a table on which there was a kerosene lamp; two chairs; and a shelf with some canisters, plates, cups, and a jug. At the rear of the cabin there was a small fireplace over which hung a bracket with a cracked iron pot. And on the back of the door there was a long board attached with five wooden pegs.

The floor was wood and scrubbed meticulously clean, and the bed was covered with a serviceable quilt.

Dayne could make do here.

She sat gingerly on the bed and listened for a moment to the rain pounding on the ceiling; the roof held fast—there were no leaks.

It was so bare, so barren; Mama Dessie had removed everything and burned it, and then saturated the eaves and the walls with protective herbs and magical incantations.

Even the bed: she could smell the faint aroma of dill and cedar and anise and cloves rising from the bedcover.

And on the table, more cloves, and mint strewn right on the top and around the base of the lamp.

And in the iron pot and all over the hearth.

Mama Dessie took no chances.

And neither would she.

She peeked into the canisters. There was flour and sugar and salt—and water outside the door—she took the jug and set it outside the door to catch the rainwater.

She had a dry place to sleep, infused with all of Mama Dessie's power, and she would have something to drink and maybe some flat cakes in the morning, mixed up and fried quickly on the hearth.

It was all she could do this day.

She lay down carefully in the bed and listened to the rhythm of the rain on the roof.

In the dark, deep in the night, the sound of the rain was like hearing voices on the roof.

Clay lay in bed, listening to the cadence of the rain, trying to imagine one little place he hadn't thought of to look for the jewels.

Two weeks—he felt an overriding desperation. It would never end, never. He needed his own indelible source of funds that he could expend whatever way he wanted.

He needed freedom from restraint and the long tether that held him to Bonneterre.

But here, too, he felt the enormity of what he had done to Meline—and then the rage that invariably followed that by her silence she had provoked him into it.

More than that, he resented that she had died knowing that the cache of jewels existed—and more than that, where they were.

Where could she or Celie have hidden them?

What the hell was that stupid rhyme?

He reached into his memory trying to pull out the rhythmic words . . .

A smattering of the rhyme came back to him—

> . . . don' look in no fields
> . . . don' look to sell
> . . . powuh come sweet
> . . . to de table
> . . . and take yo' place . . .

Power come sweet . . .

Didn't it ever?

Where on Bonneterre had he not searched yet?

The answer dawned on him early in the morning.

Celie's and Meline's cabin, a place apart and forbidden, a place a white hand would never touch and a white man would never go.

Olivia could not sleep. She listened to the sound of the rain pounding on the roof and she wondered if Dayne had met the same fate as Meline, and she wondered how she would feel if that were the fact.

I would have my house back.

She was not shocked by the thought; rather, she felt weary. She was tired of dealing with all the problems, tired of rooting around for money; exhausted by Clay and his profligate ways; and exasperated by Lydia's uncomprehending pursuit of Peter Templeton.

A woman was never free.

She had spent thirty years in servitude to her husband and who knew how much longer dependent on Flint?

She hated it—just *hated* it, and all because of that gullible Celie and her sneaking, thieving ways.

Celie had robbed her of her freedom. It was as simple as that. If Olivia had had the jewelry, she could have saved Bonneterre, paid for Verne's follies, and had something left for herself.

But stupid, innocent, trusting Celie had put paid to all that.

Well, she had fixed Celie eventually, knowing full well that the secret of the jewels would die with her.

But she had gotten inestimable satisfaction out of the expression on Celie's face as she fell backward down the stairs to her death.

A simple accident—nothing proven.

She had been reprimanding her, and Celie had scuttled backward and lost her footing—and she was gone.

She wasn't that smart, either. Olivia had been sure she was a lot smarter than Celie and that she could eventually figure out what Celie had done with the jewels.

But she had never found a clue, and Miss Queen Meline would make sly, stinging little references to it now and again, trying to provoke her into losing her temper so that Meline could perhaps prove she'd had something to do with Celie's death.

She had never ever given Meline the satisfaction.

And she had covertly searched every inch of Bonneterre and its grounds and never found anything.

But she never gave up hope. As she listened to the torrential rain pounding away on the roof, she tried to put herself in the mind of Celie yet again, and to fit herself into Celie's place and sensibility.

Where would Celie have put the jewels—?

Someplace familiar—someplace she knew she could depend upon Meline to protect them—someplace like her home—

But she had gone over and over that; she had made her tentative demeaning forays to Celie's cabin, closing her eyes to the barrenness of Celie's life which had precipitated her theft of the jewels, and she had found nothing.

There was hardly anything to search. A bed, a table, some canisters, the mattress, and always with the fear that someone would barge in and catch the Mistress of Bonneterre in this compromising place . . .

Of course she could have missed something—a chink in the wall, a creak in the floor, some secret hiding place that in her panic she might have overlooked . . .

Was it worth it—one last shot when she had about given up all expectation of finding anything?

Worth it to sneak out in the rain and the dark of the night on one last slim and amorphous hope that Celie had been naive enough to have stashed that small fortune in the place she could guard best with her life?

She felt desperate enough to take the chance—she almost had no other choice . . . nothing else could save her.

She slipped out of bed and began making preparations to go.

Nyreen couldn't sleep. She lay wide awake in that strange bed wishing she had never left Montelette.

This was definitely *not* the way to excite Peter's interest—not in the least.

He was definitely one of those men who would not be led around by his manhood; he probably hated women. He was absolutely rabid about whores.

And she was the definition of one. She ought to cut her losses and run. She ought to go straight west to find her mother and just take up residence in some likely town where there was lots of activity and rangy male flesh.

Even that thought was exciting to her, in lieu of having Peter in bed beside her.

So it had been a futile dream; maybe Harry had died for nothing and Peter had never had any intention of pursuing the life of a gentleman planter longer than it took him to convince Flint Rutledge to run Montelette and forward his share of profits to him.

A girl had a right to dream—and maybe even to hope.

She swung her legs over the bed just as dawn was breaking over the wet horizon.

Of course there was still the thought that if he owned Montelette outright, he would change his mind about staying.

She had thought perhaps she could engineer that little bargaining chip, but Dayne Templeton Rutledge was damned hard to kill.

And she had been the talk at dinner with every nerve ending at Bonneterre focused on her and why she had gone missing.

It kind of made her plans evaporate into nothingness when before it had been so easy to position herself to take advantage of

Dayne's anguish—like the day she pushed her into the bayou at Orinda . . .

She hadn't stayed to see Dayne's reaction to the missing Boy—she had taken the horse back to Orinda, and then, when she had been ready to leave Montelette, it had been an even simpler matter to bring him back and release him to run free once she entered the grounds.

And then later, easier still to lose herself in a grieving crowd around the awesome magic of Mama Dessie.

The boiling pot she thought would be her masterpiece—she had come early to Bonneterre on the day she supposedly arrived, and scouted out Dayne's whereabouts, taken a hoe from the barnyard, stolen into the kitchen, just rammed the hoe into the pot and sent it flying.

Too bad it hadn't worked.

And now—well, she would land on her feet no matter what, she was used to it, but it didn't mean she was giving up.

Not she—not yet.

Especially when Dayne had gone missing for some mysterious reason. Maybe fate had taken a hand for her.

Or maybe—maybe—

She paused as she looked out the window.

It was barely light, and still raining. Her room on the third floor faced the dependencies of Bonneterre—she had a long view of the sugarhouse, the dairy, the smokehouse, and the slave cabins.

It was quiet as death out there—except for one small unusual thing: smoke curling out of the chimney of one of the cabins—a wisp really—but well before the hour when the field gangs were awake.

She wondered why.

She wondered if Dayne could have been smart enough to seek refuge there.

And if it were Dayne—wouldn't it be wonderful for *her* to find Dayne alone and isolated away from everyone else and in a place where no one could come to help her too fast.

She liked that thought a lot, that maybe fortune hadn't abandoned her after all and had given her one last chance with Peter.

She wondered if she should take the chance and go see.

But she was never one to think things through for too long.

She had slipped on some clothes and was out the door before she even calculated the odds.

Lydia couldn't sleep. Peter—her Peter!—was in the house— and that insidious Creature.

She didn't know how she could stand it, knowing the Creature was down the hall and that Peter might go to her at anytime.

If only he knew—if only he even comprehended what she had done to insure their happiness . . .

She was not going to lose him to the Creature now.

And she couldn't just stay in her room waiting and wondering.

At the very least, she had to—*had* to—keep an eye on the Creature's door to make sure she did not lure Peter into her room for another bout of that nasty, naked grappling on the bed.

At least that—and then she would feel she was doing something . . . for both of them.

She crept out of her room and down the hallway to a little al- cove near the guest bedroom where the Creature was ensconced, and settled herself comfortably on the floor.

She wasn't there an hour or maybe two when the Creature burst out of the door and ran stealthily down the stairs.

A moment later, Lydia followed her, one hand gripped tightly around the gun she had used to kill Harry Templeton.

Peter resisted it; all night he lay in his bed, pushing away thoughts of Nyreen's tempting body a dozen yards down the long, perpendicular hallways just outside his door.

A guest did not take advantage of his hostess like that. He just didn't—and he *was* a gentleman, even if he did feel like a raging bull at the moment.

But who would know?

He could just sneak down the hallway and edge into her room and hope to hell Clay Rutledge wasn't poking her.

Damn. Shit. Hell.

The image shot into his mind like a piston, pumping away with all the energy of a man's hungry body.

He couldn't take it—not one minute longer.

He slipped out of his bedroom and furtively tiptoed down the hallway—

—just in time to see Nyreen silently close the door to her room and glide down the steps.

Damn her to hell—once a whore always a whore—

A man couldn't trust goddamned anyone.

And he sure as hell couldn't trust her.

He was going to pin her on it once and for all and get her right out of his system.

And when he caught her with the lying, cheating bastard, he was going to kill him.

Flint couldn't sleep. He had spent the whole night out on the upper gallery, listening to the teeming rain, finding no answers and no relief.

The rain was letting up now, just a little, as the dawn broke over the horizon.

And he would wake the field hands at five when Agus sounded the big brass bell in the barn. After that, they had a half hour to make ready for the day before they had to line up for the day's tasks.

So it was unusual to see a wisp of smoke curling out of one of the farther cabin chimneys.

He noted it absently, his mind on other things—like the shadows moving surreptitiously in the fog dark morning.

Shadows . . . detaching themselves from the dark trees and edging toward the outbuildings.

Determined shadows . . .

Heading toward the avenue of cabins, secretly, minutes apart, and unaware each of the other.

Damn—and what was that all about?

He lost sight of them, one—two—three as they blended in with the indistinct shapes of the night-dawn morning.

And he didn't think twice about racing down the steps to follow them.

* * *

She slept, in the fragrant bower of Mama Dessie's protection, and she felt as if nothing could hurt her here.

She awakened so early of her own volition that she thought it made sense to make her fire and her flat cakes before anyone else arose, and she lit the little fire in the hearth and mixed her batter with the rainwater she had collected the night before.

It had taken but a minute to fry up the batter into one large pancake on the bottom of the hanging pot.

She had probably sweetened it more than she ought, but at least it had some flavor, and she had the rainwater to drink.

She doused the fire and lay back down in the bed, still feeling that sense of calm and the aura of protection. She thought perhaps she had even dozed off because when she heard the noise, she thought it was in her dreams.

But then, she heard it again and she bolted into consciousness and pressed her body tightly against the wall as if she could conceal her presence by just becoming part of it.

The door shifted open and she could see the faint line of morning color against the black sky.

She noticed next that the rain had diminished to drops, so that the unremitting pounding over her head had ceased.

And then she saw the wary, dark shape slip into the doorway and edge its way into the room slowly, groping to get its bearings and maybe, luckily, find a lamp.

She was absolutely trapped and she just froze.

For all she knew, it could be Flint, seeking her out for the final reparation.

Or it could be someone else, feral and furtive in the night with other secrets, other motives, other means, a predator with no conscience who wanted no witnesses.

She heard the scrape of a match and a light flared. In the pinpoint of light, she saw his face as he removed the chimney and set the flame to the wick of the kerosene lamp.

Clay.

He looked up, and he saw her, her presence magnified by the leaping flame of the lamp which sent shadows flickering across the room.

"Goddamn hell."

They stared at each other across the small, stifling room.

"What the hell are you doing here? Flint's about to call out the militia to search for you."

She couldn't think of a thing to say; of course Flint was desperate to find her.

And Clay had, and she couldn't think of one good reason for him to be there, either.

"Clay—"

"Shit—don't say anything, all right? I have to think—I have to think what to do." But he knew already; his mind was rejecting it even if he was certain it was the only way.

This was his sister-in-law, his brother's wife, his almost-bride who would have brought him, in her dowry, all the comforts and money to which he could have laid claim.

He ought to hate her for having allowed her father to be so weak as to be coerced by Flint.

He had lost everything because of it—and now he was reduced to *this* . . . skulking around in a slave cabin looking for something he wasn't even sure existed.

He felt a simmering anger and a rising resentment. He couldn't let her see him diminished like this. She had seen too much already; in his mind's eye, she was Meline, taunting him with secrets and leading him on.

And just like Meline, she had pulled out at the last minute. So what did the slave woman and the Southern belle have in common?

Why, they were both lying, cheating bitches.

And they had both brought him to his knees by their thoughtless scheming tricks.

So why didn't Miss Dayne deserve the same fate? Who would think to look for her here any more than anyone had thought to look for Meline at Orinda.

It was sheer bad luck Dayne happened to be there—his insane bad luck that had dogged him ever since she had begged him to marry her, and he stupidly hadn't seen the obvious advantages.

Well, it was too late now, and he certainly wasn't going to let her watch him raze Meline's cabin in search of the jewels.

And he could see by her expression she was following every thought because it showed right on his face.

He took a menacing step toward her and she scuttled across the rickety bed.

"My dear Dayne, there's no other way."

"I can think of at least one other way," she whispered. "You turn around and go right back out that door and don't tell anyone I'm here."

"But you'll tell everyone *I've* been here—and maybe they'll make a connection I don't want them to make. Do you see, Dayne dear?"

She caught the lump in her throat before she swallowed it and choked.

"No, I don't."

"Well, I've come looking for treasure, and this is the last place it could be, and I intend to find it."

"Not if I find it first," said a voice behind him, and he wheeled around and froze.

"Like minds think alike," Olivia said as she pushed past him and sauntered into the small claustrophobic room.

"It's amazing, isn't it," she mused as she looked around. "Nothing has changed. What, son—you look shocked. Did you think after thirty years on Bonneterre I had never seen the inside of a slave cabin? My dear boy—it was one of the first places I began my search. As for the other—

"Well—Verne always took care of those details, didn't he, Clay? And you. He knew very well what a cabin looked like. But I tell you, I'm stunned that there's hardly a space to hide a bone, let alone a cache of jewels. Oh?—you look surprised, Dayne; what, you thought it was some kind of daydream?"

"I never thought so. I knew Celie had some of them. I just knew it. Just like Clay knew Meline had the answer—didn't you, my dear? I wonder what you bartered for her little secret and what she gave you in return that led you here."

Her eyes flickered for a moment as if she were making the connection of which Clay had spoken. And then she smiled.

"Oh, I see—she didn't tell you—and you decided to inflict the final punishment. Yes—perfectly apt. I felt that anguish myself. Celie was just as intractable and just as much a tease. I wonder if one can inherit a disposition to murder . . ."

She began walking slowly around the room and touching things—the walls, the stone hearth, the pot, the chairs, the table—

"If we could find the stones, Clay and I—we could be free. I daresay we both would leave Bonneterre and leave its fate and its patrimony in Flint's and your hands. Then I might find some meaning in my life beyond sewing slaves' clothing, making candles, and writing in journals as I have done for the past thirty years.

"I must find my jewels . . ."

"Mother—"

"What did she tell you—what did she say before she died?"

"I—I can't wholly remember—"

Olivia pushed him. "Useless! Useless and weak—you always were . . ."

"It was a rhyme," Clay said desperately, grabbing for her hands. "Something Celie made her learn as a child so she wouldn't forget—something about not looking in the cane or in the fields and power being sweet, and coming to the table—"

They both leapt on it at the same time—Olivia lifting the lamp and Clay turning it over and literally ripping it to pieces.

"Goddamn—"

"Look under the chairs—"

He did.

"—and the bed—"

He thrust Dayne off of it and he did.

"In the fireplace . . ."

He did.

"In the roof beams—"

He took the chair that he had destroyed the least and climbed up and felt around the support beams and the roof.

"And the shelf—"

He did—behind the shelf and under the dishes and in the canisters, pouring out the flour and the salt and the sugar all over the floor.

"Nothing—nothing—goddamn it—nothing . . ."

The anguish was thick in his voice and then he said, "Now my dear Dayne—you just have to die."

Chapter 20

Nyreen edged her way behind the dark bulk of the cabin. She could hear voices—a man's voice and a woman's—and she felt the thrill of having tracked down her prey.

She worked her way around to the doorway, where by the light of the kerosene lamp, she could see Clay Rutledge quite clearly, and the shadow of a woman's skirt just beyond.

Without a doubt it was Dayne—and then her voice confirmed it, and Nyreen scuttled back behind the house to exult in her luck.

Another chance—another opportunity to make Peter the sole legatee of Montelette.

And what a convenient location. All she had to do was light a fire—the thing would go up like tinder.

And maybe it would get rid of that obnoxious Clay Rutledge and his patronizing mother, too.

She knelt beside the house, rummaged for a match and struck it.

And someone tackled her from behind, knocking her over and squelching the match.

"Goddamn it to hell, whore—" his voice, his breath grated in her ear. "What the hell are you doing?"

She lay still as a statue. "I'm dying—"

"I'm going kill you myself."

"Peter . . ."

"Don't move!"

Another voice—female and familiar—laced with a different anger, coming at them from someplace above.

Peter rolled over and tried to see.

"You *cheat!*" A trembling voice, artless—God—it was Lydia—"I could *kill* you!"

"Lydia—"

"No! *No!* Don't *move* . . . especially that Creature—she had better not *breathe* . . ."

"Lydia—"

"Do you know—do you even know what I've done for *us*—us, Peter. Do you even know how long I've loved you—and then you have to come back and let this Creature get her claws into you—and you *like* it! Oh my God, my God—"

She was crying, the tears streaming down her face, her anguish palpable and a little crazed. "Do you know, do you?—do you have any idea—*Peter!* I didn't know about Dayne. Mama wrote me a letter and told me Flint was back and he had got married and that you had returned to Montelette. And I was up at Valloire—not too far away. And I thought, I'm all grown up now, and Peter is home and we'll see each other . . . and—

"And then I thought—but that stupid old feud will get in the way again. All because of Daddy and Harry Templeton. And then I thought, if there were no Harry Templeton, then—we could *really* get to know each other—finally, and I could—I could *really* love you and not worry about anything getting in the way . . ."

Peter groaned low in his throat. Dear God—

"Lydia—" he said gently.

"The gun is loaded you know. I used it to kill Harry that night. I just kind of waited to see if he would get up during the night, but really I intended to get him in the morning. So it was lucky, wasn't it, because no one saw me—and no one knew."

"I didn't know," Peter whispered.

"I thought you would. I thought maybe you'd understand once you knew how long I had loved you."

"I didn't, I couldn't—how could I know?" *My own father, for Christ's sake—Jesus!*

He felt Nyreen trembling underneath him. He heard her breath of words: "She's crazy; she'll kill us . . ."

He knew it, too. But he had to try to reason with her, even if she was a lunatic.

"Lydia—Lydia . . ."

"I saw you with the Creature, Peter. That really hurt me. I'm never going to believe your lies—not now . . ."

Oh God . . . "Lydia . . ."

"It's dark—but I know just where you are, Peter. Don't move. I'd rather you were dead than with *her* . . ."

Bam! She shot straight at him—he felt the impact of the bullet, the pain, the unreality of it—

"Jesus, God. . . . She goddamned shot me . . ."

Bam! Another shot—

Lydia fell forward onto Peter's legs, blood gushing from her back, dead on impact.

"An eye for an eye—"

Flint's anguished voice somewhere in the lightening darkness. "Are you all right?"

"Shit—she got me—in my shoulder, I think."

"Can you walk?"

"I think so . . ."

"Get the hell back to the house. I've got to rescue my wife."

Clay slammed the cabin door shut at the sound of the gun-blast.

"Holy hell—*Flint*—"

Dayne made a move—Clay shoved her back. "Jesus, you're not stupid, Dayne."

"You haven't done anything."

"My dear, I have confessed to murder and so has Mother. And I wouldn't doubt that Flint heard the whole thing. The question is, what will he do—and I don't prefer to take my chances. My big brother is a much tougher judge than any jury of my peers. Mother?"

"We have to find those jewels," Olivia whispered fiercely. "I *know* they're here . . ."

"There is nowhere they can be," Clay growled. "We can't keep looking—Flint is going to break down that door any minute."

"I *won't* leave without them . . ."

"*Stand back—*" Flint's voice at the door. "Mother—Clay—I'm coming for Dayne . . ."

"*NO!*" Olivia shrieked, grabbing hold of one of the table legs and swinging it at the door. "*NO!*"

"Mother . . ."

"I'm going to find my jewels, Flint—and I'll kill anyone who gets in my way, do you hear?"

He was silent for a moment and then, "Let Dayne come out, Mother, and you can search unimpeded for the rest of your life."

"No! No! I'm tired of you Rutledge men taking everything away from me. Now I've got something you want, and you're just going to have to wait—just like I did all these years, son—like I waited for your father to stop with the slave women; and I waited for you to come home; and I waited for Lydia to stop being so childish about Peter; and I waited for Clay to take some responsibility . . . oh, have I waited—and now I want what is mine . . .

"So now you be patient, Flint—oh, I named you well, didn't I? Clay—pull up the floorboard near the shelf and see what's under there."

But there was nothing.

Olivia was going mad before Dayne's very eyes.

Dayne moved, to stretch her cramped muscles, and Olivia brandished the table leg threateningly.

"I have to—"

"You don't have to do anything, my dear, unless I say so. Clay! Just keep going with those floorboards."

He did, ripping them up with the sheer force of his desperation until half of the room was covered with dirt.

"There's nothing, Mother—just nothing . . ."

"God, that thieving little bitch—she had them—I know she had them." She kicked at the canisters, sending them across the room, toward Dayne's feet and the bed.

Dayne heard it—Olivia did not in the throes of her rising hysteria. Something came loose in one of the canisters, the one which had landed closest to her foot.

"You've had your time to look, Mother," Flint said loudly from outside the door. "I'm coming in—"

"*Don't!*"

"It's over, Mother—" He rammed into the door with the butt of his rifle.

Wham!

"*Don't!* I'm warning you—"

Wham!

"*Don't do it, Flint*—just go away!"

Wham! The door opened partially and Dayne could see him, backlit by the rising dawn.

Wham! The door flew open—and instantly, Olivia bent and picked up the kerosene lamp and flung it against the back wall.

"Goddamn hell—"

The wall caught—like paper and roared into a sheet of flame instantly, irrevocably.

Olivia shoved him aside and raced into the cool dawn air.

"*Mother!*" Clay shouted, crazily running after her, through the thick billowing smoke.

"*Dayne . . . !*" He couldn't see a thing—he couldn't see her.

"I'm here, I'm on the floor . . ."

She was groping around, looking for the canisters—the one near her foot, the one that had made a noise when Olivia kicked it.

He fell down on the floor beside her. "Are you crazy? Stay down now, and hold my hand. We're going to crawl out of here—this place is going to collapse in one minute—"

She grasped his hand, his large, hard, warm hand, and they crawled slowly and painstakingly out of the burning cabin at the very moment Olivia came diving back in.

"*MY JEWELS!*" she shrieked and disappeared into the smoke.

"Oh my God—" Dayne moaned as Flint helped her to her feet at the head of a line of workers who had already formed a fire brigade and were hauling buckets up from the bayou.

"*Mother!*" Clay was hard on her heels, running full tilt after her—and stopping short as she vanished into the cabin. "I have to get her—I can't let her . . . *Mother!*"

He dropped to his hands and knees and crawled into the door. They could hear him beyond the crackling flames and the rolling smoke: "*Mother!*"

And then they all recoiled in horror as the flames shot up through the roof and with one last, creaking protest, the whole thing caved in with a protesting roar.

For one agonizing moment, he felt as if he had been judge, jury, and executioner. He could have pulled Clay back. He could have let Lydia live.

How did a man live with the knowledge of the wickedness that had festered in his family's bosom? He had chosen to escape it, and in the end, he had not been able to evade the truth of it. He would have to live with that for the rest of his life.

The cabin smoldered, utterly demolished. Lydia's body had been removed by Agus's gentle hands and taken back to the house to be prepared for burial.

The water brigade remained, seeking to douse every last ember so that no other houses would be endangered.

And Dayne remained by Flint's side, her dress, her face, her hair all singed, and turning over in her hands a mottled canister with the word *Sugar* partially scraped off.

"You almost got killed to save that. What the hell is it?"

"I don't know," she said, still twisting it this way and that. "Maybe the answer to an old family secret."

"We'll go back to the house," he said finally. "There's nothing more to be done."

Peter's wound was bandaged and he was sitting propped up comfortably in the parlor with Nyreen sullenly at his side when Flint and Dayne returned.

His warm blue eyes immediately shot to Flint, who looked haggard and almost ready to collapse.

"I'm so sorry."

"Nothing to be sorry for," he said, dismissing it. "Mother never took Lydia seriously. How could things have ended but tragically?"

"But Harry—"

Flint looked at Dayne. "Lydia killed Harry to remove him as an obstacle to her obsession with Peter. Mother conveniently did not tell her *who* I married—only that I was married. Mother . . . I can hardly believe this."

"And don't forget Nyreen," Peter said stoically, feeding her right to the wolves.

"How can we forget Nyreen," Flint agreed mildly. He slanted another look at Dayne. "What about Nyreen?"

"Nyreen has been scheming to get Dayne's share of Montelette. She thought a little accident might help things along, and she had no idea that Olivia was planning to burn the cabin down; she had the same idea herself—which is how I just found out what she was doing at the cabin in the first place—damn her soul to hell . . ."

"You don't have to get nasty," Nyreen said. But she couldn't look at Dayne; she much preferred looking at Peter anyway. He had hated what she told him, but he understood greed and cupidity very well. "I *did* return the Boy."

Dayne felt everything inside her cave in.

Not Flint. *Never* Flint . . .

Nyreen—because of whom everything had happened—Nyreen—who had wanted her gone, who wanted her dead.

She had gotten one of her heart's desires—and almost accomplished the other.

And still—she had landed on her feet, like a cat, and neither Peter nor Flint looked as if they were going to torment her with a litany of her sins.

Women like Nyreen always won. *Always.*

It was the thing she had never understood—the power. Nyreen had it and she never would.

"I'm leaving St. Foy," Peter went on, and Dayne looked at him sharply. He shook his head. "I'm no gentleman farmer, Dayne. And I've got to get this vile piece of baggage out of St. Foy before she tries to destroy someone else's life. I'll travel with my own *companion,* and Flint will take over the management of Montelette and forward me my share of the profits and that way, my beautiful Dayne, we'll all be happy and satisfied."

"I'll do it," Flint said and held out his hand.

"I'm damned glad it was you who married my sister," Peter said and shook it warmly.

"Nevertheless, we'll draw up some papers."

"Papers are good," Nyreen said. "We have to send one to my mother and tell her that Harry died."

"We'll do that, too," Peter said. "We'll do everything, and soon, and someday in the future, we'll come back and visit . . . when things are better and wounds are healed—"

Dayne nodded. "All right." But she didn't know if she could deal with the fact that Nyreen had taken her father and her brother from her, both.

"What's that in your hand?" Nyreen asked and Dayne looked down at the canister as if she had never seen it before.

"It was in the cabin—" Dayne said vaguely. In the cabin—and Olivia had kicked it and Dayne heard something—but there was nothing there because Clay had poured everything out of it—

But still, there was some weight to it—

Power come sweet—Clay had quoted Meline—*come to the table . . .*

The only object besides the plates that might be put on the table—and empty with weight.

She turned it upside down and shook it. Weight . . .

"I think there's something in here."

Flint's dark eyes flickered. "I have a knife."

He took the canister and dug the point of it down into the bottom. "It's wedged very tightly . . . if there's anything there."

"A false bottom?"

Power come sweet—how well she knew.

Flint jammed the knife point deep into the bottom and pried up the edge. "It's coming . . ." And up . . . and then he tilted the canister over onto the nearest table, and the jewels tumbled out— beautifully faceted diamonds, rubies, and sapphires, small, exquisite, a ransom for four lives.

The work of the plantations went on, an expiation for his sins.

He needed time to heal and time to grieve for a mother who had spent her life in bitterness and expected some final reward, and a brother who thought everything came easy and knew nothing about the life of the soil.

By July the cane was tall and leafy, ripe with juice and tasseling over his workers' heads, an unbroken greensward as far as the eye could see.

This was the time of the year when the cultivation stopped, the hoes were laid by and the sole work of the plantation was bent toward preparing the sugarhouse for the harvest.

Busy work, between the two plantations, stockpiling wood and cleaning the machinery and building the barrels in which the sugar would be shipped.

Physical work so that he would bury the past in sheer exhaustion and he would not think about his present or his future.

But the time was coming; the time was coming soon. He didn't believe the biblical injunction about the sins of the father.

Work cleansed him and made him whole.

He mourned for Olivia and he found his soul.

Not Flint.

Not Flint—

All those days of uncertainty and betrayal—and it had not been Flint, and she was so mortified, she did not know how she was going to survive.

She survived. There was always work—he was immersed in it between Montelette and Bonneterre, and she saw so very little of him after all.

He buried his mother, brother, and sister with a reverence they did not deserve in life, and if he mourned, he did it in private, while she grieved for the error of all their ways.

And when Agus brought the Boy to her, after having found him the day after the storm, floundering in the swamp, she felt as if her circle were complete.

There was no time for grieving. The work of the plantations went on. There were supplies to see to, clothes to make, mattresses to stuff, rugs to beat, furniture to repair, candles to dip, meat to cure—and sometime toward winter, the dreaded killing of the hogs.

She lost herself in the mundane work of housekeeping, healing her wounded heart and reclaiming her soul.

* * *

In September, they took the Boy to St. Francisville and entered him in his first race.

He was both swift and skittish, unused to crowds and noise and the competition with other horses.

With him, they still had a long way to go.

In September, at Bonneterre, the fertility of the earth was all around them. They were almost on the verge of the harvest of the cane. They were picking the last of the summer vegetables and planting for harvest in the fall.

Everywhere around them, a ripeness and readiness permeated the air.

Dayne had felt for weeks it was no less so with them. The horror had receded and Flint had come to some kind of balance about the past.

She was the one who could not come to terms with the fact she had not trusted him.

And she grieved for his terrible losses, for the component of his past that had never changed in all the time he had been away, and all the time since he had returned.

When they had dug into the cabin to retrieve the bodies and excavate the ruins, they had found the settings from which Celie had detached the jewels in the charred ruin of the mattress.

Small pieces: earrings especially, a necklace, and several flexible bracelets, all tucked into a corner of the feathers and straw, and shining almost obscenely in the smoke-clogged desolation.

A futile theft that had impacted lives for over thirty years and caused death and devastation.

Flint had taken the settings and the jewels and buried them with Olivia so that finally she could have in death what she could not find in life.

But as the scorching heat of July and August wafted into September, Dayne thought maybe he hadn't trusted himself.

Maybe Flint had really wanted her—so desperately he had made that devil's bargain with her father in order to insure the security of her inheritance for *her*.

How could he have stood by, after all their erotic games, and watched her father hand her over to Clay? Especially knowing what his brother was.

Maybe Flint had really meant to rescue her—to really make her his wife.

They were alone, the two of them, keeping to themselves between the two main houses; sometimes he slept over at Montelette when he was heavily engaged in work there.

Most times, he slept in his own room at Bonneterre, coming in late, leaving early.

She was so perfectly aware of him in the next room—the more so as her mind and her body healed from the pain of her losses and her guilt and her grief.

As she began to feel strong and secure, she began to feel the power of her femininity assert itself.

She began to be aware of her body, her movement, her competency in everything that she did.

She thought she felt him watching her guardedly; sometimes, when they had dinner together, she could see that little glowing light banked in the back of his jetty eyes.

She felt herself unfurling, expanding, swelling into a ripe receptiveness, almost, almost ready like the harvest which was about to begin.

She felt full to bursting with a fertile fragile need that if it were not handled with tenderness might wither and die.

She felt as if she were Eve, on the verge of discovery in her garden—her Eden.

She went to see Mama Dessie.

"Mama Dessie—I need a spell."

"You don' need nuthin', Miz Dayne; you got ever'thin' they is. You got yo' land, you got yo' man . . . whut you talkin' 'bout? Dat man got love fo' you. I seed it when he done married wif you."

"No . . ." No—she knew what he had for her . . . the obvious desire to slake his needs on her very willing body. Like animals, they both had been, wanting nothing more than to provoke each other to an explosive union.

She wanted nothing more than that now. And she wanted something very much more and she didn't know what it was.

"Nothing is happening, Mama Dessie."

"Need time fo' de healin', Miz Dayne."

"I know—I know." But it was just the two of them, alone—why not, why not?

"De hat got to fit de head, Miz Dayne."

"I know, I know."

"Ain't no use askin' de chicken fo' de egg," Mama Dessie added slyly. "All de time, you got to take it when you want it."

"Mama Dessie—?"

"I give you somethin', but you de one got to go to de hen house and find dat old rooster."

She had not been to Orinda since she had found Meline and she had the sudden restive urge to ride over, to take Mama Dessie's magic herbs and throw them in the water to nullify the evil that had been perpetrated there.

Sweet-smelling magic compounded to attract love and give protection: cloves and cinnamon, lemon verbena, violet and lavender mixed with bay and barley for leavening and the ever-present asafoetida.

"Th'ow 'em on de water," Mama Dessie had said. "Bring love and peace back to dat place. Bring 'em back to yo' own self, too, Miz Dayne."

She stood on the shore edge of the bayou, near a moss-draped tree to shade her, and she thought about the short desperate life of Meline and how finally she was free, and she took her package of herbs and lifted them high over the bayou and scattered them like ashes above the water.

It was night—a hot sultry night and her body was hot and sultry and straining against its own violent suppressed need.

He had been gone the whole day and the day before, and the more he wasn't there, the more she wanted him, and the more she thought about the power, the more her body responded with an urgency that overrode every other consideration.

She couldn't bear the feeling of cloth against her skin when she was aching for the feel of something hot and hard and muscular and possessive.

She removed her clothes the instant she entered her room now, both for her own pleasure and to obey his first command when he had married her.

Naked in her room, willing and wanting and ready for him.

Her body was like a thing separate and apart from her mind and she could not, didn't want to, subdue its treacherous memories.

When she was naked in her room, she remembered. She remembered the raw, ripe power of desire and the need to look and how the need to look exploded into the need to touch and the need to touch into the endless lust to possess and be possessed.

Her body was made for him. She was ripe for him. Nothing had changed; nothing else mattered.

And so it was true: she was a Jezebel, responding only to the urge of her own voluptuous needs.

And a Jezebel would take. A Jezebel would not sit in her room and moon at the sky because she was afraid of rejection.

A Jezebel would take what she wanted; she would rule the hen house and have all of the roosters at her feet.

She felt the languid surge of her body in the heat of the night, streaming with anticipation. She felt her nipples, so taut with excitement. She felt her skin, satin, provocative, yearning to be touched.

Jezebel didn't need leather or whips—not this time at any rate. She needed only the urgency of her desire, and her powerful feminine need.

And with that, she could go to him, and bring him to his knees.

Slowly and deliberately, she eased off of the bed, and made her way to the connecting door.

One brazen moment—and she could have what she wanted.

She turned the doorknob slowly and eased open the door.

The room was cast in shadows from a low standing light. He was laying on the bed, naked, just as she had imagined he would be, and he was thick and hard and jutting up to the ceiling.

"Hello sugar—here I am—hot and hard and ready for you."

Yes . . .

"So I see," she murmured, thinking it was best not to give him too much, too fast.

But her body said differently. Her body jolted to attention, her breasts thrusting forward as if they were begging for his caresses.

She walked slowly toward him, her eyes never moving from that prime male hard part that he displayed with such arrogant assurance with his one leg bent under him and the other up and braced against the mattress so that his body canted forward from the hips.

She was utterly enchanted with the prominence of his manhood when he lay in this position, and she eased herself onto the bed to get the perfect view.

He was just perfect; she wanted to cover him with kisses, but she restrained herself and just propped herself up against the headboard and presented herself to him in the same brazen way.

"A Jezebel to the core," he murmured.

"Isn't it true?" she agreed insolently.

She loved him looking at her. Her body reacted exactly to the heat in his eyes, the possessiveness of his response; she was his and she wanted nothing more, ever.

Her body vibrated with urgency as his eyes roamed all over her, taking her every which where, lavishing attention on all the places she wanted him to with his hot, glittering eyes.

"Naked for me, Jezebel, and only me."

It was a challenge; she shrugged—she felt the power, and anyway, how could she know?

He would have to make her. He would have to show her.

"The same rules," he went on inexorably. "Naked and waiting, and always ready for me. Anytime and anywhere I want you. A Jezebel should have no trouble fulfilling those terms."

She loved those terms, she adored those terms. Her power became absolute with those terms. Anytime, anywhere. Naked and ready.

All she ever wanted—forever.